Praise for the novels of
Heather Cullman

A Perfect Scoundrel

"A delightful, lighthearted Regency romp from a talented writer. Enjoy!"   —Kat Martin

For All Eternity

"A skilled romance writer . . . intriguing setting and highly sensual love scenes."   —*Romantic Times*

"Moves like a whirlwind . . . humor in just the right places . . . wonderful characters."   —*Rendezvous*

Stronger Than Magic

"A delightfully romantic tale."   —*Literary Times*

"Ms. Cullman weaves a magic spell with every word."
                —*Rendezvous*

"[An] enchanting message of love."   —*Romantic Times*

Tomorrow's Dreams

"Intriguing . . . steamy sexuality and well-drawn characters."   —*Romantic Times*

Yesterday's Roses

"Witty, lusty, and thoroughly delightful."
                —*Affaire de Coeur*

"Exciting . . . combines dynamic characterizations, romance, mystery."   —*Paperback Forum*

LORDS OF DANGER

Bewitched

Heather Cullman

Enjoy the magic!

Heather Cullman

A SIGNET BOOK

SIGNET
Published by New American Library, a division of
Penguin Putnam Inc., 375 Hudson Street,
New York, New York 10014, U.S.A.
Penguin Books Ltd, 27 Wrights Lane,
London W8 5TZ, England
Penguin Books Australia Ltd, Ringwood,
Victoria, Australia
Penguin Books Canada Ltd, 10 Alcorn Avenue,
Toronto, Ontario, Canada M4V 3B2
Penguin Books (N.Z.) Ltd, 182–190 Wairau Road,
Auckland 10, New Zealand

Penguin Books Ltd, Registered Offices:
Harmondsworth, Middlesex, England

First published by Signet, an imprint of New American Library,
a division of Penguin Putnam Inc.

First Printing, February 2001
10 9 8 7 6 5 4 3 2 1

*For my parents, Robert and Barbara Gordon,
for teaching me the joy of reading,
and showing me the magic in everyday life.
I must have done something very right in a
past life to have been blessed with such wonderful
parents in this one. I love you.*

Chapter 1

Whatever am I to do about Michael? Adeline Vane, dowager duchess of Sherrington, mused, absently stirring the dye vat before her. It was a question that had plagued her all morning long, one she had turned over and over again in her mind, twisting and examining it from every possible angle. And like the first few thousand times she'd belabored it, she was still no closer to finding an answer.

Desperate to vent her frustration, she gave the length of merino in the vat a particularly savage churn. It gyrated wildly, splattering dye across her skirts. The sight of those splotches, a drab, sickly yellow among the kaleidoscopic assortment of red madder, blue woad, and purple umbilicara stains that currently dappled the gown, served only to exacerbate her vexation.

Botheration! As if matters weren't irksome enough, the dye she'd worked so hard to concoct was the color of dog piddle, not at all the bright lemon yellow she'd envisioned for the tunic robe she intended to make from the cloth.

For several tense moments she continued to glare at the spots, silently berating herself for her failure. Then reason took over and she shook her head. There was no sense in frazzling herself over off-hue dye, not when she had the more pressing problem of Michael to fret over. Besides, unlike her grandson, she at least had hope for the cloth. Shaking her head again, this time in despair at Michael's lot, she bustled across what had once been the manor washhouse to act upon her hope.

Crudely built of local limestone and roofed in Stone-field slate, the weathered old washhouse now served as a haven for Adeline's favorite pastime, textile arts. It was a passion shared by her best friend, Euphemia Merriman, Dowager Viscountess Bunbury, who even now sat at a dye-stained worktable, chattering away as she wielded a copper printing plate. Though the six casement windows behind her friend had been flung open, the room remained stifling, the early July heat intensified by the low-burning hearth fire and made humid by the evil-smelling steam that billowed from the dye vats simmering over it.

Hoping to create a cooling cross breeze, Adeline opened the door as she passed by it, revealing a garden as bright and beautiful as a heaven-sent dream. The garden, in which only pigment-yielding plants were cultivated, was another of her and Euphemia's pet projects; one that served not only to ensure a ready supply of dyestuff, but to provide a respite from the heat and fumes on sultry days like today.

Though tempted by the garden's fragrant invitation to linger, Adeline continued purposefully on her mission, stopping only when she reached the cupboard near the hearth. Mopping her inelegantly sweating brow with the back of her hand, she eyed the jumble on the shelves before her.

Jars, boxes, and powder-filled papers were strewn across every available surface, carelessly tossed like debris in streets between the towers of haphazardly stacked books. To her right was a mortar of partially pestled annatto seeds, from which would seep a striking orange dye when mordanted with alum; to her left lay a cheese-cloth pouch of logwood chips, one guaranteed to produce violet when simmered with tin.

Tin? Hmmm, yes. A sprinkle of tin crystals was just the thing to brighten the merino. If she were to—

"Addy!"

Adeline jumped, startled from her preoccupation by Euphemia's indignation-peppered voice. Noticing—really noticing—her friend for the first time that morning, she smiled and rather shamefacedly inquired, "Yes, Effie, dear?"

"Ha! Just as I suspected. You haven't heard a word I've said," Euphemia accused.

"Of course I have," Adeline lied, not about to admit that her friend was right. To do so would only wound her feelings, and hurting Effie was the last thing in the world she ever wished to do.

Euphemia eyed her skeptically. "Indeed? Then what, pray tell, was I talking about?"

What the devil *was* Effie twaddling about? Adeline had been so absorbed in the problem of her grandson, Michael, that . . .

A-ha! Grandson! No, no . . . not son . . . daughter. Granddaughter. Yes, that was it. Effie had been going on about her granddaughter, the American one who was being sent to England . . . what the devil was the gel's name? She glanced back down at the table, making a show of righting a box she had toppled in her startlement at her friend's voice as she scrambled to recall the girl's name.

It eluded her. She sighed. Oh, well. She would no doubt hear it again soon enough. Indeed, if Effie was performing true to form, she was most probably still rambling on about the chit. Effie was rather like a dog with a bone when it came to conversation: she never let go of a subject until she'd worried it to death.

Now fairly confident that the discussion still rested upon . . . well, whatever her name was . . . Adeline looked back up at her friend and replied, "You were talking about your American granddaughter. You were—" Vaguely recalling Effie clucking over the erratic arrival schedules of American ships, she guessed, "You were wondering exactly when the gel is to arrive."

Euphemia sniffed. "Ha! That proves my point exactly. I have already told you twice"—she held up two plump, indigo-stained fingers—"twice!—that she is to arrive three weeks from Thursday. She's coming—"

"Because it was her father's dying wish that you find her a husband," Adeline finished for her. There! That should prove that she'd been listening . . . at least as much as it was possible for anyone to listen to Effie when she got into a natter.

"Well, I don't mind telling you that I pity the poor girl," Euphemia retorted, applying pigment to the printing plate before her. "How very terrible it must be for her to be sent from her home and family, especially so soon after her father's death. Though I dearly loved and am truly devastated by my darling son's demise, I simply cannot imagine what could have possessed him to have wasted his last breath on such an outrageous request."

"It is hardly outrageous for a dying man to charge a relative with the care of his child. Quite the contrary," Adeline replied. A-ha! The tin crystals. Carrying the earthenware jar back to where the merino soaked, she added, "If you ask me, I think his request perfectly sensible."

Euphemia shook her head, making her chocolate brown ringlets—fabric wasn't the only thing she dyed—bob beneath her beribboned home cap. "It might be sensible to send her all this way if she had no one else. But she has relatives aplenty in America, including her five older brothers. Why he didn't charge one of them with the duty of seeing her wed, I shall never understand. The boys are all married and settled, and perfectly equal to the task, while I—I am too durned old to flitter about town chasing after a miss and playing matchmaker."

Adeline shrugged one shoulder and stirred her scientifically rationed measure of tin crystals into the dye bath. "It could be that her father wishes her to wed aristocracy. Indeed, considering her noble bloodline, he might very well have thought her too fine to waste on a colonial bumpkin."

"No, no. He thought nothing of the sort. My Joseph was quite the patriot, though why I simply cannot imagine." Euphemia sniffed. "Barbaric place, America. Full of ruffians and redskins."

"Perhaps the gel agrees with you. Perhaps that is why she is being sent here. It could be that she finds American men not at all to her taste and has thus far refused to marry one," Adeline suggested, frowning down at the dye bath. It had taken on a most peculiar cast.

Euphemia emitted a noise that sounded suspiciously

like a grunt. "I hardly think that the case. Not when you consider that she has already found three men who suit."

"Three?" Adeline looked up quickly, her frown deepening. "Whatever are you saying, Effie?"

"That she has been engaged thrice," her friend replied, centering the printing plate over the rainbow-hued cambric she'd tied and dyed the week before.

For the first time since beginning the discussion, Adeline's interest was genuinely piqued. "Indeed? Do tell."

Euphemia pressed the plate against the cloth, then shrugged. "There is really nothing to tell. Things just didn't work out." Picking up a small wooden mallet, she began tapping the back of the plate.

"Didn't work out?" Adeline repeated, flabbergasted by her friend's nonchalance at what most members of the *ton* would consider a disastrous state of affairs. "Didn't work out for whom? The gel or the grooms?"

"I am not really certain." *Tap! Tap! Tap!* "Joseph never wrote much about the matter, and it would have been indelicate for me to have pried."

"Indelicate? Indelicate!" Adeline exclaimed, her voice rising in her incredulity at Effie's obtuseness. "It was indelicate *not* to have pried, especially considering that the poor gel has been motherless since birth." She shook her head, clucking her reproach. "I am ashamed of you, Effie. Really, I am. I simply cannot believe that you, of all people, could be such a widgeon."

Rather than look chastised, Euphemia positively beamed . . . not at all the response Adeline had expected. Ceasing her tapping to grin at her friend, she crowed, "Why, Addy! You truly were listening! You had to have been to remember my misgivings about her motherless state."

"Of course I was listening. I said I was, didn't I?" she retorted, taken aback to discover that she couldn't actually recall Effie airing any such concerns. Hmmm. It seemed that one didn't have to listen to Effie's prattle to absorb it. Apparently it was rather like a strong kitchen odor—it crept into your attic whether you wished it to or not. Hiding her astonishment at her discovery,

Adeline eyed her friend with reproof and pointed out, "Whether or not I was listening is hardly the issue here. Your granddaughter and her difficulty in getting a man to the alter is."

"Yes. Of course you are right, Addy, dear," Euphemia murmured, adopting a properly chastened expression. "It is a matter you can be certain that I shall explore the instant she arrives." Nodding in affirmation to her purpose, she resumed her tapping. She had tapped halfway across the plate when the mallet froze in mid-air and she gasped aloud. "Oh, my! You don't suppose that Emily is a jilt, do you?"

Emily. So that was the chit's name. Marking it in her mind, Adeline shook her head. "My guess is that the problem is the exact opposite, that it is a lack of feminine guile that has been her undoing. She was, after all, raised in a household of men. Without a mother's guidance, she most probably never learned the subtle charms of womanhood. Why, I shan't be at all surprised when she arrives to find her an utter hoyden."

"A hoyden!" Euphemia couldn't have looked more appalled. "Oh, my. Whatever shall I do if she is indeed as you say?"

"*We*. What shall *we* do, dear," Adeline corrected her, meeting her friend's troubled gaze with a reassuring smile. "After all the help you have given me with Michael through the years, you don't honestly think that I would abandon you in this, do you?"

Euphemia slowly smiled back, her aged face manifesting vestiges of the beauty that had once enchanted an entire generation of men. Her dark eyes growing misty and her voice choked with emotion, she whispered, "Oh, Addy. You truly are the best of friends. Whatever would I do without you?"

Feeling her own throat strangle on the sentimentality of the moment, Adeline, who prided herself on her rigid control, snorted and poked the merino with her stirring pole. "I suspect that you would do very much as we shall do together," she crisply countered, deliberately misinterpreting the question. "You would polish the gel's manners, deck her out like a plate from La Belle Assemblée, introduce her in the proper circles, and let matters take their own course. If she is anywhere near as fetching as you were in your youth, she shall be engaged before the end of her first season."

"Do you really think that it will be so very simple?" Euphemia inquired dubiously.

Adeline nodded and squinted into the dye bath. "Simple for two old she-dragons like us." Scowling at what she saw, she fished the cloth from the vat.

"But Addy, what if—"

"Oh, devil a bit!"

A cry of dismay escaped Euphemia's lips as well at the sight of the cloth dangling from the end of the stirring pole. It was a most putrid shade of green, nowhere near the sunny yellow Adeline had hoped to achieve. Setting aside her problem with Emily in the face of her friend's dire dye disaster, she ejected, "Ecod, Effie! It's the color of pond scum. Whatever do you think went wrong?"

"Vitriol, I suspect." Making a face, Adeline dumped the hideous cloth into the waiting vat of rinse water. "I must have mistakenly put green vitriol crystals into the tin crystal jar when I refilled it earlier. I cannot imagine how I could have done something so harebrained."

"I can," Euphemia shot back, resuming her tapping. "You've been half at sea all morning long. Indeed, I've had the distinct impression that there is something on your mind . . . something you clearly do not wish to share with me." This last was uttered with an injured air, for while she freely confided her troubles to Adeline, Adeline dithered about in distraction with hers until Euphemia was forced either to pry them from her or go mad from the annoyance her dithering provoked.

As she always did when Euphemia commented upon her dithering, Adeline sighed as if beset with the greatest of despairs. "Oh, Effie, it isn't that I don't wish to confide in you. It's just that I hate to burden you with my problems. Especially this one, since there is nothing to be done for it."

"I always burden you with my problems, don't I? Re-

gardless of how impossible they might be." At Adeline's
nod, she nodded back, logically pointing out, "Then it's
only fair that I listen to yours. Who knows? Being an
impartial party, I just might see a solution that has thus
far escaped you. You know how short-sighted you can
be when you're too close to a problem."

"Well . . ."

When she made no effort to continue, Euphemia
snorted her exasperation and scolded, "See here, Adeline
Vane, neither of us is getting any younger. So do stop
wasting what precious little time we have left and empty
the bag."

"Well . . ." her friend repeated, this time stretching
every letter of the word. Poking the cloth with the stirring pole as she stretched the last *l*, she finally conceded,
"All right, then. If you insist."

Euphemia pursed her lips and nodded. "I do."

"Well . . ." Another sigh. "If you must know, it's *The
Varlet*. He and *The Hussy* paid me another visit yesterday." As everyone in Adeline's set knew, *The Varlet* was
her despicable great-nephew, Owen Pringle, who stood
to inherit the duchy of Sherrington should something befall the current duke, her grandson, Michael. *The Hussy*
was Owen's wife, Beatrice, a vulgar, grasping creature
who made no bones about her eagerness to be a duchess.

At the mention of the Pringles, Euphemia's mallet
struck the printing plate with far more force than the
delicate task demanded.

"My sentiment exactly," Adeline remarked drily, giving the cloth another jab. "Beastly pair, the Pringles. Had
the gall to invite themselves to supper. Quite spoiled
my digestion."

"They seem to have made a habit of spoiling your
digestion of late," Euphemia observed with a grimace.
"I don't see why you do not simply refuse to receive
them and be done with it."

"I tried that already, remember? And things were much
the worse for it. Instead of annoying me at my home for
a few hours every week or so, they haunted my steps in
public. I couldn't so much as walk through my door with-

out being accosted by them. It was a nightmare! Every
time I turned around, they were there, yammering and
pecking, and making my life an utter misery." She shook
her head, her expression glum. "If only I could think of
a way to rid myself of them, permanently."

"I already thought of the perfect way," Euphemia reminded her, giving the printing plate a final tap. "Or
have you forgotten?"

"Of course I haven't forgotten. How could I? Unfortunately, we cannot really shoot them."

Euphemia sniffed and set aside the mallet. "Why the
devil not? If you were to invite them for a friendly ar-
chery match and we just happened to shoot them, well,
what court would convict us? At our age we're expected
to be half-blind and completely dotty. No doubt the Pringles would be judged deserving of what they got for
being cork-brained enough to shoot with us."

As Euphemia had hoped, Adeline laughed. "Oh, Effie!
My darling, dearest friend. You truly are a wicked old
fury," she gasped out between chuckles.

"Being a fury is a privilege of age," Euphemia retorted
primly. "A privilege, I might add, that you, yourself, delight in exercising from time to time."

"Indeed I do, and you can be sure that I take particular delight in exercising it on *The Varlet*." A faint snort.
"Bloody lot of good it does."

"Addy! Language, please." Wickedness was one thing,
cursing was quite another.

"Sorry," Adeline muttered, not looking a whit contrite
at her use of the word "bloody." "It's just that—I mean,
every time I think of—ooohhh!" She gave the cloth a
vicious shove, splashing water over the edge of the vat
and across the flagstone floor.

Euphemia gaped at her friend, stunned by her rare
display of temper. When she at last broke from her
shock, she exclaimed, "Why, Addy! You truly are over-
set! Whatever did *The Varlet* say to put you in such
a pucker?"

Adeline ejected an explosive snort. "It isn't so much
what he said. Tedious creature that he is, he never says

anything original. He first inquires about Michael's health, after which he makes noises about his neglect of his ducal duties. Those gems of cousinly concern are inevitably followed by *The Hussy's* suggestion that I have Michael declared incompetent and turn the duchy over to her husband." She gave the hideous green cloth a vicious stab with her pole. "As if I'd entrust even a shilling of the Vane fortune to that grasping pair."

Euphemia couldn't help grinning as her friend proceeded to mutter several colorful invectives that perfectly described their mutual opinion of anyone who dared to defame Michael . . . their handsome, witty, *darling* Michael.

Her grin softened into a fond smile as she lifted the printing plate from her fabric to reveal a midnight blue imprint of a pheasant among fanciful blossoms and curling foliage. She would never forget the first time she saw Michael, though twenty-six years had passed. He'd been so small and dear in his black skeleton suit, so pale, but brave, in his fear of the grandmother he barely knew. It had been a week after the tragedy that was now referred to in hushed tones as *The Incident.*

The Incident, as everyone knew, was the duel in which Michael's father had been killed by his wanton mother's lover, with whom she'd afterward fled. Michael had been two at the time. Because he'd had no one else, the task of rearing him had fallen to his recently widowed grandmother. Euphemia, who had borne six sons of her own, all long grown at the time, had adored her friend's beautiful grandson at first sight and had promptly appointed herself his surrogate aunt. Thus, together they had raised him into the glorious man he'd grown to be.

And together they now stood helplessly by, impotent to free him from the torment he currently suffered.

Thinking of his terrible state struck her with the sudden fear that he'd taken a turn for the worse. That would certainly explain Addy's distress, and her reluctance to spill the soup. For though Euphemia was, in truth, the more stout-hearted of the pair, her softer demeanor sometimes prompted Adeline to shield her from the harshness of life . . . especially when the harshness in some way concerned Michael.

Unnerved by her suspicion, yet aware that Adeline would evade her questions if she asked them point-blank, Euphemia discreetly probed, "Speaking of Michael, have you received Mr. Eadon's monthly progress report yet?" Timothy Eadon was the attendant Adeline had hired to look after her grandson.

"Yes."

"And?"

A soft sigh. "Nothing new."

A wave of relief washed over Euphemia. Expelling the breath she'd been unaware she was holding, she murmured, "Ah. Well, then we must give thanks that he hasn't suffered any spells of late. How long has it been since his last?"

"Six months."

Euphemia considered for a beat, then nodded. "Yes. I do believe that we may regard his lack of a change as good news. After all, six months is the longest he has ever gone without a spell. If you will recall, he suffered at least one a month right after his illness."

"Yes. I suppose." Adeline had ceased her assault on the cloth and now stared morosely into the vat.

"Well, then?"

"Well, what?"

Euphemia couldn't keep a note of impatience from creeping into her voice. "Well, if Michael is no worse and the Pringles said nothing out of the ordinary, what has you in high dudgeon?"

There was a brief silence, then Adeline softly confessed, "It's Michael's future. It has me terribly worried."

Euphemia gaped at her friend, wondering if age was beginning to affect her mind. "What? Why ever would you fret about such a thing? As duke of Sherrington, his position in life is secure."

"Is it?" Adeline looked up, her brow crumpled into a troubled frown. "The Pringles' last visit left me wondering just how secure it truly is."

"Indeed?" Euphemia prompted.

Adeline nodded. "You know as well as I that *The Varlet* will be in court the instant I hop the twig, petitioning for control of the duchy."

"And we both know that they will never give it to him," Euphemia countered with conviction.

"Do we? I am no longer so certain. Should I die before Michael has—er—improved, *The Varlet* stands an excellent chance of being granted the duchy."

"But how? I mean . . ." Euphemia shook her head, unable to even conceive of such a notion. "What grounds could *The Varlet* possibly bring forth to support such an action?"

"Madness," Adeline replied in a funereal tone. "He could have our dearest Michael declared mad." She met Euphemia's eyes then, and Euphemia was astounded to see them awash with tears. "Oh, Effie!" she whispered, her voice straining with anguish. "Just thinking of what might become of him if that were to happen—why, I— I—" Her voice shattered, as did her fragile hold on her composure, and a tear escaped down her withered cheek.

"Michael? Mad? Rubbish!" Euphemia ejected, distressed by her friend's show of emotion. In the seventy years of their acquaintance, she had seen Addy cry only three times: the first had been when she'd buried her husband; the second was when her son, her only child, had been killed in the duel; and the third was during the crisis of Michael's devastating illness, when the doctors had despaired for his life.

Wishing that *The Varlet* was there now so she could boil him in the ugly green dye, Euphemia rushed to where Adeline stood, declaring indignantly, "Michael is as sane as you—or I—or anyone else in the *ton*!" Giving her friend a fierce hug, she added, "Saner, even!"

"Of course he is," Adeline replied brokenly, returning her hug. "But you know as well as I that there are many in the *ton* who would argue that point. Don't forget that everyone who is anyone witnessed his awful spell at Lady Kilvington's picnic two seasons ago. And then there are those rumors that dollymop spread about." The dollymop to whom she referred was the jade who had been

Michael's mistress at the time of his illness. "Add all that to the nature of the cures he's sought and the way he has hidden himself in Dartmoor, and the rumors of him having gone mad seem quite sound."

She paused then, her expression growing rueful as she wiped her eyes with the back of her dye-stained hand. When she again spoke, her voice was hushed and as brittle as spun glass. "Of late I have wondered if I perhaps made a mistake in having myself appointed administrator of his duchy. My action could very well be seen as confirmation of the rumors should it ever become common knowledge."

"Of course you did the right thing, and to the devil with the rumors," Euphemia reassured her in a rush. "Michael was in no condition to make decisions during his illness. And now . . . well . . . your control is only temporary. The instant he proves himself fit to tend to his own affairs, it reverts right back to him."

"Yes, I know. But should I die . . ."

"Enough of such talk!" Euphemia interjected sharply, wanting to die herself at the thought of losing her dearest Addy. "You are not going to die, not for many years yet. I simply shan't allow it." She gave her friend another hug.

"I shall endeavor to remember that," Adeline murmured, managing a wan smile. "Still—"

"I know," Euphemia cut in, easily divining her friend's thoughts. "I cannot help worrying as well." Suddenly too glum to muster even a pretense of optimism, she morosely mused, "If only there was something we could do to secure his position, I mean really secure it. For now and forever."

"Yes. If only . . ." Sighing, Adeline closed her eyes. "Unfortunately, there is only one way to do that."

"Yes." Unfortunately, Addy was right.

"And that way is now impossible."

Euphemia opened her mouth to confirm her friend's bleak verdict, then shut it again as an idea began to form . . . a most intriguing and delicious one. In order to secure his duchy—to truly secure it——Michael needed an heir. That meant that he must marry, an advent that had seemed impossible because of his unfortunate condition. Impossible . . . until now. Barely able to hide her excitement, she murmured, "Perhaps that way may not be as impossible as you believe."

Adeline opened her eyes, frowning at her as if she'd lost her wits. "Of course it is. You know as well as I that there isn't a gel in the *ton* who will have Michael now, not a decent one. Those chits who aren't frightened to death of his spells are either repulsed by the notion of them, or scornful of the fact that he suffers them at all."

"Which is why he must wed a girl outside of the *ton*. One of good blood who has no choice but to do as we bid," Euphemia replied with a smug smile.

Adeline snorted. "And where, pray tell, do you propose we find such a creature?"

Euphemia gave her eyebrows a meaningful lift. "Where do you think?"

"I have no idea, but if you believe—" Adeline broke off abruptly, her eyes narrowing. After a brief pause, during which her expression of crotchety annoyance shifted to one of gleeful calculation, she said, "You aren't thinking what I think you are thinking, are you?"

"And what exactly do you think I am thinking?" Euphemia inquired archly.

A slow smile stretched across Adeline's creased face. "That we match your granddaughter to my grandson."

"Exactly." Euphemia cackled her delight at her own ingenuity. "You have to admit that is a perfect plan, for everyone. My granddaughter marries a man whom I both love and approve of, and Michael gets a suitable bride. As for this business with the Pringles, well, the very fact that Michael is wed will do much to weaken whatever claims they might ever make on the duchy. Best of all, it will unite our families. You know that that has always been our fondest wish. Just imagine, Addy, we could be sharing great-grandchildren someday."

"Great-grandchildren." Adeline's expression grew far away and she smiled dreamily. "Can you imagine how very wonderful children from our combined blood would be?"

She could imagine, easily. "They would be exceedingly beautiful."

"And charming. You know how very charming Michael can be?"

Euphemia nodded. She did know, having been twisted around his little finger for so many years. "And intelligent. I am told that Emily is quite clever, as is Michael."

"Their children would be nothing short of perfection," Adeline summed up.

Nodding in mutual agreement at that prediction, they fell silent, each smiling proudly as she envisioned her perfect great-grandchildren. After several moments of doing so, Adeline's smile began to fade, then it disappeared completely. "It is a pretty thought, but I do not think it wise that we get our hopes too high," she murmured, shaking her head.

"Pardon?" Euphemia blinked several times, frowning as she was pulled from her delightful reverie. "Whatever do you mean?"

"It's Michael." Adeline more sighed than uttered the words. "You know how difficult he has become. We shall never be able to convince him to cooperate."

Euphemia's smile returned in a flash. "Oh, I doubt if much convincing will be required once he sees Emily. After all, Michael has always had an eye for beauty, and Emily is said to be exceedingly lovely. Indeed, she is considered by many, I hear, to be the most beautiful girl in Boston."

"Ah. But there's the rub, don't you see? Michael refuses to receive anyone. I doubt if he will so much as allow himself to be introduced to her."

"Then you must force him to receive her," Euphemia declared, not about to be thwarted by Michael's brooding. "Need I remind you that the court awarded you guardianship of his person as well as of his duchy? Should he prove too intractable, you must remind him of that fact."

Adeline looked positively stricken. Hanging her head,

as if defeated by the very thought of crossing her grandson, she muttered, "Such tactics will never work, not with Michael. He's far too stubborn to bow to threats. Besides, you know how he resents it when I meddle in his life. Why, he still hasn't forgiven me for engaging Mr. Eadon."

Euphemia sniffed at her friend's weak-willed twittering. For all that Addy was a dragon in the *ton*, she was a wet goose when it came to dealing with her grandson. Deciding it high time the boy was taken in hand, she sternly lectured, "Forcing Mr. Eadon's services on Michael was the best thing you could have done for him. Indeed, the very fact that he hasn't suffered a spell in six months bears testimony to that fact. As for forcing a match with Emily, well, aside from the obvious advantages, doing so might very well improve his spirits. High spirits make for a healthy body, I always say. And there is nothing to lift a young man's spirits like a beautiful woman."

"You could be right . . . I suppose," Adeline reluctantly admitted, though she still looked far from happy.

"Of course I am. I am always right, aren't I?" That Euphemia possessed the greater sense in regards to Michael was a fact that had been acknowledged by both women on numerous occasions.

"Yes."

"Good. Then it's settled. Michael and Emily shall be wed." Euphemia smiled, well pleased with her day's work.

"Uh . . . Effie, dear. You seem to be forgetting an important factor in all of this."

"Which is?"

"Your granddaughter. She could prove as difficult as Michael."

Euphemia chuckled drily. "She could, but she won't."

"How can you be so certain?"

"I am certain because she shall be given no choice in the matter. I will simply inform her that she is to be wed, and that shall be that. If you truly love Michael and wish to preserve the Vane family name, you won't give him a choice either."

Chapter 2

Dartmoor, England

*T**his must be the dreariest place on earth,*** Adeline thought, viewing the hideous stone gargoyles with distaste. The gargoyles in question were much like her grandson's current residence, Windgate Abbey, in which she now stood: cold, eerie, and savagely misshapen. Like the gargoyles, which featured the worst possible physical attributes of the ugliest known creatures, both real and mythical, the additions to the abbey reflected the most grotesque architectural innovations of the past six centuries.

Built in the thirteenth century as a Cistercian abbey, Windgate had been confiscated by Henry VIII during his dissolution of the monasteries, at which point it had begun its metamorphosis into a country house. If legend stood correct, and Adeline didn't doubt for a moment that it did, the house had been given to a Vane ancestor as a reward for helping the king win the heart of Jane Seymour, his third queen. That that ancestor was most probably instrumental in the beheading of the king's existing wife, Anne Boleyn, was a detail that was never discussed.

Standing now in what had once been the chapel nave, but now served as the entry hall, Adeline found herself considering that very detail and thinking that the monstrousness of the house reflected the sin for which it had been a reward. She had just turned her mind to comparing it to Michael's four other estates, all exceedingly pleasant places, and wondering what had possessed him to choose this one as his refuge, when the majordomo came into view.

In keeping with the abbey's alarming image, the servant was a cadaverous-looking giant of indeterminate age with beetled black eyebrows and a twisted beak of a nose. As if those unfortunate traits weren't off-putting enough to callers, should anyone actually have the temerity to call, the man had an unnerving propensity toward baring his teeth when he spoke, the pointiness of which created the disconcerting effect of a vampire about to partake in a snack.

He was baring those teeth now as he sketched a surprisingly graceful bow. "The duke is in the summer parlor. If you would be so good as to follow me?" As surprising as his grace was his voice, which was nothing short of beautiful.

"Thank you, Grimshaw," Adeline replied, nodding cordially. For all that he was a fright to look at, he really was a dear man.

Grimshaw bared his teeth further, into what was his version of a smile, then turned on his highly polished heels and led her up a stone staircase, and into the tortured maze that was Windgate Abbey. As Adeline followed, she couldn't help thinking that perhaps the most startling aspect of the majordomo wasn't so much his barbarous looks as their astonishing contrast to his elegant attire. If ever a man was immaculately groomed, it was Grimshaw. Indeed, there was many a London buck who could stand to emulate his style.

It was the thought of London and the city's glittering denizens that dragged her mind back to her grandson. Once upon a time he had been the most beautiful and fashionable of them all. And that opinion wasn't just grandmotherly pride. Before his illness had taken its toll, the entire *ton* had acknowledged and revered him as their preeminent gallant. He was the man other men wished to be, the one the women sighed over and dreamed of wedding. Indeed, so much the rage was he that it wasn't at all uncommon for the ladies to raise their cups during tea and propose toasts to his numerous charms. Michael, who had been spoiled from the cradle by adoring females of all stations, had simply accepted their homage as his due.

Passing from the original stone abbey building into the timber and brick Tudor wing, Adeline considered how much less devastating his current situation would have been and how much easier he might have borne it had he not been so celebrated. After all, being a demigod of sorts had meant that he'd had much farther to fall than if he had been a mere mortal. It also meant that his condition had been granted less tolerance than would have been allowed a lesser man.

As a prime example of manhood, he had naturally been expected to be impervious to all weakness and imperfection. To show that he was indeed vulnerable and ultimately flawed had been viewed as a betrayal of that expectation, and was thus judged unforgivable. That his flaw should manifest itself in such a shocking manner had made the *ton,* which had once so worshiped him, turn away in disgust. As for Michael . . .

She sighed, her heart aching at his suffering. Her poor, darling Michael. For a man who flourished on feminine attention and thrived on manly sport, being ostracized by society had been the cruelest fate imaginable. Of course, not everyone had abandoned him. He'd had a few true friends who had remained loyal, or would have had he allowed them to do so. Unfortunately he'd chosen to view his condition with the same scorn as the *ton,* and his resulting shame had caused him to push away those who would have given him comfort. In the end, when it became clear that there was no cure for what ailed him, he'd shut himself away in this gloomy tomb of a house, rejecting company for fear of humiliating himself in front of others with one of his unpredictable spells.

No doubt he would have shunned her as well had she allowed him to do so. But of course, she wasn't about to allow any such thing. She loved him far too much to leave him alone in his torment. Besides, she truly believed that there was hope for him someday having a

happy and fulfilling life. And at that moment, she saw
Emily Merriman as the key to that hope.

Adeline nodded her affirmation. She'd contemplated
Effie's proposed match between Emily and Michael at
length. And after much thought and several sleepless
nights, she'd decided that her friend might very well be
right, that it was the infirmity of Michael's spirit, not his
body, that was keeping him in his invalid state. Indeed,
the very fact that he remained debilitated, despite his
lengthy freedom from spells, gave credence to her theory.
Thus, Adeline had decided that the best medicine for
him was female companionship. A hoyden, to be exact.
A beautiful one who would turn his world upside down
and shock his thoughts away from his woes. And Adeline
had no doubt in her mind that Emily Merriman was the
very hoyden for the task.

Why? Because the gel was an American. And if she
was anything like the other American women she'd met,
she was certain to be livelier and more headstrong than
her prim English counterparts. Add that natural American audacity to the fact that she'd been raised by a
houseful of men, and you were bound to get a chit with
the mettle to deal with Michael's foul moods. Indeed,
after a lifetime spent in masculine company, there was
most probably nothing he could say or do that she hadn't
already heard or dealt with before. That meant that she
was unlikely to be intimidated or shocked by him, which
gave hope to the chance that she would see the pain that
fueled his bitterness and recognize him for what he was:
a wounded man in desperate need of love and understanding.

If she possessed even a shred of her grandmother's
enormous capacity for compassion, she would strive to
befriend him and perhaps someday even learn to love
him. As for Michael, once he saw that she was no milk-
and-water miss to be scared away by his growls, there
was a chance that he would respond to her kindness and
that they might eventually become man and wife in more
than just name.

It was a chance. And she was willing to take any chance

to heal her grandson. Now she must force him to take a
chance as well.

Fully comprehending the unpleasantness of the task
before her, Adeline continued to trail the majordomo,
stopping when he signaled for her to do so. With mounting dread of the coming battle, she waited outside the
parlor door as he announced her, chanting Euphemia's
advice over and over again in her mind.

I mustn't give him a choice. I mustn't give him a choice.

Knowing how furious Michael was going to be when
she voiced her command made it the hardest advice she'd
ever taken. Breaking her chant to remind herself that
she was doing what she was about to do for his own
good, she nodded at Grimshaw, who was now motioning
her into the room, and stepped over the threshold.

Full of light and color, the summer parlor was the one
room in the house of which Adeline actually approved.
Dating from the early Stuart reign, it boasted not only
what she considered to be the most magnificent plasterwork ceiling in England, but the grandest parquet
floor as well.

Done in a palette of green, gold, and red, the room
was paneled in grained wood upon which was emblazoned the most exquisite arabesque painting imaginable.
In the northeast corner stood a white marble fireplace,
whose top was ingeniously worked into the paneling;
spanning the entire west wall was an enormous oriel
made grand by Venetian windows. Lounging on a daybed
within the oriel, his long form swathed in an emerald
damask dressing gown, was her grandson.

"Michael, my love!" she exclaimed, rushing to where
he lay. "I cannot tell you how happy I am to see you."
Grimshaw was on her heels carrying an ornately carved
Yorkshire chair, which he stood ready to deposit wherever she chose to sit. This location, of course, was right
next to her grandson, who didn't so much as open his
eyes in acknowledgment to her presence.

Settling into the chair, Adeline took his alarmingly
cold hand in hers, noting with a pang how ill he looked.
The poor, poor dear. He was so very thin, far thinner

than she'd ever seen him. And beyond pale. Why, even his lips were ashen, blanched to the same sickly grayish-ivory hue that resulted when wool was improperly bleached. In truth, the only thing about him that appeared in health was his overlong hair, which at the moment tumbled in a tangle of glossy dark waves and curls across the gold velvet pillow beneath his head.

Wanting to weep at the sight of him, she lovingly chided, "My darling boy, whatever have you been doing with yourself? You look positively dreadful."

It wasn't until Grimshaw took his leave that Michael responded, though he still didn't open his eyes. "You would look dreadful, too, if you had been purged twice, bled half to death, and forced to swallow three emetics in as many days," he snapped, the strength of his voice at odds with his wan appearance.

Adeline gave his hand a sympathetic squeeze. "I know your treatments are difficult at times, dear, but—"

"Yes, yes. I know. They are for my own good." He made a derisive noise. "So you and Eadon keep telling me."

"Yes, and it appears that they are working. Don't forget that you haven't suffered a spell in almost seven months. Even you have to admit that that fact alone marks an amazing improvement."

His lips twisted sardonically, though he still didn't bother to open his eyes. "Whether or not I have 'improved' is a subject up for debate. Indeed, as you, yourself, so tactfully pointed out just now, I look dreadful, and I can assure you that I feel ten times worse than I look."

"Michael," she began, desperately wishing that there was something she could say or do to alleviate his misery. "I—"

He cut her off with an impatient wave of his hand. His voice reflecting the brusqueness of his gesture, he growled, "What do you want, Grandmother? Has Eadon reported some transgression for which you have come to scold me? Or have you, heaven forbid, found some new cure to inflict upon me?"

Had he not been so obviously wretched, Adeline would have replied in like curt coin. Since, however, he was clearly peevish from illness, she let his surliness pass and gently responded, "Can't I visit you simply because I love you?"

His thick black lashes lifted at that, revealing the stunning jade eyes that had once caused such a fervor among the ladies. Gazing at her with undisguised cynicism, he replied, "You could, but you haven't. The only reason you ever come to Dartmoor is to make my life miserable. Why, even at Christmas, which, if I remember correctly, was the last time you visited, you couldn't resist the temptation to foist one of your quacks upon me." He snorted. "As I recall, the man was Italian, and a very merry Christmas gift he turned out to be. I couldn't stir from my bed the entire month after he had finished with me."

He smiled then, but in a way that held no humor or pleasure. "So, Grandmother, what sort of lovely surprise do you have for me this time? A Russian obsessed with the bowels, perhaps? One who will blister my belly and deluge me with yet more clysters? Or have you found an Egyptian who wishes to shave my head and cover my scalp with leeches?"

Adeline felt a niggle of guilt at his words. Several of the cures she'd insisted he try had been, in retrospect, rather harsh, though the hope they had presented at the time had made it seem worth her forcing him to endure them. Remembering that hope and telling herself that any one, or even all, of those cures could be responsible for the current abatement of his spells, she replied, "Let me assure you that I am quite content with the progress you are making under Mr. Eadon's care. And unless you start suffering frequent spells again, I see no reason to seek other cures."

Michael stared at his grandmother, not certain whether to be relieved or alarmed by her news. While Eadon's remedies weren't exactly what anyone would call pleasant, they weren't as brutal as some he had endured. Of course, had he been given a choice in the matter, which he hadn't, thanks to his grandmother and her manipulation of the English courts, he would have chosen simply to be left alone. In truth, as repulsed as he was by his spells, he was beginning to think that they were easier to bear than the hideous weakness he suffered from this latest course of treatments.

It was that weakness that now left him too fatigued to formulate a proper, stinging comeback. Hating his malaise and resenting his grandmother for forcing him to endure it, Michael closed his eyes again and testily muttered, "Would you please just say what you have come to say and leave me alone? I wish to rest."

"Of course you do, poor dear. And rest you shall. We can speak later, when you feel more the thing." Her hand moved to his hair then, gently stroking. It was a soothing gesture, one that over the years had become as familiar and reassuring as his own heartbeat. And despite his bitterness toward his grandmother and his wariness of her motive for visiting, Michael began to relax.

For a long while thereafter they remained like that: Michael drifting between consciousness and slumber, wanting to sleep but still too apprehensive of his grandmother's reason for visiting to do so; Adeline, wondering how best to approach the subject of his marriage to Emily Merriman.

It was Michael who finally broke their uneasy trance. "Grandmother?" he murmured, his eyes still closed.

"Yes, darling?"

He shifted his head slightly, urging her to stroke all the way down to his nape. When she complied, pausing to massage the back of his neck, he sighed his pleasure. "Feels good."

"Of course it does. Now hush and go to sleep." She expertly kneaded her way down to where his neck curved into his shoulder.

He released a soft moan of appreciation. "Mmm . . . can't sleep . . . not until you tell me what you wish to discuss."

"I told you that it can wait until you feel better." There was a note of gentle chiding in her voice.

He smiled faintly, another moan escaping him as her fingers found a particularly stiff muscle in his shoulder. "I doubt I'm going to feel much better than this. In fact, I cannot recall feeling so very good since the last time you did this." He moaned again to illustrate his point. "Ahhh. Think you might be able to teach Eadon to rub my shoulders like this? I promise to stop grumbling about him if you do."

She chuckled. "Unfortunately, no. He is a man, and the pleasure you are currently experiencing comes from what is commonly called a woman's touch."

Ah, yes. A woman's touch. His gut gave a sudden and painful twist. Of all the things he missed about his former life, women and their touch was what he missed the most . . . especially those touches that teased and tantalized his most intimate parts. Unfortunately, such touches and the pleasures that inevitably followed were the things he was least likely to experience again, at least in the foreseeable future.

As he dejectedly contemplated that bleak fact, his grandmother's hand stilled. "Michael, love? What is amiss?" There was a sharp note of urgency in her voice.

He grunted and shook his head. "Nothing out of the ordinary . . . well, at least nothing out of my ordinary, such as it is." Smiling at the bitterness of his own irony, he opened his eyes and gazed up at his grandmother. When he saw her expression, oddly perplexed and full of worry, he added, "What makes you ask?"

She frowned. "You look so grim all of a sudden. Why?"

"I always look grim these days, or so you and Eadon are always saying," he reminded her, evading the question. There were some things a man simply didn't discuss with his grandmother, and his sexual desire was one of them.

"True, but never while I am plying my woman's touch," she countered, outmaneuvering him.

"Mmmm, yes. Speaking of your woman's touch—" He jerked his head at her hand, which now rested on his shoulder, indicating his wish that she resume her stroking and massaging.

She shook her head and folded her arms over her chest. "Oh, no. Not until you tell me what had you looking so devastated just now. Something is clearly distressing you, and I want to know what it is."

Michael sighed, easily recognizing the expression on her patrician face. How could he not? He'd seen it hundreds of times while growing up. And as it had back then, that expression now told him that she expected an immediate answer to her question and that she would brook neither argument nor evasion.

He returned her gaze for several moments, trying to concoct an appropriate lie. Then he remembered her uncanny talent for seeing through fibs and resigned himself to telling the truth. Feeling as if he were fourteen again and had been caught with his hand up the chambermaid's skirt, he muttered, "If you must know, your mention of women's touches reminded me of my past mistresses and how much I miss their—er—physical intimacies."

Rather than looking shocked or embarrassed, as he had expected, she smiled faintly and nodded. "Of course you do. You are a young man, and young men have certain appetites that need to be satisfied on a regular basis."

"Indeed?" he murmured, for lack of a better response. What else could he say to that?

She nodded again. "Yes. It is something that Effie and I were discussing—"

"You and Effie discussed my—my appetites?" he sputtered, genuinely appalled. That two such respectable old dragons would even consider his sexual needs was a notion that utterly staggered his mind.

"Of course we discussed them," she retorted primly, eyeing him as if he had just asked a very stupid question. "I discuss everything with Effie, especially those things that concern you. She is, after all, my bosom-bow, and she loves you almost as much as I do."

"Be that as it may, my manly needs are hardly an

appropriate subject of discussion for women," he pointed out stiffly.

She snorted. "Pshaw! Don't be such a prig, Michael. You know as well as I that men discuss women in such a manner all the time and see no harm in doing so. What is wrong with us women doing the same?"

A prig was he? A prig! Michael met his grandmother's steady gaze with indignation, his eyes narrowing as he noted her sparkling amusement. All right, then. If she indeed saw nothing wrong with discussing sexual matters, then he would forget that he was a gentleman and do so. Carefully donning his most blasé expression, the one he always assumed when discussing such matters at his club, he nodded and replied, "Fine. If you truly wish to have this conversation, then perhaps you would be so good as to tell me what you and Effie decided should be done about my appetites."

"Why, they must be satisfied, of course, and we have just the plan to help you do so."

"What!" He more roared than said the word. So much for being blasé.

She nodded, clearly unperturbed by his towering outrage. "We decided that your grimness stems from your spending much too much time alone in this dreary heap of stones. And that the very thing to raise your spirits is a lovely gel."

Michael's eyes narrowed at her response. "You didn't, by chance, just happen to bring a 'lovely gel' with you, did you?" Heaven help him, but he would strangle her if she had.

"Of course not."

He exhaled a sigh of relief.

"But one will arrive next week."

"What!" The walls practically shook from the force of his shout.

His grandmother nodded, smiling as if she hadn't heard his eruption. "The gel is Effie's American granddaughter, Emily, and she is reputed to be quite a beauty."

For several moments Michael remained too stunned to reply. When he finally managed to speak, his words came out in a hiss. "Are you telling me that Effie wishes me to satisfy my manly needs on her granddaughter?" And here he'd thought he had been shocked before.

She couldn't have looked more pleased with herself. "Yes, but not until after you are wed, of course."

Michael's mouth opened and closed soundlessly several times; then he bolted upright and thundered, "Good God, woman! Have you gone mad?"

"Of course not," she returned calmly, "and if you don't wish all of England to continue to believe that you have, you will wed the gel and get her with child." Firmly grasping his shoulder, she tried to force him back down on the daybed. "You really must lie down and rest. You are going to need your strength for when your bride arrives."

"Like hell I am," he spat, resisting her efforts. "If you think that I am going to wed some American chit whom I have never even met, you can think again. I will not do it!"

"You will," she shot back, her eyes growing hard as their gazes clashed. "I command you to do so."

Michael glared at her, too incensed to do more. After a beat he found his tongue and bit out, "You have heard the rumors, I assume? The ones my most recent mistress has been spreading?"

She shrugged. "Of course. Everyone has."

"And has it ever occurred to you that they might be true?"

Another shrug. "You know that I never heed such gossip."

"You bloody damn well should, because in this instance it just happens to be true!" He spat the words through gritted teeth.

His grandmother recoiled slightly, but never lost her air of composure. Not that he'd expected her to. As far as he knew, nothing had ever shattered her aplomb. True to form, she shrugged yet again and coolly replied, "True or not, it hardly matters now. That episode happened over two years ago and much has changed since that time, including you. Given your improvement, I am certain that such a thing will never happen again."

"You are damned right it won't, because I refuse to put myself in the position to suffer that kind of shame again. Ever!"

She made a clucking noise behind her teeth. "Such stuff and nonsense. You don't really expect me to believe that you intend to remain celibate, do you? Why, the very notion is absurd."

Michael snorted. "Tell that to your quacks. According to their expert opinion, excitement of any kind can provoke spells. Because of the incident with my mistress, I have been specifically instructed to avoid sexual arousal at all costs."

His grandmother snorted back. "Pshaw. They were simply being cautious. If their theory of excitement provoking spells were indeed true, you would be having one now."

"Be that as it may, there will be no wedding." Michael gave his head a firm shake, determined to squelch her outlandish plan once and for all. "When Effie and the chit arrive, you will explain that it was all a mistake and send them on their way. And you will never—I repeat, never!—so much as even consider such a scheme again. Do I make myself clear?" He more roared than uttered that last line.

Oh, he'd made himself perfectly clear. Adeline, however, had no intention of abandoning her plan or her last hope for his happiness. Again reminding herself that the marriage was for his own good, she adopted her most authoritative mien and decreed, "There will be a marriage, and that is that. I command it."

"Of course you do. You do nothing but command me these days," he flung back, meeting her gaze with cold, resentful eyes. "However, unlike the cures you have forced upon me in the past, you cannot have me held down and simply inflict this marriage on me. I have to speak the vows willingly, you know."

"Yes. And you will." Despite her exasperation with

him, she was pleased to see a spot of color rise in his cheeks.

"And if I refuse?"

She let his inquiry dangle in the air for a moment, then brought it crashing to earth with, "Then I shall have you declared mad and you shall be committed to Bamforth Hall." Bamforth Hall was the genteel asylum where he had been confined during several of his more aggressive cures. It was a place he both despised and feared.

As she had expected, he looked horrified. So horrified, in fact, that she felt her resolution waver. It was just a threat, of course. She would never send Michael back to Bamforth, no matter the circumstances. Unfortunately, it was the only threat she knew powerful enough to sway him to her will.

After several moments, during which what little color he had gained during their argument drained from his face, Michael recovered himself and said, "You know as well as I that you would never do such a thing. Not when it means handing the duchy over to the Pringles."

"Wouldn't I?" she softly challenged.

He smiled rather smugly. "No. Never."

She smiled back. "You are wrong. I would if the Pringles relinquished their infant son into my care, which we both know they would do in a heartbeat if it meant gaining the duchy."

His jade eyes narrowed, and to Adeline's relief, she saw a flicker of uncertainty in their depths. "I don't believe you. Why would you do such a thing? You always said that you would die before you would allow a Pringle to assume the Sherrington title."

"I will do it because you shall give me no choice, not if you refuse to marry. You know as well as I that if you die without issue, which is exactly what will happen if you do not wed, the title will automatically go to the Pringles. And we both know how disastrous that will be. However, if I were to take their son, Benjamin, now, while he is young, I might be able to raise him into an heir worthy of the Sherrington duchy, thus ensuring the continued eminence of the title."

He raised his eyebrows, visibly skeptical. "Indeed? Well, then, if you are indeed so very worried about the duchy, why take a chance on my marriage to this . . . this . . ." He snapped his fingers. "What is the chit's name again?"

"Emily," she supplied. What was it about the name that made it so difficult to remember?

"Ah, yes. Emily." He shook his head, as if thinking the same thing. "Anyway, as I was saying, if you are so very set on ensuring the Sherrington duchy, why take a chance that my marriage to this Emily chit will bear fruit? As I have explained, there is a good chance that I will be unable to consummate the union. And even if I can, there are no guarantees that my seed will produce an heir."

Adeline shrugged, hiding her grin as she sensed victory close at hand. "There are no guarantees that the Pringle boy can be made worthy of the Sherrington duchy, either. However, given the choice, I'd wager on a Vane against a Pringle any day of the week. Unfortunately, you refuse to give me that choice, so I must cast my lot with the Pringles."

"But why now and why this Emily chit?" he inquired softly.

"Because I am old, and I wish to have things settled." She sighed, suddenly feeling every one of her eighty-two years. "I—"

"Good heavens! You aren't ill, are you?" he interjected, his gaze frantically searching her face. If he had looked horrified by the threat of Bamforth, he looked doubly so now.

"No, no. Of course not. I'm in as fine a feather as I was at twenty," she replied, touched by his concern. Despite his current resentment of her, she never doubted for a moment that he loved her. Patting his wan cheek in a way that conveyed her own love for him, she added, "To answer your question, I have selected Emily because Effie's recently deceased son left her charged with the duty of finding the gel a husband. If you could push aside your stubbornness for a moment, you would see that she is a perfect match. She is, after all, a Merriman, which means that she comes from noble blood, and you know what a dear our Effie is. By all accounts, Emily is every bit as lovely and kind as her grandmother."

"That and the fact that there isn't a gently born girl in all of England who will have me," he added, wearily. Rubbing his temples as if they throbbed, he sighed and lay back down again.

"Yes, that too," Adeline agreed quietly. "Emily Merriman is my last hope for you." As she uttered the words, she began lightly stroking his temples.

He made a soft sound and closed his eyes. She had continued the soothing action for several moments when he murmured, "Will you really have me committed to Bamforth if I refuse to wed the girl?"

Though it pained her to utter the words, she replied, "Yes. I am sorry, but I shall have no choice. The only way the Pringles will hand over their son is in trade for the duchy. And in order for me to give it to them, I must declare you mad and prove the point by sending you to Bamforth."

"And here I thought you loved me," he muttered.

"I do," she exclaimed fiercely. "Do not ever doubt that I love you. Unfortunately, I know where my first loyalty must lie, and that is with the duchy. Were your priorities in order, yours would lie there as well, and I wouldn't be forced to make such a heartbreaking choice. But make it I must."

He heaved a heavy sigh and slowly opened his eyes. Looking as if he were going to a particularly excruciating death, he murmured, "I suppose you must, which leaves me with no choice but to wed this Emily chit."

"No choice at all, unless, of course, you prefer life at Bamforth," she briskly replied.

He grimaced. "I think you know my preference."

Indeed Adeline did, and she smiled.

Chapter 3

"Married!" The girl couldn't have looked more flabbergasted. Indeed, by her expression you would have thought that she'd just been informed that her house had burned down with her entire family inside, not that she was about to be wed.

Euphemia smiled and nodded, certain that her next revelation would soften her granddaughter's shock. "Yes, married, and to a duke, no less. Your groom-to-be is Michael Vane, duke of Sherrington, and he is quite a catch, I assure you. Not only is he young and handsome, he is exceedingly wealthy. In short, he is everything a girl could wish for in a husband." She nodded again, noting with a prick of irritation that the girl appeared unappeased. If anything, she looked even more dismayed.

Oh, botheration! The chit was going to be difficult about this marriage business, and she had so hoped to avoid an unpleasant scene. In fact, she'd been confident of doing so, convinced that the lure of a title and wealth would crush whatever objections her granddaughter might have to wedding a stranger. The ploy most assuredly would have succeeded with any of the girls in the *ton,* had the chosen girl, of course, been ignorant of Michael's spells, which Emily was.

Euphemia surveyed her granddaughter with displeasure, wondering what in Hades ailed her. Then it struck her: Emily wasn't a member of the *ton.* She wasn't even English; she was an American. Could it be that she simply didn't understand the significance of what she was being told?

Deciding that that must indeed be the case, Euphemia pointedly clarified, "Just think, Emily, you shall be a duchess. A duchess! An enviable title by anyone's account. Imagine your American friends' envy when you write them of your grand new station in life."

The chit was either the most contrary creature on earth or the most witless, though Euphemia preferred to believe the former, given the fact that Emily was family, for she stubbornly shook her head and replied, "I can't marry him. Surely you know that?"

"Bosh! I know no such thing. You can marry him, and you will. It is all arranged. You shall be wed tomorrow morning, and that is that." Euphemia fixed Emily, who sat in the opposite coach seat, with her most uncompromising stare, one she was certain would squelch her mutiny.

Again she misjudged the girl. Unlike the misses at Almack's, who could be cowed into quivering silence with that look, Emily remained undaunted. If anything, she looked all the more determined. Her naturally rosy cheeks flaming to the crimson of strong madder dye, she shook her head again and argued, "I can't. It's impossible—"

"You mean you won't, that you intend to be contrary," Euphemia interjected harshly. At her age she had little enough patience, and none whatsoever for disobedient misses.

"No! I—"

"Silence!" The command was accompanied by an imperious hand motion. To Euphemia's supreme satisfaction, the provoking chit actually did as she was told and bridled her wayward tongue. Good. She was beginning to learn her place. Resolved to reinforce the lesson, she again pinned her granddaughter with her glare, this time leaning forward in her seat as she did so to heighten the impact. In a clipped voice that brooked no argument, she said, "You might as well save yourself the trouble of being difficult, girl, for I can assure you that it will do no good. I said that you will wed the duke of Sherrington, and wed him you shall. You have no choice in the matter."

Emily's cheeks flamed a shade brighter, an advent that astounded Euphemia, who was unaware that such a vivid red existed in nature. "I'm not being difficult, Grandmother, truly I am not," she countered, her voice soft and laced with appeal. "I am simply trying to explain why I cannot marry. If you will just listen, I am certain that you'll agree that I can't wed your duke, or anyone else for that matter."

Euphemia, however, was far too appalled by her granddaughter's outlandish color at that moment to listen to anything she had to say. Pointing accusingly at the offending blush, she ejected, "Ecod, child! Your cheeks are a most singular shade of red. If I hadn't seen them flush that color with my own two eyes, I would suspect you of painting."

"My cheeks?" Frowning, Emily raised her yellow-gloved hands to her face, cupping her cheeks in her palms as if to shield their shameful ruddiness from sight. "Oh, the hateful, awful things! They turn this color every time I get the least bit angry or upset . . . they are my cross to bear. I know I look dreadful, but nothing I do seems to repress their color."

Dreadful? Euphemia eyed her granddaughter critically. "Dreadful" most certainly wasn't the word she would have used to describe how Emily looked at that moment. No, seeing her like this, flushed and rather breathless, with her full red lips in a pout and her exotically slanted eyes shadowed by her lowered lashes, brought a far different, and in Euphemia's mind, far worse word to mind. That word was "provocative." In truth, she looked positively wanton, rather like a woman who had just arisen from a tumble with a particularly lusty lover. Not at all a seemly way for an innocent miss to look, or any decent woman, for that matter.

Rather than be distressed by her observation, which she most assuredly would have been had she been faced with guarding Emily's virtue for a Season, Euphemia was

pleased. How could Michael resist her? As a man of the
world, he was certain to appreciate her seductive beauty.

And Emily was undeniably beautiful. Lovelier even
than she had been in her youth, and she'd once been
proclaimed the beauty of the eighteenth century. Secretly
relieved that the girl hadn't been born eighty years earlier, Euphemia leaned back in her seat and viewed her
granddaughter with discriminating eyes.

The ensemble she wore was perfection, which Euphemia had known it would be when she'd selected it for
her. Made of geranium red Gros de Indes silk through
which was worked narrow pistachio stripes, the carriage
gown was sumptuously embellished with trellis trim over
which was embroidered climbing pink and yellow roses.
At the modest neckline was a dainty lace collerette,
pinned with a gold and citrine brooch; matching earrings
dangled from her ears.

Euphemia paused a beat to consider the triple-puffed
à la Marie sleeves, noting with a faint nod of approval
how their fullness accentuated the willowy curves of Emily's torso. Michael would definitely find no fault with that
fine bosom and tiny waist, or with the rounded hips and
long, slender legs she had glimpsed when the dressmaker
had measured the girl for her new wardrobe. As for Emily's face . . .

Her gaze swept upward to her granddaughter's face,
which was charmingly framed by a beribboned and
flower-bedecked leghorn hat. Peeking from beneath that
millinery masterpiece were several glossy curls, their
ebony darkness a stunning contrast to her flawless ivory
skin. Then there were those tip-tilted dark eyes and those
lush red lips. One glance at that exquisite face and Michael was certain to be eager to bed her, thus solving
the problem of an heir. Of course, in order for him to
bed her, the chit would first have to cooperate with the
plan.

That thought pulled her mind back to Emily's refusal
to wed, and her own duty to force her. Determined to
do exactly that, and with as little fuss as possible, Euphemia waved dismissively and said, "Never mind about

your color. A dusting of rice powder should remedy it right enough. The issue at hand is your obstinate refusal to marry the duke of Sherrington."

Emily dropped her hands from her cheeks with a sigh. "Yes, and I am trying to explain why I cannot wed him."

Euphemia echoed her granddaughter's sigh with a heavy one of her own. Vexing, tiresome creature! It was clear that she wasn't going to be silenced until she'd had her say. Feeling the beginnings of a megrim at the prospect of the unpleasantness that was sure to follow that say, she sighed again and crossly relented. "Fine, then. Go ahead and explain if you must. But be warned: your reason shall in no way alter the outcome of this matter. Make no mistake about it—you will marry the duke, exactly as planned. Need I remind you of your father's final request?"

"No, and were I not cursed, I would gladly honor it. Of course, I would insist on selecting my own husband."

Euphemia promptly dismissed the latter part of the statement, focusing instead on the irregularity of the former. "Cursed?" she echoed, caught completely off-guard. She most certainly had to give the girl credit for originality. Of all the objections she had thought her granddaughter might voice, this one had never even entered her mind. Her astonishment momentarily banishing the throb of her impending megrim, she ejected, "Egads, Emily! What the devil sort of nonsense is this?"

"I'm cursed. You know . . . by a witch? Surely Father wrote you about it?" By the girl's expression, it was clear that she expected Euphemia to know exactly what she was blathering about.

Euphemia snorted. "Of course not. He knew better than to write such gibberish."

"But it isn't gibberish. The curse is real." She was shaking her head now, over and over again in a frantic manner that made Euphemia quite dizzy to watch. "Oh, dear. I was sure Father had written you about it. It's the reason I wasn't wed in Boston."

Another snort from Euphemia. "Is that so?" And here

she'd been thinking that it was because the chit was a queer card.

The head shake jerked into a nod.

"Indeed? And what, pray tell, sort of curse is it that it would bar you from marriage?" Heaven help her, she had to ask. There was no help for it if she wanted to settle the matter.

"The witch said that I shall be a plague to any man I love. And I am! The most awful things happen every time I fall in love. Why, my three fiancés were lucky to escape with their lives. When the other gentlemen realized that the curse is indeed real, they avoided me like the plague I am."

"Fools, the lot of them," Euphemia declared with a sniff. "No doubt your father recognized that fact, which explains why he wished you sent here. Being an Englishman himself, he knew that our gentlemen are far too sensible to be frightened off by superstitious twaddle."

The chit was shaking her head in that giddy manner again. "He sent me here because he read somewhere that a curse can't follow a person over water, and he hoped that I might be safely wed here."

"Are you saying that my Joseph actually believed in the curse?" Euphemia exclaimed, incredulous that a fruit from her loins would engage in such folly. Why, were he not already dead, she'd have strangled him for his own stupidity.

Emily bobbed her head to the affirmative . . . goodness! Was it really too much to ask that the child's head remain still for a moment? Watching her was making her own head spin, which did nothing to mitigate her burgeoning megrim.

Continuing her infernal bobbing, Emily soberly replied, "After everything that happened, he had no choice but to believe it. You would too, had you been there."

"I doubt it," Euphemia snapped. The chit was most definitely bringing on a megrim. Deciding it high time that she put an end to her twaddle—and her frightful head gesticulations—before the throb in her temples exploded into a full-blown pounding, she added, "However, whether or not I believe it is neither here nor there. It most certainly doesn't change the fact that you will wed the duke."

"But the curse—"

"Is drivel. There are no such things as curses." Emily opened her mouth, no doubt to argue, but Euphemia silenced her with a stabbing hand motion. "Even if they did exist, which they *do not*, you should be safe enough. You said yourself that a curse cannot follow a person over water." There! That should resolve the matter.

But of course it didn't. "That is what my father believed, but he was wrong." Emily's head was shaking again, desperation edged her voice. "It is demons and ghosts and such that cannot travel over water, not curses. Why, there have been instances of witches cursing people halfway around the world. So you see? I really cannot marry the duke."

Euphemia paused in rubbing her now pounding temples to cast her granddaughter a jaundiced look. "And who, pray tell, fed you that rubbish?"

"Gitta Czigany."

"Who is?" she prompted with an impatient snap of her fingers.

"She's the gypsy I consulted after I was cursed. Her notice in the newspaper said that she is all-knowing in such matters. She was supposed to break the curse, but she left town rather suddenly."

"I see." And she did. She saw that the chit was going to persist with her jabber if she didn't settle the ludicrous matter once and for all. Intent on doing exactly that, she brusquely stated, "The very fact that the woman is a gypsy proves that this curse business is rot. Notorious liars, gypsies. Couldn't spit out a truth if you stuffed one in their mouths."

"But—"

"Enough! Not another word!" She more barked than uttered the command in her annoyance. "Your natter has given me a monstrous megrim. Since I wish to be rid of it before we arrive, you will remain silent until you are again spoken to. I suggest that you use the time to reconcile yourself to the fact that you are to be wed on the morrow." With that she extracted a vial of lavender water from her reticule, a commodity kept on hand for such emergencies, and doused her handkerchief. Darting a final warning glance at her granddaughter, whose cheeks were now the color of raspberry cordial, she tipped her head back against the satin upholstery and draped the damp cloth over her face. Within moments, she was asleep.

Emily stared at her grandmother, her stomach knotting with despair. She couldn't marry the duke of Sherrington! She just couldn't! Even if she weren't cursed, which she most assuredly was, she couldn't wed him on the fundamental principle that she simply didn't know him. Why, the very notion of marrying a stranger was nothing short of shocking. That her grandmother actually expected her to be amenable to such an arrangement made her wonder precisely what sort of people these English aristocrats were.

It most certainly made her question the duke of Sherrington's character. Indeed, the very fact that he, whom her grandmother had touted as being young, rich, and handsome, should resort to an arranged marriage suggested some kind of character flaw on his part. A dreadful one.

Trying to imagine exactly what that flaw might be, Emily rested her warm cheek against the cool window glass, watching the glorious Devonshire countryside unfold as she thought.

Hmmm. It could be that her husband-to-be was eccentric, like Robbie Wolf back home in Boston, who wandered about town in a judge's robes and wig, appealing absurd legal cases to himself. Or he might be a lecher. Was the duke the sort of man who ogled one woman's breasts while groping beneath the skirts of another? Emily shuddered. Surely her grandmother wouldn't be so cruel as to wed her to such a lout?

Would she?

No, of course not, she told herself. Her grandmother might be overbearing, and cantankerous to a fault, but she was hardly what one would call cruel. Well, at least not intentionally so. Despite her own aversion to wedding a stranger, Emily could tell from her grandmother's demeanor that she truly believed the marriage to be for the best.

Yes, and the best most definitely did not include a groom who was a lecher or an eccentric. Or a drunkard or a brute, for that matter. Or someone who engaged in any of the more heinous of the seven deadly sins.

Hmmm. That meant that the defect must be minor . . . yet off-putting enough to make the duke objectionable to women. A defect like, say, an aversion to soap, or a perpetually dour disposition. Yes. Something of that nature seemed more probable. Who knows? He could even be like those popinjays she'd seen lounging about Bond Street in London: vain, powdered, and ridiculously over-dressed. Or . . . or . . . he might be cold and arrogant.

Well, maybe not, she amended, remembering the gentlemen she'd met during her brief sojourn in London. By all appearances, chilled arrogance was considered a sign of breeding by the English . . . as were insolence, clipped speech, and the use of ludicrous terms that she couldn't even begin to understand.

Why, she had yet to figure out what "mulligrubs" meant. And what in the world was a "maddening mull"? In truth, there had been times during the past two weeks when she'd found herself wondering if the conversation around her was actually being conducted in English.

Sighing, Emily glanced at her grandmother, whose lusty snores now stirred the handkerchief covering her face. She hadn't dared ask her grandmother to translate. To do so would merely have validated the woman's opinion that all Americans were heathens, a view she'd made no bones about voicing the instant Emily had stepped off the ship. Indeed, her grandmother had no sooner clapped eyes on her than she began her incessant pecking.

Emily made a face at the memory of that pecking. According to the crabby old tyrant, everything about her was disastrous. Her accent was atrocious, her hair a barbaric mop, her hats frumpish, and her shoes nothing short of plebeian clodhoppers. Oh, yes. And her gowns, which had been so smart back in Boston, had been dismissed as impossibly démodé. She smiled faintly at that last word. It was French, which, unlike much of the English these British spoke, she understood, having learned the language in what her grandmother invariably referred to as the wilds of America.

America. Home. Her smile grew wistful. How she missed it, and what she wouldn't give to return there. Everything she loved was there . . . Boston . . . her friends . . . her brothers.

Tears stung her eyes at the thought of her five older brothers, all of whom she adored to distraction. Would she ever see them again? And what of their children, her darling nieces and nephews? Would they remember her in the years to come? Some of them were so young. Why, little Katie had just started to walk when she'd left, and two-year-old Oliver had finally learned to pronounce her name. Because she'd been certain that she would never have children of her own, what with the curse and all, she had taken her role as aunt to heart and had actively shared in their lives.

As Emily lovingly pictured those she'd left behind, the tears she'd held in check since arriving in England silently escaped down her cheeks. When she came to her father, a soft sob tore from her throat. He had been everything to her—mother, father, teacher, heart, and soul. And when he'd died, her whole world had crumbled. Not only had she lost the only parent she'd ever known, she had been torn from her home and whisked across the ocean before she'd had time to mourn and heal. Her only comfort during those dark days was that the ship that had brought her to England had belonged to her father, one of a large fleet that regularly sailed the world in trade, and had been captained by her middle brother, Daniel.

Though she loved all of her brothers equally, she was particularly close to Daniel. In fact, her earliest memory was that of him teaching her to fly a kite, his strong arms holding her securely as he dashed across Boston

Common, laughingly chiding her to hold tight to the line as the kite sailed into the air above them. To this day she adored kites, and one of her greatest delights was building them. It was a hobby she shared with Daniel, who had always found time to indulge her, even after he'd had a family of his own and a demanding position in their father's shipping business.

To her eternal gratitude, Daniel had remained with her during her first few days in London, his jovial presence doing much to ease the initial shyness she'd felt around their grandmother. All things considered, their time together had been good, unmarred, as it was, by the mention of marriage to the duke. But, of course, it made perfect sense that their grandmother would refrain from mentioning it. She no doubt knew that Daniel would object to the notion of his sister wedding a stranger, and that he would most probably have spirited her back to America if their grandmother had so much as hinted at such a thing.

Or would he? Emily frowned, suddenly uncertain. Of all her brothers, Daniel had chafed the hardest against her prospective spinsterhood. Having found bliss in his own marriage, he'd often expressed the wish that she might someday experience the same joy. Could it be that he had known about their grandmother's plan and had seen this arranged marriage to the duke of Sherrington as her one and only chance to do exactly that?

Her frown deepening, she repositioned her hat, which suddenly seemed intolerably hot and heavy atop her overburdened head. If what she suspected were indeed the case, what of the consequences? In order to find the sort of happiness Daniel wished for her, she would have to love the duke. And he knew as well as she that her love was a hazardous proposition. Surely he wouldn't risk the life and limbs of this unknown duke on the scant chance that their father had been correct and the curse hadn't followed her?

In her heart she knew he would.

The rutted road had now sunk below the level of the ripening fields by which it ran, its increasing roughness

evidenced by the erratic lurching of the carriage. Despite
the violence of the bumps, her grandmother snored on,
her enormous black velvet hat dragged askew as her
head slowly slipped to a rest in the padded coach corner.

Bracing herself more securely in her seat, Emily considered what was to be done about her predicament.
Hmmm. As much as she loathed the idea of wedding a
stranger, she adored the thought of the children the
union would bring. And there would be children. If she'd
learned anything at all about the aristocracy during her
short time in England, it was that they placed an extreme
importance on securing the family name. Remembering
that detail awakened a whole new possibility.

Could it be that the duke wanted not a wife, but an
heir? Did he wish children without the trouble of court-
ship or the obligation of love? Was she to be nothing to
him but a belly to be filled? That motive would certainly
explain his desire for an arranged marriage.

Rather than being dismayed by that prospect, she
found it . . . tempting. So much so that for several moments thereafter she envisioned herself with babes, a luxury she hadn't allowed herself since the advent of the
curse.

Her babes would be beautiful, of course, even if her
grandmother had lied and the duke was frightfully ugly.
And clever. Yes, the duke's flaw could be stultifying stupidity and their children would still be brilliant. And
graceful. And witty. And charming. And everything else
that was good and wonderful . . . regardless of their
father's faults. In short, they would be her children and
that would make them perfect. So perfect, in fact, that
it wouldn't matter a whit that her marriage was loveless.

Loveless? Emily's breath caught in her throat. A beat
later she slowly smiled. Perhaps it was a perfect arrangement after all. If she didn't love the duke, which she was
almost certain would be the case, then the curse couldn't
touch him, and she could have her babes without worry
or guilt. Well, she could if he wasn't vile. Even the joy
of children couldn't balance the misery of marriage to a
vile man. However, if he turned out to be tolerable . . .

well, tolerable she could endure. Easily. And who knows? Just once in her ill-starred life she might get lucky and the duke could be a man she actually liked.

Emily crossed her fingers, hoping for that last. Like would be ideal. If she liked the duke of Sherrington, even the slightest bit, making babies with him wouldn't be such a terrible ordeal. Liking would also give them a chance at a pleasant life together. Of course, like or not, she couldn't wed him without first informing him of the curse and the fact that she could never love him. It was only fair that she do so. For though it seemed unlikely, there was always a remote possibility that he wished a loving marriage.

She nodded once, satisfied with her decision. If the duke of Sherrington was tolerable, she would wed him.

And if he proved to be insufferable? Another nod. Then she would use the curse to dissuade him from the marriage. A little embellishment on the facts should scare him off effectively enough.

The crisis of her marriage thus resolved, Emily commanded herself to rest, deeming it best to be refreshed when she faced whatever awaited her at her journey's end. Doggedly ignoring her lingering hopes and fears, she shifted into a more comfortable position, then gazed out at the passing landscape. They had just entered Dartmoor, or so the weathered wooden sign proclaimed—a land, Emily quickly discovered, as dramatic as it was diverse.

The flower-strewn meadows and lush green pastures, which had thus far made up the bulk of the Devonshire scenery, soon gave way to sylvan forest, the land growing wilder with each mile they traveled. Then they entered the moor. The unpaved road was narrow now, made all the more so by the encroaching ferns and briars. In the distance, set against the golden late-afternoon sky, swept peak after peak of vast jagged hills, their shadowed bleakness portending the desolation that lay before them.

It was a land unlike any Emily had ever seen . . . remote, brooding, and utterly alien. The very sight of it filled her with loneliness. This was where she would live if she chose to wed the duke. She swallowed hard, the prospect giving her pause. Surely not all of Dartmoor was so very bleak?

On they advanced, past wide stretches of fen and through deep, narrow valleys. Over rocky bluffs and through tangled coppices. Now and again she saw moss-covered ruins, the ravaged testimony of man's surrender to the harshness of the land.

It was a bleak place, yes. And primitive. And forsaken. Yet, despite its foreboding starkness, Emily had to admit that it held a certain native beauty. There was the sparkling clarity of the numerous streams, for example, and the way the heather and furze splashed purple and yellow across the otherwise drab stretches of desert. Yes, and the charming, ivy-draped moonstone bridges that linked the more precipitous hills. Then there were the hills themselves, each one magnificent in its striking contrast to its companions.

Some of the hills rolled gently, clothed in verdant herbage; others stabbed at the sky, the brutality of their barbed peaks and sheer rises masked by crystalline waterfalls. Still others appeared almost mountainous with their boulder-strewn valleys and fantastical rock formation crowns.

After traveling for some distance, Emily ascertained that those grayish-brown rock formations were a dominant feature of the moor. They were now everywhere, each one different in its tortured shape. As she studied a particularly arresting configuration, an enormous one with a strangely human shape, she was reminded of the biblical tale of Lot and his wife.

His wife looked back from behind him, and she became a pillar of salt.

Hmmm. Could it be that the formations had once been giants who had been turned not to salt, but to stone as punishment for sins against their creator? She smiled faintly at her fanciful thought. Her father had always teased her about her imagination, fondly declaring it to be the most vivid one in Boston. Still, in a land such as this, anything seemed possible. Even magic.

After spending what felt like the proverbial forty years wandering in the wilderness, they abruptly came upon signs of civilization. First it was an uneven stone enclosure, covered with gray moss and lichen, then a partially cultivated field. After that they passed several neatly tended farms, each boasting a low stone cottage with a thatched roof and a wide, arched doorway. Another two miles and they were in a village.

Curious as to where they were and how far it was from their destination, Emily glanced at her grandmother. She still slept, sleeping the deep, sound slumber that embraced only the very young and the very old. By now the handkerchief had slipped from her face and her hat hung at a drunken angle, its lavish lavender plumes bobbing to the erratic rhythm of the coach wheels striking the road ruts. Every now and again she issued a spirited snore, followed by what sounded suspiciously like a belch.

Emily grinned at the picture she made. Garbed in that fussy lavender and black gown, with her obviously dyed brown hair tortured into a mass of tiny ringlets, she looked like one of those sweet but dotty old dears one often saw dozing in the corners of aristocratic drawing rooms. In her grandmother's case, however, looks were deceptive, for Euphemia Merriman was neither sweet nor dotty.

Wondering if the wily old tyrant would ever approve of her, Emily looked back out the window. They had just left the tiny village and were turning onto a road that was even narrower and rougher than the previous one. A blink of the eye later, they entered the most dismal area imaginable. Unlike the moor through which they had passed, this land was nothing but span after span of marsh, followed, at length, by a series of boulder-strewn knolls. Everywhere were more of the bizarre rock formations; nowhere was there a sign of life.

After traveling several more miles, they turned upon yet another road. A short distance later the moor abruptly gave way to a dense stand of trees. Beyond the trees stood a towerlike gatehouse, flanked by tall, crenelated stone walls.

Windgate Abbey, of course. It had to be.

Emily gaped in wonder. With its battlemented parapets and cruciform-shaped window, the gatehouse looked like something out of a fairy tale. As she stared, the window captured the last of the sun's dying rays, its stained glass panes glittering in the blaze like jewels tumbling from a treasure chest. Magnificent! If the house behind those massive walls was anywhere near as grand as this, it would indeed be a castle fit for a duke . . . a prince even.

Forgetting everything but her eagerness to see that castle, Emily gawked about her like a child at a fair, taking in everything as they advanced through the passage of the gatehouse. The building was old, that much was certain. Far older than anything they had in America.

The carriage had slowed now, its pace decorous as they emerged from the gatehouse upon a long, tree-lined drive. Skirting the drive was an immaculately kept park, surrounded by yet more trees. Cranking her head this way and that, Emily tried to catch a glimpse of the house ahead. When she finally did, her heart dropped to the floor of her belly.

It looked like a fairy tale castle all right . . . one upon which had been cast a dark curse.

More than a little taken aback, she eyed the slightly off-center front portion of the house. With its monastic starkness, it looked every bit the medieval abbey the name suggested it to be. Hmmm. And here she'd thought that the use of the word "abbey" was nothing but a romantic conceit. Obviously she'd been wrong, for it appeared that the house was exactly what it claimed to be.

Well, at least part of it, she amended, looking first to the right, then to the left.

Constructed of the same weathered gray-brown granite as the gatehouse, the curious structure was indeed part church, as evidenced by its magnificent tracery windows and inlaid crosses. It was also part fortress, the fortress portion being the battlemented towers flanking the

church segment. Hmmm. And then there was that porch.
A grotesquely ornate affair, the covered porch jutted aggressively from the austere church front, its—baroque,
wasn't it?—styling clearly proclaiming it a later addition.

Not quite certain what to make of what might possibly
be her new home, Emily let her gaze roam over the rest
of the house, growing more and more bewildered as she
took in the jumble that was Windgate Abbey.

Like many of the country houses her grandmother had
pointed out along the way, it was a veritable catalog of
architectural styles. Exactly what those styles were, Emily
couldn't even begin to guess, not being familiar with British architecture. All she knew for certain was that it was
enormous, and ungainly, and foreboding to the point of
being terrifying. Indeed, it looked exactly like the sort
of place one would find the ghosts of which the British
were so fond of boasting.

"Hideous, isn't it?"

Emily jumped in startlement, glancing quickly to
where her grandmother now sat upright. She had that
squinty-eyed, rather cranky look of someone who had
been awaken prematurely. Uncertain whether or not it
would be rude to agree, Emily diplomatically responded,
"You say that the duke's grandmother is a friend of
yours?"

The older woman paused in removing the hairpins that
anchored her hat to nod. "For more years than I like to
claim. Known her since we were girls. Been thick as glue
ever since." Hairpins now extracted, she swept the hat
off her head and examined it. Frowning at what she saw,
she promptly set about puffing the crushed fanlike bow
and straightening the bent plumes.

Adjusting her own hat, Emily murmured, "Then you
must know her grandson . . . the duke?"

Her grandmother emitted a faint sniff and deposited
the now-restored hat back onto her head. "Know him?
I practically raised the boy." She expertly jabbed a hair-
pin into place. "His grandmother has been his guardian
since he was just a babe. Being bosom-bows, I naturally

helped with his rearing. I don't mind telling you that I love the boy as if he were my own."

Having experienced her grandmother for the past two weeks, Emily wasn't at all certain whether that last was a good or a bad sign. Especially given the fact that she had yet to meet anyone under the age of sixty of whom the woman actually approved. Hmmm. Did that mean that the duke of Sherrington had a particularly fine character? Or was he, perhaps, coldly correct, like her grandmother, and old before his time?

Before she had time to ponder the question, the coach came to a stop. There was a shout, after which the door was opened by the waiting footman.

Emily sighed. She was only moments away from finding out.

Chapter 4

Gargoyles? In the entry hall? Oh, my!

"Emily!"

Emily jerked her startled gaze from the pair of gargoyle statues to glance at her grandmother, whose expression at the moment rather resembled that of the glowering, dragonlike gargoyle to the left of the door.

"Do stop goggling those horrid creatures and come along," her grandmother admonished, sniffing, as she always did whenever Emily was guilty of a faux pas, which was most of the time.

Emily didn't move. She couldn't. She was frozen by the sight of the man who now stood beside her grandmother. Speaking of horrid creatures! Never in her life had she seen such a barbarically fierce-looking being, or one so monstrously tall. Why, he was a veritable giant.

Giant? Her mouth went suddenly dry. Could it be that her whimsy about the rock formations wasn't whimsy at all? Had a race of giants indeed inhabited the moors in bygone days, and was this hulking being one of their last living descendants?

For several moments Emily continued to gape at the man, too aghast by her flight of fancy to do more. Then her common sense rallied and she felt her cheeks flame at her own foolishness.

What a peagoose she was! Of course the man wasn't a giant. Indeed, now that she really looked at him, he wasn't all *that* tall. Well, at least not tall enough to be considered a true giant. True giants were at least ten feet tall, everyone knew that, and this man looked only to be somewhere between six and a half and seven feet tall.

She nodded, pleased at the logic of her rationale. Yes, and giants, at least the mythical kind, didn't wear such elegant suits of clothing. And this man was undeniably dressed up to the nines. Besides that, what would a giant be doing at the duke of Sherrington's home . . . unless . . . unless . . .

The giant was the duke. The warm infusion of color promptly drained from her cheeks.

"Emily, really! Didn't anyone ever teach you that it is rude to dawdle in doorways?" her grandmother reprimanded.

Emily shifted her horrified gaze back to her grandmother, whose gargoylelike glower had mutated into a scowl that was almost as intimidating as the notion of marrying the giant.

Almost. After a moment longer, during which she made no move to desist in her dawdling, her grandmother clapped twice, producing a sharp, staccato thwack that echoed eerily in the sepulchral vastness of the entry hall. Curtly signaling for her errant granddaughter to join them, she barked, "You will obey me, girl, and do so this instant. I have had quite enough of your nonsense for the day."

Miserably seeing no escape, Emily slowly did as she was instructed, warily eyeing the giant as she advanced forward.

So was he the duke?

The more she thought about it, the more sense it made. He was, after all, particularly well-dressed. And he had displayed a certain air of grandiose command when he'd directed the household footmen to assist her grandmother's servants with their baggage. Then there was the matter of his intimidating appearance. It would most definitely explain his need for an arranged marriage.

Wretchedly certain now that the giant was indeed her intended, Emily came to a dutiful stop before her grandmother. After a beat, she forced herself to smile. Just because the duke was ugly was no reason to be rude. Besides, she was beginning to feel rather sorry for him. He'd no doubt suffered much misery on account of his dreadful looks, and she'd be blasted before she'd add to his pain by revealing her aversion to him.

Despite her charitable intentions, she came alarmingly close to being blasted in the next instance when he abruptly bared his teeth in response to her smile. Goodness! As if the poor man weren't cursed enough, he had the most wicked-looking teeth she'd ever seen on a human. They were like fangs—very large, very pointed, very white fangs—a whole ghastly set of them. A shiver ran down her spine. She couldn't marry him. She simply couldn't! Not with those teeth. Why, the very act of kissing him would be hazardous, and didn't people always kiss when they made babies?

She was darkly imagining the gruesome perils of kissing him when her grandmother said, "Emily, this is Grimshaw, his grace's majordomo. Grimshaw, this is Miss Emily Merriman, my granddaughter. As you have no doubt heard, the duke and Miss Merriman are to be wed on the morrow."

Majordomo? Emily's forced smile broadened into a wide, genuine one in her relief. "It is a pleasure to make your acquaintance, Mr. Grimshaw," she responded sincerely.

The man sketched a courtly bow. "I assure you that the pleasure is all mine, Miss Merriman. Please do accept my felicitations on your upcoming marriage." His fangs were completely bared now, a sight that Emily might have found unnerving had it not been for the gentleness of his cultured voice and the twinkle in his surprisingly lovely blue eyes.

Deciding that she rather liked the majordomo, despite his unorthodox looks, she nodded and murmured, "Thank you. You are most kind."

Her grandmother nodded as well, eyeing Emily with what would have passed for approval had her grandmother been anyone else. "Yes, well, I am sure the marriage will be a splendid success." Another nod. "Now then, Grimshaw, please do inform his grace of our arrival. I am certain that he is anxious to greet his bride."

"He has already been informed, my lady. Your outriders alerted us to your impending arrival just over an hour ago. His grace's grandmother instructed me to direct you to the blue drawing room the instant you appeared. If you would be good enough to follow me?" When her grandmother had inclined her head in assent, he bowed again, then turned on his exquisitely shod heels and led the way down the long corridor to their left.

Like the dreary, gargoyle-infested entry hall, the cavernous corridor had a high-domed, rib-vaulted ceiling that appeared to be carved from the same grayish-brown stone that littered the moors. The floors, too, were of stone, as were the roughly hewn walls. Disrupting those craggy walls at irregularly spaced intervals was door after closed door, each in the Elizabethan style with geometrical panels and nail-head ornamentation. The only reason Emily was able to identify them as Elizabethan was because she'd heard her grandmother refer to a similar door at—had it been Lady Moreland's house?—as an Elizabethan abomination. Secretly, Emily had thought the door charming, as she did these.

Unfortunately, those doors were the only thing she had thus far found charming about the house. And as she continued to follow her grandmother and the majordomo deeper into the convoluted bowels of Windgate Abbey, she was again reminded of her initial impression of the house. With its dark corners and pervading gloom, the house most definitely looked to be a haven for ghosts.

And gargoyles, Emily added to herself, glancing nervously up at the vaulted ceiling. Despite the numerous wall lanterns lighting their way, the uppermost reaches of the ceiling remained shrouded in sinister shadow. She shivered and looked away. Why, there could be a dozen gargoyles perched up there, and who would be the wiser?

Though she knew she was being ridiculous, she suddenly had the uncanny sensation that she was being watched from those shadows; watched by gargoyles who even now flexed their great batlike wings, malevolently preparing to swoop down and carry her off to their nest. Envisioning the hideous—and hungry—gargoyle hatchlings that most probably inhabited that nest, Emily quickened her step, rushing to catch up to her grandmother, who now seemed miles ahead of her. She had no sooner caught up than the majordomo turned down a different corridor.

A far pleasanter corridor, Emily noted, viewing the gilded cream-colored walls, and glossy red and cream tiled floor with infinite relief. Unlike the murky hallway they had just left, this one was full of light and warmth. Best of all, the plasterwork ceiling was rather low, its every sculpted corner glowing golden in the light from the candle-laden wall sconces.

She had just relaxed enough to actually notice the portraits lining the hall and to wonder if the handsome subjects were ancestors of the duke, when the majordomo stopped before a pair of wide double doors. After nodding at her and her grandmother, he scratched at one of the Pompeian-painted panels.

"Yes?" demanded a voice. Though that voice was muffled by the door, it was unmistakably female.

"Viscountess Bunbury and Miss Merriman, your grace."

"Enter!"

The voice was not only female, but aristocratically tart. Emily grimaced. But of course the dowager duchess of Sherrington would be a fury; she would have to be in order to be her tyrannical grandmother's bosom-bow. Before Emily had time to fully inure herself to that dismal certainty, Grimshaw opened the door.

Her grandmother promptly stepped into the room, her previously scowling face now the picture of genteel congeniality. When Emily didn't automatically follow suit, she hissed, "Come along now, girl. Don't forget to curtsy, and do try to be a credit to me for a change," just loud enough for her and the majordomo to hear. Never once during her terse rebuke did her grandmother's smile slip even the tiniest bit.

Blushing at being taken to task yet again before the servant, Emily moved forward, only to stumble over the threshold in the next instant. She no doubt would have fallen headlong had Grimshaw not caught her.

"There now, miss. Careful of the threshold," he murmured, deftly steadying her.

Emily felt her flush deepen in her mortification, and though she knew it unnecessary to do so, she felt compelled to justify her bungle to the servant. "I'm sorry. I-I'm not usually so very clumsy."

The hand that braced her arm gave it a reassuring squeeze. "No need to apologize, miss. The fault lies entirely with the uncommon elevation of the threshold. In truth, I tripped over it countless times myself before becoming accustomed to its height."

Touched by his kindness, Emily glanced up at what she was rapidly beginning to consider his rather pleasant face. Hoping that her voice reflected her heartfelt gratitude, she whispered, "Thank you, Grimshaw." She thanked him not just for rescuing her from her near spill, but for his gallant words.

He nodded and bared his fangs in what she now realized was his version of a smile.

She smiled back, revealing a goodly portion of her own teeth in the process. She most definitely liked him. Why, even his teeth weren't so very dreadful, not now that she was getting accustomed to them.

"You are most certainly welcome," he replied, releasing her. As he did so, he added under his breath, "I always find it best to remember that the nobles, too, occasionally use the chamberpot."

Before she could respond to that irreverent bit of wisdom, the imperious voice exclaimed, "Devil a bit, Effie! Is the chit always so dashed clumsy?"

Having had her carriage branded as "unspeakable" by her grandmother, Emily hung her head, wretchedly expecting her to respond in the affirmative. To her amazement, her grandmother replied, "She isn't clumsy. It's that beastly threshold. Mark my words, Adeline Vane, someone is going to break their neck vaulting it one of these days. And then where will you be?" She finished with one of her disapproving little sniffs.

Her bosom-bow sniffed back. "Whether or not she is clumsy has yet to be seen."

"Well, at least she is here to be seen, which is more than I can say for your grandson," her grandmother countered. "I must say that it is exceedingly bad form on Michael's part not to be here to greet his bride."

"He would have been here had you not arrived early," the duchess retorted. "According to your outriders, we weren't to expect you for at least another quarter hour."

Another sniff from her grandmother. "Everyone knows how devilishly impossible it is to predict exact travel times, even for experienced outriders, like mine. Thus, it is established convention to be prepared to receive one's guests at least a quarter hour before they are expected. You obviously know that rule since you are here. Exactly why you never bothered to impart the lesson to Michael, I shall never know."

"If I remember correctly, it was you who drilled him in etiquette. Indeed, you begged me to allow you to do so," the duchess pointed out, matching her friend sniff for deprecating sniff. "Had I known that you would make such a lamentable bungle of it, I'd have taken matters into my own hands."

With that they began to debate the methods for instructing boys, each trying to cast the other's mode into the wrong.

Uncertain what to do, Emily lingered by the door of the gaudily gilded blue and white room, nervously awaiting her grandmother's instruction. Where she had been apprehensive before, she grew doubly so now as she beheld the dowager duchess of Sherrington.

Unlike her grandmother, whose faded prettiness and comfortable plumpness gave her at least a facade of cherubic benevolence, the duchess's angular face and spare figure projected a cold, patrician elegance that was as forbidding as it was regal. At the moment she sat enthroned on a floridly gilded white settee, her head held high and the full skirts of her simple, but exquisitely cut gray silk gown draped around her with a precision that called to mind an idealized portrait.

"Austere"—that was the word that came to Emily's mind as she viewed the woman. Indeed, everything about her, from her ramrod straight posture to the rigid perfection of her severely coiffed white hair bespoke a nature of exacting formality. Even her jewels, which sparkled from each of her gnarled fingers, her wrinkled throat, her ears, and both bony wrists, seemed calculated to intimidate rather than dazzle the observer with their glitter and flash.

And here she'd been thinking that her grandmother was a terror! Why, compared to the dowager duchess of Sherrington, her grandmother looked as harmless as a newborn lamb.

As she watched, the lamb plopped down on the settee next to her bosom-bow, wagging one plump finger beneath the duchess's high-bridged nose as she scolded her for spoiling their beloved Michael. The duchess snorted and responded in a voice far too low to carry to where she stood. Whatever it was the woman said apparently had something to do with Emily, for in the next instant both gazes were turned upon her.

Her grandmother promptly frowned, as she usually did when she observed her granddaughter, while the duchess's sharp-eyed gaze swept Emily's length, her thin lips pursing as if she didn't at all approve of what she saw. When that gaze came to rest on Emily's face, her steely gray eyes narrowed and she ejaculated, "Really, Effie. I simply cannot imagine what could have possessed you to allow the chit to go about looking so."

"Looking how?" her grandmother inquired, visibly perplexed.

"Like a dollymop. Why, just look at her!" The duchess flung her hand in Emily's direction, the enormous gems in her rings exploding with fire as they flashed through air. "She's painted brighter than a Covent Garden harlot. If you cannot see that for yourself, then you're in worse need of spectacles than I suspected."

"My granddaughter most certainly does not paint. She doesn't have to," her grandmother rebutted, looking genuinely offended. "Like all the women of my blood, Emily is a natural beauty. If *you* cannot see *that,* then I suggest that *you* get spectacles."

"Natural? Bah! My sight isn't so far gone that I don't know rouge when I see it."

Rouge? Emily raised her hands to her face. Oh, my! She'd completely forgotten about the problem of her cheeks, but of course they were a horrid shade of red. They had to be after all she'd endured in the past few moments. Prompted by her embarrassment to explain, she blurted out, "It's true, your grace. My color is natural. My cheeks blush like this whenever I am in any way overwrought." As an afterthought, she curtsied.

"Indeed?" The duchess seemed to consider her words, then beckoned for her to approach with a brusque flick of her index finger. Obediently, Emily did as she directed. When she stood before the woman, the duchess icily inquired, "Do you also always speak so rudely out of turn when you are overwrought?"

Emily started, taken aback by the woman's censure. Not quite certain what else to do, she stammered, "I-I'm sorry. I didn't mean to be rude. Truly I didn't. I just wished to explain about my cheeks."

"Did I ask you to explain?" the duchess quizzed, eyeing her as if she were an insect she wished to squash.

"No, but—"

The woman cut her off with a stabbing hand motion. "There you go again, speaking out of turn. If you will recall, I did not ask you to explain, I inquired as to whether or not I had asked you to explain about your cheeks, to which the correct response is a simple no." She transferred her hateful gaze back to Emily's grandmother. "I see that I was correct in assuming that her father had neglected her training. She is an utter hoyden."

Emily's back went up at the horrible woman's criticism of her beloved father, and she felt her cheeks burn yet hotter.

"Of course, it is to be expected that she be somewhat gauche," the duchess continued in her cold, clipped voice. "She is, after all, an American, and everyone knows that Americans are barbaric creatures. Add that unfortunate fact to the even less auspicious one that she was raised amongst men, and it is a wonder that she doesn't take snuff and curse like a sailor."

Gauche? Barbaric? "How dare you say such dreadful things about Americans!" Emily exploded, filled with patriotic indignation. "Why, we are no more barbaric than you English with your arranged marriages and your archaic social order. In many ways we are far more civilized. In America—"

"Silence!" her grandmother barked. "You will bridle your tongue this instant, and apologize to her grace."

"I will do no such thing!" Emily shot back, too incensed to be checked. "I am tired of being ordered about, and insulted, and treated without the least bit of consideration, just because I happen to be young and an American. For your information, I am exceedingly proud of being American—doubly so now that I have seen your *polite* English society. Indeed, I can now see why America fought so hard for its independence."

"Emily—" her grandmother growled.

But Emily wasn't finished yet. Far from it. Ignoring her grandmother, she continued, "Never in my life have I seen such a rude, narrow-minded, insufferably pretentious group of people as you English nobles. You and your kind have made me despise it here! So much so, that had I any choice at all in the matter, which of course I haven't, I would return to Boston this very moment. Boston might not be as elegant as London, or have as many comforts and amenities, but at least I was treated with respect there and allowed to speak my mind. In truth, I pity you aristocratic English women—"

"Emily—" her grandmother interrupted again.

"No, no, Effie. Do not hush her. I truly wish to hear her out," the duchess interjected. Rather than look insulted, she seemed almost pleased by Emily's outburst. Nodding, she added, "Pray do enlighten us as to why we are so pitiful, Miss Merriman."

Emily nodded back. "I pity you because you are raised to be little more than shallow, supercilious ornaments; ornaments who are afraid to speak your minds or follow your hearts for fear of breaking one of the stupid, oppressive rules set forth by your society. Those rules, which you follow so blindly, leave you utterly impotent, something that frustrates you so much that you must empower yourselves in the only way allowed by your noble circle: by controlling and meddling in the lives of those more vulnerable. You prey upon women younger, or poorer, or more inexperienced than yourselves, using your petty gossip, snubs, and civilized threats as weapons of intimidation to bend them to your will. What saddens me most is how easily those women bend. Having been raised to view expulsion from the *ton* as a fate worse than death, they honestly believe it better to tolerate your bullying than to take a stand and risk having to face the frightening unfamiliarity of freedom." By now she was out of breath, having spoken in an impassioned rush.

As she caught her breath, the duchess inquired rather drily, "Are you quite finished?"

Emily shook her head. Gulping in a deep breath, she added, "Furthermore, on the point of my brothers and father, unlike your fine English noblemen, they never once took snuff or cursed in my presence. They always behaved in a manner befitting the title *gentleman.*"

There was a chuckle behind her, then a very masculine, very genteel voice drawled, "You must concede that she does have a point there, Grandmother. We British noblemen do have a most regrettable habit of cursing in front of the ladies."

Emily gasped and swung around, her cheeks burning almost to the point of incineration at the sight of the man standing just inside the door. The duke, of course. It could be no one else. Her mouth went as dry as it had been the time she'd sampled a sea biscuit. Goodness! Was everyone in Dartmoor so very tall? Though he wasn't as tall as Grimshaw, the duke of Sherrington stood at least two inches above six feet.

"Michael, my dearest boy. Do come and give me a hug. It has been a very long while since I last saw you, and I have missed you dreadfully," a dulcet voice cooed.

Emily frowned. Surely that wasn't her grandmother's

voice she was hearing, so kind and full of warmth?
Stunned by the very notion that the tyrant could sound
so benevolent, she glanced quickly at her grandmother.
She now stood with her arms outstretched and her plump
face soft with doting affection. When the duke strode
over and dutifully obliged her with the requested hug,
she positively glowed with delight.

"My dearest, darling love. Whatever have you been
doing with yourself? You are so very thin," her grandmother tenderly scolded, enfolding him in her eager
embrace.

He *is* thin, Emily thought, noting the hollows at his
temples and beneath his cheekbones as he swooped
down to kiss her grandmother. Far, far too thin. And
pale. Why, his skin was positively ashen, as if he were
desperately—

Ill? Her breath caught in her throat. Of all the flaws
she had imagined the duke might have, it had never even
crossed her mind that he might be an invalid. Now that
she saw him, she perceived that that very well might be
the case.

Was this arranged marriage, then, not a wish on his
part, but a necessity due to his ill health? As he straightened up again and stepped from her grandmother's arms,
she judged the answer to be yes. At the same time, she
also couldn't help noticing that her grandmother hadn't
lied about his looks. The duke of Sherrington was indeed
a handsome man. Beautiful, really, or at least he would
have been had his comeliness not been marred by the
effects of his illness. Nonetheless, he was still more attractive than any man had a right to be. Aware that she
stared, yet too fascinated to stop, Emily gloried in the
splendor of the man before her.

His hair was a dark, rich brown, the kind of brown that
captured the light and gleamed with molten highlights of
copper and gold. Though he wore it longer than the current fashion, it waved and curled over his high, starched
collar in a way that gave it a distinctly romantic air. One
thick curl had tumbled over his forehead when he'd

dipped to kiss her grandmother, and now called attention to his eyes.

Not that she could have missed those eyes. Fringed with the longest, most enviably lush lashes she had ever seen, those eyes were the brilliant, blue-tinged green of fine jade. They were, without a doubt, the most gorgeous eyes she'd ever seen. Framing them to perfection was a pair of thick, but finely arched eyebrows.

True, the face that surrounded those remarkable eyes was far too thin and pale. Yet, despite that detraction, it was still stunning with its straight nose, high cheekbones, and strong jaw. As Emily traced the line of that jaw with her gaze, she noted that his chin had a shallow cleft. The sight of that charming feature quickened her already racing heart. She'd always had a weakness for cleft chins—and nice mouths, she added, shifting her attention to his lips. And the duke of Sherrington had a very nice mouth indeed.

Suddenly wondering what ailed this magnificent man, Emily dropped her gaze from his face to inspect his form. His clothing, while of excellent material and cut, had clearly been made for a man with more flesh. As she eyed his loose tobacco-brown coat and green striped waistcoat, she summoned up a picture of how he would look if they fit.

Hmmm. If they had been tailored for him when he'd been in health, it was apparent that he'd once been a fine figure of a man. Perhaps he would be so again when he recovered from whatever sickness had left him so wasted.

Perhaps. But what if the nature of his illness was such that he never recovered? What if it was chronic . . . or even fatal? That last, hideous notion spawned a new and very distressing thought: Could the haste of the marriage be due to the fact that the duke was dying, and that he wished to secure his title with an heir before he expired? The tragedy of that theory wrenched at her heart, and she abruptly turned her head, not wanting him to see the tears that had suddenly flooded her eyes.

What Michael saw was what he had seen countless

times in London following his spell at Lady Kilvington's picnic: a beautiful woman staring at him with morbid fascination, then turning away in disgust. It was the sort of reaction that had at last driven him to hide away in Dartmoor. Though it had thus been almost two years since he'd last suffered such a response, the resulting sting hadn't lessened with absence or time.

"Michael, love. As you have no doubt ascertained, this fetching young lady is my granddaughter, Miss Emily Merriman," Euphemia cooed, clearly oblivious to what had just passed between the couple. "Emily, this dashing fellow is Michael Vane, the duke of Sherrington."

"Your grace," Emily mumbled, dropping into a curtsy.

Bloody hell! The chit was so repelled that she couldn't even look at him to acknowledge the introduction. Worst yet, she sounded on the verge of tears. Silently, he damned Euphemia Merriman. Judging from the vehemence of the girl's reaction, it was clear that she'd spilled every last, unsavory detail about his spells. Either that, or he looked even worse than he believed.

His mouth hardened into a bitter line. Whatever the case, it was obvious that she was no more thrilled about this marriage than he. Then again, why should she be? She was being forced to marry a man whom no one in England would wed.

Though Michael knew he should sympathize with her plight, he couldn't. Her reaction had reminded him far too painfully of how undesirable he'd become, cutting him in a way that was impossible to ignore. Exactly why he should be so stung by her aversion to him, he couldn't say. It wasn't as if he actually cared what she thought of him, or anything else, for that matter. He was marrying her simply because his grandmother had given him no choice.

Well, at least no real choice. Sly old dragon that she was, his grandmother had guessed that he'd do anything to escape returning to Bamforth Hall, even take a wife who was bound to abhor him. And she'd been right, of course. Though he hardly relished the thought of a life-time spent suffering Miss Merriman's snubs, it was a far more pleasant prospect than what he knew awaited him at the asylum.

It was remembering the asylum and the misery he had suffered there that made Michael mask his resentment and cordially utter, "Welcome to Windgate Abbey, Miss Merriman. I do hope you will be happy here." After all, as his grandmother had pointed out, the chit was his last hope for a proper marriage. She had also warned him that she would swiftly, and without further discussion, make good her threat to commit him to Bamforth Hall should he do or say anything to turn the chit from the match. Michael didn't doubt her word for a moment.

As he now gazed at Miss Merriman, waiting for her to respond to his greeting, he was struck with a sudden and chilling realization: His whole future rested upon this girl agreeing to wed him. And agree she must. She must freely speak the words that would bind her to him forever, and nothing—nothing!—in either his or their grandmothers' powers could force her to do so if she was truly set against the marriage. And if she refused to say "I do"—

Gripped with a sickening panic at exactly what would happen in such an instance, he frantically scrambled for something more to say, anything that might make her view him with even a modicum of favor. When his mind remained paralyzed, he saw no choice but to resort to banal pleasantries. Praying that it would be enough, and that his voice wouldn't betray his desperation, he said, "I realize how very difficult this situation must be for you, my dear. Thus, if there is anything I can do to make matters easier, anything at all, please do not hesitate to ask. As I said before, I wish you to be happy here."

The chit actually looked at him then. After several beats, during which her brow creased and she worried her full lower lip between her small, white teeth, she murmured, "In truth, your grace, there is something you can do."

Almost afraid to ask, certain that she was about to cry off from the wedding, he stiffly replied, "I believe that I said that you weren't to hesitate to ask for whatever it is you wish."

"So you did. All right then. What I wish is to know if—if—" Where she had looked distressed before, she looked a hundred times more so now as she shook her head over and over again, visibly grappling for her words. Her already flushed cheeks darkening to a rich, velvety crimson, she finally stammered out, "Your g-grace, I understand that this is an indelicate question, but I really must know: Are you—dying?"

"Dying?" Michael and his grandmother echoed in shocked unison.

"Of course he's not dying," Euphemia snapped. "I cannot even begin to imagine what could have prompted you to ask such an unseemly question."

The girl's cheeks blazed yet brighter. "I'm sorry. It's just that—I thought—" She shook her head again and made a helpless hand gesture. "I mean, he looks so ill that I couldn't help wondering if perhaps the haste of this marriage is due to the fact that he is dying, and that he wishes to sire an heir before he dies."

Rather than be offended by her question and its suggestion that he looked bad enough to be at death's door, Michael was relieved. The very fact that she would ask such a thing was a sure sign that she was at least considering his suit. By the same token, her question rather perplexed him, making him wonder if perhaps—

"Good heavens, Effie! Do not tell me that you failed to inform the chit of Michael's condition?" his grandmother expelled, eyeing her friend with consternation.

Michael, too, stared at Euphemia. His question exactly.

"W-e-l-l . . ." Euphemia shifted uncomfortably beneath their querying regard. "I really saw no reason to mention it."

"Condition?" Miss Merriman glanced first at him, then at her grandmother, clearly seeking an explanation.

"Yes, condition," Euphemia confirmed. "And the reason I didn't say anything about it is because it is hardly worth mentioning. Michael hasn't suffered a spell in ever so long."

"Nonetheless, you should have told her, if only to save Michael the discomfort of having to explain matters," his grandmother rebuked.

"What sort of spells?" Miss Merriman interjected, frowning.

Euphemia and his grandmother stared at her for a moment, then looked at him, as if uncertain what to do. When he merely returned their gaze, his eyebrows slightly raised, Euphemia sighed and muttered, "They are the sort of spells where he falls to the ground and thrashes about. Since it is impossible to predict when one will occur, they have been known to transpire at some rather . . . ur . . . inopportune moments. Needless to say, such moments are distressing for both Michael and those around him."

"I see," the girl murmured, regarding her grandmother gravely. "Is there anything else?"

"Well . . ." Euphemia drew out the word as she glanced at his grandmother, clearly reluctant to continue. At her nod, she disclosed, "He does . . . uh . . . foam a bit at the mouth."

His grandmother nodded again, and added, "Yes. He also makes frightening faces and emits some . . . a-hem! . . . rather alarming noises. Of course, as Euphemia mentioned, he hasn't had a spell in ever so long."

"I see," Miss Merriman replied. She contemplated him briefly, as if not quite certain what to make of what she had been told, then quietly inquired, "Is that all, then?"

Michael stared at her, incredulous. All? As if everything she'd been told wasn't damning enough. Though he knew he should be relieved by her response, there was something about her easy dismissal of his torturous affliction that rankled him. And before he could bridle his irrational surge of anger, he snapped, "Aside from the fact that I usually soil myself and have to be carried off to my bed, yes, that is all."

"Michael, really! There is no call to be vulgar," his grandmother chastened, shooting him a threatening look.

Damnation! Of course she was right. It hardly served his cause to disclose the vile detail that he soiled himself, especially in such a brusque manner. Wishing that he could turn back time and swallow the outburst before he uttered it, he smoothly justified his response by explaining, "I sought only to answer Miss Merriman's question as truthfully as possible. If I in any way offended you ladies in doing so, please do accept my most humble apologies." His regrets thus tendered, he ventured a glance at Miss Merriman, fully expecting to see her gaping at him in disgust, or at the very least, slowly inching away from him.

She did neither. She simply looked at him, her expression thoughtful. For some odd reason, he found her calm regard far more disconcerting than the revulsion he'd expected.

"Well?" he inquired, far more curtly than he intended. "Did I answer your question?"

She shook her head. "You still haven't told me what ails you. I mean"—another head shake—"what causes your spells? Are you an epileptic? Or are they due to something else?"

The question took Michael aback. Could it be that she still contemplated marrying him? He considered for a moment, then slowly acknowledged that it was possible. Having never witnessed one of his spells, she had no idea how truly repulsive they were. Once she did, and she was bound to see one if they wed, she would no doubt view him with the same disgust as the spectators of his episode at the Kilvingtons' picnic.

Not that it matters, he reminded himself. His grandmother had demanded only that he wed the girl; a harsh demand she had softened by promising to sign back his ducal rights upon his marriage . . . on one condition. With his grandmother, there was always at least one condition. In this instance the condition was that he remain under Mr. Eadon's care and continue to take his treatments, which his grandmother believed were of benefit to him. Though the treatments were far from pleasant, he would gladly endure them for the satisfaction he would derive from regaining his other freedoms.

"Well, Michael? Are you going to answer Miss Merriman's question, or must I?" his grandmother prompted, visibly annoyed by his prolonged silence.

Swallowing the bitter response that sprang to his lips, he said, "She asked me, therefore I shall reply." With a polite nod, he directed his attention back to the girl, who still gazed at him with unsettling thoughtfulness. "To answer your question, Miss Merriman, no, I am not an epileptic. At least not in the traditional sense, though my spells do manifest themselves in a similar manner. Or so I have been told." He shrugged. "Having never witnessed an epileptic episode, I cannot say with any great certainty whether or not it is true." Another shrug. "At any rate, my spells are the result of an infection of the brain, an unfortunate complication of the measles I suffered just over two years ago."

"Yes, and a terrible infection it was. Why, he is lucky to be alive, much less in possession of his wits," Euphemia chimed in. She took his hand and gave it a fond squeeze. "Poor, poor darling. The doctors predicted that if he lived, and they doubted very much that he would, that his mind would be hopelessly scrambled. Fortunately he proved stronger than they believed, and the only adverse effect he suffered is a proclivity toward spells. And as I have said before, even those are improving."

To Michael's amazement, the chit actually smiled. "I see. Then his spells are nothing we need worry about passing on to our children."

Children? Good God! Did she really expect him to consummate the union? One glance at her face told him she did. He quickly looked away again, uttering a silent oath. He was so close . . . so damn close to ensuring his freedom. All it would take was a simple nod.

Yet . . . yet . . . it was clear that the girl hoped for a real marriage, one complete with lovemaking and children. That being the case, could he, in good conscience, marry her with the knowledge that consummation was most probably impossible? To be fair, he should at least mention the problem. Then again, if he did mention it, she might very well refuse to marry him. And he was all too aware of what awaited him if she did.

Caught between fear and honor, he deliberated for a beat longer. Then his desperation overrode his scruples, and he nodded to the affirmative.

Her smile, a dazzling display of straight, white teeth and luscious red lips, grew positively radiant, and she seemed about to say something when that smile abruptly faded and she whispered a distressed, "Oh, my."

A fist of dread slugged hard into Michael's belly. Had she suddenly come to her senses and realized what a wretched prospect for a husband he was?

Meeting his gaze with eyes as anguished as her utterance, she murmured, "You have been so honest with me, your grace, that it is only fair that I am equally so with you, though I fear that you shan't wish to wed me after you hear what I must say."

"Indeed?" he intoned, breathless with relief. Not wed her? Hell, she could tell him that she had two wooden legs, false teeth, and had been compromised by every man in America, and he would still take her.

She flushed a rather interesting shade of maroon and nodded.

He nodded back. "Pray do continue."

After a brief moment, during which she solemnly contemplated him, she transferred her gaze to the vicinity of her feet and haltingly confessed, "You see, your grace, I'm—I'm—uh—cursed. By a w-witch."

"What?" he ejected, certain that his ears were playing tricks on him.

"I'm cursed by a witch," she repeated, miserably.

Euphemia expelled an exasperated grunt. "That will be quite enough, Emily. I already told you that there are no such things as curses or witches."

"But there are!" Emily protested, shaking her head. She looked up then, her dark eyes earnest as she met his gaze. "Your grace, you must believe me. The curse is real. In truth, it is the reason I wasn't wed in Boston."

As engrossed as he was in his own dilemma, it had never occurred to Michael to wonder why a chit with Miss Merriman's spectacular looks and rich dowry would have difficulty procuring a husband. And she *was* having difficulty. That she was here, relegated to an arranged marriage with an invalid who was subject to fits, bore testimony to that fact. Now that she'd called her plight to his attention, the answer as to why she was suffering it was abundantly clear: she was an eccentric, one with an absurd belief in superstition and a penchant for outlandish flights of fancy.

Not that it mattered. He shrugged. "I am afraid that I am of the same mind as your grandmother, Miss Merriman. I, too, do not believe in curses."

She shook her head. "Neither did my three fiancés, and the most dreadful things happened to them."

"I said enough, Emily!" Euphemia growled.

Three fiancés? Michael frowned. Bloody hell! She must be as mad as May-butter to have scared off three prospective husbands. Not that it mattered.

"The curse is that I shall be a plague to any man I love. And I am!" the chit urgently persisted.

Love? If she had to love him in order for her fictitious curse to strike, then neither of them had anything to fear. After all, who could love him now?

Feeling suddenly ill and wanting nothing more than to end what was quickly becoming an exhausting interview, Michael sighed and said, "If what you say is indeed true, Miss Merriman, then we are a perfect match. I am cursed by illness and you by a witch. If you will wed me and suffer my curse, I will gladly brave yours."

"She's perfect. Exactly what Michael needs," Adeline declared to Euphemia.

Michael had since retired with a headache, and Emily had been led away to freshen herself for dinner, leaving the women alone. At the moment Adeline stood before the gaudy gold and white rococo sideboard, pouring them each a glass of gin. Good, strong gin was their favorite beverage, a secret vice they fostered whenever in each other's company.

Rising from the settee, Euphemia moved to the sideboard, replying, "So it seems, though I must admit that I did have my doubts. Indeed, until she blasted you, the child gave no indication whatsoever that she had any spirit at all. And you should have seen how I bullied her." She came to a stop next to her friend, shaking her head. "I tweaked and nagged and criticized her mercilessly the entire time we were in London, trying to provoke a response, and never once did she so much as raise her voice."

"Well, she certainly raised it when I insulted her precious America." Adeline chuckled at the memory of the chit's impassioned performance. "I cannot remember the last time anyone dared to dress me down like that."

"She was magnificent, wasn't she?"

Adeline nodded. "Very. And did you see Michael's face when she began that curse business?"

Euphemia guffawed. "I haven't seen that much color in his cheeks since before his illness."

"Yes. Which, in my opinion, proves how right we are in forcing this match." She handed her friend a dainty crystal cordial glass containing a healthy ration of gin. "Indeed, if I do not miss my guess, and I seldom do, Emily is going to do exactly what we hoped she would do: shake Michael up and chase away his doldrums."

"Shall we drink to Emily, then?" Euphemia inquired, raising her glass in a toast.

Adeline nodded and followed suit. "To Emily, the future duchess of Sherrington. May her chase be merry."

Chapter 5

Michael and Emily were married the following morning at the Windgate chapel, a small, but picturesque medieval structure that stood in an idyllic grove of elm trees at the far edge of the park. The ceremony was a short one, presided over by the dour Reverend Bellamy, rector of the tiny nearby village of Talrose. Acting as witnesses were their equally dour grandmothers, and a brawny, blunt-featured man of middle years named Timothy Eadon, who, as far as Emily could ascertain, was some sort of companion to the duke. All in all the wedding was a quiet affair, one that would have been downright dreary had it not been for the Windgate servants.

Unlike the grave wedding party, the servants appeared to be genuinely thrilled by their master's marriage and had done their best to make it a gay event. To that end they had decked the simple chapel with garlands and nosegays, an act which had visibly stunned their employer, transforming it into an Eden of ambrosial fragrance and riotous color. After the couple had uttered their vows and had sealed their pledge with a brief, sterile kiss, they had stepped outside to yet another surprise . . . the thunderous applause and cheers of the entire household. At least Michael said that the assembly was the household, though Emily had trouble fathoming the notion that a single dwelling, even one as enormous as Windgate, could employ so many people.

Garbed in what was clearly their Sunday finery, the servants proceeded to accompany the newlyweds to where a simple, but bountiful feast had been laid in the manor park, strewing flowers in their path and shouting heartfelt wishes for their happiness as they went. Their joyous display did much to revive Emily's wilted spirits, soothing the nagging qualms that had plagued her the entire night, robbing her of her sleep. After all, it only stood to reason that a man who was kind to his servants would be considerate of his wife. And judging from the way his servants adored him, it was apparent that he was the best of masters.

The rest of the warm, early August morning and much of the hot afternoon passed in a blur of lighthearted activity. The wedding breakfast, which was served on long, posy-festooned tables beneath a shady stand of oak trees, went on for hours, with everyone, except the bride and groom, glutting themselves on roast beef and plum pudding, and drinking astonishing volumes of ale. Emily refrained from eating out of nervousness, being uneasy about the intimacies she knew inevitably followed wedding festivities, while Michael barely touched the oddly spartan repast of broth, toast, and weak tea that Mr. Eadon had served him.

He also remained silent and almost grimly aloof throughout the meal, seldom smiling and speaking only when courtesy required him to do so. It was the same polite, but perfunctory manner in which he had responded to Emily when she'd sought to engage him in conversation during their stroll from the chapel.

Wishing to acquaint herself with the enigmatic stranger whom she had just promised to love, honor, cherish, and obey, 'til death did them part, Emily had shyly mentioned that she knew nothing about being a duchess and that she hoped he would guide her in her duties. Sparing her only the briefest of glances, he had civilly, but succinctly, replied that he knew little about women's work and that she would thus be better served in seeking his grandmother's counsel. He had then resumed his brooding silence.

Stung, Emily, too, had retreated into silence, wondering if she had breached yet another tiresome rule of British protocol by requesting his help. Grudgingly deciding it best to find out . . . after all, she was now a member of the British nobility so she might as well learn their rules . . . she had finally asked Michael if she had unwittingly committed a faux pas, to which he had replied, "No." And that had been that. No explanation, no attempt to ease her mind, nothing.

Smarting at his slight, yet bullishly determined to make the best of her difficult situation, she had tried twice more to draw him into conversation. Twice more he had discouraged her efforts. At last giving up, she had occupied herself watching the servants' frolics, a pleasant enough diversion that was occasionally interrupted by comments from her grandmother, who sat to her right at the bridal table.

Though her grandmother's demeanor toward her still wasn't what Emily would have termed affectionate, it had softened somewhat since the marriage ceremony and she now treated her granddaughter with a certain measure of courtesy. Indeed, not once since leaving the chapel had Emily been subjected to what had previously been her grandmother's relentless criticism. Then again, why would the old tyrant bother? Emily was no longer her problem or her responsibility. She was Michael's, who clearly wanted no more to do with her than her grandmother did.

When, at last, everyone had eaten their fill and many toasts had been drunk to the health and happiness of the newlywed couple, each servant came forward in turn and introduced themselves to their new mistress.

As Emily now acknowledged the last of their astonishing number, a young, freckle-faced scullery maid called Mary, as were at least a dozen other of the female servants, she despaired at ever remembering all their names. How in the world did Michael manage to keep them all straight? Especially the plump twin sisters, Phoebe and Agnes, who were the cook and baker, respectively? Amazingly enough, he did manage, splendidly, somehow remembering not just their names, but small details about them that enabled him to inquire after each person in an individual manner.

Something he did now. Cordially nodding to Mary,

who had just bobbed a rather wobbly curtsy, Michael inquired, "How fares your mother, Mary? I believe that she has been ill with an ague this past fortnight?"

Mary flushed, visibly flattered by his notice, and curtsied again. "Much better, yer grace. She bid me to thank ye fer the food basket, and asked me to give ye her best wishes fer a long and happy marriage."

He smiled faintly and nodded again. "I am pleased to hear of her improvement. Do let me know if there is anything else she requires."

"Yes, yer grace." Yet another curtsy. "Thank ye, yer grace. Ye are most kind," she stammered, backing away.

When the girl had rejoined the ranks of the other servants, who stood at easy attention before them, Michael rose to his feet.

"You must rise as well, Emily," her grandmother whispered. "It is time for you and Michael to retire."

Retire? Emily thought with dismay, automatically doing as instructed. Why, it couldn't be much past four o'clock. Surely her husband didn't intend to bed her until after dark? Indeed, from what she had ascertained from the snatches of conversation she'd eavesdropped from her brothers, and from the giggling confidences she'd shared with her friends, babies were always made under the cover of darkness. Unless, of course, the British nobility did things differently, which she supposed was always possible.

As she numbly accepted her husband's proffered arm, forcing herself to smile as he graciously thanked the servants and invited them to remain for an hour of dancing, she tried to recall all she had heard about the wedding bed.

Hmmm. Let's see now. They would kiss . . . yes, there would be lots of kissing involved. She stole a glance at her husband's mouth. It was a nice mouth, strong and firm. She particularly liked the curve of his lower lip and the way it was ever so slightly fuller than his perfectly bowed upper one. In truth, she liked it so much that she rather relished the thought of kissing it, despite what should have been the off-putting fact that he was a stranger.

Shamed that she would contemplate, much less experience, such wanton urges, Emily dropped her gaze from Michael's mouth, her face growing warm as she suddenly remembered some of the other things she'd overheard her brothers boasting about doing with their mouths. Of course, they had been in their cups at the time . . . drunk, actually. Still—

Goodness! If British dukes were anything like her brothers, Michael would be kissing her all over. And touching her . . . in all sorts of secret, private places . . . but not until after he had removed her clothes . . . all of them. Her cheeks burned as the provocative scene played out in her mind. Of course, he would remove his own clothes as well, after which he would lie naked beside her in the bed. That particularly fascinating visualization heated her face to the point of scorching.

Having been raised in a household of men, the male body wasn't exactly a mystery to her. Indeed, unlike most of her friends, who had had more conventional upbringings, she had known the differences between men's and women's bodies from a very early age. And though she would never have dared voice the disgraceful fact, she was scandalously intrigued by those differences.

She was just envisioning those diverting differences and wondering if British noblemen's differences looked the same as other men's, when Michael murmured, "Shall we retire now?"

Emily's breath caught in her throat. Apparently she was about to find out. Unnerved by the prospect, she nodded once, taking care to keep what she was certain was her cranberry-colored face averted as she did so. Even if it turned out that her husband did look like other men, and she suspected that he would, she still wasn't exactly sure what to do with his differences. Especially the one between his legs.

Her best friend, Judith, who had been married for two years when Emily had left Boston, had whispered to her that that particular difference made some rather startling

changes when a man was near a naked woman; changes
that men found uncomfortable and expected women to
sooth by allowing them to thrust it into her private female place. Just how she was supposed to make it fit in
there was something she had never quite understood.

Utterly disconcerted now, Emily allowed Michael to
lead her from the revelry, forcing herself to smile as he
murmured thanks to their well-wishers as he went. She
had so much to learn. Hopefully her new husband would
be more amenable to instructing her in wedding bed matters than he had been when she'd requested his guidance
in learning her aristocratic duties.

By now they had left the merry crowd behind, and
Michael had again lapsed into silence, seeming to lose
himself in his thoughts as they strolled down the pleasant, yew-lined path that led to the abbey. Whatever those
thoughts were, they must have been very dark indeed,
for his expression was exceedingly grim.

Hmmm. Could it be that he found the notion of bed-
ding a stranger as daunting as she did? Or was it something about her, personally, that he found so displeasing?
She suffered a pang at that last. As much as she hated
to admit it, she supposed that it was entirely possible
that she wasn't to his taste. After all, everyone had their
own opinion as to what made a woman appealing, and
just because the men in Boston had considered her so
didn't necessarily mean that Michael automatically
shared their view.

Absurdly wounded by that very real possibility, Emily
stole a peek at her husband, noting with another, rather
bittersweet pang that she found *him* appealing to the
extreme . . . even more so than she had yesterday, and
she had liked what she'd seen then immensely.

The illogicality of her discovery gave her a start. Considering that he'd been less than charming to her all day,
you would have thought that his appeal would have di-
minished, not increased. Frowning, she stole another
glance. Hmmm. Perhaps the increase had something to
do with his clothes. After all, everyone knew that men
always looked doubly dashing in formal dress. Wonder-

ing if the doubly dashing factor was the culprit here, Emily surreptitiously studied the man beside her.

Though his dark blue tail coat wasn't what she would call a perfect fit, it came closer to fitting his thin frame than the coat he had worn the previous day, as did his white and silver patterned waistcoat and dove gray trousers. True, the snugger fit did emphasis the alarming gauntness of his form, but it also displayed the perfection of his proportions, which remained spectacular despite his excessive leanness.

After pausing to admire the manly breadth of his shoulders, Emily shifted her gaze to his face. He was looking at her as well, his expression unreadable. For an instant their gazes locked, his glimmering jade one piercing her entranced dark one, then she abruptly looked away, shivering. There was something in his eyes, something disturbing yet compelling that sent a tingle down her spine—an odd, but pleasurable tingle that now terminated in a strangely delicious tickle low in her belly. She shivered again in response.

He snorted. "Never fear, dear wife. I excused us from the festivities because I was tired, not out of some uncontrollable urge to ravish you."

Emily started at his words. "What?" she ejected, quickly glancing back at him. His face was hard and etched with bitterness. Taken aback by his sudden animosity, she frowned and stammered, "I—I don't understand what you mean."

"Of course you do," he snapped. "Your feelings were quite transparent just now. You were looking at me and shivering, clearly dreading the moment when I claimed my husbandly rights."

Stunned, she simply gaped at him, too floored by his outlandish allegation to do more. Then she began shaking her head over and over again in denial. "You are wrong, your grace. I was having no such thoughts. What ever makes you think I was?"

"What the hell am I supposed to think when you make it so damn obvious that you cannot bear the sight of me?" he retorted, grinding the words out from between his teeth. "Those times when you somehow do manage to spare me a glance, you instantly look away again, shivering as if you had just seen the devil."

Emily continued shaking her head, unable to believe what she was hearing. "That is ridiculous! All of it!"

"Is it?"

"Of course it is. I can assure you that I have no trouble whatsoever looking at you."

"Oh?" He halted abruptly in his steps. A muscle flickering angrily at his tense jaw, he folded his arms over his chest and harshly inquired, "If what you claim is indeed true, then how do you explain your response to me when we were introduced? If I remember correctly, and I assure you that I have an impeccable memory, you could barely look at me. When you did, you appeared ready to burst into tears."

"Your grace—" she began, wanting to explain.

He silenced her with a brusque hand motion. "Then there was the way you shivered at the sight of me just now. And do not try to tell me that your shiver was a figment of my imagination. Unlike yourself, who believes in witches, and curses, and God only knows what other sort of drivel, I have no imagination whatsoever."

Drivel! Of all the rude, pompous, insolent. . . . ! Incensed by his sneering disparagement of her beliefs, she hurled back, "Apparently you have more imagination than you know to so preposterously misinterpret my actions."

"Indeed? Pray do tell." He tipped his head to the side and regarded her with an infuriating air of superiority.

She prickled beneath his stare. Really! These British nobles had to be the most insufferable beings on the face of the earth. Deciding that she had suffered quite enough from this particular noble, Emily braced her hands on her hips and heatedly replied, "For your information, I was on the verge of tears yesterday because I thought you were dying. I was saddened by the terrible tragedy of someone so very young meeting an untimely end. Surely you can understand why I would feel so?"

He shrugged. "Of course. I am not completely lacking in feeling."

He could have fooled her. Eyeing him in a way that she hoped conveyed her skepticism, she continued, "As for my shivering just now, you are correct in that I was thinking about the marriage bed. However"—she added a punch of emphasis to the word "however"—"contrary to what you believe, I didn't shiver out of dread, rather, out of apprehension. Even you, with your professed lack of imagination, should be able to perceive how distressing a prospect it is for a girl to be bedded by a stranger."

"I can, though I must confess to being perplexed as to why you didn't consider that prospect and properly come to terms with it before agreeing to marry me. And do not try to tell me that a chit with your talent for fancy failed to imagine what lay beyond the altar."

"I never said that I didn't imagine it, or that I hadn't come to terms with my marital duties," Emily shot back, her palms itching to slap the sneer from his face. "I did and I have. Unfortunately, simply imagining something and coming to terms with it doesn't always erase all of one's reservations toward it."

"Oh?" His dark eyebrows arched in sardonic query. "And would you care to tell me exactly what you imagined that has incited such dire reservations?"

"I would not. I will, however, tell you something that I did fail to imagine and that is now inciting the direst of all reservations. And that is the fact that I have married a hopelessly disagreeable man." She added a sniff for good measure. A sniff? Oh, my! She was beginning to sound like her grandmother.

He chuckled darkly. "There was hardly any need for you to imagine something about which our grandmothers were so forthcoming. Indeed, I cannot recall anyone mincing words in describing my condition. And if a man described as an invalid plagued with fits isn't hopelessly disagreeable, then, pray tell, who is?"

"A man conceited enough to believe that a woman's

every action is in some way influenced by him, that's who," she rebutted.

"Ah, but I didn't say that I influenced your *every* action, just the ones I stated," he replied in an infuriatingly reasonable tone. "And you admitted that I was correct."

"Yes, I did. And it is only fair now that you admit that my responses to the stated situations were perfectly justified," she countered defensively.

He shrugged one shoulder. "Were they?"

Her eyes narrowed at his condescending reply. "I suppose you think that you would have been better able to hide your feelings, had you been in my position?"

"I did do better, damn it," he snarled, savagely rounding on her. "Do not forget that I was in your same position, that I, too, was faced with marrying a stranger. The very fact that you never suspected how much I despised being forced into this marriage more than proves the superiority of my control."

"Forced?" Emily gasped, her shock at his words staggering her mind. She had naturally assumed that he had wished the match. Indeed, she'd been under the distinct impression that he had sought it. That he had been forced into the marriage was an entirely new, and devastating, concept.

"Yes, forced," he spat back. "Regardless of what you might have been told, I had absolutely no desire to marry you, or anyone else. Unfortunately, my meddlesome grandmother took it into her head that I needed a wife, and since she saw an arranged marriage to you as her only hope of satisfying that ambition, she threatened me with some rather unpleasant consequences should I refuse to cooperate."

"I—I had no idea," Emily murmured, her emotions spinning in a sickening maelstrom of chaos.

While she understood and even sympathized with his bitter resentment, a part of her couldn't help feeling hurt and betrayed. For though she had neither expected nor wished to find love in this match, she had assumed that she would at least be wanted. It was that assumption, and that assumption alone, that had given her the courage to utter the marriage vows. Now that that assumption had been shattered, she felt a crushing sense of hopelessness and loss. Given her husband's fierce animosity toward her and their marriage, there was little chance that he would wish to consummate their union. That meant that there would most probably be no children.

For several seconds Emily remained wretchedly silent, grieving as she buried her dreams of children and the joy they would have brought to her life. Then fury born of sorrow swept through her, and she began to rage against the injustice of her lot. Irrationally placing the sum of that injustice on Michael's shoulders, she lashed out, "You bastard! How dare you use me in such an unconscionable manner!"

His eyebrows rose a fraction. "Such language. I suppose it is considered acceptable in America for women to call their husbands bastards?"

She shot him a withering glance. "It is if the husband in question merits the title, which I assure you you do."

Instead of being insulted, as she had fervently hoped he would be, the hateful man chuckled. "In light of how many women have assigned me that very designation, I suppose I do indeed merit it." Another chuckle. "How comically ironic. Those women called me a bastard for *refusing* to wed them, and you call me one *because* I wed you. It seems as if I am damned if I do, and damned if I don't."

"Indeed it does—doubly so when you consider the consequences of marrying me as you did. Were you anywhere near as clever as you fancy yourself to be, you would have had the sense to marry one of your adoring throng and been done with it."

"Meaning?" he prompted, looking genuinely intrigued.

Goodness! Was that another sniff that had escaped her? "Meaning that you would have been better served by marrying a woman who knew what a bastard you are and thus understood what a despicable husband she was getting. Had you done so, you wouldn't now be saddled with a disappointed wife."

His eyes narrowed almost imperceptibly at her words.

"Come, come now, dear wife. Can you truly claim to be disappointed? Let us not forget that this was an arranged marriage between strangers. Surely even you, with your rampant imagination and nonsensical fancies, didn't honestly expect to find bliss in such a match?"

"Bliss? No. I already explained about the curse and how it is impossible that I love you," she snapped. "I had, however, expected to be wanted and welcomed as your wife. To be utterly honest, I thought you were marrying me to bear your heirs."

His eyes narrowed a fraction more. "And where, pray tell, did you get such a notion?"

"From your aristocratic peers. From what I ascertained from their conversation in London, the only reason a nobleman marries is to secure his family line. And since I desire children," she shrugged, "such an arrangement seemed agreeable enough."

His eyes were little more than slits now. "Am I to understand that you married me out of a wish to bear children? And that you were willing to wed any man, even a total stranger, to achieve your end?"

Emily winced. When spoken out loud, her motive did sound rather . . . unsavory. Still, was it really any more contemptible than his reason for marrying her? Deciding the answer to be no, she nodded, defiantly refusing to deny his disgraceful charge.

"I see." He contemplated her in silence for several beats, his jade eyes opaque and unreadable, then his mouth pulled into a sour grin and he said, "How very droll. It seems that you used me as well. Unfortunately, we used each other at cross-purposes, a misadventure in which, I am sorry to say, you have come out the loser."

"Oh?" she intoned, her hands balling as she was overcome with another, stronger urge to slap him. He really was a bastard.

He nodded. "While I have succeeded in my purpose, which was to satisfy my grandmother's demand that I marry you, the chances of you succeeding in yours are marginal, at best. In case you are ignorant of the fact, it takes more than marriage vows to get a woman with child."

"I know perfectly well how babies are made," she returned, haughtily. It wasn't a complete lie. She knew, she just didn't understand the mechanics of the act.

"Then you know that a couple must copulate in order to produce a child, an act which takes a great deal of stamina on the man's part." He leaned forward then and impaled her with his vengeful gaze. "In case it escaped your notice, my dear, I happen to be an invalid."

Her jaw dropped at the meaning behind his words. "Are you saying that you are incapable of fathering a child?" she expelled on a gasp.

A strange shadow passed over his face, one that disappeared in the next instant when he straightened up again, chuckling harshly. "I am saying that doing so would require far more of my meager supply of strength than I wish to expend on you."

Emily recoiled as if slapped, her pulse thundering and her breath huffing out in rapid, shallow puffs as she sputtered her blistering anger at his insult. Once, twice, three times her mouth wrenched open before she finally managed to snarl, "You really are a bastard."

He shrugged, clearly unperturbed. "So we have established."

"And I hate you," she added, throwing the words as if they were stones.

Another shrug. "Good. If you hate me, you'll be inclined to leave me alone."

"Oh, I will leave you alone, all right," she spat, her eyes filling with scalding tears. "I shall stay out of your way so completely that you will wonder whether or not I am still about. I just hope that—that—" Her voice became strangled then, choked by virulent emotion. Trembling with mute fury, she spared him one last contemptuous glare, then lifted her skirts and fled down the path toward the sanctuary of her chamber. As she ran, tears of pain and impotent rage spilled down her cheeks.

What should have been a day filled with promise and joy had turned out to be the beginning of a lifetime of emptiness and broken dreams.

Chapter 6

Damn the chit to hell! Damn her for being beautiful, and desirable, and spirited. Damn her for reminding him of what he had lost and how very much he missed it. Most of all, damn her for being so bloody provoking.

Michael smiled grimly at the irony of that last. In this instance the consequences of Emily provoking him had turned out to be bloody to the extreme. Indeed, Timothy Eadon had taken one look at his agitated state when he had come upon him in the park, scowling after Emily's retreating form, and had promptly declared an immediate need to bleed him of at least twenty ounces. Bleeding was, of course, the prescribed remedy for any emotional or physical state that might be deemed sufficiently stimulating to trigger a spell; a treatment effective in that it left the patient too weak to do or feel anything at all. Besides that, it hurt like hell, a prospect that went far in keeping the patient properly subdued.

Having tightly bound Michael's upper arm, making the veins in his lower arm bulge bluish-purple against the pale skin of his forearm, Eadon now positioned the wickedly sharp ivory and steel spring lancet over a thick vein just below the inner bend of his elbow. Glancing up at his patient, he inquired, "Ready, your grace?"

Closing his eyes, Michael gave a single curt nod, his breath hissing out from between his gritted teeth as the blade stabbed into his flesh. His arm jerking away in agonized reflex, he muttered, "Ouch, damn it!"

"There now, hold steady, your grace," his tormentor coaxed, wrestling his patient's arm back to the table with one strong hand. Bracing it firmly in place, he dug yet deeper to open the vein, adding in a soothing voice, "It will be over soon. Just relax and think of something else."

Michael opened his eyes just enough to shoot the man a disgruntled look. It was easy for Eadon to tell him to relax, he didn't have someone slicing up his arm. Still—

He sucked in another quick breath of pain as the man rotated his now throbbing arm to allow the open wound to drain freely into the silver bleeding cup he held below it.

Still, regardless of how miserable Timothy Eadon made his life, he was nonetheless easier to bear than would have been one of the other assorted physicians, quacks, and butchers who had sought the prestigious position as his attendant. Eadon at least treated him with respect, something which most definitely could not be said about the other candidates, all of whom had spoken to Michael as if he were a half-wit and had pompously cited their intention to deal with him as such. And though Michael truly despised and dreaded Eadon's treatments, he was able to take some comfort in the fact that the man genuinely wished to help him. He was also more than qualified to do so.

Having spent many years observing the seizure-plagued wretches at Guy's Hospital in London and examining the effects of various therapeutics on their fits, Timothy Eadon had become an acknowledged expert on convulsive conditions about which he had written countless treatises. It was one of those treatises, one published in a volume amid the mountains of medical tomes his grandmother had combed since the onset of his spells, that had led him to be offered the lucrative position of Michael's caretaker.

Though Eadon had at first been reluctant to accept, having been desirous of continuing his studies at the hospital, Michael's grandmother had finally offered him a sum of money that no sane man could turn down. Thus, he had now been with Michael for a year and a half, ever since Michael's release from Bamforth Hall.

As he always did when he thought of Bamforth, Michael winced.

"Your grace, please! You really must hold still," Eadon chided, his large, square-palmed hand tightening on Michael's arm. "It will make matters ever so much easier for you if you will just relax and imagine something pleasant."

Imagine. Michael winced again at the word. After today he would forever associate it with Emily, and thoughts of her most definitely were not what he would call pleasant.

"There, there, your grace. Only ten more ounces to go," Eadon murmured, clearly mistaking Michael's wince as one of pain at his ministrations.

Michael ignored him. Once upon a time, before he had become what he now was, he would have found imagining Emily pleasant to the extreme. How could he not? She was exactly the sort of woman he had always fancied. And there lay the problem. The very sight of her, with her lush figure and exotically beautiful face, stirred feelings in him he hadn't felt in a very long time—torridly sensual ones that aroused urges he was no longer allowed to experience or able to satisfy.

He wanted her . . . God! How he wanted her! He couldn't recall ever wanting a woman as badly as he'd wanted Emily as she stood by his side in the chapel, a sultry temptress in virginal white silk and Brussels lace. Indeed, so strong was his desire that it had almost brought him to his knees in devastated need when she had lifted her face to his at the close of the ceremony, chastely offering her lips for the bridal kiss.

Michael groaned softly at the remembrance of those lips, so full and red, prompting another pacifying murmur from Eadon.

Never in his life had he seen such a lusciously ripe mouth; never had he felt one so pliant or tasted one so honeyed. And the way she'd smelled . . . mmm . . . sweet, like garden carnations beneath the hot summer sun. It was a pleasant fragrance, one rendered irresistible by the bewitching alchemy of her wondrous skin.

Now oblivious to Eadon's ministrations, Michael's thoughts lingered longingly on Emily's skin. It was porcelain perfection blushed with the most provocative shade of red he had ever seen. Strawberries and cream. Mmm, yes. It reminded him of strawberries and cream. And it just so happened that he adored strawberries dipped in sugared cream. No doubt he would adore the taste of her skin beneath his kisses even more.

No doubt at all, he thought ruefully, brutally forced back to his wretched reality by yet another shock of pain as Eadon prodded his arm wound, encouraging it to continue bleeding. Too bad he would never have the pleasure of finding out exactly how scrumptious she tasted.

Gritting his teeth as Eadon continued his relentless poking, Michael grimly considered the cruel paradox that was his life. He'd married the most desirable woman in the world, which meant that she was his for the taking. And damn it! He wanted to take her, more than anything else in the world. But he couldn't, not now. Humiliating experience had taught him that. And it was that memory, coupled with the bitter frustration born of the knowledge that he was unable to satisfy his urgent masculine need, that had made him treat Emily so abominably in the park.

Oh, yes. He knew that he had been wrong in behaving as he had, that he had been unjust in blaming and punishing her for his futile desires. He had known even as he'd lashed out at her that she had done nothing to provoke his lust.

Nothing but be beautiful, he amended with a grimace, and beauty was quite enough to arouse him these days. Indeed, when one considered the fact that he, who had once been known for his voracious sexual appetite and amorous escapades, hadn't had a woman in over two years, was it really any wonder that the sight of Emily would affect him so? He shook his head, groaning in despairing response.

"Easy now, your grace. I know it hurts," Eadon murmured, referring, of course, to his torturous manipulations.

Michael spared him a wan smile. Compared to the anguish of his mind, the pain in his arm was negligible. Now too mired in that anguish to escape, he slipped helplessly back into his thoughts of Emily.

No, he meditated, taking up where he had left off. Emily wasn't to be blamed for his lust, any more than she was to be blamed for their marriage. Like himself, she'd been nothing but a pawn in his grandmother's insidious little scheme to ensure the duchy. That she'd entered the marriage with a plan of her own, well, what did it matter? He should simply be grateful that she'd saved him from Bamforth, and let it go at that.

Unfortunately, what he should feel and how he felt were two entirely different matters. And he couldn't say that he was particularly proud of how he felt at that moment.

Had his arm not been otherwise engaged, he would have raked his fingers through his hair in his chagrin. Damn it. Why couldn't Emily have been someone he could ignore, some plain, spinsterish creature with thin lips and a flat bosom? When he'd grudgingly agreed to this marriage, he'd never—ever!—suspected that his bride would be an enchantress. Not that he'd given the matter a great deal of thought. In truth, he'd been so wrapped up in his own woes that he hadn't really cared what she would be like. Not that it would have mattered if he had. It wasn't as if he'd had the power to veto his grandmother's choice.

And if he had been given the option, would he have said nay to Emily Merriman?

Michael didn't have to think twice to find the answer. There was no way in hell he would have wed her, not when the very sight of her brought him such grief. Then again, if his wife were true to her word, he would be seeing precious little of her in the future, which should settle the problem neatly enough. If only—

"Ow!" he spat abruptly, pulled from his musings by a sudden, intense burning in his arm. Jerking his abused limb from Eadon's grip, he barked, "What the hell are you doing? That stings!"

Eadon smiled indulgently and reclaimed his patient's arm. Pressing a thick, clean linen pad against the viciously throbbing incision, he replied, "I treated your wound with Dr. Antell's latest tincture. Not only is it supposed to prevent infection, it is said to reduce healing time by half."

"Wonderful," Michael muttered as the man deftly bandaged his arm. "That means you can cut it back open again twice as often."

Eadon chuckled. "Bleeding you once a week should continue to be quite sufficient, your grace, unless, of course, you work yourself into another state. There." He gave the knot he'd tied in the bandage a final tug.

Michael grunted. "You can rest assured that I shall take the utmost pains to avoid anything," or anyone, he added silently, "the least bit stimulating in the future." And he would. He'd do his damnedest to make certain that his and Emily's paths crossed as seldom as possible.

Eadon dipped his head in acknowledgment to his vow. "Very good, your grace. Do you wish to rest now?"

Michael nodded and started to stand, only to fall back into his chair again as his knees gave out. As always, Eadon was there to aid him, his strong hands bracing beneath Michael's arms to help him rise. Now shivering uncontrollably, Michael gratefully allowed the man to half carry him to the enormous, domed tester bed a short distance away. Worse even than the pain of the bleeding was the debilitating weakness it left in its wake. His teeth were chattering now. That, and the unnatural coldness.

Having already disrobed his patient to the waist for the bleeding, Eadon sat Michael on the edge of the bed and efficiently stripped his lower body. After garbing him in a warm flannel nightshirt, he tucked him beneath the covers.

Utterly drained now, Michael rolled onto his side, gingerly cradling his sore arm in his uninjured one as he curled into a tight ball, desperately trying to get warm.

"Would you care for a hot brick, your grace?" the ever solicitous Eadon inquired, draping a thick blanket atop the heavy velvet counterpane cocooning Michael's violently shaking body.

"Several, please. I'm freezing," Michael somehow managed to force out from behind his chattering teeth. With that he curled yet tighter and closed his eyes. Unbidden, a vision of Emily sprang out of the darkness, smiling at him in a way that made fire jolt through his loins. Groaning at the resulting ache, he cracked open his eyes. "Eadon?" he called hoarsely to the man, who now stood at the fireplace warming bricks.

Eadon glanced over his broad shoulder, one thick, tawny eyebrow raised in query. "Your grace?"

"I would like one of your sleeping draughts as well. The strong one."

"But that one leaves you senseless for days," his attendant protested, frowning at the peculiarity of his patient's request. So violently did Michael object to being drugged, that he consented to take the potion in question only after he had passed several sleepless nights and everything else had failed to bring him rest.

"Exactly," Michael muttered. Several days of senselessness was exactly what he needed to erase Emily from his mind.

In a region as contrary in climate as it is in its appearance, the sunny Dartmoor afternoon dwindled into an unseasonably cold and rainy night, sending its inhabitants scurrying to seek the warmth of their hearths. The hearth Euphemia sought was the magnificent carved wood and brick Tudor one in her bosom-bow's bedchamber, before which they now sat cozily ensconced in a pair of century-old easy chairs, toasting their stockinged feet and nursing their rheumatism with the aid of the decanter of gin they had filched from the library sideboard.

Thoroughly pleased by her day's work, Euphemia settled contentedly back in her chair, declaring, "The wedding was a rather agreeable affair, I think, considering the circumstances of the marriage."

"Indeed it was," Adeline concurred, pausing in donning the shabby red knit cap she always wore on cold nights to nod. "I was particularly pleased by the pains the staff took to make everything so festive. As you know, neither Michael nor I bid them to decorate the chapel, and the gala following the ceremony was entirely their doing." Nodding again, she began tying the frayed ribbon straps beneath her chin, her age-gnarled fingers flexing awkwardly in their arthritic stiffness. "I knew the servants were fond of our boy, but I had no notion they adored him so very much."

"The servants have always doted on Michael, ever since he was an infant," Euphemia reminded her, lifting her glass to her nose to savor the crisp, juniper berry–nuanced scent of the gin. "And why should they not? He has always been the best of masters, unfailingly fair and considerate . . . exactly as we taught him to be."

"Mmmm, yes. We did do rather well by him in that regard," her friend acknowledged, lifting her own glass from the graceful Chippendale tea table they had had the footman set between their chairs. Tippling a lusty swallow, she added in a liquor-choked voice, "Under Michael's tutelage, Emily should make an admirable duchess. She most certainly looked the part today."

Euphemia smiled faintly, a wave of fierce, familial pride sweeping through her at the well-deserved praise of her granddaughter's beauty. "Yes, she did. Indeed, was she not quite the most stunning bride you ever saw?"

"Apart from you, who was and shall forever remain the loveliest bride England has ever seen, yes," Adeline replied, always the loyalest of friends. "Everything about her was sheer perfection, even that gown, which I must admit to having had reservations about when you first showed it to me." Shaking her head, she took another quaff of gin. "With that barbaric coloring of hers, who would have guessed that the chit would look so very well in white?"

"Oh, I rather suspected she would, though, of course, I cannot take credit for selecting the color. White has become quite the rage for wedding gowns, you know, and according to the dressmaker, no other color would do."

Adeline shrugged. "Nonetheless the gown was a masterful stroke on your part. Decking Emily out in proper wedding attire added a certain . . . er . . . seemliness to the affair, making it appear as if the bride had actually anticipated and rejoiced in her upcoming nuptials. What I do not understand is how you managed to have a gown so obviously meant for the altar made up right under her nose. Surely she suspected that something was afoot when she saw the design?"

Euphemia shrugged back. "She never suspected because she saw nothing of the gown until I presented it to her this morning."

"Oh?"

Another shrug. "Since her American wardrobe was a provincial abomination, she naturally required a new one. Thus, I had the gown made up with the rest of her garments. Of course, I did have to explain to Madame LeCroix that it was to be a surprise and asked that it not be brought forth during fittings. In view of the fact that it was never adjusted to her form, I think that it fit rather admirably."

"Indeed it did. It made her figure appear quite spectacular."

"Her figure is spectacular," Euphemia corrected with a sniff. "Do not forget that she is my granddaughter."

"She is at that, every lovely, impertinent inch of her," her friend agreed amiably, draining her glass.

Mollified, Euphemia followed suit, after which she tossed in, "If you ask me, Michael is lucky to have her."

"Very lucky . . . not that he is particularly appreciative of his good fortune." Adeline emitted one of her signature snorts, the loud, forceful one she reserved for excessively exasperating situations. "The way he looked at her during the wedding, you would have thought that Emily was a hangman about to string him up."

Euphemia shrugged, unconcerned. "It is only natural that he look so. After all, we did force him into this match. I have no doubt whatsoever that he will appreciate her in time, after his resentment has had time to cool."

"Yes, yes, I know. But—damn it!" Adeline slammed her empty glass violently onto the tea table. "I expected him to be at least somewhat appeased by the gel's beauty. If you will recall, nothing used to lift his spirits like the sight of a pretty face." Her expression grim, she picked up the decanter and sloshed another ration of gin into her glass. Shaking her head, she muttered, "I must confess that I am beginning to fear that Michael's illness affected him even worse than we suspected. Did I tell you that he admitted to the truth of that dollymop's rumors?"

"You did," Euphemia confirmed, presenting her own glass to be replenished.

"Did I also mention how very pained he remains over the episode?"

Pained was he? Hmmm. Euphemia's eyes narrowed. A hunch slowly dawning, she inquired, "What exactly did he say?"

"Oh, it wasn't so much what he said. In truth, he said very little about the episode," her friend replied, pouring the refill. "It was the hostility with which he spoke— well, you know how he's been since his illness. How he masks his pain with anger?"

Indeed she did. After several beats of contemplation, she picked up her glass, murmuring, "It makes perfect sense, really, all of it."

"What makes sense?"

"Michael's behavior toward Emily. As you, yourself, pointed out, he hides his pain behind anger."

Adeline frowned. "I—I am not entirely certain what you mean."

"Think, Addy, think! And consider everything . . . that unfortunate episode with the molly-mop, those Bamforth doctors' warnings against libidinous excitement. Then remember the Michael of old, how he used to conduct himself around women and how unfailingly charming he was to them, regardless of his mood." Nodding sagely, Euphemia lifted her glass to her lips and sampled her gin. "It is entirely possible that Michael fancies his pockets to be empty and is simply refusing to window-shop."

Her friend considered her words, the furrows in her brow deepening as she lifted her own glass to her lips. After taking several meditative sips, she mumbled, "You could be right."

Euphemia sniffed. "Of course I am. I am always right. It is as plain as the nose on your face that Michael is refusing to admire what he thinks he can never have. Speaking of what he can and cannot have"—she shot her friend a querying look—"I believe you were going to discuss this very matter with Mr. Eadon?"

"I did and I have. I spoke to him three days ago." Adeline shook her head, chuckling drily. "Poor man. He was beyond shocked that I would broach such a subject, and it took ever so much prodding on my part to make him speak with candor."

"And?" Euphemia quizzed, indulging in some prodding of her own.

"And unlike the doctors at Bamforth, he sees no reason whatsoever why Michael cannot sire an heir. In fact, he believes that a moderate romp in the marriage bed might actually benefit his health. He said that like the blood, bowels, and digestive tract, a man's male parts, too, accumulate bad humors, which is why male patients often spill their seed during spells. Since such humors cannot be bled away, or cleansed through clysters and purgatives, the only answer is to allow the patient sexual release."

The theory made sense, still ... "If what Mr. Eadon says is indeed true, how did he explain what happened with the dollymop?" She glanced quickly at her friend, frowning. "You did tell him about the episode, did you not?"

Adeline snorted and took what could only be inelegantly described as a swig from her glass. "Of course I did. Have you ever known me to mince words?"

Euphemia waved aside the question, not about to be drawn into that particular discussion. "So?"

"So, he believes that the episode was due to Michael attempting relations too soon after his illness. If you will recall, the boy had no sooner left his sickbed than he went to the jade."

"Indeed I do," she replied, satisfied by the explanation. "I suppose you asked Mr. Eadon to relay his theory to Michael?"

"I did."

"And?"

Adeline snorted again and drained her glass, an act which provoked a most undignified belch. Ignoring her peccadillo, she responded, "Stubborn whelp! He refused to listen. He is certain that the episode will repeat itself should he attempt to make love again, and he balks at putting himself in the position to suffer more such humiliation." Clearly at her wit's end now, she dramatically clutched her empty glass with both hands and moaned, "Oh, Effie! Whatever is to be done? We shall never get our heir at this rate."

Not believing the situation to be so very desperate, Euphemia gave her bosom-bow's arm a pacifying pat. "There, there now, Addy, dear. All is not lost. Many a man's firmest resolution has been broken by the temptation of a woman's charms. And Michael can hardly avoid being tempted by Emily's when they will be constantly under his nose."

Adeline shook her head, unconvinced. "I am not so certain. You know how stubborn Michael is."

"Yes, but I also know of his weakness for beautiful women. My guess is that if we leave them alone, nature will take its course and that weakness will eventually triumph over his stubbornness." Nodding her confidence in what she said, she picked up the decanter and poured what little gin was left into her friend's glass. Indicating that Adeline was to drink, she reiterated, "The way I see it, the question isn't whether or not Michael will succumb to Emily's charms, but how long he will be able to withstand them."

Her friend remained silent for several moments, somberly contemplating the contents of her glass. Finally she sighed and murmured, "I can only pray that you are right."

"Of course I'm right. I am always right, remember?" Euphemia playfully reminded her, trying to tease the despair from her face.

To her satisfaction, a faint smile lit Adeline's face. "So you have been telling me for over half a century now." As quickly as the smile appeared, it faded, and she sighed again. "Oh, Effie. I do so want Michael to be happy . . . Emily too, of course. In truth, I want it above all else. If they find happiness together, I shall strive not to be too terribly disappointed if they fail to produce an heir."

"If they find happiness, they cannot help but to produce a dozen heirs," Euphemia retorted with a chuckle. "And mark my words, Adeline Vane, they shall be very happy indeed. Ecstatically so. How can they not be? They are our grandchildren, which makes them a perfect match. If you ask me— Adzooks!" she expelled abruptly, startled by an unearthly moaning that seemed to resonate from the house itself. "What the devil is that ghastly noise?"

Adeline shrugged, unperturbed. "Just wind in the chimneys. There are close to a hundred chimneys here at the abbey, so it makes quite a noise on stormy nights like this."

Euphemia remained silent for a moment, listening, her blood chilled by the eerie keening. Outside the storm raged across the seemingly endless blackness of the moors, screaming as it worked itself into a fury that threatened to shatter the windows as it hurled rain against the ancient glass panes.

Shivering, Euphemia snugged her paisley wool shawl tighter about her shoulders, forcing herself to ignore the hellish bluster as she resumed their conversation. "As I was about to say," she half-shouted over the wind, "the best thing we can do to promote the match is to simply leave them alone. If we aren't about, they shall undoubtedly feel freer to go about their business."

Adeline eyed her thoughtfully. "You could be right at that."

"Of course—"

"You are right. You are always right," her friend finished for her.

Euphemia chuckled. "Exactly."

"Well, then. In that instance we must take ourselves off on the morrow. Since I told Michael that we would be staying for at least a fortnight, we shall require a plausible excuse for leaving."

"Indeed we shall. Hmmm." Euphemia drummed her fingers against her now-empty glass as she pondered. "Let me see now. Well, there is always that series of dye lectures being presented in Leeds next week. Remember?" She glanced at Adeline. "We received a notice for it last month."

Her friend nodded. "Mmm, yes. Fascinating stuff. I had rather hoped to attend."

"Then we shall. We will say . . . hmmm . . . yes. We will announce that since matters are so well in hand here, that we feel free to attend the lectures. Considering the piece of work we have done here, I doubt if either Emily or Michael will object too strenuously to us going." At that moment a particularly bone-chilling moan slithered down the chimneys. Shuddering, she added, "I, for one, shall be glad to be shot of this place. How ever does Michael bear this ungodly noise?"

It sounded like a lost soul, wandering down the halls, wailing its woe.

No, not wandering. Ghosts don't wander like live people, they float about in the air—and drift through walls, and doors, and such, like—like evil mist, Emily fearfully revised, slanting a nervous glance at her closed bedchamber door. As she peered, half-expecting to see an eerie white haze seeping through the door panels, another ghastly cry rent the air, this one terminating in a hideous moan seemingly right outside of where she stared.

Oh, heavens! It was coming to get her! Emitting an involuntary cry of her own, she ducked her head beneath the bedcovers. Not that she actually believed that she could hide from the ghost, or that the elegant damask coverlet could shield her from it should it choose to murder her. No, she hid because—because—

Well, she didn't know why. Hiding beneath the covers was just something people did when they were frightened. And now that she thought about it, it seemed a rather silly and futile thing to do. Still, lying all snug and warm like this at least made her feel more secure. Besides, if a ghost did fly through the wall, she would rather not see it coming.

For a long while she lay shivering beneath the covers, envisioning a wraith—a headless one—melting through the wall—*drip!—drip!*—dripping droplets of spectral blood as it came to steal her soul. Incorporeal in body, but corporal in deadly purpose, it swooped through the air like a—a—well, there was no describing its horribleness as it flew nearer and nearer—*drip!—drip!— drip!*—wailing the language of hell.

Ar-o-o-o! E-e-e! It seeped beneath the blankets, its vaporous being swirling and coiling about her in a frigid embrace, engulfing her in phantom ice as it slowly leeched her soul from her terror-paralyzed body—

No, no, no! Stop! she commanded her runaway imagination. *Stop your nonsense this very instant! There are no such things as ghosts. Papa used to say so . . . so did Daniel . . . and—and everyone else. It's just the wind . . . yes, just the wind tangling among the chimneys and blustering beneath the eaves. Just the wind . . . just the wind . . . no such thing as ghosts . . . just the wind . . .*

Chanting that mantra to herself, Emily lowered the covers an inch and peeked about the room. It appeared free of unearthly beings. She heaved a gusty sigh of relief and pulled the covers below her chin. Assuming an air of casual bravado, she folded her arms behind her head, struggling to erase her lingering disquiet as she warily surveyed her surroundings.

Decorated in pale purple, white, and celadon green, and trimmed with what must have been all of the gold fringe in England, it was a very grand chamber indeed, too grand in Emily's estimation, though she did rather like the fireplace. It was an enormous white marble affair, one that quite dominated the purple silk–paneled wall opposite the bed, its chimney piece a sculpted wonder of mythological figures, scrolls, fruit, and foliage, all surrounding an oblong medallion portraying the Three Graces. Whoever decorated the room had had an inordinate fondness for mythology, for it was a recurring theme throughout, though nowhere did it occur more gaudily than in the design of the bed upon which she lay.

Like the chimney piece, the scrolling gold and white rococo headboard, too, was carved with mythical flora and fauna, all framing a colorfully painted scene of Cupid shooting a sleeping Psyche with his magical arrow. Suspended from the ceiling above was a tentlike pavilion of gold-fringed purple and green silk, intricately draped in a series of puffs and crescents to form a billowing canopy and side curtains, the latter of which were held back by a pair of lascivious-looking brass cherubs.

Matching drapery, which had been drawn against the storm for the night, hung at the row of windows to her left, before which sat an elegant writing desk, flanked by a dainty pair of needlework-upholstered sofas. It was to one of those sofas that her gaze was now drawn, her eyes widening in panic at the sight of the diaphanous white figure draped across it. Oh, heavens! It was—it was—

Her wedding gown. Left exactly where she had tossed it. Her terror-tensed body went instantly limp with relief. Goodness, what a ninny she was! She really must learn to bridle her imagination, before she scared herself into an early grave and became a ghost herself. Then again—

She grinned with sudden, wicked amusement. Then again it might be rather enjoyable to be a ghost if she could haunt the duke of Sherrington. Hateful man! After the beastly way he'd scoffed at her curse, it would serve him perfectly right to suffer supernatural torment.

Her fear of ghosts now replaced by the droll fancy of actually being one, she indulged in a particularly satisfying fantasy where she mercilessly plagued her ill-tempered husband, driving him to the brink of despair with her otherworldly mischief. Hah! She could just picture his comical chagrin as his narrow little mind grappled to explain the uncanny happenings it could not and would not accept. The more she imagined, the deeper she sank into her thoughts, at last slipping into the dark domain of sleep.

And she dreamed of Michael—desperate, impossible dreams of longing; of frantically seeking and at last finding him, only to discover that the man she had found wasn't Michael at all, but a stranger who promptly turned to wind that carried her wails of disappointment across the storm-torn moors. It was one of those queer dreams where she knew she was dreaming and tried to wake up, only to find herself trapped in yet another fruitless chase of a tall, shadowy figure she desperately yearned to be Michael.

On she chased, only to be thwarted in her quest time after frustrating time, growing wearier and more heartsick as she went. Just when she was certain that she would die from exhaustion—

Crash! Clang! She was rescued from her slumbers by a sudden, loud metallic bang. "W-w-what!" she ejected, bolting upright in bed, blinking rapidly in groggy disorientation.

"Oh, yer grace! I beg yer pardon! I dinna mean to wake ye. The coal shovel just slipped from my hands. I swear it did!" a voice apologized in a rush. It was a young, female voice, possessing the same soft intonation that Emily had noticed marked the majority of the servants' speech.

Stretching, she replied on the tail of a yawn, "It's quite all right." She yawned again, then squinted at the bracket clock that sat on a bombé-shaped commode a short distance away. Unable to see the dial through the shadows, she murmured, "Mmm—what time is it, anyway?"

"Just past noon, yer grace."

Emily broke off amid her third yawn. "Noon!" she gasped, shocked from her drowsiness by the lateness of the hour. "Why wasn't I awakened earlier?"

"Beggin' yer pardon, yer grace, but no 'un instructed us to wake ye." Though the woman's features were obscured by the darkness of the room, Emily could see her shadowy form rise from where she kneeled before the hearth. "Would ye like me to open the drapes then?"

"Yes, please," Emily replied, frowning. Not a morning had passed since she'd arrived in England that her grandmother hadn't sent her haughty French maid, Mademoiselle Gremond, to awaken Emily at precisely seven, after which the old tyrant would sweep into her room and commence in her scolding instruction. Of course, now that she was married, she was no longer subject to her grandmother's dictates. Still—

Mystified that the woman hadn't at least inquired after her, considering the hour, she asked, "You haven't, by chance, seen my gran—uh—Lady Bunbury this morning?"

"Oh no, yer grace. She 'n' Lady Sherrington were off 'fore sunrise—to Leeds, I believe," the young woman replied, dragging open the heavy drapery. The wind had swept away all traces of the storm, leaving behind a sky blinding in its sun-drenched brilliance.

Emily squinted against the glare. Leeds? Rather than feeling liberated by the departure of her grandmother, she felt . . . abandoned. Struck by sudden anxiety, she clutched at the damask coverlet. Oh, dear. Whatever was she to do now? She knew nothing about being a duchess. And after what had passed between her and the hateful duke, well, she had counted on the bosom-bows for guidance. Feeling as lost as the proverbial lamb, she forlornly inquired, "Did they, by chance, say when they would return?"

The woman shook her mob cap–topped head. "Nay, yer grace. But they might've left a message fer ye with Grimshaw. Would ye like me to ask him?"

"No. I shall ask him myself—uh—" Her eyes now adjusted to the light, she stared at the servant hard, trying to recall her name. Though she vaguely remembered the woman's broad, freckled face from the wedding feast, the name that went with it escaped her. Shamed by her lack of talent for remembering names, she finished lamely, "I'm sorry, I cannot seem to recollect your name."

The woman smiled, a wide, good-natured sort of grin, and bobbed a quick curtsy. "Mercy Mildon, yer grace.

Mrs. McInnis, the housekeeper, instructed me to see to yer needs.''

"Did she?" Emily replied, for lack of a better response.

Mercy nodded. "Aye. 'Tis 'cause I've a bit of experience as a lady's maid. I worked fer Lady Pearcy o'er at Hookway manor, ye see, 'fore she died a year 'n' a half ago.'' There was a note of pride in her voice as she made the declaration, one that dampened in the next instance as she added, "Of course, I've been workin' as a chambermaid at the abbey since then, there not bein' much call fer lady's maids on the moor. Bein' a duchess 'n' all, ye'll probably be wantin' to send to London fer one of those fancy Frenchy maids.''

Emily suppressed her urge to grimace. After her dealings with the disdainful Mademoiselle Gremond, the last thing she wanted was a French maid. That prejudice firmly in place, she swept Mercy's stocky form with her gaze, considering her for the position.

Hmmm. She appeared to be a decent sort of woman. And clean. Emily eyed the servant's neat blue dimity gown and spotless white apron with approval. Cleanliness was an attribute of the utmost importance in selecting a personal maid. To her credit, Mercy also seemed of a pleasant disposition, and Emily liked her copper penny red hair. Her best friend, Judith, had hair that exact same color.

Pausing now on Mercy's plain face, which was visibly downcast, no doubt in expectation of being displaced from a position she badly wished to keep, she slowly replied, "Being from America, I had rather hoped to hire someone local . . . someone who can tell me about Dartmoor and help me learn Dartmoor ways. Are you such a person, Miss Mildon?''

It took a moment for the meaning of her words to sink in. When they did, Mercy's glum face brightened and she again smiled, this time revealing a set of white, albeit slightly crooked teeth. Clasping her hands together in her excitement, she exclaimed, "Oh, aye, yer grace. Aye! I was born 'n' raised near Newleycombe, so I know everything there is to know 'bout Dartmoor. I also went to the village dame's school, so I can read 'n' write a bit."

"All the better," Emily replied, deciding that Mercy Mildon would do very well indeed. "It appears that you are exactly the sort of maid I had hoped to hire. How very lucky for the both of us that you are already at the abbey."

"Do ye mean it, yer grace? Truly?" Mercy expelled breathlessly, looking as if she hardly dared to believe her own good fortune. "Do ye really want me fer yer maid?"

Emily rotated her shoulders, which were impossibly stiff, grimacing at the resulting pain. "I shouldn't wish anyone else."

Apparently Mercy also possessed the qualification of having excellent eyes, because she exclaimed, "Is somethin' amiss, yer grace? Are ye feelin' ill?"

Emily smiled at the genuine concern in the servant's voice. It appeared that she had indeed chosen wisely. Reaching up to rub the aching muscles, she replied, "No, not ill. Just"—another grimace as she kneaded a particularly sore spot—"stiff. I am afraid I didn't sleep very well last night."

Mercy made a clucking noise behind her teeth. "Well, 'tis hardly a wonder, what with the wutherin' 'n' all."

"Wutherin'?" Emily paused in her massaging, frowning at the unfamiliar term. "What is wutherin'?"

" 'Tis what the wind does when it blows o'er the moors," the servant informed her, returning to the coal-blackened hearth to finish her sweeping. "There's more wutherin' that goes on here in Dartmoor than anywhere else in England, 'n' it wuthers worst of all at the abbey. 'Tis why it's called Windgate Abbey." She glanced up then, her blue eyes wide. "Surely ye've heard the legend?"

"Legend?" she prompted, though she wasn't so very certain she wished to hear the tale. If it was anything like the other English legends she had heard, it was bound to be macabre.

Nodding, Mercy dumped a shovel full of soot into her empty coal scuttle. " 'Tis said that the sort of wind ye heard last night, the wutherin' kind, isna wind a'tall, but the souls of sinful people condemned to blow 'bout the moors. 'Tis their penitence, ye see, to wuther. Come Judgment Day, they'll be pardoned fer their wickedness 'n' let into heaven. 'Til then, they have to wuther.''

"How awful," Emily murmured, shivering at the notion of evil spirits howling at her windows.

Mercy nodded, her expression grave. "Oh, aye. 'Tis a dreadful torment, bein' the wind, 'specially since wind-souls aren't allowed to rest except once every hundred years. That's why they howl so, they're terrible fagged. They howl worse in Dartmoor than anywhere else, 'cause they haven'a rested fer o'er five hundred years. They canna. They can only rest in a secret place deep beneath the moors, but they canna get to it anymore. The monks that built the abbey built it o'er the gate to the place.''

"Hence the name 'Windgate Abbey,' " Emily mused, speaking more to herself than to Mercy.

"Aye. The winds rage 'round the abbey like they do, 'cause they're tryin' to tear it down. They're desperate to go through the gate 'n' rest." Mercy stood then, shaking her head. " 'Tis said that the wind's fury was so bad when the abbey was first built that its howlin' drove the monks mad. Some of 'em were so crazed by it that they hanged themselves to escape the wutherin'.''

"What!" Emily ejected in shock.

Mercy nodded. "They hanged themselves from the oak tree that used to stand in the courtyard of the cloisters. The cloisters are the ruins at the west edge of the grounds, in that forest of trees. Ye can still see the tree stump there.''

"Oh, my!"

"Aye." Another nod from Mercy. "The tree's been gone fer centuries now—it was cut down after the monks hanged themselves—still, on nights when the moon is full 'n' the wind is wutherin', the tree is sometimes seen standin' there again, with the ghostly monks hangin' from its branches, their corpses swayin' in the wind. Everyone avoids passin' that place on such nights, 'cause seein' the monks means that you'll die 'fore the year is out.''

"What a terrible tale!" Emily exclaimed, shivering again as she envisioned the tree in question. You could bet she wouldn't venture anywhere near that place at night, full moon or no.

"Aye. Terrible," Mercy somberly agreed. "But then, there are all sorts of strange tales told here on the moors. Why, just 'bout every village 'n' house has a ghost, or a witch, or a demon, or a pixie, or some other sort of uncanny bein'. 'Tis why many people call Dartmoor the most haunted place on earth." Nodding, she picked up her hearth-cleaning tools. "Now then, yer grace. I suppose you'll be wantin' yer breakfast?"

Emily merely stared at her. The most haunted place on earth? Heaven help her! She was even more cursed than she'd suspected.

Chapter 7

Her laughter drifted through the open dressing room window, merry and melodic, like joyous music floating on the warm morning breeze. Michael paused in toweling his freshly washed hair to listen. Emily's laughter had become a familiar sound, one he'd heard almost daily for the past three weeks, ever since she'd discovered the water cascade and miniature Venetian canal, both of which just happened to be in the private garden that spread beneath the windows of his suite of rooms.

Not that she knows I am near, he thought wryly as he resumed drying his hair. Had she known, he doubted if she'd have adopted the garden as her playground.

True to her word, Emily had avoided him since their wedding day, taking the promised pains to stay out of his way. And he was grateful. For though he'd been unable to obliterate her beautiful face and luscious form from his mind, as would have been his preference, he at least hadn't had to suffer the proximity of her alluring presence. Thus he'd resumed his peaceful, if humdrum, existence, passing his days as he had done before her arrival.

Existence? A sardonic smile twisted Michael's lips. Hmmm, yes. "Existence" was the perfect word for what his life had become. Indeed, no one in their right mind would consider his day-to-day continuation to be living.

Living was going interesting places and meeting fascinating people. It was days filled with wonderment and diversity; it was the freedom to experience all the exhilarating adventures the world had to offer. Living was what made a person rejoice in waking up morning after morning; it gave their days meaning and made them thrill at being alive. To live was to seek love and to savor the heady rush of its discovery. It was the sharing of passion and the sweet, intimate murmurings of well-pleasured lovers. Living was feeling, really feeling . . . joy, sorrow, anticipation, regret, anger, and all the other richly complex emotions that made up the lush tapestry that was life.

Existing, on the other hand, meant to breathe and endure, nothing more, which summed up his life to perfection.

Infused with a sudden, bitter sense of futility at his dreary lot, Michael uttered a foul oath and tossed aside his wet towel. Picking up a fresh one, he stepped from the cooling bath in which he stood, and began drying his body in agitated swipes.

When all was said and done, his days amounted to little more than a series of monotonously routine vignettes in which he read, played chess or cards with Eadon, walked near the old cloisters, surveyed the sky through his telescope, or sat brooding in his study, merely passing the time between Eadon's rigid schedule of treatments. One day slipped into another, days melding into weeks, weeks into months, all without a single defining moment to distinguish itself from the others.

True, there was the diversion of his grandmother's sporadic visits, and Euphemia's weekly letters did serve to amuse him for a quarter hour every Tuesday afternoon. Still, those moments weren't exactly what he would call "defining," for they failed to make a significant or memorable impact on his barren existence.

Now dry, Michael stepped into his comfortably worn leather mules, then slipped on the burgundy, gold, and black paisley patterned silk dressing gown Eadon had left draped over the French chair beside his dressing table. As he tied the sash belt, another trill of laughter drifted up from the garden, followed by the sound of Emily's voice gaily calling to someone.

Or something, Michael added to himself, remembering the times he'd glanced out the window to see her romping with the gardener's enormous black hound. Like the gray-striped stable cat, which he sometimes saw cradled in her lap as she sat reading high in the beech tree near his sitting room window, the hound seemed to have taken an immense liking to his young wife. As had Bennie, the coachman's young son, whom he'd spied with Emily the day before, the pair of them companionably engrossed in building miniature ships from an odd assortment of twigs, flowers, and leaves.

Closing his eyes as yet another arpeggio of mirth tickled his ears, Michael pictured his wife as she had looked then, sitting with Bennie on the lush green grass beside the water cascade.

She wore a simple, but form-flattering day dress, one in a rich shade of crimson that suited her vivid coloring to perfection. Her hair, which was tied back from her face with a wide red ribbon, tumbled down her slender back, forming a riotous cascade of glossy jet curls. For a long moment Michael allowed his mind's eye to linger on those curls, his fingers aching to caress them. Then he reluctantly pulled back to observe the entire scene.

Of course she was smiling and laughing, as was Bennie, a sturdy, sandy-haired lad of eight, as they shifted through their treasure trove of foliage, searching for the ideal mast twig or a leaf to serve as a sail. Now they admired each other's handiwork, both masterpieces of nautical whimsy; now they launched their creations upon the gentle water of the canal, shouting and cheering their triumph when the flower-bedecked boats remained afloat.

It was a charming panorama, one that filled him with a sense of bittersweet longing that made him yearn to step into the picture and partake in the jollity. It was the same sensation he'd experienced of late every time he looked outside and saw Emily engaged in her merrymaking . . . something he did often these days, despite his initial resolution to remain dissociated from his all-too-tempting wife. In truth, he'd come to look forward to seeing her in the garden and enjoyed watching her lively capers. So much so, that he now suffered crushing disappointment that shadowed his entire day on those occasions when she failed to appear.

Cued by a particularly gleeful shriek to commence in his spying, Michael wandered over to the small casement window, smiling pensively at the sight that met his eyes. She wore a green round dress today, a modest one with a lacy chemisette-tucker and long, puffy gigot sleeves. Like all the gowns he'd seen her wear, this one became her quite admirably. Then again, he couldn't imagine any garment that wouldn't suit her, not with her vibrant beauty. Even the silly creation she wore on her head, a newspaper which she'd cleverly folded to resemble a cocked hat, made a fetching frame for her perfect oval face.

As he watched, she and Bennie, who wore a matching hat, bowed to each other, then launched into what appeared to be a mock duel. Each brandishing a long stick, which, knowing Emily's fertile imagination she had declared to be swords of the finest Toledo steel, they thrust, slashed, and parried with sprightly ebullience, sometimes circling, other times chasing each other around the topiary pillars of Irish yew that defined the borders of the small garden. After several moments the gardener's dog entered the melee, its yipping barks of excitement mingling with their happy shouts.

For a brief, irrational moment Michael envied the animal and the ease with which it was accepted into the game. Lucky bloody beast! He could just imagine what would happen if *he* were to try to join in the fun. The reception he'd received from the *ton* after his disgusting display at Lady Kilvington's picnic would no doubt seem warm in comparison to the welcome he would receive from Emily.

Not that he would be able to blame her for her coldness. After the disgraceful way he'd behaved on their wedding day, he couldn't expect any better. Hell, he didn't *deserve* any better. He deserved to be treated exactly as she was currently treating him, to be despised and ignored . . . a state of affairs that suited him just fine. Indeed, he preferred matters as they stood and wished them to continue in a like manner.

Or did he? Michael rested his head against the stone window dressing, taking care to remain out of sight as he shifted through his tangled emotions.

While it was true that he still desired Emily—more than any woman he'd ever met—the overwhelming salaciousness of his lust had mellowed over the weeks. No longer were his thoughts of her the carnal visions of hot, naked flesh and animalistic couplings that had haunted him in the days following their marriage ceremony; no longer did the sight of her provoke the excruciating urgency he'd suffered on their wedding day and the first few times he'd seen her in the garden. No. Ever since he'd glimpsed the bright, buoyant spirit that possessed her luscious body, he'd begun to view her as a person rather than as an exquisite vessel upon which he wished to spend his lust.

Thus, what he felt now when he saw her was a lonely, almost desperate desire to befriend her—an emotion accompanied by an effervescing sensation of warmth that stirred not his groin, but his heart. He yearned to talk and laugh with her, to play her silly games, and yes, even listen to her queer nonsense about curses. In short, he wanted to be a part of her exhilarating life; he wanted to be energized by her vivaciousness and inspired by her joy of living.

Michael smiled ruefully at that last. Unlike himself, Emily had chosen not to simply exist in her isolation at Windgate Abbey, she had elected to live. She had taken what was an admittedly less than auspicious situation and had found countless ingenious ways to brighten and enrich not just her life, but those that touched it.

And it seemed that she had touched many lives at Windgate. Judging from what he'd seen and heard . . . the way the gardeners all smiled and greeted her when they happened upon her in the garden . . . the pleasure in both Grimshaw and Mrs. McInnis's voices when they uttered her name . . . the chambermaids' praise of her kindness and generosity . . . well, it was apparent that

Emily had quite won over the household staff. Raking his fingers through his damp hair, Michael had to admit that she had inadvertently won him over as well. So much so that he often found himself wishing that he'd met her before his illness.

Back then he'd been a worthy match for her . . . strong and handsome and charming. And he had no doubt whatsoever that she would have been every bit as taken with him as he currently was with her. She would have been thrilled to be courted by him, the rich and desirable duke of Sherrington, and he would have felt honored by the privilege of her allowing him to do so.

Michael swallowed hard, his heart contracting painfully at the thought of wooing Emily. How very splendid it would have been to court her. How perfectly wonderful to whisper in her ear all the sweet romantic nothings that so delighted the female heart. What pleasure to steal kisses from her ripe, red lips. They would have been perfect together, quite the most dashing couple London had ever seen. And when they finally wed, they would have done so with love and joy, forming a blissful union from which would have sprung all the beautiful babes Emily so desired.

But, of course, such a dream was impossible now. He was no longer the man he'd once been.

As he bleakly contemplated that dispiriting fact, Bennie playfully jabbed Emily in the side with his stick, to which she responded by dramatically clutching her middle and slowly crumpling to the ground. When she finally lay still, pretending to be slain, the boy began hopping around her prone form, spinning and whooping in what appeared to be a harum-scarum victory dance.

Michael smiled wistfully at the sight. Once upon a time he'd loved nothing more than a good romp. Indeed, it had often been remarked upon in the *ton* that nobody could turn a dull affair into one of gaiety and excitement quite as handily as the duke of Sherrington. The remembrance of those occasions made his chest feel suddenly taut and achy.

How he missed the *ton*! He'd thrived on society, nur-

tured by the noise, gaiety, conversation, and intrigue provided by the endless round of entertainment. Having
been crowned as London's most desirable bachelor, he'd
naturally been invited everywhere, which meant that he'd
hardly spent a moment alone during his reign. Indeed, if
he weren't being pursued by the virginal misses at Almack's, or being tendered ribald invitations by older,
more worldly women everywhere else he went, he was
enjoying the sensual pleasures of his mistress or one of
the many alluring members of the demirep.

And when he wished to escape the constant female
fawning? He could always take refuge in one of London's
many temples of manly amusement: White's, Tattersall's,
the boxing school on New Bond Street, the fencing
rooms in Haymarket, the gambling hells in St. James, or
any of the other numerous places where he could bask
in the camaraderie of his sometimes envious but always
admiring peers. It had been a marvelous life, a full and
exciting one . . .

One from which he'd been banished, much as Adam
and Eve had been cast out of the paradise that was Eden.
Unlike Adam and Eve, however, his eviction came not
from any sin on his part, but from a weakness he had
never courted and was now powerless to control.

And it hurt. Dear God, how it hurt! Nothing in his
previously blessed life had prepared him to endure the
devastation he had suffered at being ostracized by the
people he had thought to be his friends. Nor had it left
him with the grace to bear his lot without soul-shattering
shame and bitterness.

As always happened when Michael recalled his rever-
sal of fortune, he raged against fate, the *ton*, and himself,
looking to place blame for his misery and growing frustrated when doing so merely deepened his despair. It
seemed so futile, this existence of his. Hardly worth the
effort it took to breathe.

At that moment Emily returned to life, laughing in a
way that embraced his heart as she jumped up and began
to chase Bennie around the garden. Despite his desolation, Michael smiled. Perhaps, just perhaps, his existence

wouldn't seem so hopeless if he had someone like Emily in his life. Someone gay and amusing to divert him from his torment, a companion to ease the loneliness that constantly plagued his days.

Michael's smile faltered. Emily . . . his companion? What the hell was he thinking? As much as he longed for her company, actually acting upon his hankering and befriending her were utterly out of the question. Why, the very notion was absurd . . . impossible even.

Or was it? His brow furrowed in his consternation. The concept that he might be friends with a woman to whom he was so powerfully attracted was nothing short of astounding. Indeed, never in his life had he imagined doing such a thing. Then again, there had never been any reason for him to do so. Not when he'd always been so sexually vigorous and had had so many beautiful women eager to warm his bed. Now that all that had changed . . .

Hmmm. Could he be friends with Emily, *just* friends? Could he ignore his baser instincts and simply enjoy her company?

Standing there now, a distant spectator of his wife's alluring beauty and seductive presence, he could honestly reply yes. He felt at least somewhat confident that he could bridle his lust and behave in a civilized manner. He was also certain that any discomfort he suffered in doing so would be well worth enduring, considering the color and texture her friendship was sure to bring to his drab life. She was a whole new world to explore, one full of whimsy, charm, and magic.

With Emily by his side, he might learn to live again.

The temptation of that hope made him long to dash out to the garden and—and—what? He might want her company, but she most decidedly did not want his. She loathed him.

He raked his fingers through his hair, utterly disconcerted. After the contemptible way he'd treated her, was there anything he could possibly do or say to win her forgiveness?

Before he could consider, there was a soft rap at the

dressing room door, followed by, "Your grace? Is everything all right?"

Michael cast the closed door an exasperated look. Eadon was worse than a mother hen with one chick when it came to leaving his charge alone, always fearful that he would have a spell and do himself damage during one of those rare unattended moments. He was especially apprehensive when Michael bathed, an ablution Michael insisted on conducting in utter privacy.

Though he had once been like every other nobleman in England, never thinking twice about having his valet bathe him like a babe and attend to his most personal needs, his stint at Bamforth had left him jealous of his privacy and rendered him unable to bear the sort of intimate handling he'd once taken for granted. Thus, upon his release from the institution, he'd refrained from hiring a new valet, preferring to tend to himself and allowing the first footman or Eadon to help him only when absolutely necessary. It was a state of affairs that suited him splendidly, though Eadon had made it clear that he would have preferred his patient to adhere to a more traditional, hence less solitary, arrangement.

"Your grace?"

Michael sighed. Ah, well. As annoying as he found Eadon's smothering, he had to acknowledge that the man was only doing his job. Having thus reminded himself of that fact, he injected a cordial note in his voice as he replied, "I am fine, Eadon. I shall be finished directly."

"Very good, your grace."

Taking one last glance at Emily, who now lay sprawled on her back, chatting with Bennie, he reluctantly moved from the window. So, would she ever forgive him?

The only way to know for certain was to ask her.

Chapter 8

Vut! Vut! Vut!

Emily gasped, her hands flying to her chest in her startlement. Oh, heavens! C-could it be . . . w-was it . . . elves? Her palms clasped yet harder against her heart, which thundered and raced in horror at the thought of encountering supernatural beings.

Mercy had said that these ancient woods were populated by elves, wickedly mischievous ones, who danced among the cloister ruins at night and slept in the tree trunk hollows by day. She'd also cautioned that the creatures were jealous of their sleep and had related several local legends that detailed their vengeance against humans foolhardy enough to disturb their rest. Though skeptical about the existence of elves, bitter experience had taught Emily not to dismiss the threat of curses out of hand, so she'd tread carefully along the derelict path, taking care to avoid stepping on the many fallen twigs and dry leaves, or anything else that might produce a noise sufficiently sharp to awaken the spiteful woodland denizens. She thought she'd been successful but—

Vut! Vut! Vut! But apparently elves had far keener hearing than she'd imagined . . . well, they did if an elf were indeed the perpetrator of that queer call . . . which she very much d-doubted. Her hands still clutching her chest, despite her dogged determination to dismiss the notion of fairy folk, Emily anxiously searched for the source of the sound, her apprehensive gaze shifting from tree to tree, all of which sported the glowing tints of early autumn.

Yellow tinged the beech, birch, and elm; the maples

flaunted orange. The great spreading oak trees, most of
which appeared to be as old as England herself, wore
tawny mantles edged in bronze. To her right grew ash
and elder, dotted with plump fall berries; to her left
flourished larch, spruce, and pine, their scaly cones ripening with the season. Across the sun-dappled ground
splashed purple saw-worth and pale crimson betony,
bright shocks of color against the muted carpet of nature's mulch. Emily was suspiciously eyeing what appeared to be a fairy ring when—

Vut! Vut! Vut!

She jumped, then whirled around, her wide-eyed gaze
flying in the direction from which the babble had come.
The oak tree. Yes, whatever had voiced the noise was
most definitely in the gnarled oak just behind her.

Though common sense told her to flee in the face of
possible danger, to run as far and as fast as her feet
could carry her, she didn't move. She couldn't. Her curiosity, which was every bit as potent as her imagination,
warred with her prudence, and at the moment it was
winning the battle. Thus she remained rooted to the spot,
goosebumps tiptoeing up her arms as she uneasily surveyed the tree.

There! Yes. Something moved . . . around at the back
of the tree trunk. Fearful of what she might see, but now
too inquisitive not to investigate, she took a cautious step
nearer. Oh, she knew she was being reckless, stupid even,
but—but—

Helpless to stop herself, she took another step. Then
another, and another—

Vut! Vut! Vut!

An involuntary scream escaped her lips and she froze.
There followed the scraping sound of scurrying feet, then
a plump red squirrel scampered into view. Its plumed
ears cocked and its bushy, foxlike tail bristling, it clung
to the fissured side of the tree, scolding her fiercely
around the nut in its cheek.

Emily gaped speechlessly for several beats, her mind
scrambling to process what she was seeing. Then her

shoulders began to shake and she doubled over, laughing helplessly.

Elves indeed! What a widgeon she was to take such nonsense to heart. The squirrel, looking insulted at being laughed at, bound up the tree, discharging a final *vut! vut! vut!* as it disappeared into the autumn-bronzed foliage.

Still chuckling and shaking her head at her own folly, Emily wiped her mirth-dampened eyes with her kid-gloved hand and resumed her pilgrimage to the cloister ruins. Goodness! She really must stop listening to Mercy's wild tales. They were fueling her already overactive imagination and not in a manner she found agreeable.

Why, just last night she'd been certain that she'd heard the chanting of the hanged monks' phantom funeral procession, which Mercy claimed paraded down the ancient stone hallway of the abbey and into these very woods on dark, moonless nights. As it turned out, the music was just the tuneless humming of Ralph, the fourth footman, whose duty it was to tend to the wall lanterns in the hallway in question. Unfortunately for the both of them, she hadn't discovered that fact until after she'd worked herself into a panic and had almost caused the house to be burned down.

Emily cringed at the memory of the mortifying episode. It had occurred around nine o'clock, an admittedly early hour for a haunting, as she had returned from the library with the book she'd selected to read in bed. Upon hearing what at the time had sounded like eerie chanting, she'd remembered Mercy's ghostly tale and had panicked. After all, as with seeing the hanged monks, encountering the phantom funeral procession, too, portended death. And so she had run, tearing blindly down the hall in her desperation to escape the uncanny cavalcade. When she'd come upon Ralph, she'd screeched her irrational terror, making him drop the taper he carried, the flame of which had ignited the carpet runner.

Though the damage had been minimal, the incident had served to illustrate how dangerously out of control her imagination was in regards to the Windgate legend, thus prompting her to take her current course of action:

She was visiting the scene of the alleged tragedy, hoping to exorcise her fear by removing the mystery of the place from her mind.

Her father had always said that the only way to banish one's fears was to squarely face and explore them, and that once the unknown became known, it inevitably ceased to be frightening. It was a theory that had proved correct in all instances . . . save that of her curse. The more she'd explored it, the more alarming it had become.

Lifting her now dusty skirts, Emily stepped over a moss-mottled log that lay rotting across the path, sighing at the thought of the curse. The only good thing she could say about her marriage to the master of Windgate Abbey was that it had alleviated her fear of the curse. It was, after all, impossible to fall in love with a man she never saw, especially one whose very memory prickled and galled her.

As always happened when she thought of her husband, Emily's ire kindled. He really was a bastard, tricking her as he had done. And the way he'd spoken to her after the wedding . . . o-o-o! How dare he woo her into a marriage he'd never had any intention of honoring! Why, when she thought of how deceptively pleasant he'd been during their introduction and the way he'd played upon her sympathy with his candor about his condition . . . o-o-o! Hateful man! If anyone deserved fits, it was he.

Though Emily knew she should feel shame at thinking such an uncharitable thought, she couldn't help herself. He had wounded her far too deeply for her to muster the slightest bit of compassion for his suffering. Indeed, after all the wretched things he'd said and done, he could fall into a thrashing, foaming heap at her feet, and she doubted if she would feel anything for him but a bitter sense of justice. She most certainly wouldn't lift a hand to help him nor would she comfort him in the aftermath of his fit, as she would be inclined to do for anyone else. No. Were he to be overcome in her presence, she would simply walk away.

Well, not without first summoning help, she amended. He might be a bastard, but she couldn't in good conscience leave him alone at such a moment. After all, were he to choke to death or suffer some other grievous damage because of her neglect, she would be forced to feel guilt. And the last thing she intended to do was spend her life plagued with guilt over the demise of a man she disliked as much as she did the duke of Sherrington.

She also had no intention of wasting any more thoughts on him, a resolution she found easy to honor as the woods came to an abrupt end and she caught her first glimpse of the ruined cloisters.

They looked much as she'd imagined, jaggedly fragmentary and overgrown with vegetation. The feeling they invoked in her, however, was utterly unexpected. Instead of being clutched with dread, as she'd anticipated, she felt an odd sense of serenity. Surely a place where the sun shined so brightly and where the birds sang with such gladness couldn't be so very evil?

Careful not to trip over the scattered rubble, Emily slowly advanced forward, her gaze moving over the crumbling remains of the foundation and walls, trying to gauge the size and arrangement of the time-ravaged buildings. That the cloisters had once been expansive was clear from the dimensions of the groundworks; that they had been splendid was evidenced by the segments of green and yellow mosaic flooring she spied between the thick patches of encroaching weeds.

With almost every step she took, Emily found something new to arrest and intrigue her. Thus, as had happened in the woods, her curiosity quickly overrode her wariness and she was soon engrossed in her exploration.

It was a fascinating place, sprinkled with all sorts of clues to the mysterious lives lived there so very long ago. There was what she guessed to be a stone altar, carved with strange symbols and letters. And the hand of a white marble statue, which clasped the shattered remains of what she decided had once been a cross or a staff. Then there was the immense hooded fireplace, still blackened by ancient fires, and the enchanting assortment of illustrated wall fragments that, while faded and scarred by the elements, provided evidence of a once great mural.

Now coming to what appeared to be the heart of the ruins, Emily carefully wound her way down the debris-littered remnants of a long corridor and through an arched doorway, stopping when she entered what had once been the courtyard.

Constructed in a square of the same grayish-brown stone that dominated Windgate Abbey, three of the four courtyard walls remained erect, two of which spanned three stories with one still retaining a portion of its graceful tracery window. Judging from the fractured pillars and the fingers of rib vaulting protruding from the walls, it was clear that the courtyard had once boasted a covered walk, beneath which still sat several remarkably well-preserved stone benches. After pausing a beat to pick up and examine a shard of thick, crude ruby glass, a souvenir from the tracery window, no doubt, Emily reluctantly surveyed the once grassy, but now weed-choked center court.

According to Mercy, it was here that the legendary oak tree had once stood. Now clutched by the dread she'd expected to feel upon her first glimpse of the ruins, Emily scanned the rubble-strewn grounds, forcing herself to search for the stump that her maid claimed still remained.

Hmmm. There was what looked to be the shattered remains of an enormous, elaborately carved font; several thick slabs of granite, the purpose of which she couldn't even begin to guess; an abandoned well; and—and—

Her heart plunged to the pit of her belly. There it was, the tree stump.

Though she wanted nothing more than to flee, Emily forced herself to move forward, determined to prove to herself that the stump wasn't any more sinister than the one upon which she'd often sat in the yard of her Boston home. Nervously wadding the skirt of her violet French merino pelisse in her trembling hands, she slowly approached the object of her nightmares, trying to talk herself out of her fear as she went.

It was ridiculous, really, the very notion of a ghost tree . . . absurd to the extreme. Why, just because there happened to be a tree stump here, exactly as described by the legend, didn't automatically authenticate the tale. Besides, if Windgate was really as haunted as Mercy claimed, no one would want to work there. And as far as she'd been able to ascertain, most of the servants had been at the abbey for many years and were perfectly content to remain there. Then again this *was* Dartmoor, the most haunted place in England, so the servants, nearly all of whom were Dartmoor natives, were no doubt used to ghostly goings-on.

Not particularly comforted by that last thought, Emily came to a stop before the stump. Her hands still worrying her skirts into rumpled balls, she peered down at it.

Judging from its diameter and the numerous growth rings still evident in its center, despite the wood's darkening with age, the tree had been ancient when it had been cut down. That meant that the cloisters had been built around it. She paused to consider her discovery, then removed her gloves to touch it. Touching was an essential part of the facing and exploring process, the part she had been dreading most in this particular instance.

Her breath catching in her apprehension, she tentatively brushed her trembling fingertips across the exposed heartwood, half-expecting to be struck down where she stood. Nothing happened. After waiting several more beats, she released her breath on a sigh of relief and forced herself to touch it again, this time allowing her fingers to linger for a moment. When all remained calm, she bit her lip and flattened her palm against the chopped surface, which felt smooth and hard from centuries of weathering. Again nothing happened. Slowly she smiled. It was just a stump, a perfectly ordinary one. Why it was no more menacing than—

Crack! A sharp snap splintered the silence behind her.

Emily froze. Oh, heavens! No squirrel could have made that noise. Jolted by a surge of panic, she jerked her hand from the stump and whirled around, her already wide eyes almost popping from their sockets in her dismay at what she saw.

The duke of Sherrington. And of course he was scowling, the recipient of which was the piece of rotting wood beneath his boot, the apparent culprit of the noise.

A soft groan escaped her. Either there were truly elves and this was their revenge for her disturbing their rest, or the stump possessed some sort of evil power that brought a plague upon those bold enough to touch it. For several seconds Emily simply stared at her plaguesome husband, too taken aback by his unwelcome presence to do more. Then her hostility pierced her surprise and her spine instinctively stiffened.

As if sensing her sudden change in demeanor, he glanced up. When he saw her staring, his strong jaw tensed perceptibly and he jerked his head in a curt nod of acknowledgment.

She bristled. O-o-o! Wasn't he the polite one, deigning to spare her a nod? The tyrant and her bosom-bow could certainly be proud of the job they had done of drumming manners into his aristocratic little brain. Thoroughly despising him, she turned away, flagrantly snubbing him. Well, to hell with manners. She'd be damned before she would return his dubious courtesy and acknowledge his presence. He didn't deserve to be recognized, the arrogant bastard! Besides, wouldn't acknowledging him qualify as going against his wish to be left alone—a wish she had vowed to honor?

Contemptuously deciding it would, she stuck her nose in the air and lifted her hems. Without sparing him so much as a parting glance, she started toward the nearest opening in the foundation of the demolished wall.

She was halfway there when his hateful voice lashed out. "Stay!" It was an order, naturally, a brusquely uttered one.

Emily paused, more out of annoyance than in obeyance of his command. Stay indeed! How dare he bark at her like that . . . like she was a dog or a horse or some other poor dumb creature to be mastered and directed? Though she was sorely tempted to ignore him, to show him exactly what she thought of him and his high-handedness, she couldn't resist tossing over her shoulder, "If you think that I am going to stay and suffer more of your insults, then your illness has damaged your brain far worse than anyone suspects." Adding a sniff to emphasize her disdain, she resumed her retreat.

"Emily, stop." Another command, this one edged with fury. Or was that frustration?

Who cared? Rather enjoying her defiance, she continued on her way, making a show of ignoring him.

"Emily would you . . . oh . . . bloody hell!" From behind her she heard the rustle of the tall, dry weeds and the grating of pebbles beneath his boots as he began to stalk after her.

She quickened her pace.

Judging from the sound of his footsteps, he followed suit.

She accelerated a fraction more, practically running now.

"Damn it, Emily! Will you stop . . . please? I am trying to apologize." There was no mistaking the tone of his voice this time: it was frustration laced with a distinct note of pleading.

Astonished, as much by his tone as by his words, she did as he requested. What was this? The hateful duke of Sherrington pleading to apologize? Impossible! Certain that she had heard amiss, Emily shot him a sharp glance over her shoulder and snapped, "What did you say?"

"I wish to apologize," he repeated tautly. "I have treated you abominably, and I am sorry."

She remained motionless for a beat, appraising his words, then slowly turned to face him, frowning her consternation. "Why?"

He paused, as if taken aback by her question, then took several more strides forward, stopping a scant yard from where she stood. His handsome face a mask of impeccable cordiality, he politely inquired, "Why what? Why did I treat you so abominably, or why am I sorry?"

"Why do you wish to apologize? I mean"—she shook her head, her hands spreading in a gesture of perplexed query—"you made it perfectly clear that you neither like me nor want me for your wife. Why bother to apologize to someone you so clearly despise?"

Though his expression didn't change, a shadow darkened his stunning jade eyes, dimming their jewel-like brilliance. "I do not despise you, Emily. I never did," he softly replied.

She made a skeptical noise. "You most certainly could have fooled me, your grace. It seems to me that a person wouldn't speak to another in the manner in which you spoke to me and then banish them from their sight if they didn't despise them."

"A person wouldn't, no, but a bastard would. Bastards are stupid, thoughtless creatures with a regrettable tendency to utter asinine things that they usually do not mean and inevitably live to regret." A wry smile tugged at the corners of his exquisitely sculpted lips. "And as you, yourself, pointed out, I am a dreadful bastard."

"Yes, you are," she readily agreed, not about to be mollified by his display of charm. "However, being a bastard is no excuse for your behavior, nor does it explain why you wish to apologize now, a full month after the offense."

He stared at her for several beats, as if grappling for a response, then heaved a heavy sigh and closed his eyes. Pressing his fingers against his forehead, as if his thoughts had made it ache, he murmured, "What can I say? There is no defense for the way I acted. I was angry and resentful over being forced into this marriage, and I unfairly took my bitterness out on you. It was a vile thing to do, I know that, and I shan't blame you if you never forgive me. However, if you do choose to hate me for the rest of your life, please know that what I said and did on our wedding day in no way reflects my true feelings for you."

There was an oddly frayed quality to his voice, a note of weary, almost dejected resignation that thawed the icy edge of Emily's hostility. Nonetheless, she was nowhere near forgiving him, so she kept her tone deliberately frigid as she inquired, "Oh? And what, pray tell, are your feelings for me?"

He sighed again and dropped his hand from his forehead. Opening his eyes to meet her suspicious gaze with one of naked candor, he softly confessed, "Quite simply, I admire you."

Of all the things he might have said, that he admired her was the last one she expected to hear. Drawing back slightly in her incredulity, she demanded, "How can you admire someone whose beliefs you hold in such contempt? And do not insult me by trying to tell me that you actually respect them, not after the viciousness with which you attacked them."

"Again, what can I say?" He shook his head, his upturned palms extending in a gesture of helpless supplication. "I am a bastard. Someone should have done the world a favor and shot me years ago."

"So we have established," she tartly countered, though something inside her softened at the sight of him dining on humble pie.

"We have also established that bastards are stupid, thoughtless creatures who have a tendency to say things they do not mean, remember?"

She nodded.

He nodded back, his lips crooking into a sheepish smile. "Well then, there you are. I was simply doing what bastards do best. And like most bastards of my ilk, I genuinely regret my words. The truth is . . . and please do not take this as an insult, for I have quite enough to apologize for as it is . . . I honestly do respect your beliefs."

"Indeed?" she murmured, his unorthodox apology thawing her another degree. For all that he was a bastard, he could be rather engaging when he put his mind to it.

Another nod. "Oh, I admit that I do not share your views in some matters, but I do respect your right to hold them. Truly. And should you ever learn to trust me enough to discuss them again, I promise to listen thoughtfully and respond in a civil manner. If you wish proof of my sincerity, you may have my pistol and my permission to shoot me should I transform into a bastard during any conversation you choose to grant me.''

Emily started to smile at the charming absurdity of his offer, catching herself in the very nick of time. No! No! She couldn't forgive him yet. She wasn't ready to do so, not after all he'd said and done. Besides, he had yet to explain his sudden wish to make amends. Until he did, how could she possibly trust him enough to befriend him? Firmly ignoring the softening of her heart, she coolly replied, ''You may rest assured that I will take you up on your offer should I ever decide to engage you in a tête-à-tête, though I think it only fair to warn you that I am quite adept with a pistol.''

He grinned in a way that reduced the remaining ice of her hostility to a rapidly melting slush. ''Excellent. You shall be far more inclined to chat with me if you aren't worried about missing your shot.''

''I am afraid not, your grace,'' she retorted, shaking her head. ''The only thing that could induce me to chat with you is trust, something I cannot even begin to feel until I understand your reason for wishing to secure my forgiveness. Even you must admit it odd for a man to have such a sudden change of heart.''

His smile faltered at her words, though it was apparent from the strain around his lips that he was trying hard to maintain it. ''If you must know, the change wasn't so very sudden. I have wished to make amends for some time now.''

''You have?'' She drew back, staring at him in astonishment.

''Yes.''

''Then why didn't you do so? I mean ...'' She shook her head, frowning her incomprehension. ''Your apology would have been ever so much easier for you to tender and for me to accept had you not allowed the animosity between us to fester.''

He managed to preserve his smile for a beat longer, then let it slip with a sigh. Looking suddenly weary and defeated, he admitted, ''I did not apologize simply because I didn't know how. There seemed nothing I could possibly say or do to make up for the way I treated you. As I said, I admire you immensely, which made what I did seem all the more deplorable."

The slush of her once-frigid wrath dissolved completely in the face of his humility. Tempted to forgive him, but wishing to understand and solidify the terms of their truce before doing so, she countered, "You admit that you disagree with my views, yet you claim to admire me. How can that be?"

"Just because we differ in our beliefs regarding witches and curses doesn't automatically doom us to disagreement on every other subject. Indeed, I wouldn't be at all surprised to learn that we agree on a great many matters." He nodded once, smiling in a way that left little doubt in her mind as to his conviction in what he said. "In fact, it is one of those many other matters, your view of life to be precise, that prompted my admiration."

Again he took her aback. "What?" And again she frowned, this time eyeing him as if he'd taken a leave of his senses, which at that moment she rather suspected he had. "I do not recall discussing any such view with you. Ever."

He shrugged. "You didn't have to. It is obvious. It was from the very moment we met."

"It was?" Her frown deepened, as did her bewilderment.

He nodded. "By your willingness to make the best of our marriage, you demonstrated a remarkably optimistic outlook on life. That you were able to maintain that outlook in the face of what I know was an immensely difficult situation for you illustrated both courage and an amazing strength."

"Do you really think so?" she murmured, reluctantly flattered by the portrait he painted of her character. No one had ever referred to her as strong and courageous before, both traits she had always considered highly laudable.

Another nod, this one adamant. "I know so. Why, I can only imagine how daunting it must have been for you to be shipped off to a foreign land and forced into marriage with a stranger . . . especially when that stranger turned out to be me, a man who even I must admit is no bargain. That you were willing to accept me and my shortcomings, and still hold out hope for a successful marriage, well"—he shook his head—"it leaves me breathless with awe every time I think of the courage it must have taken for you to do so."

"It really didn't take all that much courage," she demurred, remembering her own breathless awe of his beauty the first time she saw him.

He snorted. "It took more than I can claim, obviously."

So bitter, so full of pain and self-loathing, was the utterance that Emily, whose heart had always been too tender for her own good, was moved to show him compassion. Resisting the urge to reach out and take his hands in hers, she gently replied, "I daresay it wasn't so much a want of courage, but a lack of health that made you behave as you did. No doubt you would have handled matters differently were you not so ill."

"Were I not so ill, neither of us would have been forced into this marriage. I would have remained free to choose my own bride, and Euphemia most probably would have allowed you to wed whomever you pleased." He shook his head, chuckling harshly. "Do you want to know the real irony in all of this?" Apparently it was a rhetorical question, for he answered without pause, "Given the choice, I would have chosen you."

"What!" she gasped, stunned.

He nodded. "It is true, Emily. If I were still in the position to choose and you were offered as a choice, I would take you in an instant. How could I not? You are brave, strong, kind, intelligent, and gracious, not to mention more beautiful than any woman has a right to be. It would be an honor and a pleasure to court you. Who knows? Were I still the man I once was, you might even look upon me with favor."

"I—I don't know what to say," she stammered, rendered utterly speechless by his flattering disclosure.

He shrugged. "There is nothing left to be said. That being the case, I will take my leave and let you enjoy the remainder of your walk in peace." After sketching an elegant bow, he turned on his heels and started back in the direction from which he had come.

Dumbfounded, Emily stared at his retreating back, an odd sense of longing tightening her chest as she watched him go. She forgave him. Oh yes, she forgave him . . . with all her heart. Suddenly desperate to tell him so, she blurted out, "Your grace?"

He halted, then slowly turned, his face a study of urbane politeness as he waited for her to continue.

She swallowed hard, silently cursing as her already warm cheeks flamed. Feeling strangely shy and uncertain, she stammered out, "I just wanted to say . . . um . . . that . . . that . . ." What? What should she say? What *could* she say? She struggled to think of something, anything at all to express what she felt. When nothing came to mind, she forced herself to begin again, making up the words as she went along. "I mean . . . uh . . . I was wondering if . . . if you would . . . er . . . care to walk with me a bit?" So what if the utterance wasn't a gem of eloquence? It conveyed her forgiveness.

To her gratification, he smiled, really smiled, the first time she'd ever seen him do so. The effect was dazzling, making her already skipping heart turn giddy cartwheels across her chest. Beaming as if she'd just granted him his fondest wish, he huskily replied, "I can think of nothing in the world that would give me greater pleasure."

Chapter 9

Ah, yes. These would make perfect angel wing feathers.

Emily separated the six gold-shot sheets of white tissue from the thick folio before her, nodding her satisfaction with her selection. The folio, which held what she estimated to be at least a hundred sheets of exquisitely colored and printed Chinese paper, had been a parting gift from Daniel, along with a chest containing all the other necessary tools and materials required to continue her kite making.

It was a marvelous gift, the best one he could have given her, for designing and making, not to mention flying, kites was her greatest delight. Indeed, nothing raised her spirits quite like building a new kite, which was why she always turned to the pastime whenever she felt sad or lonely, or was troubled and needed to think. In view of that fact, she had spent much of her time since her wedding day ensconced here, at the long sewing room cutting table, building kite after splendid kite, each design more ambitious than the last. The one she currently constructed, an angel built on the principles of a Chinese bird-kite, was without doubt the most impressive yet.

After pausing a moment to consider how best to simulate feathers, Emily picked up her shears and began cutting the delicate tissue into long strips. What occupied her mind as she worked, however, wasn't her project, but her husband.

Though he had flitted through her thoughts frequently over the past month, despite her best efforts to keep him at bay, he now firmly possessed her mind. How could he not? After a month spent ignoring her, he had made a sudden, but what at the time had struck her as a sincere gesture toward friendship, only to resume avoiding her immediately afterward.

Or so it seemed. Emily frowned, not quite certain what to think. Despite her machinations to contrive another meeting, she hadn't so much as glimpsed her enigmatic husband in the two days following their initial encounter. Why, she'd even spent several hours of both those days lingering about the ruins, where he'd said he walked daily, but he had never appeared. That he would remain so conspicuously absent after taking the pains to mention his strolls had to mean that he was avoiding her . . . what other explanation could there be?

None, she decided for the tenth time that hour. At least none that made a whit of sense. She shook her head, sighing over her conclusion. What made his absence all the more confounding, not to mention exceedingly disappointing, was that he had been so charming during their brief walk. In truth, she couldn't remember the last time she'd enjoyed a man's company more. He'd been so warm, so very unaffected in both manner and conversation.

Indeed, unlike most men in her acquaintance, whose idea of conversing with a woman was to pretend to hang on to her every word and respond with banal pleasantries, Michael had listened, really listened to her. He'd thoughtfully considered everything she said and had replied in a manner that paid homage to her intellect, something as refreshing as it was flattering. Best of all, he had patiently answered her questions about the legend, explaining the tale with an engaging logic that had had her smiling at her own foolishness in ever believing it.

The story of the hanged monks, it seemed, had come about as a result of the abbey's lay-brothers' custom of drying laundry on the branches of the infamous oak tree. On the authority of an account written by the abbot of the time, one which Michael had said still remained in the abbey library and that she was welcome to read any time she so desired, the legend was started by two local youths, who had sought shelter at the cloisters after being caught in a storm while hunting on the moors.

Because the monks lived in seclusion and little was known about their activities, they had taken on a mysterious, almost sinister aspect in the primitive minds of the neighboring peasants, thus prompting rumors of nefarious goings-on behind the forbidding monastery walls.

The truth of the matter was that this particular abbey was devoted to the care of the order's elderly and infirm members, which was why the cloisters had been built a distance from the main monastery buildings, something that Michael had explained was highly irregular. The intended purpose of this separation was to allow the ailing brothers to spend what was often their final days in peace and quiet, away from the normal hustle-bustle of the ever-industrious Cistercian monks.

At any rate, it was late afternoon when the tempest that had prompted the legend had struck, hitting suddenly and without warning, streaking the storm-blackened sky with lightning and furiously pelting the moors with hail and rain. According to the abbot's report, it had been wash day, and though the brothers had managed to collect most of the laundry from the oak tree, the fierceness of the wind had caused several sheets to become entangled in the branches, thus making it impossible for the monks to free them without risking hazard to themselves. Hence, they had been left in the tree.

The youths, having arrived just after vespers, were extended every humble hospitality the monks had to offer, after which they were shown to a chamber in which they were invited to pass the night. The chamber, as fate would have it, had a window that overlooked the courtyard. When the youths peeked out that window later that night, no doubt attempting to gauge the storm, they beheld the sodden sheets swinging from the tree branches, illuminated only by the eerie bursts of lightning.

Because of the speculation about the Cistercians, some of it involving madness, they had imagined the sheets to be the corpses of hanged monks; a macabre vagary that had made them flee the cloisters in horror without awaiting either confirmation of their suspicion or an explanation of what they saw. Their report of the incident to the other peasants had planted the seeds of the legend, which had thrived and grown over the centuries to include wind spirits, ghosts, and curses.

When Michael had at last fallen silent, Emily, whose mind had been eased by the explanation, had pensively smoothed her hand over the time-glossed surface of the stump, speculating aloud as to the fate of the once mighty oak. Pointing to the nearby well, Michael had explained how the tree's roots had threatened the cloister's water source, thus necessitating that it be chopped down. At her prompting, he had then given her a most fascinating tour of the ruins, detailing the original purpose of each building and describing how it was reported to have once looked. He was telling of the fire that had reduced the cloisters to their current rubble when Mr. Eadon had appeared, informing his employer that he had business requiring his immediate attention.

And that had been that. After escorting her back to the house, Michael had disappeared into the bowels of the abbey, from which, as far as she knew, he had yet to emerge.

Wondering if, perhaps, he'd secretly thought her questions about the legend ridiculous and was now avoiding her for fear of being roped into another silly tête-à-tête, Emily picked up one of the paper strips she'd cut and began clipping it into a featherlike fringe. It was possible, she supposed, just as it was conceivable that he'd deemed her a peagoose and had judged her friendship not worth his while. She paused mid-snip, crushed by the notion. Truth be told, she found him extremely worthwhile. Not only was he charming, intelligent, and amusing, but he was a pleasure to behold.

As always happened when she envisioned her husband, Emily felt the queerest tingling in her belly. He was such a handsome man, too handsome, really. It ought to be illegal for a man to look so. She sighed. He was especially stunning when he smiled, flashing what had to be the most perfect set of teeth God ever granted a mortal man.

And then there was the improvement in his color. As if he hadn't been far too attractive before, his smooth cheeks had boasted a faint, but extremely becoming hint of pink the last time she saw him, an enhancement that rendered him devastating.

For several heartbeats her mesmerized mind's eye remained riveted on Michael's exquisite face, glorying in its perfection. Then she shook her head and tried to tear it away. To her dismay, his provocative image remained firmly fixed in her thoughts. After several more fruitless attempts to banish him, she gave up and surrendered to her daydream.

Hmmm. All and all he'd looked better during their walk around the cloisters . . . healthier. Not only had his color improved, there had been a spring in his step and strength in his arms, something she had noted when he'd helped her over the rubble during their tour of the ruins. Yes, and she mustn't forget the sparkle in his eyes . . . his beautiful, extraordinary eyes.

Another sigh escaped her. Never in her life had she seen eyes that color, that brilliant bluish-green. Why, they perfectly matched the jade in the bracelet her oldest brother, George, had brought her from Turkestan . . . the one that currently graced her left wrist. Emily glanced at the exotically wrought piece of jewelry, her cheeks heating with embarrassment at the romantic fancy that had led her to don it.

How very missish of her to wear it, just because the color of the stones happened to match the eyes of a man she admired. One would have thought that she was a schoolgirl with a crush to behave so, which she most assuredly was not.

Shaking her head, she resumed her cutting. No. Just because she liked looking at Michael didn't mean that she had a crush on him. Indeed, she couldn't imagine anyone not finding the sight of him pleasurable. He was, after all, an exceptionally beautiful man, and viewing him was rather like beholding a stunning work of art. That she also enjoyed his company . . . well, thinking him handsome and agreeable was a long way from the breathless captivation one felt for the object of a crush. Another head shake. No. She hardly suffered a crush. The long and the short of the matter was that she liked Michael Vane and wished him for a friend.

Too bad he didn't share her feelings.

A pang of disappointment tightened her throat. Despite her camaraderie with Bennie and her cordiality with the servants, she was lonely. And not a day had passed since her arrival in Dartmoor that she hadn't wished for a friend, a special someone with whom she could exchange thoughts and confidences. After the rapport she'd shared with Michael, she'd thought that he might be that someone. The fact that he'd seemed as starved for company as she, displaying the eager, almost desperate animation of a person who was alone too often, had merely strengthened her belief.

Obviously she had been wrong. Obviously he wasn't starved enough to overlook her silliness and adopt her as a friend. Obviously he preferred Eadon's company, though judging from the grim expression on his face when the man had appeared, he found the relationship less than enjoyable.

She was just trying to imagine exactly what that relationship might be, having no clear idea as to Mr. Eadon's actual position in the household, when there was a scratching at the door. Frowning, more at her thoughts than at the interruption, she called out, "Yes?"

It was Francis, the first footman, a pleasant-faced man in his late twenties whose main duty seemed to be leading her about the house and seeing to it that she didn't get lost in the impossible maze of halls. As always, he was immaculately garbed in elegant dark green and gold livery, his hair, which Emily had never seen, neatly tucked beneath a formal powdered wig. Smiling with an ease that was at odds with his decorous appearance, he sketched a stately bow and uttered, "Dinner, your grace."

Dinner? Emily's scissors froze mid-snip as she stared at him in surprise. Was it really so late? One glance at the shadows outside the row of round-headed windows told her that it was. "Oh, my. Wherever does the time go?" she murmured, laying her project on the table. The answer, of course, was obvious. The time, which had dragged up until two days ago, now flew whenever she thought about Michael.

Wondering if her cheeks were as red as they felt, another discomfiting consequence of thinking about Michael, she self-consciously smoothed what she was certain was her impossibly mussed hair, adding, "I am afraid I'm rather a mess. Perhaps I should freshen myself before going downstairs." Why she should bother, she didn't know. Except for Francis, who stood stationed behind her chair at meals, and the other footmen who served the food, she always ate alone.

The footman bowed again—all the servants in England bowed overly much in Emily's opinion. "Unless you would feel more comfortable in doing so, I hardly think it warranted. You look quite splendid, as always, your grace."

"Well, if you are sure I am proper," she slowly replied, dubiously eyeing her simple pomegranate-and-black-checked jaconet gown. "I wouldn't wish the other footmen to think their mistress a slovenly frump."

"I can assure you that they will think no such thing, your grace. Indeed, it is often commented upon in the servants' hall that we have the loveliest mistress in all of England."

If Emily's cheeks weren't red before, they most definitely were now.

"Besides," he continued, "we mustn't keep, er"—a faint, uncharacteristic flush stained his fair cheeks—"uh, what I mean to say is that dinner is ready, and that since I was detained from my duty of escorting you downstairs, well"—a head shake—"I needn't tell you what a terror Cook can be when she is kept waiting to serve."

Indeed he did not. Judging from the crashing and scolding she'd heard coming from the kitchen on those occasions when she'd been late for a meal, and the redness of the footmen's faces afterward as they had come racing forth bearing trays of plain but hearty food, it was clear that the cook, plump Phoebe Swann, ruled the kitchen with an iron spoon.

Not wishing to subject the footmen to the tribulation of Cook's temper, Emily rose, pausing only the briefest of moments to smooth her rumpled skirts with her hand. Dismissing them as hopeless, she nodded at Francis, who bowed yet again and ushered her from the room.

The sewing room was located in what was referred to as the new wing of the house, new being seventy years old, which in comparison to the original sections of the abbey was very new indeed. Being new meant that it was far removed from the dining areas, all of which were situated in either the old abbey or the addition built by the first Vane owner sometime during the reign of Henry VIII.

In accordance with Emily's preference, meals were always served in the breakfast room, a cozy nook at the end of the Tudor wing, rather than in the enormous banqueting hall, which was where her first dinner at Windgate had been served and which she had found far too large and grand for her comfort.

Thus when they reached the hall where the breakfast room was quartered, Emily was surprised to be led in the opposite direction. Wondering if perhaps the footman's mind was on other matters and that he had inadvertently taken a wrong turn, she pointed out his mistake.

He smiled a cryptic smile and shook his head. "Dinner is being served in the Italian dining room this evening, your grace."

She frowned at the oddness of his information. She had seen the Italian dining room only once, while on a tour of the house with Grimshaw. And while not as vast as the banqueting hall nor as formal as what was referred to as the little dining room, it was still far too imposing for her taste. Indeed, all that marble, those florid wall murals, and the numerous alcoves with Romanesque statues were quite enough to take away one's appetite with the confusion they caused the eye. Add the gaudy shell-shaped buffets and the long table, neither of which were Italian at all, but yet more of the rococo monstrosities that blighted the abbey, and you had a room in which she'd hoped never to dine.

As they stopped before the door, Emily murmured, "How very irregular that dinner should be served in here. Are you quite certain that you aren't mistaken?" That last was uttered with a note of forlorn hope.

"Quite certain, your grace."

"But why? I mean"—she shrugged her puzzlement— "why the sudden change? I was quite content dining in the breakfast room."

Another cryptic smile. "You shall see." With that, he flung open the double doors. Indicating with a sweeping hand motion that she was to enter, he murmured, "If you please, your grace?"

Not quite certain what to make of his queer conduct, Emily did as directed, only to stop on the threshold in the next instant. Michael was there, sitting at the far end of the long table.

At her appearance, he rose unsteadily from his seat, his whole body visibly trembling from the effort. Pressing his palms against the linen-draped table to brace himself, he nodded, smiling weakly. "Good evening, dear wife." His voice sounded hoarse, as if it had been skinned raw.

Emily stared at him in shock, more taken aback by his appearance than by his presence. Good heavens! What had happened to him? He was so pale, far paler than she'd ever seen him. And thinner, if such a change were possible in only two days' time. In truth, he looked positively wasted. Then there was the way he trembled with weakness and the fragility of his voice. All and all he looked and sounded like a person who had recently suffered a grave illness and had barely survived to tell of it.

Alarmed, she lifted her skirts and rushed to him. Unmindful of the footmen, who stood at attention along the wall, pretending not to notice her harum-scarum entrance into the room, she came to a skidding stop beside him. "Your grace . . . oh! What has happened? You look terrible." It was no lie. Up close he looked even worse, bad enough to drop where he stood.

His ashen lips curved into a semblance of a rakish smile and he even managed a rasping chuckle. "I must say that that is hardly the sort of greeting I envisioned.

Then again, I am unfamiliar with your American customs." He tipped his head to one side, his stunning eyes, the only thing about him she found unaltered, dancing with amusement as he gazed down at her. "Tell me, wife. Is blurting out the brutal truth about another person's poor appearance an accepted convention in America?"

"Only when the person in question looks as if he should be on his death bed, which you do," she replied, frowning as he swayed precariously and had to clutch the edge of the table to steady himself. Though he continued to smile, his face blanched a shade whiter and a fine sheen of perspiration misted his brow. Certain that he was about to faint at any moment, Emily thumped the arm of his chair and sternly ordered, "Sit down this instant, your grace. Before you topple over and put yourself into a worse state than you are currently in."

Michael out and out grinned at her scolding tone, stunned and pleased by her genuine show of concern. Though they had been companionable during their walk, he'd hardly expected her to care enough about him to fret over his welfare. That she did made him all the more determined to improve on their tentatively cordial relationship, which was the reason he'd dragged himself from his sickbed to dine with her this evening, despite both Eadon's and his own infirm body's vigorous protests against him doing so.

Truth be told, he'd been afraid to stay away from her for any longer, worried that the fragile bud of their blossoming friendship would wither from a lack of nourishment. The required nourishment was, of course, conversation and companionship, the administration of which necessitated him being near her as often and for as long as she would permit. It was nourishment he was eager to provide . . . so eager, in fact, that the prospect of doing so had done much to sustain his spirits as he'd lay recuperating from the debilitating effects of Eadon's latest course of treatments.

Now determined to make the most of his hard-won moments with Emily, Michael replied in as teasing a tone as his emetic-traumatized throat would allow, "I shall sit only if you promise to call me Michael. I wish to be friends, you know, and friends refer to each other by their given names."

She sniffed. "By the look of you, you shan't live long enough to be friends with anyone if you don't start taking better care of yourself."

"Perhaps, perhaps not." He shrugged one shoulder and broadened his smile. "Then again, what is the purpose of living if you refuse to be my friend?"

She flushed a glorious shade of red, visibly flustered by his flattering response. "I never said that I didn't wish to be friends with you . . . Michael. There." She nodded. "I called you by your name. Now do sit down and tell me what has happened." Nodding again, she motioned to his chair, demanding his immediate cooperation.

Which he gladly gave. In truth, it had taken the last of his meager strength simply to stand; thus he more collapsed than sat back down in his chair. Disregarding the fact that her place had been set at the opposite end of the table, Emily pulled the chair at his right as close to him as she could get it, then plopped down, scrutinizing his face with a frown. The instant her backside hit the chair seat, the footmen sprang into action, gathering up her place setting and moving it to her selected spot at the table.

Ignoring them, or perhaps she was merely oblivious to their bustling in her concern for him, she laid her hand over his, which continued to more clutch than rest on the edge of the table, and began stroking it in a soothing manner. After several moments of doing so, she softly inquired, "So?"

"M-m-m?" he murmured, the tranquilizing sensation of her caress having made him lose his train of thought. It was her woman's touch, of course. Nothing robbed him of his senses quicker than a woman's touch.

"What ails you?" she clarified.

"Ails?" He met her intense stare with his glassy, so-pited one.

Her brow furrowed. "Perhaps I should summon a doctor. You are clearly even worse off than I imagined."

His daze of contentment shattered at her mention of

a doctor. Shaking his head to fully restore his wits, he muttered, "No . . . no need for a doctor. It's just Eadon's treatments. They always leave me like this."

"Treatments?" The furrows deepened. "Then Mr. Eadon is your physician?"

"More or less. Though he doesn't actually bear the title of doctor, he has studied seizure disorders and knows more about treating them than anyone else in England, or on the continent, for that matter. My grandmother engaged him as my nursemaid."

Rather than lighten her frown, his explanation darkened it, and she shook her head. "Whatever his experience, I cannot say much for his cure. Indeed, I cannot even begin to imagine what sort of treatments would leave you looking so dreadful."

"Bleeding, emetics, purging, and clysters," he supplied with a grimace. "They were the pressing business that interrupted our walk."

"What!" She couldn't have looked more shocked had he informed her that he had the plague and had just infected her. "You cannot mean to say that you endured all that at once!"

"No. Not all at once. Eadon always gives me a day to recover from my bleeding before administering the emetics." He shrugged. "Since a person can only use a chamberpot at one end at a time, he waits several hours for the effect of the emetics to pass before inflicting me with his purgatives and clysters."

She looked positively appalled. "But—but to what purpose? I mean"—she shook her head—"I know you suffer spells, but I cannot think such harsh treatments to be necessary, nor can I see how they could be in any way beneficial."

"They are beneficial in that they rid my body of morbid humors." At her look of incomprehension, he explained, "Eadon believes my spells to stem from my body's inability to rid itself of morbid humors."

"What sort of morbid humors?"

"The ones that have resulted from my brain infection. According to Eadon's theory, the humors are carried by my blood to my digestive organs and bowels, where they stagnate into some sort of poisonous matter. When that matter is allowed to build up, my body goes into violent convulsions in an attempt to cleanse itself. Thus, the only way to prevent the seizures is to regularly evacuate both the humors and the matter, something Eadon does weekly."

"Weekly?" She gasped. "You poor man! How ever do you bear it? I was bled once and it hurt so much I thought I would die."

"Were you?" He studied her prettily flushed face with a smile. "Somehow, I cannot imagine a girl with such rosy cheeks ever requiring a bleeding."

"Rosy? Oh my!" Her hands flew to her face. Fingering her cheeks as if trying to feel their color, she anxiously inquired, "Are they so very red then?"

Michael frowned, taken aback by her dismay. He'd meant the remark as a compliment, which was exactly how every other woman in his acquaintance would have taken it. Deciding that a bit of clarification must be in order, he smoothly annotated, "I only meant that I have never seen anyone so aglow with health."

"Aglow?" Her expression of dismay heightened into one of wide-eyed distress and she flattened her palms against her cheeks, hiding their becoming blush. "O-o-o! Then they are red, hateful things!"

For several seconds he merely stared at her, at a loss as to how to extract the foot he'd so clearly stuffed into his mouth. Uncertain how it had gotten there in the first place, he gestured his bewilderment and helplessly tried to redeem himself by venturing, "There is nothing the least bit hateful about red cheeks. I do not know about America, but here in England they are counted as quite lovely and desirable. Indeed, many women paint in an effort to achieve the very effect that comes naturally to you."

She snorted, thus proclaiming that he'd managed only to shove his foot yet deeper. "Not according to our grandmothers. My grandmother said that my color is vulgar, and yours remarked on how it makes me look like an overpainted dollymop."

Grandmothers, was it? That explained a lot. Snorting

back to illustrate his disdain for their grandmothers' criticism, he scoffed, "Dragons, the pair of them. Ignore their fustiness. It is just their way to pick and scold. They mean nothing by it. I should know, I have endured more than two decades of it. Besides, I happen to be privy to the fact that they both think you the loveliest and most charming girl in the world."

"They do?" She eyed him dubiously.

"They do," he confirmed, resisting his urge to sigh as he felt his foot begin to slide from his mouth. "If you would like proof, I shall gladly show you the letters they have sent me over the past month, all of which are full of praise for you."

She seemed to consider taking him up on his offer, then slowly shook her head. "No, no. That shan't be necessary. I believe you."

He nodded. "Good. Then I hope that you will also believe me when I tell you that I, personally, have a preference for women with high color and that I find yours particularly glorious."

"You . . . do?"

He nodded again. "Most definitely."

She smiled then, something else he found particularly glorious, and dropped her hands from her cheeks. Sighing, as if the weight of the world had been lifted from her shoulders, she murmured, "I'm glad you like it. I shall feel ever so much more at ease in your company if I needn't consistently worry about offending you every time my cheeks grow red."

"In that instance I am glad that you are glad, because I intend to spend a great deal of time in your company and wish you to be comfortable around me."

She laughed her melodious laugh, another of her many glories. "That news makes me even gladder, for I enjoy your company immensely."

"Which makes me gladder than glad," he countered, letting his own hoarse chuckle mingle with the music of her laughter. Slanting her a playful look, he teased, "You aren't saying that you like my company just because I look terrible and you pity me, are you?"

"No." She shook her head over and over again. "Oh no, Michael. I was beyond crushed when you disappeared for two days. To tell you the truth, I feared that you had found my questions about the Windgate legend foolish, and that you had decided that you didn't wish to be friends with such a ninny."

He smiled tenderly at her confession. "I found your questions charming to the extreme. And since we are being so frank, I must confess that I was worried that I might have bored you with my pontifications about the cloisters. As you no doubt ascertained, I am fascinated by the abbey and have spent a great deal of time studying its history."

She was shaking her head again. "I wasn't bored for a second. Not only were your accounts interesting, they eased my fears about living here. Why, I have slept quite soundly ever since you explained matters."

He took her hand, which still lay over his, and gave it a warm squeeze. "That you are comfortable at Windgate makes me gladdest of all." And it was true. He wished nothing more than for her to be happy with her new home . . . and him.

Her cheeks darkened to crimson velvet. "You are most kind, your grace."

"Michael," he reminded her with a smile. "You promised to call me Michael, or must I stand up again?"

"Michael, yes." She nodded. "I was thinking Michael, truly I was, but it came out as your grace. Habit, I suppose. And don't you dare stand up. If you so much as try to rise, I shall have Francis bring me a rope with which I will tie you to that chair."

Michael chuckled, not doubting for a moment that she would do as she threatened. "And is tying up one's husband to ensure his compliance yet another of your quaint American customs?"

"Only when the husband in question is in danger of doing himself harm through his own stubbornness."

"Indeed?" At her nod, he heaved a mock sigh of defeat. "In that instance, I suppose I have no choice but to surrender to your petticoat government."

"None whatsoever," she retorted, the tartness of her tone belied by her grin. "Furthermore, I shall brook no more argument on the matter. Exactly how you managed to make it down here in the first place, I shall never know, but I can assure you that I shan't allow any more of such foolish behavior in the future."

In truth, it boggled his own mind that he had been able to stagger this far. Even with the aid of the clucking and scolding Eadon, it now seemed an impossibly long distance to have walked in his current state. Not about to admit such a thing to Emily, he grinned back and gallantly replied, "I found all the strength I required in my anticipation of your enchanting company."

As he'd hoped, she blushed again. "Be that as it may, you should never have left your bed. Why, if I were any kind of a wife at all, I would order the footmen to carry you back there this very instant."

"Ah, but then I would be bereft of your company and all my efforts would have been in vain," he countered, exercising the charm that had once made him a favorite among the *ton*.

She sniffed. "If my company was truly all you wished, then there was no need for you to leave your bed. I would have gladly made a sickroom call. All you had to do was ask."

"You would?" He frowned, taken aback by the notion of her sitting at his bedside. It had never occurred to him to ask her to do so. Had it, he'd have instantly banished the thought. Pride would have forbidden him to allow her to see him at such a disadvantage. For though he might never be able to demonstrate his virility, he desperately wanted Emily to view him as a man, not as an invalid to be coddled and pitied. Besides that, it hardly seemed proper to extend such an invitation to a woman he barely knew, even if that woman happened to be his wife.

Emily nodded in response to his startled query. "Of course I would have come. You are my husband, so it is quite proper that I attend you. And lest you worry that I would be shocked by something I might see, please be aware that I tended my father the last two years of his life and am thus inured to both the sights and smells of the sickroom."

"He was a lucky man to have such a lovely and devoted nurse," Michael commented, not missing the catch in her voice when she mentioned her father.

She shrugged in a way that was clearly meant to be nonchalant, but instead tugged at his heart. "I did what I could."

"Which I am certain did much to ease his last days." He again enfolded her small hand in his large one and gave it another squeeze. "You were no doubt a great comfort to him."

She met his gaze then, her beautiful dark eyes shadowed by the soul-deep pain of her loss. "I tried my best, but in the end I think that he was eager to go and join my mother. She died when I was born and not a day passed that he didn't miss her terribly. He loved her so very much." A small smile touched her lips, and from the look of nostalgic longing on her face, it was apparent that she would have liked to have spoken of her family.

Wanting nothing more at that moment than to share her memories and learn more about the exquisite woman who was now his wife, Michael gently prompted, "It is clear that you loved your father a great deal."

"Yes. I did. More than I can ever say." Her smile broadened and her face took on a faraway expression. "He was so big and strong and handsome. And jolly. No one was more amusing than Papa. He had a special talent of making people smile, even those who were determined to remain glum. Of course, he was rather old when I was born, almost forty."

"So very old?" he teased, thinking how impossibly young she must be to think forty old. Truth be told, he had no notion of her age. He'd never thought to ask, and his grandmother had never volunteered the information. Deciding it high time he found out, he gently inquired, "How old are you, Emily?"

"I was twenty-two in June, the third, to be exact. You?"

"Twenty-eight last March."

"I have a brother, Henry, who is twenty-eight. You would like him—everyone does."

"If he is anything like his sister, I am certain I would," he replied, and he meant it. "Is Henry your only brother?"

"Oh, no. I have five. All older. George is the oldest, followed by Roger. Then there are Daniel, Henry, and Peter. I am the only girl, which, I suppose, is why everyone doted so on me." She paused to smile up at Francis, who had just come to a stop beside Michael.

Michael glanced up at him in query.

He bowed. "If it pleases your grace, Cook would like us to serve now."

So captivating did he find Emily's company, that Michael had quite forgotten about dinner. After nodding his consent, to which Francis bowed and signaled to the other footmen, who instantly sprang into action, he returned to their conversation. Picking up where they had left off, he said, "My guess is that your family doted on you because you are charming and it gave them pleasure to spoil you." A pleasure he fully intended to enjoy himself, now that it was apparent that she liked him enough to allow him to do so.

Her cheeks flamed, though it was clear from her smile that she was pleased by his words. "Whatever the reason, they are the best family in the entire world."

At that moment the parade of footmen reappeared. Emily and Michael looked up in unison, their attention drawn by the savory dishes the men carried.

There was the usual starter of soup—Mulligatawny this evening, judging from its curried scent—followed by buttered prawns, pigeon pie, ragout of celery, mushroom fricassee, and Michael's personal favorite, roast leg of lamb in crust with wine sauce. Everything looked and smelled delicious. So delicious that Michael's stomach, which hadn't been treated to anything but the blandest of fare for the past two years, let out a loud growl of appreciation.

Emily glanced up at the undignified sound, smiling.

"That you have an appetite is a very good sign indeed, Michael."

"I suppose," he murmured, well aware that he couldn't indulge in any of the delicacies the footmen were arranging in the center of the table. No. Any moment now someone would present him with his usual two-days-after-bleeding fare of beef broth, shank jelly, biscuits, dried raisins, and ass's milk. Like everything else in his monotonous life, his meals were unsatisfying and dismally predictable.

No sooner had the thought popped into his mind than John, the third footman, set his pessimistically anticipated bowl of broth and plate of biscuits before him. Unlike the rich Mulligatawny being ladled into Emily's bowl, the smell of which had his mouth watering, the insipid broth held absolutely no appeal for him.

For several moments thereafter, no one spoke. Emily, who had discovered herself to be ravenous, busied herself doing justice to her soup, while Michael more picked at than consumed his dreary broth. When Emily had at last spooned her bowl clean and declined a second helping from the ever-solicitous Francis, she glanced back at Michael. He sat listlessly swirling his spoon in his soup, his face set in lines of distaste as he stared down at it.

She frowned at his sudden lack of appetite. "Michael?"

He glanced up, smiling politely.

"You really should try to eat, you know. If the soup isn't to your liking, there other dishes from which to choose. Perhaps you would prefer some pigeon pie?" She pointed to the plump, egg-glazed pie. "Or maybe some lamb?" She shifted her hand to indicate the beautifully dressed platter in question. "Cook has a particular talent with lamb."

An almost pained look crossed his face. "I know. I love Cook's lamb."

"Well then . . ." She glanced up at Francis, who in turn looked at Michael.

Michael shook his head. "Unfortunately, I cannot indulge in the lamb, or in any of Cook's other delicacies. Eadon's orders."

"What?" Emily frowned again, taken aback by his words. "But why? I would think that he would wish you to eat, especially after all you have endured the past two days. Without proper nourishment you will never regain your strength."

He shrugged one shoulder. "I don't think he is so much concerned with improving my strength as with preventing fits." Another shrug. "Indeed, I sometimes think the reason his treatments are so effective is that I simply lack the strength to have a seizure."

"But that is terrible!" she exclaimed, genuinely appalled. "Surely there must be a better way to control them, one that doesn't require you to go about half-starved and feeling miserable all the time?"

Yet another shrug. "Not that I have experienced."

"Well, I, for one, have always disapproved of any treatment that makes a patient feel worse rather than better." She nodded firmly to emphasize her point. "When I tended my father during his final illness, I refused to allow the doctors to do anything that would in any way weaken him, despite their protests that such measures were necessary. And do you know what?" Without waiting for his response, she continued, "He lived far longer than anyone ever expected. Instead of living several weeks, which was his doctors' prediction, he survived for two years. And though he was never truly well, he was at least comfortable and well fed."

"As I said, he was lucky to have such a lovely and devoted nurse," Michael replied, smiling in a way that left no doubt as to the sincerity of his words.

She felt herself flush at his praise. "I could do the same for you, you know. Perhaps if I spoke to Eadon, we could find some sort of compromise that would allow you a bit more comfort."

"You would do that for me?" He looked and sounded positively stunned by her offer.

"Of course," she countered stoutly, unable to resist the urge to reach over and give his hand a squeeze. "You are my husband, and it is a wife's duty to see to her husband's needs. Besides that, I like you and I wish to help you."

He continued to gaze at her, as if in wonder. "I like you, too, Emily, very much, and would like your help. Unfortunately, I fear there is little you can do. Unlike with your father's doctors, you cannot simply nay-say Eadon's treatments and chase him from the house. He is attending me by order of my grandmother, and for reasons I would prefer not to discuss now, I have promised her to grant him my full cooperation."

"But doesn't she see the toll his treatments are taking on your strength?" she demanded, astounded that someone who was supposed to love him as much as his grandmother reportedly did would allow him to suffer so.

He nodded. "She has also seen the price of my spells. After weighing the two, she has determined that the treatments are the less costly in terms of my welfare, though I must admit that I do not agree with her conclusion." He made a wry face. "As horrible as the frequency of my seizures was, I at least felt much myself in the times between them."

"Have you told your grandmother of your preference?"

"Countless times, but, well"—a head shake—"you have met my grandmother."

"She's a terror, yes," Emily murmured, making a face herself at the thought of the imperious old duchess.

"Exactly. And I must, unfortunately, abide by her dictates. At least for now and on this matter."

"But—"

"But enough of such dreary talk," he interjected smoothly. "Your dinner awaits you, and I believe that John wishes to serve me my feast of shank jelly and ass's milk."

Emily didn't miss his grimace as he uttered that last.

He might have promised to abide by his grandmother's dictates, but she had made no such vow.

Chapter 10

Michael was going to be so surprised. And pleased. Emily hugged the basket she carried tighter to her side, thrilled as she envisioned Michael's delight when he saw his dinner that evening.

After seeing his dreary meal the night before and his lack of appetite for it, she had resolved to speak to Mr. Eadon and see if there wasn't some way to improve his menus. After all, Mr. Eadon was a man, which meant that he most probably knew nothing about cookery and was thus unaware that light, wholesome fare could be made to taste delicious.

She, on the other hand, had spent the past two years in the kitchen creating dishes to tempt her father's invalid appetite, and had learned all sorts of ways to make a restrictive diet appealing. During that process she'd concocted many recipes she felt certain would please Michael's palate—ones she very much wished to make for him. In order to be allowed to do so, however, she knew that she must first advise Mr. Eadon of her experience, after which she must convince him of her competence to oversee Michael's meals.

With that ambition in mind, she'd sent for the man early that morning, remaining closeted with him in the library for well over an hour, during which she'd quizzed him about Michael's condition and medical regimen. Expecting him to be like her father's physicians, who had dismissed her and her queries out of hand, she'd entered the meeting prepared for a fight. To her astonishment, Timothy Eadon proved not only receptive, but sensitive

to her concerns, answering all of her questions with a
thoroughness that had completely disarmed her.

The logic for Michael's current diet, he'd explained,
stemmed from the belief that highly flavored foods ex-
cited the senses, while heavy ones slowed the digestion,
both states which were thought to bring about seizures. It
was an opinion shared by many of the leading authorities
on conditions such as plagued Michael. Thus, Michael was
allowed only the blandest and most easy-to-digest foods,
such as the meat broths and jellies she'd seen him pick
at the night before, with the addition of an occasional
poached egg, some boiled beef, mutton, or fowl, and
dried fruits on those days when he was deemed strong
enough to tolerate them. Those days, it turned out, were
the two or three days between the end of his recovery
from his weekly treatments and the beginning of the next
round, which meant that he was afforded very little nourishment indeed for a man his size.

When Mr. Eadon had finished telling of his theory and
Emily had carefully noted Michael's dietary constraints,
she had presented her own case. Speaking with as much
authority as she could muster, she had told him of her
experiences with her father and her success in his care,
after which she'd outlined ways in which she thought
Michael's meals could be improved.

After gravely considering her suggestions and asking
further questions, he'd agreed to allow several additions
to Michael's diet, all of which Emily had argued would
improve his constitution, stipulating that he did so with
reservations and that the changes would be made on a
trial basis only. He had then asked her to make up several menus for his consideration. This she'd done
promptly, and within an hour had had half a dozen
menus planned, all of which promised to be not only
delicious, but nourishing and gentle on Michael's digestion.

Eager to surprise Michael with one of the meals that
very evening, she'd requested Mr. Eadon's immediate
approval of the menus, which he'd given with a warm
smile and liberal praise for her epicurean savvy. Despite

her disagreement with his methods, Emily had to admit that he genuinely cared about Michael and seemed as anxious as she to improve his lot. His approval of her menus left only one obstacle to the success of her quest to build Michael's strength: Cook.

Since the preparation of Michael's new menus would demand a much lighter touch than the woman normally employed, including a clever substitution of herbs for the heavy sauces and highly spiced gravies she routinely depended upon to flavor her meats, she would be required to drastically alter her cooking methods. Knowing that such a suggestion was bound to send her into one of her legendary rages, which she would in turn take out on the other servants, Emily had approached her with caution.

In hopes of appealing to her vanity, she'd presented the menus with lavish praise for the woman's skill, pointing out the difficulty of such delicate cooking and expressing her confidence that she, Phoebe Swann, and she alone in England, would be equal to such culinary mastery. As if that weren't enough, which it most probably would have been, judging from Cook's look of puffed-up self-importance at her flattery, she'd played upon her devotion to Michael, a devotion she knew the woman shared with every other servant at Windgate and which had had her barking orders at her helpers in her eagerness to do her part in bettering her beloved master's lot.

In short, all had gone far better than Emily had dreamed possible. Indeed, the only real hurdle she'd encountered thus far was the one she now sought to overcome: a lack of tansy for the tansy pudding she wished made for Michael's dessert. Not only was tansy reputed to help in the prevention of seizures, but everyone knew that nothing built an invalid's constitution like eggs and cream, both of which were principal ingredients in the dish. Hence, she now searched the moor for the herb, where it was said to grow wild.

True, she could have sent a servant on the errand. Or asked one of the kitchen maids, all of whom had reported seeing patches of tansy on the moor, to accompany her and help her locate it. But she had declined doing either, wishing to perform the task herself. Truth be told, she was restless for something to do, something productive and ultimately satisfying. It was a restlessness that had plagued her ever since her father's death.

During her father's illness she'd been constantly busy, her days hectically engaged in his care and in promoting his comfort. So accustomed had she become to being thus occupied, that her relative idleness in the weeks following his death had left her feeling oddly fidgety and bored. To put it bluntly, she was at loose ends in regards to her life. After two years of forsaking her personal interests for her nursing duties, she had quite forgotten what her interests were. When she'd rediscovered them, she'd found that they no longer held the appeal they once had.

Oh, she'd gone through the motions of doing them, and had even derived a small measure of joy from their execution, but beneath her pleasure had gnawed a need to do more. She'd missed being useful and had hungered for the satisfaction she'd derived from caring for her father. That she again had someone to tend, someone who needed her as clearly as Michael did, made her feel happier and more alive than she'd felt in a very long while. It renewed her purpose in life. And her purpose at that moment was to find tansy.

Her mind drawn back to the task at hand, Emily glanced around her, trying to establish her location. Several of the kitchen maids had reported seeing a particularly fine patch of tansy in the pasture of an abandoned croft a mile or so east of the formal gardens, and had said that if she walked in a straight line toward the twin tors that crowned the third hill in the distance, that she was certain to come upon it.

Tor, she'd learned, was the proper name for her stone giants. And as with everything else in Dartmoor, each had its own legend and significance. This particular pair of tors was rumored to have been used by the Druids to count sheep and other herd animals, the theory being that the beasts could be driven only one at a time through the narrow passage between the enormous rock piles, thus affording an accurate count. Whether or not the tale was true, Emily didn't know. All she knew was that there were no hauntings, murders, suicides, or anything else even remotely sinister associated with them, something she found an enormous relief . . . especially now, as she stood staring at them, wondering where she was and how she had gotten there.

Why, she could have sworn that she'd been on the left side of the tors only moments ago. Yes, and the hill over there, which had looked to be a stone's throw away at last glance, now appeared to be at least a mile away. Frowning her bewilderment, she lifted her hand to shade her eyes from the glare of the harsh noonday sun, turning a complete circle as she searched for signs of the abandoned croft. By all accounts she should have come to it by now, or at least be near enough to see the ruined cottage.

What she saw was an utterly different landscape than she was certain had been there only a heartbeat before. Her senses reeling, she again surveyed her surroundings hoping to see something to untangle her snarled bearings. The sight that met her eyes merely deepened her disorientation.

Hmmm. Hadn't there been another hill over there, a barren one scattered with forlornly stunted trees? And that queer circle of mossy stones, hadn't she passed it a quarter hour earlier? As for the abbey, it seemed to have vanished completely.

Wondering how she could have wandered so dreadfully off course without noticing, she changed directions and looped back toward the opposite side of the tors, certain that she would catch sight of both the house and the hill at any moment.

She didn't. All she saw was a wide, shimmering lake . . . one that moved with every step she took, and then evaporated altogether. As for the tors, they seemed to shift shapes, first appearing magnified, then dwarfed, the dark, stone-strewn ridges upon which they sat seeming to flatten and elevate in turn.

On Emily wandered, going first this direction, then that, her alarm steadily creeping toward panic when she could find nothing the least bit familiar. She'd thought to climb the tors, thinking to perhaps spy the abbey from atop their lofty height. But alas, she couldn't even find her way to them, though they were constantly before her. What she found instead was a luxuriant expanse of purple melic grass, its liberal dotting of fluffy white cotton grass and spear-shaped rushes alerting her to the unnerving fact that she'd stumbled upon a moorland marsh.

Having been warned about the hazards of the bogs, Emily jumped back, half-expecting the spongy ground to magically slither beneath her feet and suck her down to a filthy, suffocating death.

Thwack! "Ouch!" She slammed into something rough and hard, the bruising blow to her calves collapsing her legs from beneath her.

Thud! "Oomph!" She landed hard on her backside, so hard that she saw stars from the pain radiating up her spine. Too sore and stunned to do more, she simply sat atop what felt like a throne of cold, damp stone, certain that she'd shattered her tailbone. When, at last, the stars cleared and her pain had receded to a dull ache, she glanced warily down at her seat, almost afraid of what she would see.

It was the same circle of moss-draped stones she'd passed twice before, only—only—a sob of frustrated desperation escaped her—like everything else on the moor, it appeared to have moved. A quick glance around her verified that it had indeed migrated, as had she, apparently, for the bog had disappeared and in its place stretched a wide field of bright pink harrow, purple teasel, and daisylike ragwort.

Afraid to move for fear that the bog might reappear and swallow her up, Emily sobbed drily several more times, her despair rising with every fractured breath. A couple of sniffles and she burst into tears. She was lost, hopelessly lost! Heedless of the fact that her gloves were stained with the odious-smelling moss that slimed the stones, she buried her face into her hands and wept in earnest.

Oh! Why hadn't she brought one of the kitchen maids? Or had one of the grooms guide her, as she'd promised Francis she would do? She had been a peagoose to come out here alone . . . no, not a peagoose, the description allowed her far too much credit. She was a paperskull. She nodded and sniffled her approval of the title. Yes, she was a flighty, beetle-witted paperskull and it would serve her stupidity perfectly right if no one ever found her . . . something that was beginning to seem more and more a possibility, what with the way the scenery constantly shifted and changed. The whole situation was—was—phantasmagoric!—yes, rather like being stuck in a nightmare in which she thought she was awake, but wasn't.

Emily paused midsob, wondering if such could be the case now. She'd been trapped in dreams before, more times than she could count. Thinking back now, it had felt exactly like this. Deciding that that must indeed be the case—what other explanation could there be for the bizarre scenery changes?—she screwed her eyes shut and willed herself to wake up. After counting to twenty and pinching herself twice for good measure, she slowly opened them again, hoping but not really expecting to find herself snug in her bed.

She was still on the moors, except now the field was gone and she sat facing what appeared to be the back side of the tors. Not even daring to speculate how she'd gotten there, knowing that there was no explanation, save a sudden bout of madness or magic, neither of which she cared to ponder at that moment, Emily swiped at the tears that again welled in her eyes.

Sniffling several times in quick succession, she tried to comfort herself with the knowledge that a search party would be sent when she failed to return to the abbey. Of course, even if the party somehow managed to find her, she would never locate the tansy in time for dinner and Michael wouldn't get his pudding.

Exactly why something as trifling as Michael not getting his pudding should distress her at such a moment, she didn't know, but it did and she resumed weeping. She had cried what felt like an ocean of tears when she heard, "It's the pixies, you know."

Emily looked up with a start, half-expecting to find the voice yet another trick of the moors. It wasn't.

Or was it? She gaped at the being before her, uncertain what to believe. The being was a young woman, a tall, beautiful one, who looked quite unlike any human she'd ever seen. Everything about her seemed drenched in silver . . . her lustrous pale hair, her glistening gray eyes . . . even the sheen of her flawless skin, which summoned up the image of moonlit pearls.

Certain that the creature was one of the fairies Mercy claimed dwelled on the moors, and almost afraid to speak for fear of what she would do, Emily hoarsely whispered, "Who—who are you?" She'd almost asked what she was, but had refrained from doing so for fear of offending the being and invoking her wrath, the consequences of which, at least according to Mercy, would be very grave indeed if the woman truly was a fairy.

The fay creature smiled, revealing teeth every bit as perfect as Michael's. "My name is Rebecca Dare," she replied in a voice as uncannily beautiful as everything else about her. "I live in the dale just over that hill"— she pointed to her right—"at Greenwicket cottage. And you are Emily Vane, the new duchess of Sherrington." Unlike everyone else she'd met thus far, Rebecca didn't curtsy in deference to her lofty title, which in Emily's mind simply gave proof to her suspicion of the woman's otherworldly origins.

Feeling obligated to reply, but uncertain what to say for fear of inadvertently angering her—after all, what did she know about conversing with fairies?—Emily murmured, "You know who I am, then?" It seemed an innocent-enough question.

Apparently it was, because the fairy laughed, a sound like—what else?—silver bells. "Of course. Everyone in these parts knows who you are. How could they not? The duke's marriage to an American was quite the most interesting thing to happen around here in at least a decade. Indeed, the topic has dominated every conversation for over a month now."

"But how did you know that I am the duchess in question?" she cautiously ventured, not wholly satisfied with the explanation. After all, she could have been anyone, yet the woman had instantly identified her as Michael's bride.

The fairy shrugged. "You look exactly as Mercy Mildon described. Besides, your accent is similar to the one of an American who came to study our moor plants two years ago." Another shrug. "So you see? There was no mistaking you."

"Oh. So you know Mercy." Emily more sighed than uttered the words in her relief. Mercy would most definitely have told her if she were personally acquainted with a fairy, which meant that Rebecca must be an ordinary human being after all. Well, not so very ordinary, perhaps, she amended, as the woman again smiled her enchanting smile.

"Mercy visits me from time to time."

"Oh," was all Emily could say in response, for she suddenly felt rather silly. Now that she really looked at Rebecca, she wasn't so very unearthly. Indeed, who ever heard of a fairy wearing a black and yellow calico day dress? Or sturdy boots, she added, catching a glimpse of what her grandmother would most definitely pronounce as clodhopping horrors were she to see them. Smiling back now, the sight of those boots inexplicably endearing Rebecca to her, she asked, "What did you mean when you said that it was the pixies?"

"You are lost, are you not?" At Emily's nod, she quizzed, "And did your surroundings keep changing in a queer manner?" When Emily again nodded, she explained, "You were being pixie-led, or mazed, as some in these parts like to call it."

"What! Are you saying that there are really pixies out here, and that they were playing tricks on me?" Emily exclaimed, once again revising her opinion of Rebecca. Perhaps she wasn't entirely of this world after all.

Rebecca shrugged. "Maybe."

Emily eyed her warily, her evasive response suddenly making her wonder if the woman was somehow in league with the spiteful sprites. Forgetting all prudence in her rush of suspicion, she narrowed her eyes and pointedly inquired, "Just how is it that you happened to spy me out here?" The instant the words flew from her mouth, she wished she could take them back, miserably aware that she might possibly have just tempted more fairy mischief.

Rebecca shrugged yet again, clearly unperturbed by her insinuation. "I was returning from gathering peat when I saw you walking in circles and concluded that the pixies were up to their naughty tricks again. When you collapsed on the stones and began to weep, I was certain of it."

Emily felt her cheeks flame at the woman's reply, embarrassed by her ridiculous suspicion. And she was again reduced to responding with a weak, "Oh."

"What I do not understand is what you are doing out here alone," Rebecca continued, frowning in a way that did nothing to diminish her stunning looks. "The moors are a dangerous place, especially for the unwary. Do not tell me that no one has warned you of the hazards?"

"I was looking for tansy," she muttered, her cheeks heating another degree. Even to her own ears the excuse sounded lame.

"But alone?" Rebecca shook her fair head. "Surely his grace doesn't condone such recklessness? Indeed, by all accounts he is extremely protective of those beneath his care."

"He doesn't know I am here," Emily miserably confessed. "I wished to surprise him with tansy pudding for dinner." Her cursed cheeks were blazing now. "I know I should have brought one of the servants, but"—she shook her head—"what can I say? I wished an outing by myself and simply did not stop to consider the consequences." The real truth was that she'd wanted to be alone with her thoughts about Michael.

Rebecca studied her for a second, the keenness of her

silvered gaze giving Emily the disturbing sensation that she looked into her mind. Then she smiled faintly and nodded, as if satisfied with some conclusion. "Ah, well. I suppose that there is no need for him to ever learn about any of this, eh? From what I've heard, the poor man has troubles enough without having to worry about his wife getting lost on the moors."

Indeed he did, as did the rest of the household. Not wishing to add to those troubles by raising an alarm with her prolonged absence, she stood, ignoring the ache in her tailbone as she replied, "Thank you, Miss Dare. You are most kind. Now, if you would be so good as to direct me, I should probably be returning to the abbey."

"Rebecca, please. And I shall be glad to direct you. But wouldn't you like to collect your tansy first? It seems a shame for you to return empty-handed after all you have gone through to procure it."

"Do you know where I might find some nearby?" Emily inquired, her mood instantly brightening at the prospect of obtaining the coveted herb.

Rebecca nodded. "It so happens that I have a particularly fine batch of tansy growing in my garden . . . the wild sort, which is considered best for helping reduce seizures, which is the reason, I assume, you are so set on making his grace tansy pudding?"

"Yes," Emily admitted, struck anew by the woman's uncanny ability to divine her thoughts.

"Well, then. As I said, I live just over that hill." She again indicated the verdant hill to her right. "It is but a short walk to my cottage."

Emily started to nod her consent to the plan, then hesitated, suddenly wondering at the time. Better for Michael to be deprived of his pudding than to suffer the agitation he would no doubt experience were the kitchen staff to raise hue and cry over her delayed return to the house.

As if again reading her thoughts, Rebecca reassured her, "It is early yet. You have plenty of time before anyone at the abbey will even think to miss you."

"All right then," Emily acquiesced with a nod, accepting the woman's verdict without reservation. Some-how, she just knew that Rebecca was correct in her assessment.

Nodding back, Rebecca shifted her keen gaze to a point behind Emily, scowling abruptly at something she saw. "Magellan! Stop eating that groundsel this instant! You know it gives you wind."

Curious as to who Magellan was, yet almost afraid to look for fear of what she might see, Emily stole an un-easy glance over her shoulder.

A goat. Magellan was a plump goat with dusky gray fur and curly horns. At the moment he was rigged rather like a pack horse with large baskets full of what she assumed was peat strapped to either side of his bulging body, heedless of his mistress's command as he continued to chomp away at the dainty yellow weeds before him.

"Magellan," Rebecca called again, this time injecting her voice with a note of warning. "You take one more bite and I shall make you sleep outside tonight. I swear I will."

The goat lifted its head and emitted a belligerent bleat.

"Oh, no. We will have none of that," Rebecca re-sponded, shaking her head. "Now come along, we have a guest."

To Emily's amazement the animal began trotting toward them, as if it had actually understood the com-mand. Then again, maybe it had. She glanced away with a shrug, surprisingly unperturbed by the notion. After all the queer happenings she'd experienced during the past hour, there was nothing particularly fantastical about a goat understanding a simple command.

"Shall we then?" Rebecca inquired politely of Emily, gesturing toward the hill.

"A-a-a-a!" the goat bleated, as if in response.

"I wasn't speaking to you," Rebecca tartly replied, shooting the animal a sharp glance. "And I will thank you to stop where you are. After all the groundsel you ate, I have absolutely no desire to walk downwind from you."

Again the beast bleated and again Rebecca responded,

this time with a sigh. "Her name is Emily Vane—her grace, the duchess of Sherrington to you. And no, you may not be introduced. You are hardly in a state to be meeting nobility." Shaking her head, she looked back at Emily, explaining with another sigh, "Magellan has always had an eye for the ladies. Apparently he is quite taken with you." By her nonchalance, you would have thought that being able to converse with goats was the most ordinary thing in the world. Then again, in Rebecca's instance, perhaps it was.

Genuinely taken aback now and not quite certain what to say to such strangeness, Emily helplessly sputtered, "He, er, seems to be a rather—uh—pleasant sort of goat."

The animal fixed her with a beady-eyed stare and let out a soft, quivering bleat.

"No, you may not show her just how very pleasant you can be, wicked beast. Now enough of such talk!" Rebecca hissed. Casting Emily an apologetic look, she said, "Let us proceed to my cottage now . . . your grace." By the look she darted at the goat, it was apparent that she'd used Emily's title as an example to it, rather than out of deference for her rank.

Emily nodded, keeping a wary eye on the goat, who was now staring at her backside as if contemplating either biting or butting it.

"Oh, just ignore him," Rebecca exclaimed, apparently noting her misgiving. "He might look, but he wouldn't dare touch. For all that he is a goat, he's no fool."

Not about to even contemplate the meaning of that queer statement, Emily lifted her moor muck–soiled hems and trailed after Rebecca, who had already started toward the hill, her thick, flaxen braid bouncing jauntily against her slender back as she walked. Behind her she heard the goat begin to follow, occasionally making muttering bleats, which she wouldn't have been at all surprised to learn were complaints. Judging it best to heed Rebecca's advice, she ignored the beast, not sparing it so much as a backward glance as she quickened her pace to catch up with her guide.

Easily falling into step beside her, despite the fact that Rebecca was a good four inches taller than she and had a much longer stride, she walked in silence for several moments, her curiosity multiplying with every passing second. Finally unable to contain the thousand or so questions swirling in her mind, she discreetly probed, "Have you always lived in Dartmoor?"

"Oh, no. I am originally from Gloucestershire."

"Hmmm. That explains that," she murmured, more to herself than to Rebecca.

Rebecca slanted her a querying look. "Explains what?"

"Your accent. You sound nothing like any of the Dartmoor natives I have met." It was true. Rebecca's voice was cultured and genteel, rather like the nobility she'd met in London.

Nobility? She stole another quick glance at the woman beside her, her eyes narrowing with speculation. Could it be that Rebecca, too, was a duchess? Or some other such title . . . one with a penchant for rustication, as the Londoners referred to a preference for the country? It would certainly explain her lack of awe for the Sherrington title.

The duchess or fairy, or whatever she was, smiled. "I must admit to being somewhat surprised by your observation. After living here for three years, I would have thought that I'd have adopted at least a trace of moor accent."

Emily smiled back, deciding that she liked Rebecca despite her uncertainty of what she was. "Perhaps you have and I simply do not hear it. I haven't been in England long enough to separate the subtler differences in accents, though I am told they vary from county to county. I—oh my!" She stopped abruptly in her tracks, gawking down the hill at the vision that had to be Greenwicket cottage. It was lovely . . . like something out of a lushly illustrated storybook.

Unlike the moor dwellings she'd spied on her journey to Windgate, which had been crude, squat structures, Greenwicket was as neat and cozy a house as Emily ever hoped to see. Constructed of the inevitable Dartmoor stone, the cottage stood two stories high, its gracefully curving thatch roof extending downward in front to encircle the three second-story dormer windows, and then dropping sharply down on one side to embrace the attached garden shed. Ivy grew everywhere. It twined around the twin chimneys and festooned the golden roof; it tumbled riotously over the eaves to clothe the drab grayish-brown walls in a mantle of leafy green.

Like sections of the abbey, the cottage boasted stone mullion casement windows, these fitted with diamond panes that reflected the early afternoon sun with a brilliance that recalled their more precious namesake. Above each jeweled window curved a horseshoe-shaped cornice, a motif echoed in the stone hood suspended above the red front door. Like the rest of the cottage, the hood and door frame, too, were draped in vines, these burgeoning with prismatic blooms. Dramatizing the breathtaking beauty of the cottage was its setting.

Somehow Rebecca, or perhaps a previous owner, had tamed the wildness of the moor to create a garden unlike anything Emily had ever seen. Why, it practically exploded with color, even this late in the season, engulfing the spacious area within the bordering box hedges in a variegated blaze of scarlet, blue, yellow, pink, and white, and what appeared to be a hundred gradient shades in between. Adding a finishing touch of perfection to the idyllic picture was the merry little brook that wound past the front of the house.

"This land has been in my mother's family for over five centuries now, a gift to be handed down from mother to daughter," Rebecca commented, indicating the acreage in question with a sweep of her hand.

"Then your family built the cottage?" Emily inquired, barely able to speak for the awe clogging her throat.

"Oh, no. It was here at the time of the land grant. It has always been here, as has the garden," Rebecca replied, beginning her descent down the hill.

Emily followed at her heels. "Always? Like in forever?"

"Well, perhaps not so very long as that," Rebecca

countered with a laugh. "It is quite ancient, though. Indeed, according to legend both the house and the garden were created by the Dartmoor fairies as a gift for their very first go-between."

"Go-between?" She frowned, not certain what to make of the queer information. "What is a fairy go-between?"

"A human who serves as a link between the other-worlds and the mortal one. It is usually someone who was blessed by the fairies at birth and has thus been granted special powers."

"W-what sort of powers?" Emily inquired nervously, slowing her pace to put distance between them. Considering the grim outcome of her last brush with special powers, she was more than a little reluctant to risk another.

Rebecca stopped several yards ahead of her, slowly turning as she recited, "Divination, healing, and the ability to see into otherworlds and communicate with their beings. Some go-betweens are given additional odds and ends of magic as well."

"And—and do you believe in the legend?" What she wanted to ask was the obvious question: Was Rebecca a go-between? But of course, she couldn't. Not only would it have been rude to the extreme, what with the briefness of their acquaintance, it could prove dangerous. Why, for all she knew the identity of a go-between might be considered a grave secret among the fairies, the discovery of which merited swift and grievous retribution.

Rebecca considered her thoughtfully for a beat, then turned to survey her kingdom. "One cannot help but believe it once one has lived here. It is a remarkable place, full of enchantment and wonder. Especially the garden. Things that shouldn't logically grow in moor soil miraculously flourish there and continue to thrive during seasons in which they lay dormant everywhere else in England. There are even plants there that no one has seen in well over three hundred years."

"Then this place truly is magic?" She more squeaked than uttered the inquiry in her dismay.

"Yes, but it is good magic," Rebecca tossed over her shoulder, along with a reassuring smile, as she resumed her descent. "No harm has ever befallen anyone here, nor will it ever."

At that moment Magellan bleated, a sound that came from a place uncomfortably near her backside. Forgetting Rebecca's advice to ignore the goat, Emily glanced behind her, still leery of the animal despite its apparent tameness. She could have sworn it winked at her. Looking quickly away again, she hastened after Rebecca, who had reached the stream and now hopped from stone to broad, flat stone across it.

Given the choice between the goat and Rebecca, she'd cast her lot with Rebecca any day. At least she had some inkling as to what she might be, which, if Rebecca was to be believed, was a benign being. She had just followed Rebecca across the stream and was jumping onto the bank when Rebecca called out, "Careful now, Magellan. Do not get the peat wet. You know how it smokes when it is wet."

Emily shot another glance at the animal, this one in involuntary response to Rebecca's warning, her gaze arresting at the sight of it expertly navigating the stones. That the beast possessed both the wit and the skill to cross in such a manner simply confirmed her suspicion that he was no ordinary goat.

When he had successfully reached the bank and Rebecca had ordered him around to the back of the house, where she promised to come directly and relieve him of his burden, she ushered Emily into her garden. It was even more magnificent up close than it had been at a distance.

There was bed after bed of artistically planted flowers, some she could identify, others she had never seen, most of which, as Rebecca had mentioned, were blooming out of season. The trees and berry bushes, too, flourished, their branches heavy with the most succulent-looking fruit Emily had ever seen. As for the herbs and vegetables, well, she'd never seen such an abundance.

"Ah, yes. Here it is. Tansy." Rebecca stopped before

a patch of tall plants with wing-shaped leaves and buttonlike yellow flowers. "Do take as much as you like, and anything else you desire as well. As you can see, I have more of everything than I can possibly use." Nodding in affirmation of her invitation, she added, "Now if you will excuse me, I really must tend to Magellan. He gets cross when I keep him waiting."

Well able to believe that, Emily nodded back.

Now alone, she drew her shears from the basket she carried and clipped several particularly leafy stalks of the tansy, after which she strolled about the garden, delighting in its splendor. Not only did it look glorious, it smelled heavenly, the fusion of fruit, herbs, and flowers creating a scent far sweeter than any ever captured by man in a perfume.

She was just examining a small bluish herb that smelled rather like mint, but was unlike any mint she'd ever seen, when she heard Rebecca say, "Calamint, yes. How very astute of you. A decoction of calamint might help his grace at that."

"Pardon?" Emily murmured, rising from her crouch with a smile.

Rebecca advanced toward her, nodding. "A decoction of calamint often proves helpful to people troubled by convulsions. Of course, having never met his grace, I cannot be certain that it would aid his particular case. I can, however, assure you that it shan't harm him in any way should you care to try it."

"Perhaps I will at that," she replied, kneeling back down again.

Standing over her as she clipped, Rebecca instructed, "The decoction must be strong if it is to be effective, so do take a goodly bunch. Oh, and do not forget to add sugar when you boil it. Calamint turns bitter when boiled and the sugar will make it so much more pleasant on his grace's palate."

When Emily had at last harvested what Rebecca deemed an appropriate amount of the herb and again stood, Rebecca said, "I would offer you tea, but I fear there isn't time. You shall be missed soon. Besides, you must start your pudding if it is to be ready in time for dinner."

"Yes, of course," Emily murmured, genuinely sorry to go. There truly was something magical about Green-wicket cottage, something that made her feel serene and safe. And despite her initial misgivings about Rebecca, she suddenly somehow knew that she could trust her. How could she not when it was so very clear that she had only her and Michael's best interests at heart? Deciding then and there that she would like to further their acquaintance, she shyly added, "If it is agreeable to you, I would like to come again. Perhaps we could have tea then?"

Rebecca smiled what was by far her most beautiful smile of the day. Indeed, it was so radiant that it almost hurt to look at her. "Nothing would please me more. Come anytime. I shall be here ready to receive you."

"I will. Soon," Emily promised, joy bubbling within her at the prospect of a new friend. "I shall ask Mercy to guide me so I shan't be lost again."

"You shan't be lost at any rate, I promise. Never again," Rebecca countered, still smiling.

Emily eyed her curiously. "How can you be so certain?"

"Because I am the go-between and you are my friend. That means that from this day forth you are under the protection of the otherworlds. You have only to ask and the pixies will safely lead you anywhere you wish to go on these moors."

Chapter 11

It had been so long since he'd enjoyed a decent meal, that he had forgotten the delight to be had at the table. Now that he'd rediscovered it, he hoped he'd never again be deprived of it.

For what must have been the hundredth time since beginning his dinner, Michael groaned his appreciation. Luscious. Exquisite. It had to be the most delicious meal he'd ever eaten. So delicious, in fact, that Emily had teased him that there would be no need to wash his dishes, so clean had he thus far left them.

Right now he sampled what he silently christened as the tastiest onion and herb stuffed salmon in the entire world. Closing his eyes in ecstasy at the delicate explosion of flavor on his palate, he more moaned than uttered, "M-m-m, heaven. I cannot believe that Eadon approved this." It was the same comment he'd made upon tasting each dish that evening, for it seemed impossible to him that such succulent fare could be made from the wretched foodstuffs allowed him on Eadon's diet.

As she'd done each time he made the remark, Emily chuckled and responded, "I can assure you that he did. It meets with all of his requirements." She sounded as happy as his stomach felt.

Opening his eyes again to shoot her both a look and a smile of everlasting gratitude, Michael turned his attention to devouring the salmon, along with its superbly seasoned side dishes of cabbage and rice, and dressed asparagus, a feat he accomplished in record time. When he'd eaten every last morsel and scraped his plate clean, he settled back into his chair, purring his gastronomic gratification. "That was excellent, Emily. Thank you," he murmured, patting his stomach to exemplify his satisfaction. For the first time in what felt like a century, it didn't ache with emptiness.

Emily, who ate her own meal at a ladylike pace, made a dismissive hand motion. "Oh, that was nothing. Just wait until you see what I have planned for you tomorrow, starting with breakfast."

"I look forward to it." The words slipped out so easily, so naturally, that Michael's breath caught in his throat, arrested by the startling truth of the utterance. For the first time in over two years, he genuinely did look forward to a tomorrow. He had something to contemplate with pleasure, a reason to get out of bed.

And that something wasn't the splendid meal Emily vowed to provide, tempting though the prospect was, it was the lure of Emily herself. It was the promise of her fine company, the enticement of her friendship. It was her unspoken invitation to share in the wonders of her world and to rediscover the glories of life. It was the joy of simply being near her, of basking in the warmth of her smile and thrilling to the exhilarating joy of her laughter.

Oh, true, he still suffered a certain measure of lust for her. How could he not? Despite everything, he was still a man, and she was the most beautiful and provocative woman he'd ever met. Unlike on their wedding day, however, when he'd viewed her as nothing more than a carnal temptation, he was now able to control his physical desires, difficult though it was at times, and content himself with delighting in the charms of her spirit. Oddly enough, doing so gave him immense satisfaction, a warm sense of fulfillment that lingered and continued to kindle his heart long after they had parted. In truth, the satisfaction he gleaned from just being near her was greater and gave him far more pleasure than that which he'd derived from making love to his many women.

Suddenly feeling happier than he could recall ever feeling before, Michael nodded to Ralph, who indicated a wish to remove his empty plate, then glanced back at Emily. She was staring at him, her expression a million miles away as she absently licked the back of her fork. Wanting to share in whatever had her so preoccupied, to better understand the woman who was not only his wife, but his savior, he leaned forward and murmured, "A penny for your thoughts, Emily."

She paused midlick, her eyes widening briefly as if trying to recall both time and place, then she smiled sheepishly. "I'm sorry, Michael. How very rude of me to woolgather like that."

He smiled back, tenderly. "Hardly rude, considering that I have barely spared you a word the entire meal. Of course"—his smile broadened into a teasing grin—"my lack of conversation is entirely your fault. Had it not been for your delicious food, my mouth would have been quite free to entertain you."

She laughed, something that was quickly becoming his favorite sound in the world. "In that instance, I suppose I must be prepared to amuse myself at every meal in the future, for I fully intend to see your mouth thus occupied from this day forth." Smiling with a warmth that incandesced her beautiful eyes into pools of midnight luminance, she saucily added, "You see, I have my own theory on what ails you and my own plan for treating it."

"More treatments?" He emitted a mock groan.

Her smile broadened, revealing a slightly crooked back tooth. Rather than detracting from her beauty, the flaw merely endeared her all the more to Michael. "Unlike Mr. Eadon's treatments, I promise that you shall find mine most pleasant and vivifying. Indeed, if all goes as planned, you should be feeling much the better and have regained a goodly portion of your strength in several weeks' time. If nothing else, my treatments will reduce the toll Mr. Eadon's bleedings and other such horrors are taking on your body and spirit."

"Treatments for Eadon's treatments, eh?" Michael murmured, more thrilled than he could say by her interest. That she had given him so much thought and was prepared to go to such trouble on his behalf spoke volumes of the warmth of her feelings for him.

She nodded. "I have seen how weak and miserable

they leave you, and have surmised that you will be better able to endure them if your constitution is improved. In my opinion, your want of constitution comes from being half-starved. You also appear to suffer a malaise, which I believe to result from a lack of pleasure. In short, darling husband, you must endure more tempting meals and several hours of daily amusement if you are to ever feel yourself again. Do you think you shall be able to bear all that?"

Darling husband. How he liked the sound of that. Wanting to shout his delight at her casual use of the endearment, he grinned and countered, "I shall gladly suffer any treatment you choose to inflict upon me . . . darling wife." Hmmm. It seemed that he liked uttering endearments even more than he liked hearing them.

"Excellent." She nodded again. "If you progress as I hope, which I am certain you will, I might be able to convince Mr. Eadon to reduce the frequency of your harsher treatments."

"Indeed?" he drawled, liking her plan immensely. He couldn't help but be improved by her gentle nurturing.

Another nod. "To my way of thinking, your bowels, digestion, and blood will eliminate bad humors on their own if they are strengthened enough to do so, thus reducing your need for weekly cleansing. A properly balanced diet paired with a lightening of your spirits should do the trick handily enough."

At that moment William, the second footman, set a bowl of prettily garnished pudding before him. Michael gazed longingly at it for several beats, then shot Emily a querying look.

She laughed. "Yes, of course Mr. Eadon approved it. I wouldn't have had it served if he hadn't."

"It is just that it looks so wonderful," he replied, eyeing the treat almost reverently as he picked up his spoon. "It hardly seems possible to make something so marvelous from the dreary foods he allows me."

"It wasn't, not until I convinced him to allow a few additions to your menus, such as sugar and cream. Of course, they will only be allowed at one meal a day and in moderation, but that should be enough to build your strength."

"A miracle," he sighed, referring to both Eadon's allowance of the foods and the silken sweetness embracing his tongue as he tasted the confection.

Emily smiled and took a bite of her own dessert. "He has also consented to allow you a caudle on the days you are bled, which should do much to revive you, what with the heartening properties of the eggs and milk. As for the rest"—she grinned—"you shall see. I wish to surprise you."

"I look forward to being surprised, though I doubt any future surprise will be able to match the excellence of this one." He consumed another spoonful of the pudding, an involuntary moan of pleasure escaping him at the taste. "M-m-m. What sort of pudding is this, anyway?"

"Tansy. And it is counted as most healthful for someone in your condition. Not only does it have the benefits of cream, eggs, and sugar, tansy is said to help with seizures." She paused to lick a dollop of pudding from the back of her spoon. "Since you like it, I shall make certain that you get it every week."

For the next few moments they ate in companionable silence, Emily's appetite for the pudding almost matching his. Unlike the night before, when they had dined in the formal Italian dining room, Emily had had the meal laid in the tiny breakfast room, a change he had to admit he liked. There was a homey sort of coziness about the room that seemed to encourage their growing intimacy. Deciding that he would order every meal served here, Michael glanced around him, inspecting the room in which he'd dined hundreds of times, but had never really seen.

It was modest, almost austere, with its creamy yellow walls and worn brick floor. The fireplace, unlike most of the other ones in the house with their ornate chimney pieces, was a simple stone arch, above which hung a pastoral landscape in a gilded frame, flanked by a pair of heavy black wrought iron sconces. The chandelier above their heads, too, was of black wrought iron, as were the andirons upon the hearth, which currently held several cheerily burning logs.

Like the room itself, the furnishings were spare and for the most part utilitarian. Indeed, aside from the bright Turkish rug beneath the polished oak refectory table at which they sat and the tapestry upholstery on the chairs, the only ornamental touches were the mish-mash of paintings on the walls, ones clearly banished from other rooms. Those, and the decorative blue-and-white ware displayed upon the heavy oak sideboard that sat near the fireplace. Michael paused briefly to consider the low-beamed ceiling, then glanced over at the wall of leaded windows, beyond which stood the formal garden, now shrouded in evening shadow and rising autumn mist. Looking outside made him all the more aware of the welcoming warmth within the room. Most of the warmth, of course, was due to Emily.

Smiling, as he always did of late at the mere thought of Emily, Michael shifted his gaze to admire the charming picture she made as she sat bathed in firelight, daintily eating her pudding.

In keeping with the casualness of the meal, she wore a simple but delightful dinner gown of green and pink striped taffeta, one with a wide, square neck and short puffed sleeves. He particularly liked the fit of the bodice, the cut of which clung to her lush curves, and the way her jewelled-buckle belt whittled her already narrow waist into nothingness.

Her hair, which she usually wore hanging down her back in a profusion of gypsy wild curls, had been swept up this evening in a fashionable coiffure of glossy puffs and braids. Though he secretly preferred it unbound, he had to admit that her current style emphasized the exotic beauty of her face and gave her a certain air of sophistication. Indeed, were she to appear in the *ton* looking exactly as she did now, she most certainly would have been declared quite the thing and become the toast of the Season.

As Michael sat admiring Emily, imagining the pleasure of showing her off in London, she glanced up. When she saw him staring at her, she smiled and said, "I had the most amazing adventure today. Would you like to hear about it?"

Thrilled to hear anything she wished to tell him, he smiled back and nodded. "Please."

"It happened when I was on the moor searching for tansy to make the pudding. I lost my way and—" She broke off with a soft gasp, her cheeks flooding with vibrant color. Darting him a guilty look, she rushed to amend, "I was just a little lost, mind you. And only for a moment. I'm certain—"

"What!" Michael roared, unnerved by the thought of the woman who was quickly coming to mean everything to him lost on the moors. "Are you saying that you went out on the moors alone?"

Her cherry cheeks darkened to the color of garnets. "Well, yes. But it turned out that I really wasn't so very far from the abbey after all."

He shook his head, not about to be pacified. "Be that as it may, you are never—ever!—under any circumstances to again set so much as a toe on the moors without one of the grooms for escort, preferably Abraham or Josiah. Both were born and raised in these parts and know the land as well as they know the back of their own hand." Leaning forward to emphasize his point, he bore his gaze into hers and forcefully demanded, "Is that understood, Emily?"

She smiled weakly and nodded. "Yes, of course."

"Do I have your promise?" he thundered, not about to let the subject drop until he was certain of her compliance.

"I promise. Now please, Michael, do calm down." She reached over and gave his hand a placating pat. "You know you aren't supposed to excite yourself."

He snorted. "And how exactly did you expect me to respond to the news of your folly, if not with excitement?"

"I hadn't expected you to respond at all, since I had no intention of telling you about that part of my adventure. It somehow just"—she shook her head, gesturing her bewilderment—"slipped out. I still do not know how it managed to do so."

"Well, I'm glad it did. At least now I will know to keep a closer watch on you." And he meant it. He'd be damned before he'd allow her to endanger herself in such a manner again.

"Yes, fine. You may follow me everywhere I go if you so desire. Just please, do calm yourself." She patted his hand again, this time rather frantically, casting an anxious glance at the door as she did so. "If Mr. Eadon sees you in such a state, he will think you in need of another bleeding, and I shall never forgive myself if you have to suffer so on my account."

She was right, of course. Eadon would no doubt deem his current pique worth opening a vein and draining a good twenty or thirty ounces. Nevertheless, it was a price he would gladly pay if it was what it took to curb her recklessness. Shaking his head, he growled, "I will survive a bleeding. You, on the other hand, might not survive another outing alone on the moor. Indeed, you were exceedingly fortunate to have found your way home this time. Countless people have been lost on the moors through the years, some of whom have never been found."

"Oh, I admit I was lucky. In truth, had Rebecca and Magellan not found me, I might very well have stayed lost." Her hand was over his now, gently stroking it in the way he found so soothing.

Michael sat very still for several moments, mesmerized by her woman's touch. When he realized what was happening, he shook his head hard, determined to break her spell and continue her well-deserved dressing-down. Remaining bewitched despite his efforts, he scowled and muttered, "Who the devil are Rebecca and Magellan?"

"They are the real part of my adventure. Rebecca is a woman—a young, beautiful one—who lives in a magnificent cottage on the moor. And Magellan is, well"—a faint frown creased her smooth brow—"he appears to be her pet goat, but I suspect that he isn't really a goat at all."

Michael's frown mirrored hers. "Whatever do you mean?"

"Magellan looks like a goat, but he doesn't act like one."

His frown deepened at the oddness of her response. "How does he act then?"

She returned his gaze in silence for several beats, then bit her lip and looked away. Flushing again, she murmured, "He acts almost . . . almost . . . human."

"What?" Michael exclaimed, staring at her as if she were the most eccentric chit on earth, which at that moment he believed she was.

"He acts human," she repeated, her cheeks skipping the garnet stage entirely to blush a rich burgundy. Stealing a glance at him from beneath her thick lashes, she said, "I know this is going to sound absurd, but I could have sworn that the beast winked at me."

"He what?" Surely he'd heard wrong? She hadn't really said that the goat had winked at her, had she?

"He winked at me," she confirmed with a nod. "And you should have seen the way he stared at me. It—it, well, it reminded me of the way men sometimes look at women when they think they are paying them no mind. You are a man, so I suppose you know the look?" She was gazing at him earnestly now, her face the picture of innocent appeal. "It's that intense, hungry look, as if the man is imagining the woman in her chemise?"

Oh, he knew the look well enough, and he could have told her that those men weren't imagining the women they were staring at in their chemises. They were picturing them naked and moaning beneath their thrusting loins. He should know—he'd spent enough time casting her that very look out his window.

Not wanting to think about the groin-wrenching lust he'd suffered during those moments, much less discuss it, he frowned and said, "Are you saying that the goat leered at you?" Better an absurd conversation than a provocative one.

"Yes, but as I mentioned, I do not think that he is

really a goat. Not only doesn't he act like one, he can talk."

Michael drew back, floored by her latest bit of queerness. "Are you telling me that the beast actually has the power of speech and that you understood it?" And here he'd just been thinking that the conversation couldn't possibly get any more outrageous.

"I didn't understand him, but Rebecca did. They carried on several conversations. You should have seen them. It was most amazing."

"How can you be so certain that they were conversations if you couldn't understand them?" he demanded incredulously.

"By the way the goat responded. It actually followed her commands. I have never seen a goat that would do such a thing. And you should have seen the way it crossed the stream. Like this." Using her hand as the goat, her center finger extended forward to represent the head and the other four operating as the legs, she demonstrated how it had carefully hopped from stone to stone across the water.

It was all he could do to bridle his snort of cynical disbelief. "Perhaps the beast simply doesn't like to get wet. Animals will do extraordinary things to avoid situations they find unpleasant. A case in point is a hound I had when I was a boy. It hated wet grass so much that it would run along the top of our stone enclosures to avoid walking in it when it rained."

She shook her head, stubbornly unconvinced. "That was a hound, Magellan is a goat. Everyone knows that goats aren't nearly as clever as hounds."

"True, but it is possible to teach them tricks. I have seen several trained-goat acts at village fairs, some of them quite clever."

She seemed to consider his argument for several beats, then slowly conceded, "I suppose you could be right. Still—" She shook her head, her expression sweetly wistful. "I could have sworn that they understood each other." By the forlorn note in her voice, it was apparent that she had very much wished to believe in her fancy and was crushed at having it shattered by his logic.

Suddenly feeling like an ass for spoiling her fun, Michael took the hand that still lay atop his and gave it an affectionate squeeze. "Regardless of the case, this Magellan sounds most remarkable, as does—Rebecca, is it?" At her nod, he nodded back, adding, "She must have quite a talent with animals to train him in such a manner."

"Rebecca has a talent for everything," she replied, instantly brightening. "Why, you should see her garden! I have never seen such bounty. It is where I got the tansy to make your pudding. I also clipped some calamint, which I am going to decoct to make you a tonic. Rebecca says that calamint is sometimes helpful in preventing seizures. I thought we might try it."

Michael's eyes narrowed slightly at her words. "You told her of my condition?" he quizzed, feeling strangely betrayed by the notion that she would gossip about his fits. Not that they were a secret. Still, he'd somehow expected better of her and had thought that she would respect his privacy.

"Of course not," she retorted, visibly stung by his query. "I have never nor shall I ever speak of your condition to anyone. Not unless you wish me to do so. I know how uncomfortable a subject it is for you." She shook her head to stress her denial. "Rebecca somehow already knew about it, and it was she who broached the subject of the calamint."

"I am sorry. I should have known that I could trust your discretion. Still, you must admit it odd that a stranger should know about me," he murmured, genuinely perplexed. Hmmm. He supposed that one of the servants could have mentioned his spells, though he seriously doubted that to be the case. Not only did Grimshaw and Mrs. McInnis have a strict policy against gossip, he knew everyone in his employ to be completely loyal to him.

"It is strange," Emily agreed. "Then again, if Rebecca

is truly a go-between, as she claims, then it would make perfect sense for her to know."

Though he hated to do so, sensing that he would receive an outlandish answer, Michael asked, "What exactly is a go-between that my spells would be her business?"

"A go-between is a human emissary between the mortal world and the fairy world. According to Rebecca, such people have been blessed by the fairies, which gives them all sorts of magical powers, like divination, prophecy, and the power to heal. If she is indeed such a being, then she could have divined your condition from my worry for you. I was thinking of you when I became lost."

Michael opened his mouth to denounce such nonsense out of hand, only to clamp it shut again in the next instant as he suddenly remembered his vow. That day at the ruins, when he'd begged Emily for a chance at friendship, he'd pledged to listen to everything she said thoughtfully and to respond in a civil manner. Since she had more than met his requirement for friendship, he owed her the courtesy of considering her views, no matter how contrary they were to his own. Having thus reminded himself of his promise, he replied with a soft, "Perhaps."

Apparently his response met her requirement for civility, for she smiled. "I must admit that I was rather taken aback by the notion of Rebecca's magical powers at first, given what happened the last time I encountered someone with supernatural abilities."

Remain thoughtful . . . civil . . . "I assume that you are referring to the witch who cursed you?" he politely quizzed, feeling exceedingly silly asking such a question. It made him sound as if he actually believed in superstitious twaddle.

She nodded. "Yes. Unlike the witch, however, who was a terribly wicked creature, Rebecca claims to use her magic only for good." She paused then, eyeing him shyly. "If I tell you something, will you promise not to laugh?"

There was something in her voice, a tremulous uncertainty, that made his heart melt into a puddle of tenderness. Squeezing her hand, which he still held, he quietly vowed, "I swear it on both my life and my honor."

"I believe in Rebecca's power. I—I felt it . . . its strength and its goodness. I also enjoyed her company. So much so, that I was wondering . . . well"—she slanted him another bashful look—"if you have no objections, I would like to visit her again."

As if he could deny her anything at such a moment. Giving her hand another squeeze, he replied, "If you like her, then by all means visit her. Just make certain that you remember your promise and take Josiah or Abraham with you. You may also ask her to call upon you here, if you so desire."

"Really? You truly wouldn't mind if I invited her to come?" she exclaimed, visibly stunned by his concession. "I know how you value your privacy and I wouldn't wish to do anything that might make you uncomfortable."

It was on the tip of his tongue to tell her that he valued her more, but he instead replied, "You may invite anyone you wish to visit. The abbey is your home now and your friends are more than welcome here. Indeed, I would very much like to meet your go-between and her leering goat. Perhaps you could ask them to dine with us some evening." Oddly enough, he really did wish to meet the unorthodox duo.

She was looking at him as if he had just done something exceedingly noble. "Oh, Michael. I would love that," she enthused, the radiance of her smile attesting to the truth of her statement. "And I know that Rebecca would enjoy meeting you. Who knows? She might be able to help your spells. If what she says is true, she is blessed with the power to heal."

"I was rather thinking that she might help you with your curse," he smoothly countered, not about to submit to magical mumbo-jumbo. Continuing to steer the conversation lest she decide to pursue the notion of a fairy cure, he added, "You have never really told me about your curse. I know that it condemns you to being a plague to any man you love, but you have never told me how it came about."

The radiance of her smile dimmed, then disappeared completely. Looking positively grave now, she murmured, "Are you certain you wish to hear about it?"

"I wouldn't have asked if I didn't." Oddly enough, he did want to know. For though he hardly dared to hope for such a miracle, the day might come when he was well enough to love her, really love her, at which time he would wish her to love him back. In order for her to do so, he must understand and somehow find a way to banish her fear of the curse.

"W-e-l-l." She drew the word out, her brow furrowing as if she considered how to proceed. Then she slowly began, "It happened when I was just sixteen, at a confectionery shop I used to frequent."

"A confectionery shop?" Michael echoed in surprise. He'd expected a tale involving cackling crones and bubbling cauldrons, maybe even some newts and toads, but most certainly not a confectionery shop.

She nodded grimly. "It was owned by a mother and daughter who were witches. Of course, I didn't know they were witches until they cursed me. They seemed so respectable."

Leave it to Emily to be cursed by a pair of bonbon-baking sorceresses. Suppressing his urge to smile, Michael prompted, "What made them curse you?"

"I fell in love with a gentleman I met at the shop, the son of a prominent banker. When we became engaged several months later, they cursed me. It turned out that the daughter wanted him for herself."

"Why couldn't she have just cast a love spell on him and taken him away?" he inquired, more disturbed than he liked by the thought of Emily loving another man. "It seems to me that anyone worthy of the designation of witch would be up to such a trick."

"A love spell only works when the person the spell is being cast over isn't in love with someone else. Love spells are powerless to dissolve true love, and ours was true."

Michael frowned at that last piece of news. Tamping down his jealous urge to grill her about the man she claimed to have truly loved, he more growled than asked, "How did you learn about the spell? Did the witches tell you about it? Or did something happen to make you suspect it?"

"Worse. They cast it when Jonathan and I stopped at the shop for an ice shortly after our engagement was announced. The shop had the best ices in the entire city, and Jonathan adored ices."

Jonathan, was it? Michael snorted his disdain for the man. If he were ever fortunate enough to find true love with Emily, no witch in the world could keep him from her arms. Not caring if his voice reflected his scorn for the clearly unworthy banker's son, he retorted, "Do not tell me that Jonathan believed in the curse and abandoned you?"

"Oh, no." She vigorously shook her head. "He didn't believe in it at first. Neither did I. I was long past believing in such things. But after what happened"—she shook her head again—"I couldn't help believing. Neither could Jonathan, poor man."

Poor man indeed. Refraining from snorting again at what he was certain was her unwarranted sympathy for the fiancé who hadn't had the pluck to keep her, he quizzed, "What happened?"

"Everything. Every time Jonathan was around me, something awful happened."

"Such as?"

"Well, it started when our maid tripped and spilled an entire pot of scalding tea in his lap." She blushed. "Of course I didn't see his injury, but I was told it was quite bad. So bad that he was unable to leave his house for almost a week after."

Michael partially revised his opinion of Emily's sympathy for her ex-fiancé. He truly was a poor man to have been burnt so badly in such a place. Indeed, just thinking about it made him cringe. Nonetheless, it wouldn't have been enough to have frightened him away from Emily.

"Of course, we all thought the accident nothing more

than a strange coincidence," Emily continued. "Then it happened again, the next time he came to call."

"He was scalded again?" Michael choked out, genuinely appalled by the thought of being burnt in such a manner twice.

"Oh, no. He was knocked senseless. He was strolling up to our door when a bolt of lightning appeared out of the bright blue sky and struck one of the trees lining our walkway. It so happened that Jon was beneath that very tree when it struck and was clouted over the head by a falling branch. His doctors all said that it was a miracle he survived the blow. It was then that I began to believe in the curse."

"What of Jonathan?"

She heaved a weighty sigh. "I think that he was beginning to believe in it as well, though he wouldn't own up to it. It wasn't until the next disaster that he was finally forced to do so."

"Which was?" He was too fascinated not to ask.

"The next time we were together was when he escorted me to my father's warehouse to examine some newly arrived silks. He was standing outside of his gig, waiting to help me down, when the ropes binding a dozen barrels of dried cod snapped. Before he could react, the barrels fell on him, almost crushing him to death."

"And that was that?"

"Yes. I never saw him again. When he was mended enough to travel, which was several weeks later, his mother took him to Italy to convalesce. While there he met a girl from New York, whom he eventually married. Last I heard they were living in Philadelphia, where he has opened several branches of his father's bank."

"Did things go as badly for your other two fiancés?" he gently inquired. He might as well hear the whole harebrained tale if he was to fully understand her fear.

She nodded. "I met my next fiancé almost two years later. Since the witches had left town, I assumed that the curse was no longer in effect. But it was. I had no sooner

discovered that I loved Luke and had accepted his proposal when awful things began to happen to him."

"How many incidents did it take to scare him away?"

"Four. His accidents weren't as serious as Jonathan's,
but they were bad enough to frighten him away."

"What finally did in your engagement?" Again, he just
had to ask.

"Hogs," she pronounced in a tragic tone. "We were
on a picnic at a friend's farm just outside of Boston when
Luke was assaulted by the beasts. We never found out
what provoked them into attacking him, or how they
escaped their pen. At any rate, he suffered two broken
ribs and a ruined suit. From then on, he went to great
pains to avoid me. Though I couldn't blame him for
doing so, it used to hurt me terribly to see him cross the
street every time he spied me."

Michael gave her hand a sympathetic squeeze, though
what he longed to do was strangle the cowardly bastard
for treating her like a leper. For despite all that she'd
told him, he was still no closer to believing in the curse
than before. Indeed, to his way of thinking, the accidents
were just that, accidents, the causes of which could no
doubt have been attributed to the primitive conditions
in America had the men squelched their superstition long
enough to have fully investigated them.

"As for my third fiancé, Russell," Emily continued,
heaving her heaviest sigh of the evening, "I never wanted
to fall in love with him. In truth, I tried my best to avoid
doing so, fearing what would happen if I did. But he was
so persistent. Why, I could hardly turn around that he
wasn't there, ready to charm me. He quite stole my
heart."

"Hadn't he heard of the curse?" Michael asked, unable to blame the man for his tenacity. The exertions he
would expend to win her should the occasion to do so
ever arise would make Russell's efforts seem petty in
comparison.

"Yes, of course. Everyone had. But unlike the other
gentlemen in Boston, who no longer dared to court me,
Russ refused to believe in the curse." She looked away

from him then to bleakly contemplate the remains of her pudding. "In the end, it was a pincushion that scared him away."

"What!" He'd never heard anything so absurd in his life.

"No matter where we were, he always ended up sitting on a pincushion full of pins. His backside was pricked progressively worse each time it happened. After a while, he, too, refused to come near me. So you see?" She glanced up again, her face the picture of woe. "I cannot fall in love ever again."

"What I see is that the curse worries you," he returned with a gentle smile, "which is why I think you should seek Rebecca's counsel. If she truly does possess magical powers, she might be able to help you."

"Perhaps, though I must confess to being almost afraid to ask. What if it turns out that there is no hope for me?" She couldn't have looked more distressed.

"If she cannot help you, then I shall comb all of England, the world even, until I find someone who can," he vowed. And he meant it. He would do anything to restore Emily's peace of mind. If that meant finding someone who could convince her that she was a witch and was able to lift her curse, then so be it. He would do it.

For several beats she simply stared at him, as if she couldn't quite believe her ears. Then she smiled one of her stunning smiles. "You would do that?" She more whispered than uttered the words in her breathless wonder.

He smiled back. "Of course I would. You are doing your best to cure my curse, so it is only right that I help you lift yours."

Chapter 12

It was a delightful day. Not too warm, not too cool, with a steady but gentle wind that swept the rustling leaves from the amber-flecked ground and scattered them across the moors.

St. Martin's Summer, Mercy had called this early October day as she'd flung the windows wide to admit the balmy, sun-dappled morn. Back in Boston such fine fall weather would have been christened Indian Summer. To Emily, it was simply a perfect day for testing her latest kite.

Standing now on the wide strip of fallow land that formed a border between the lush abbey park and the desolate moor, Emily found herself fully appreciating the beauty of the morning. Though she adored all the seasons, she had always loved autumn best. To her it was a season of boundless riches—a treasure trove of color when everything in nature appeared dusted with precious metals and dipped in melted jewels. And the way it smelled . . .

She closed her eyes and deeply inhaled. Earth. The air smelled of earth; of its life, of its death; of its sepia-tinted summer memories now framed by the stark promise of winter. It carried tales of chilled twilights and cozy midnight fires, of countless harvests and the ancient rites that followed. It whispered of the decay beneath the gloriously gilded landscape, a pungent portent of the demise of the aging year.

Slowly opening her eyes again, Emily gazed up at the pure cerulean sky, across which frothed clouds as delicate as a bridal veil. As she studied those gossamer wisps, a flock of swans passed overhead, their snowy whiteness bathed in gold as they winged their way toward the sun. The magnificent sight filled her with bittersweet longing.

Oh, what she wouldn't give to be able to fly like that, to experience the freedom and exhilaration of soaring above the earth. To do so was her greatest wish, her fondest dream, the deep desire that fueled her passion for kites. Someday she would build a kite that flew so high that it would touch heaven.

That was her fantasy, to touch heaven. After all, if the angels saw such a kite, they couldn't help but marvel at the virtuosity of its construction, something which would most certainly entice them to follow its line down to earth, curious to see its maker. When they did, she would beg them to carry her high into the sky and to once, just once, allow a mortal to know the grandeur of flight. It was a silly fancy, she knew, but one that was dear to her heart. It was what prompted her to incorporate an angel into all of her kite designs.

Contemplating her latest creation now, the one she had been working on the evening Michael had first joined her for dinner, Emily couldn't help believing that the angels would be impressed were they to see it. How could they not? It was her most beautiful angel yet. It was a perfect portrait of Michael.

Staring at the skillfully painted seraph, with its striking jade eyes and long, dark hair, she found herself wondering what Michael was doing at that moment. Since he devoted most of his mornings to ducal business, she seldom saw him until three o'clock, when they met by the hallway gargoyles for their daily walk together. After an hour or so of strolling about the grounds, they would then retire to Michael's favorite room, the cheerful summer parlor, where they would play cards or chess, or simply talk and laugh until dinner.

Except, of course, on the days of his treatments. On those afternoons she carried a hot caudle to his chamber, where she sat by his side, gently coaxing him to drink the nourishing brew and doing her best to distract him from his misery.

Sighing her despair at his suffering, she turned her back to the wind and cast the kite into the air, slowly feeding out the line as the wind caught and carried it. Pulling on the string to foster lift, she ran, not stopping until the kite had reached a height where the wind was brisk enough to continue carrying it aloft. As she carefully released more line, watching it soar higher and higher into the endless blue sky, she reflected upon her sickroom calls.

She had been beyond shocked by the sight of Michael during her first visit, something she had thought impossible after the dreadful way he'd looked that evening in the Italian dining room. But he had looked worse, far worse, making her all the more aware of how badly he needed her help. His skin, which had been merely ashen during their first dinner together, had had a waxen, almost cadaverous pallor. His eyes had been sunken and ringed with shadows, their jade brilliance dulled by suffering. And the way he shivered!

Just remembering the sight of him, huddled into a quivering ball beneath a mountain of blankets, his teeth chattering uncontrollably and his handsome face contorted in his torment, had made her long to weep. Truth be told, it had been all she could do to bridle the sob that had risen into her throat at the sight of his wretchedness and go about her sickroom business with a cheerful smile. But smile she had, speaking to him with a blitheness she hadn't felt and doing what she could to give him comfort.

As for Michael, he'd been initially displeased by her presence, growling and snapping at her attempts to aid him, and finally ordering her from the room. Not that she'd been particularly surprised by his conduct. She knew from being near him and from the bits she had learned about him from her consultations with Eadon that he was a man with a strong sense of pride, one whose illness had robbed him of much of his dignity and had shattered his self-respect. Armed with that knowledge, she'd understood that it was shame that had made him behave so—shame of his weakness and embarrassment at having her see him in such a reduced state.

Though she hadn't wished to add to his chagrin, something her presence clearly did, she couldn't bring herself to leave him, not when he so desperately needed the nurturing she knew she could give him. And so she had ignored his demands to be left alone. Stubbornly remaining by his side, she'd serenely countered his peevishness with kindness and wit, wheedling and teasing him until he'd finished every last drop of the caudle she'd brought him and had allowed her to wrap him in a firewarmed blanket, something which had done much to ease his shivering. By the time she had finally left him, long after he'd fallen into an exhausted sleep, he had reluctantly resigned himself to her coddling.

From then on her visits were easier. Not only did he gradually grow more comfortable with her presence in his sickroom, but her efforts to strengthen his constitution were proving effective and he now better tolerated Mr. Eadon's treatments. So much so, that when she'd visited him after his treatments earlier that week, she'd found him not in bed as usual, but reading in a comfortable wing chair before his bedchamber fire.

Seeing him sitting there in his blue velvet dressing gown, with his hair neatly brushed and his jaw freshly shaven, had filled her with a gladness such as she'd never known before. It was a gladness that had exploded into elation when he'd looked up to greet her. Not only was he smiling, visibly pleased to see her, but his glorious eyes sparkled and his face retained a touch of color, despite the horrendous ordeal she knew he had recently endured. Setting aside his book and the caudle she carried, he'd taken both her hands in his and had quietly, but fervently thanked her for all she'd done.

Oh, it wasn't the first time he'd expressed gratitude. Not a day passed that he didn't voice his appreciation for his meals or acknowledge his pleasure in her company. But those thanks by the fire, well, they had been different, somehow more intimate. Perhaps it was the way he'd looked at her, so frank and admiring, his eyes illuminated with fondness. Or his voice. Despite the rasping hoarseness he always suffered in the aftermath of Mr. Eadon's emetics, his voice had held a profound and touching tenderness that had struck a vibrant chord in her heart.

And that chord still hummed, even now warming her heart as she remembered the moment. Over the past month she had come to care deeply about Michael and had carried him constantly in her thoughts. Thus, when she wasn't creating a new dish to enthrall his long-deprived palate, she was inventing entertainment for after their walks, or struggling to recall an amusing tale or two to divert him after his treatments. On those occasions when her mind wasn't occupied with promoting his comfort, it turned to other, somewhat more disquieting thoughts. Thoughts that involved children and the act it took to make them.

She still craved children . . . even more now, since they would be sired by Michael. How could she not? With him as their father, they were bound to be beautiful, and witty, and utterly charming. Well, at least they would be if they ever had the chance to be born.

Tugging on the line to urge the kite yet higher and to guide it more squarely into the wind, she wondered if he ever gave the matter any thought. But of course he did, she decided in the next instant. He was a nobleman, and all noblemen wished for an heir to secure their family name. No doubt he was waiting to regain more of his strength to ensure that he was physically equal to the baby-making act before broaching the subject with her.

And when he did?

Emily fed the kite another length of line, watching as it rose almost out of sight. She would, of course, encourage him, again expressing her eagerness to bear his babes. As for the act itself, well, except for her brief wonder about it on her wedding day, she'd never really given it much thought . . . at least not any *serious* thought.

Like every other girl she knew, she had a natural curiosity about the ways between men and women, and had listened intently when the subject was giggled about among her set of friends. For the most part, however, she'd assumed that her husband would know what to do and would simply go about it. But now, with Michael, she suddenly wanted to know everything. Not only did she want to know what to expect from a man, she wished to know what to do with his male parts when they made the changes that Judith had mentioned.

Releasing yet more line, Emily wondered at her sudden thirst for carnal knowledge. Never once during her engagement to any of her three fiancés had she speculated about the act . . . how it would feel or what it would be like to lie naked in their arms. She most certainly had never imagined how they would look without their clothes on. But with Michael, well, she found herself thinking about such things more than she cared to admit . . . especially at night.

Many nights of late, as she lay in that safe, twilight place between consciousness and slumber, she found herself picturing Michael naked, her belly taut and her private place growing damp and achy as she imagined the feel of his bare flesh pressed against hers. Judging from the satiny smoothness of his face and the flashes of body she'd glimpsed beneath his nightshirt the times she'd wrapped him in heated blankets, his skin would be beautiful . . . as would his form. True, he was still too thin, despite the fact that he had gained some flesh during the past month, but his natural physique was splendid, so he was certain to please the eye.

As for how it would feel to actually engage in the act, hmmm, considering how close she and Michael had become, it might not be so very bad. Indeed, she no longer found the notion of him touching and caressing her female differences embarrassing, nor was she flustered by the notion of fondling his male ones. Truth be told, she rather relished the idea of doing so.

Smiling her bemusement at her newfound wantonness, Emily let out several more feet of line. Come to think of it, the only thing she knew about the act that gave her any alarm at all was the thought of him sticking his male part into her female place. That was bound to hurt terribly, considering how small she was down there and how large she knew men to be. But if that was what it took to make babies, she would gladly endure it. Besides, knowing Michael as she now did, how kind and thoughtful he was, she had no doubt whatsoever that he would be gentle. Besides that, just having him near, holding and coaxing her as he would most certainly do, would make the whole ordeal easier. In fact, she couldn't think of anything she couldn't endure if he was near. To her Michael was . . . was . . . everything.

Everything? Stunned, Emily abruptly ceased in feeding the line, causing the kite to take a perilous dive to the left. Oh, heavens! Could it be . . . was she . . . falling in love with Michael? For several horrified moments she considered the possibility, weighing what she felt for him against her feelings for her hapless fiancés. When she'd finished, she heaved a long sigh of relief. No, she couldn't possibly be in love with him. She had none of the symptoms she always experienced when in love.

First off, she felt none of the giddiness she had felt around her fiancés. Nor did she suffer the delirious sort of infatuation that had made her feel as if she were walking on clouds whenever they were near. She also didn't waste her time imagining Michael in romantic vignettes, as she'd done with Jonathan, Luke, and Russell. Unlike those men, whom she'd delighted in casting in fairy tale roles, Michael wasn't a knight in shining armor. Nor was he a prince to sweep her off her feet, or a dashing buccaneer to save her from Barbary pirates. Michael was . . . well, he was simply Michael. And what she felt for him had nothing whatsoever to do with romance.

In contrast to her fiancés, all of whom had desired her but had never really required anything she had to offer, Michael needed her. He was so sad and lonely, and suffered such terrible anguish, both inside and out. How could her heart not respond to him?

And respond it had. Powerfully. Seeing his suffering had awakened a potent sense of protectiveness within her, one that had fostered an almost desperate urge to rescue and nurture him, an urge she'd never felt with any of her fiancés. The result of her acting upon that impulse was the creation of an intimacy unlike any she'd ever known. It strengthened and empowered her, making her feel like a real part of Michael's life, a vital one, rather than a mere decoration whose consequence lay solely in her beauty and her ability to say the proper thing at the correct moment. Michael had made it clear that he liked and admired her, no matter what she said or did, or how she happened to look on any given day. And she felt the same about him. Theirs was a relationship with only one condition, and that was that they put no conditions on their caring. They accepted each other for what they were, flaws and all, and in their eyes the other was perfect.

They were friends, Emily decided, tugging on the line as her kite made another erratic dive. The dearest of friends. Theirs was an alliance made up of the best and purest elements of every friendship she'd ever had, one fused by a bond as strong as the one she shared with her brothers. As for her physical attraction to him, well, as she'd pointed out to herself a million times before, Michael was a gorgeous man. What woman wouldn't desire him?

As she continued to rationalize her view, her kite made several quick loops, followed by a violent flip, then spun into a sharp, uncontrolled spiral toward the earth. Frantic to save her masterpiece, Emily ran across the wind, letting out extra line in a desperate attempt to create drag. Sometimes the drag would return the kite to the correct flight angle, thus allowing it to stay aloft. And if she could get it to remain stable for a short time, she could reel it to safety.

For several moments the kite seemed to respond to her rescue measures, making a sudden lift and straining at the line. Then it took another dive from which Emily was unable to recover it. Her heart sinking, she watched it crash upon the moors, far in the distance. From what she could ascertain from where she stood, it had fallen near or among the tall grouping of tors that loomed on the near horizon.

Though she knew that the kite would most probably never fly again, that it might even be smashed to bits, considering the dizzying height from which it had plunged, she couldn't bring herself simply to leave it. Not only might one of the moor animals become caught in the line and be harmed, the thought of abandoning anything bearing Michael's image was unthinkable.

Mindful of her promise not to venture onto the moors alone, Emily hastily located Josiah, a plump, jovial man of middle years who had accompanied her to Rebecca's cottage on several occasions during the past month, after which they set off. Using the line as a guide, which Emily neatly wound around the attached spool as they went, they soon located her fallen angel. It had indeed plummeted upon the tors and now dangled forlornly from the tallest one. As she stared up at it, wondering how in the world to retrieve it, a hand appeared and snatched it from sight.

For several beats she merely gaped, uncertain what to make of the theft. Then her spine stiffened with outrage ... this was no ordinary kite, this was her Michael angel ... and she hollered, "You! Return that kite this instant! It is mine!" As she stood glaring at the tor, her clenched fists braced upon her hips, a blond head appeared. Instantly recognizing that head, she expelled, "Mr. Eadon? It that you?" Apparently Mr. Eadon was quite skilled in climbing rocks, because he was already halfway down.

"Your grace," the man responded with a polite nod.

"Who is it, Eadon?" called a voice she would have known anywhere, followed by what sounded like the splash of water.

"Michael?" Emily ejected in surprise.

"It is your wife, your grace, and Josiah," Mr. Eadon informed his master.

There was brief pause, during which there was more splashing, then, "Emily?"

Smiling her delight, Emily handed the spool of line to Josiah, then slipped through the arched opening between the tors, following her husband's voice. There was a pool within the stone circle, a hot one, judging from the rising steam, fed by a spring that bubbled up from the stones at her left and spurted forth in a misty fall. Standing half-submerged at the far end was Michael. The instant she saw him, her eyes widened and her gay cry of greeting strangled in her throat.

He was naked. Well, at least the top part of him was, and she had been right. His body was beautiful, even more so than she'd imagined. He was lean, yes, but stripped of his ill-fitting clothes, which emphasized his devastating loss of flesh, he no longer appeared unhealthily thin. No. He was all trim lines and sleek, chiseled muscle . . . a born athlete, judging from the natural definition of the muscle beneath his smooth, taut skin. Stunned that he would look so after being an invalid for two years, Emily couldn't help gaping at his impressive form.

His shoulders were broad and capped with starkly delineated muscles; his arms were sinewy and strong. As for his torso, what could she say? It was perfection with its wide, sculpted chest and rippling belly. She had just dropped her fascinated gaze lower, brazenly trying to penetrate the water and steam to see if he was naked below, when Josiah shouted something to Mr. Eadon.

Snapped back to time and place by that shout, Emily promptly looked away, mortified by the blatancy of her ogling. Uncertain what to say or do in the wake of her immodest display, she stood awkwardly staring at a spray of golden gorse that sprouted from a fissure near her feet, her face growing progressively warmer. It was Michael who finally broke their tense silence. "I am sorry, Emily."

Emily glanced at him sharply, frowning, taken aback not only by his apology but by the fractured harshness of his voice. His shoulders were tense and his features rigid, with bleakness reflecting nakedly in his eyes. "Sorry? For what?" she softly inquired, advancing a step to the edge of the pool.

"For—for—this!" He more spat than uttered the words as he brusquely indicated his naked torso. "I know how shocking I must look to you."

"What?" She deepened her frown, as perplexed by his manner as by the preposterousness of his assumption. "Why would I be shocked? I was raised in a household of men, remember? The sight of a bare male chest is neither unfamiliar nor shocking to me."

He made a derisive noise. "Mine obviously is, and do not try to deny it. I saw your expression when you beheld me just now, the way your eyes widened and how you averted your gaze in disgust. Not that I can blame you." Another snort. "I know what I look like these days, all scraggy and withered. I am hardly a maiden's dream."

Where Emily hadn't been shocked before, she was now. Hardly a maiden's dream? With his spectacular looks? Oh, if only he knew! Aching at the self-loathing in his voice and desperate to reassure him, yet aware that the fragility of his confidence might make him reject her efforts as pity, she shrugged and countered as dispassionately as she could manage, "You are right, Michael. I was shocked by the sight of you, but not for the reason you think. In truth, I had expected you to be all scraggy and withered, as you so inelegantly phrased it, and was stunned that you are not."

"Oh?" He raised one eyebrow, visibly incredulous.

She nodded. "If you must know, I was utterly shocked to find your body so"—dared she say it?—"lovely." Yes. She did dare. Anything to ease the unwarranted shame he so clearly felt for his body. Anything to erase the bitterness from his voice and to restore the self-esteem of which he'd been so tragically robbed. Anything for Michael. Besides that, it was the truth. He *was* lovely.

He merely stared at her, his eyes slowly narrowing into slits as if weighing her sincerity.

She met his narrowed gaze with a smile and a nod. "It's true, Michael. Believe it. I think you quite the loveliest-looking man I have seen. Ever."

His taut lips curled faintly at the corners. "I fear that that says little of the men in America. They must be a very sorry lot indeed if I look handsome by comparison."

"Ah, but I said the loveliest-looking man ever . . ." She now skirted the edge of the pool, moving nearer to where he stood. "Which includes the scores of exceedingly elegant English noblemen I met in London." Unable to advance further for the narrowing of the stone embankment between the tors and the water, she knelt down, bringing herself eye level to him as she finished, "None of whom were anywhere near as handsome as you, my darling husband."

He contemplated her in silence for several beats, then tipped his head to one side, his brow furrowing as if genuinely mystified. "What a queer card you are, Emily. I do believe that you truly mean what you say."

"I said I did, didn't I?" she retorted, steadily returning his gaze. "What makes you think that I would I lie?"

He smiled, gently and with unmistakable tenderness. "Your generous nature. You, sweet wife, are the kindest person in the entire world. And I think that you would do or say just about anything to avoid hurting a person."

"Perhaps. But I wouldn't have said that you are lovely if I didn't mean it. Had I found you as scraggy and withered as you seem to perceive yourself, I would have answered your charges by pointing out how ill you have been and reassuring you that your flesh would be restored with time. I would then have suggested increasing your caudle consumption to one every day, rather than just on the days of your treatments, thus accelerating the process. As matters stand"—she shrugged—"I am most pleased with your progress."

What didn't please her, however, were the scars she could see marring the perfection of his body now that she was nearer, cruel souvenirs of the terrible cures he'd endured over the years. More appalling yet was the lividity of the half-healed wounds defiling the flesh on his arms. Good heavens! It was a wonder he was able to use them at all for the pain they must cause him. As she watched him swim toward her, exposing a back red and raw from a recent blistering, she decided that he was not only the handsomest man in the world, but the bravest and most patient one to endure all he was forced to suffer with such grace.

Feeling an almost unbearable tenderness for him now, Emily smiled as he dove beneath the steam-shrouded water, reappearing a scant yard from where she knelt, his lush eyelashes spiky with moisture and his dark hair sleeked back from his stunning face. Smiling in a way that sent her heart skipping across her chest, he said, "I must admit that I am pleased with my own progress. A month ago the very notion of walking this far and still having the strength to swim would have been unthinkable. Of course, the credit for my improvement must all go to you." His smile broadened to reveal his teeth in all their pearly splendor. Drifting yet nearer, he softly inquired, "Have I thanked you for everything you have done for me yet?"

"At least a thousand times," she replied, though how she managed to speak, she didn't know. Her heart had somehow become lodged in her throat.

"Only a thousand?" He out and out grinned, looking younger and more carefree than she'd ever seen him look before. The effect was devastating. "Then I must tell you a thousand more times. And then a thousand more, and a thousand more after that, and—"

She laughed at his buffoonery and splashed him with water, playfully cutting him off. "Silly man! Just seeing color in your cheeks and a smile on your lips is quite thanks enough for me."

"No. It is not." His smile faded then and his face grew intensely serious. "Nothing will ever be enough, Emily. Nothing." He shook his head, his eyes burning like jade fire as he captured her gaze with his. His voice frayed by the depth of his emotion, he hoarsely declared, "I am forever in your debt. If there is anything I can ever do to repay you—anything at all—you have only to ask and it shall be yours."

The next few moments were suspended in time as Emily stared into those compelling eyes, her heart crying out in longing. All she wanted was him—to see him smile and to hear his voice every day for the rest of her life. He made her feel cherished . . . special. And over the past month she had come to need him every bit as much as he needed her. He had become the center of her world. Unable to deny her heart's desperate plea a second longer, she abruptly blurted out, "Just never leave me, Michael."

He remained very still for several beats, staring at her as if stunned by her appeal. Then he smiled gently. "Emily, my sweet," he murmured, taking her hands in his warm, wet ones. "Don't you know that I could never leave you? You are the dearest thing in the world to me."

"As you are to me," she softly confessed. "You are the best friend I have ever known."

"Friend . . . yes." His smile tightened, turning strangely brittle. "Well, my friendship, for what it is worth, is something I can truly and freely pledge to you. And I do so with the greatest of pleasure." His eyes filling with a deep, curious yearning, he lifted her hands to his lips and kissed them. After several moments during which she offered him a small, shy smile and he clasped her hands to his water-beaded chest, he began slowly shaking his head. "Emily. My dear, sweet Emily. Whatever am I to do?" The words were uttered on a broken sigh, shadowed by a sorrow she didn't understand.

"Michael? What is it?" she urgently begged, searching his face, seeking a clue to its sudden, terrible bleakness.

He smiled again, this time tenderly. "It is nothing that you need fret about."

"But I wish to help you. Perhaps if you tell me—"

He cut her off with a firm shake of his head. "It is nothing I wish to speak of, or anything you need to know. At least not now."

"But—"

"Your grace?"

They glanced up in unison to see Mr. Eadon and Josiah standing just inside the opening into the circle. Josiah was proudly displaying her kite, which was in surprisingly fine condition considering its misadventure. "We have managed to retrieve your kite without breaking the line, your grace," Mr. Eadon said with a polite bow. "And a very fine kite it is. I cannot say that I have ever seen anything quite like it. Did you get it in America?"

"No, I made it myself—from Chinese paper and bamboo my brother gave me," she replied, feeling strangely bereft when Michael released her hands. Seeing no choice but to properly thank the men for their services, she graced Michael with a final, rather worried smile, then rose and walked over to where they stood.

As she graciously tendered her thanks, quizzing Mr.

Eadon about his rock-climbing skills, to which he confessed a childhood fondness, Emily heard the lapping of
water, followed by a faint splash. When she casually
glanced back at Michael, she saw him climbing from
the pool.

His lower body was clothed, but barely, in a pair of
loose cotton breeches that rode low on his hips and clung
soggily to his flesh. Indeed, he might as well have been
nude for all that the garment hid. As if that fact weren't
quite distracting enough in itself, his lower body was
every bit as magnificent as his upper one.

Mindful of her disgraceful performance earlier and not
caring to repeat it, especially with the servants looking
on, Emily pretended to study a tear in the angel's robe,
the whole while stealing furtive glances at Michael from
beneath her lashes.

His legs were long, impossibly so, with strongly curved
calves and lean but muscular thighs. His hips, too, were
trim, as she had expected, the belly beneath the wet cloth
taut and flat. Intrigued by the shadowed line of hair trailing neatly from his navel, she dropped her gaze yet
lower, inquisitively following its descent. In the next instant her face flushed scarlet.

Good heavens! His main male difference was enormous. Why, she could only imagine the size it must be
when it made the changes Judith had described. As she
covertly gawked, unable to tear her tantalized gaze away,
Eadon appeared beside him with a blanket. Ever attentive to his charge, he promptly tucked it around Michael's body, obscuring his startling charms from her
scrutiny.

Drying his hair with a corner of the blanket as he
walked, Michael strolled over to where she stood. Stopping beside her, he murmured, "You made this, you
say?"

Emily stole a guilty glance at his face, relieved to see
that he appeared preoccupied with her kite. Good. Then
he hadn't noticed her studying his scantly veiled private
parts. Just the thought that he might have observed her
indecent interest stained her cheeks a shade darker. Hop

ing that she wouldn't sound as flustered as she felt, she replied, "Yes. It is a hobby of sorts. I suppose it seems a rather silly amusement for a woman my age, but it is something I enjoy immensely."

"It isn't silly in the least. In fact, I think it a perfectly wonderful pastime," Michael retorted, casting her a look that made her flush all the more from its warmth. "Unlike a piece of needlework or a watercolor painting, both of which just lie there, kites can fly and do the most cunning tricks."

"Then you like kites, too?" she inquired with a shy smile.

"I love them. I hate to brag, but I used to be rather good at building and flying them myself, though I fear it has been a rather long while since I last made one." Smiling faintly, he traced the line of the angel's face, then slanted her a meaningful look. "As skilled as I was, I never made anything nearly as remarkable as this. You, my dear, are a true artist."

Of course he would notice the resemblance. How could he not? It was a perfect likeness. Certain that her face would burst into flames from the heat radiating from it, she confessed, "I simply painted the loveliest face I have ever seen. You don't mind, do you?"

"Mind?" He grinned that devastating grin again. Hmmm. Next time she would make the angel smiling. "I am flattered. However, if you truly wished to give your angel the loveliest of all faces, you should have painted your own."

Emily smiled back, thrilled by his compliment. "You are too kind," she modestly demurred.

"Not at all," he protested, the frank admiration in his eyes corroborating the sincerity of his words. "You would make a most fetching angel. Indeed, I would very much like to have such a kite. Perhaps you would be kind enough to help me make one sometime."

She returned his heartwarming gaze with one of kindling affection. "Nothing would give me greater pleasure, Michael. You know how I love your company."

Mr. Eadon, who had retrieved Michael's clothes from

the other side of the pool, cleared his throat then, breaking the unexpected intimacy of the moment. "Er, excuse
me, your graces. But I think it time his grace got dressed
and returned to the house. There is a distinct chill in the
breeze, which I fear might bring on a fever."

Michael's fond gaze never left hers as he replied, "I
will get dressed only on the condition that my darling
wife wait for me and allow me to escort her back to the
abbey. I would very much like to hear more about her
delightful hobby."

"And I would very much like to tell you about it,
darling husband," she countered softly. "I will await you
just outside the tors." Taking one last look at his handsome face to sustain her while she waited, she followed
Mr. Eadon and Josiah through the stone arch.

Once outside Mr. Eadon came to stand by Emily's
side, while Josiah busied himself with rewinding and
straightening her kite line. After several moments, during
which Emily stood basking in the lingering warmth of
Michael's smile, Mr. Eadon cleared his throat and said
in a confidential voice, "I must congratulate you, your
grace. You have done quite well with your husband. I
have never seen him so happy. To be perfectly frank, his
lack of spirit has worried me for a long while now, far
more than anything that plagues his body."

She glanced at him with a slight smile, gratified by his
praise. "I am glad to help him. If anyone deserves happiness, it is Michael. He has had such a bad time of it."

"Indeed he has, though"—he slanted her a measuring
look—"I have a feeling that those days are firmly in the
past. I shouldn't be at all surprised if we see a continued
improvement in him in the coming weeks."

"Do you think so?" Her smile widened at the wonderful prospect of Michael restored to health. "I am doing
everything I can possibly think of to aid in his recovery."

"I know so," he confirmed, his broad, pleasant face
made all the more agreeable by his answering smile. "In
fact, he is coming along so well that I have decided to
give in to his constant objections to the frequency of
his bleedings and clysters, and decrease them to once a

fortnight rather than weekly. I must, however, insist that he continue his schedule of emetics and purgatives."

"Why—why—that is marvelous news!" she exclaimed, beyond thrilled by her small victory. While the bleedings took the greatest toll on Michael's strength, the clysters were the treatment he dreaded most. Clasping her hands together in her delight, she added, "He will build his strength ever so much quicker if he isn't bled so often."

"He will . . . if he doesn't suffer an increase in seizures, which is always a danger," he cautioned her. "Though I suspect that his grace is now better able to tolerate the humors in his blood and lower bowel, what with the improvement of his constitution, my suspicions could very well prove false and he could relapse into monthly or even weekly spells again."

"And if he does?" she quizzed, instantly sobering at the horrible thought.

"I will be forced to increase all of his treatments to thrice weekly, maybe even daily for the first week or so, until his seizures are again under control. At that point I will gradually reduce the frequency until we again find a balance."

Emily shook her head over and over again, unable to bear the thought of Michael suffering so. Better he continue his weekly bleedings, as barbaric as she found them, than risk what could amount to months of terrible torment. "Perhaps it would be best to simply leave well enough alone," she concluded softly.

"Perhaps. Then again, how are we to gauge his grace's progress if we do not test his strength?"

"But if we are risking harm—" Emily protested.

"I can assure you that he shan't be harmed in the least. The reverse will only be temporary." When she continued to look troubled, he smiled gently and added, "Even should the worst occur, which, in my professional opinion it shan't, his grace cannot help but to make a swift recovery with you by his side. Why, I have never seen a man respond so to a woman's care. It is obvious that he sets quite a store by you."

"And I by him. Indeed, all I can think about these

days is his comfort and welfare, which makes the very notion of him suffering seizures and enduring yet more treatments most distressing.''

Mr. Eadon reached over and gave her arm a squeeze, his hazel eyes kind and filled with compassion as they met her anxious gaze. ''It shan't be easy for him, no, but the prospect isn't so daunting that it will deter him from taking the chance. I have warned him of the dangers of decreasing his treatments on numerous occasions, and he has always expressed a willingness to take the risk. If it eases your mind any, I have written several of my colleagues regarding his case and they all agree that his improvement in spirit and strength merit a change in therapy.''

''I am sure you are all correct,'' Emily slowly responded, ''though I still cannot help worrying.''

''Worrying about what?'' Michael inquired from behind them.

Emily turned to smile at him, her misgiving increasing a hundredfold at the sight of him. He looked splendid, healthy, with his flushed cheeks and sparkling eyes. Even the gray trousers and blue-and-red-patterned waistcoat he wore weren't so pathetically loose. More importantly, she knew that he actually felt good. It quite broke her heart to think of him robbed of his newfound vigor.

''I was just telling your wife that I have decided to decrease the frequency of your bleedings and clysters to once a fortnight, your grace,'' Mr. Eadon replied with a nod. ''And she was expressing concerns.''

''He says that doing so could result in an increase in your spells,'' Emily anxiously elaborated.

''Indeed? And does the prospect of my spells worry you so very much?'' Michael asked, a strange shadow passing over his face.

''Anything that causes you pain or distress worries me,'' she declared, moving forward to loop her elbow through his. Gently hugging his arm close, mindful of its damaged flesh, she added, ''Of course, the final decision in this matter must be yours. It is you who will be taking the risk.''

"Not just I, Emily. You, too, will be taking one."

She frowned and indicated herself with her free hand. "Me?"

He nodded. "Yes. Should I choose to decrease my treatments and the worst happens, you risk witnessing my fits, something, which I can assure you, is not an attractive sight. 'Repulsive,' 'appalling,' and 'obscene' are the kindest terms I have heard describing the spectacle thus far." The bitter note of self-loathing that had tainted his voice when she'd glimpsed him in the pool was back.

Again compelled to banish it, she shook her head and earnestly reassured him, "It isn't the sight of your spells that worries me, but their effect on you. I simply do not wish you to be hurt. Surely you know that by now?"

He seemed to consider her argument, his expression guarded and his eyes unreadable as he studied her face. Then he sighed. "Of course I know it. How can I not after all you have done for me?" A faint smile curved his sculpted lips. "Indeed, were it not for your care, we wouldn't even be having this discussion."

"If I might interject here, your grace, I would like to present my opinion for your consideration," Eadon petitioned.

Michael nodded, though his now warm gaze never wavered from Emily's face. "Please do, Eadon."

When the man had stated his views and answered all of Michael's questions, Michael, whose gaze had remained steadily on Emily throughout the entire exchange, tipped his head to one side and murmured, "You know my inclinations in this matter, Eadon. However, it is those of my wife that shall be the determining factor. I must know her feelings before making a decision."

"I cannot see why they should influence you so," she retorted, shaking her head. "As I said, it is you who must take the real risks . . . you who must endure the spells you might have and abide the pain of the treatments it will take to relieve them."

"All risks I will gladly take for the chance to decrease Eadon's bleedings and clysters." His gaze bore into hers now, searching. "What I will not risk is you suffering the irrevocable disgust for me that seems to result in everyone who witnesses my fits. Truth be told, I would rather have my arms slashed and my backside abused a hundred times a day than risk losing you. And so I ask you, Emily, and please think carefully before you reply to make certain that you are confident of your response: Do you truly believe that you can witness one of my fits without forever turning from me in disgust? As I said, they are not a pleasant sight. If you wish details, I am sure that Eadon will be glad to furnish them."

But Emily didn't need details, nor did she need time to think. "I shan't be disgusted, Michael, not a bit. And I most certainly will not abandon you. Ever! I care for you, deeply, and all the fits in the world shan't change that fact in the least." Compelled by a fierce surge of emotion, she impulsively threw herself against him, hugging him in an embrace that imparted the strength of her feelings far more eloquently than words alone could express.

He stiffened briefly, as if stunned by her action, then relaxed, his strong arms encircling her to return her hug. Beneath her cheek, which lay burrowed in the crisp folds of his linen shirt, she felt the faint rumbling in his chest as he began to chuckle. "Well, Eadon. You heard the lady." He couldn't have sounded more pleased.

"Indeed I did. Once a fortnight it is, your grace." The delight in Mr. Eadon's voice was unmistakable. In the next instant he raised that voice and called out, "Ho there, Josiah! It looks like you could use a hand with that line."

As he walked off, the tall, autumn-bleached grass whispering against his boots as he went, Michael murmured, "Emily?"

She tipped her head to look up at him, her chin resting against his hard chest as she met his gaze in query. Smiling gently, he dipped down and lightly kissed her forehead. "Thank you, my dear."

"For what?" she whispered, thrilling at the tenderness and joy in his eyes.

"For being you."

Chapter 13

"They cannot possibly come in this storm," Emily lamented, turning from the rain-splattered sewing room window with a dispirited sigh. "Even if it stops in time for dinner, the moors will be far too muddy for them to venture forth."

Michael looked up from the angel he sketched on what would eventually be his kite, his heart aching with tenderness at the disappointment lacing her voice. Rebecca and her pet goat were to have dined with them that evening, making what would have been their first visit to the abbey. But as Emily had so dejectedly observed, it would be impossible for them to transverse the moor in such foul weather.

Wishing that there was something he could do, that he could make a road magically appear on the moors so he could send his coach to fetch the pair, he gently replied, "I believe you are correct, Emily, and I am sorry. I know how you were looking forward to their visit. You must make certain to extend another invitation the instant the rain clears."

"I will," she murmured, listlessly trailing her hand along the smooth cutting table surface as she wandered back to her own kite. After pausing a beat before it, a frown forming as she studied it, she sank into her chair opposite from where he sat, her gaze never wavering from her handiwork as she seated herself.

Watching as she picked up her well-used India rubber eraser and began vigorously erasing a wide area, he responded with a nod, "Good. I look forward to meeting them."

"Yes, I know, but not nearly as much as I look forward to them meeting you." She paused to blow the soiled eraser fragments from her drawing, then glanced up with an impish smile. "After all the bragging I have done about you to them, I cannot wait to show you off. They are going to adore you."

"I do hope that you haven't bragged overly much, or they shall think you quite mad when they finally meet me. As I have pointed out on numerous occasions, I am hardly a bargain when it comes to husbands, though I must admit that my value has increased somewhat, thanks to your improvements," he countered, shaking his head when he realized that he'd inadvertently used the term "they," thus endowing the goat with the human distinction of being able to determine madness. Then again, perhaps the beast could.

Michael started in astonishment at his own preposterous conclusion. Damn if Emily's tales about the goat hadn't made him start viewing it as the person she was convinced it was. According to his ever-fanciful wife's imaginative theory, Magellan was a man who had been transformed into a goat as punishment for some transgression against the fairies. It was a ludicrous theory, of course, ridiculous to the extreme. Still—

He paused to consider the concept, *really* consider it. Slowly he smiled. Who knows? If the beast turned out to be even half as amazing as she claimed it to be, perhaps . . . just perhaps . . . he might actually be persuaded to view her theory as a possibility.

Perhaps. Michael out and out grinned, absurdly pleased by his new sense of whimsy. If anyone in Dartmoor possessed magic, it was Emily, which she had clearly used to bewitch him. What other explanation could there be for the way she was making him, the rational, urbane, ever-logical duke of Sherrington, believe in enchantment?

At his grin, Emily grinned back, playfully tossing her eraser at him as she accused, "It is you who are mad not to see how very wonderful you are, Michael."

"Indeed?" he drawled, dexterously catching the projectile with one hand. Inspired by her beautiful smile to put it to use, he began carefully erasing the mouth he'd drawn, wanting to broaden the curve of his angel's luscious lips a fraction more.

"Yes, my darling husband," she confirmed. "You are all that is good and kind, not to mention intelligent, charming, witty, and too sinfully handsome for your own good." By her impassioned tone, it was apparent that she meant what she said.

Michael's hand stilled mid-erase, her words flowing over him like ice water. Charming, witty, intelligent. Too handsome for his own good. He must have heard those bombastic descriptions ascribed to him at least a thousand times before his illness, always uttered with the utmost sincerity, accompanied by long, worshipful stares. How he had loved hearing them! He'd adored being epitomized by the *ton,* hungrily feeding off their admiration and thriving on their adulation. After a time he'd come to actually believe their hyperbole and had taken to fancying himself the perfect archetype of the quintessential gallant.

But that was then; this was now. And now, after shamefully tumbling from grace, after paying the devastating price for his betrayal of society's faith in his lionized perfection, hearing such praise fall so sweetly, so easily from Emily's lips served only to shrivel his soul.

Damn it! He didn't want her to idealize him as the *ton* once had, to view him as some sort of bloody demigod. He wanted her to see him for what he was: a man, just an ordinary man with all the weaknesses and failings that went with being human. Doing so was her only chance to honor her vow—their only chance at a future together.

Though Michael knew that Emily genuinely believed herself immune to the disgust that inevitably arose in those witnessing his fits, he doubted if she would be able to maintain her conviction if she continued to view him in such a rarefied light. Indeed, he'd always suspected that the *ton*'s cruel rejection of him hadn't been prompted so much by the fits themselves, loathsome though they were, but by the shock of seeing him, their

crowned prince of perfection, stricken with such an appalling imperfection. Had he been someone else, someone less favored, they might have been more forgiving,
perhaps even sympathetic.

Given his belief in that view, the only way he could
see to protect Emily from suffering a terrible shock, and
to save himself from losing the woman he loved more
with every passing day, was to dash her innocent illusions
about him and force her to see him as he really was.

Determined to do exactly that now, he shot her a sardonic look and curtly scoffed, "Bah! Missish rubbish, all
of it! I am no such paragon. While I pride myself on
being reasonably intelligent, I possess only moderate wit
and charm, and my looks are ordinary, at best." When
she opened her mouth, clearly about to protest, he cut
her off with a brusque wave of his hand. "Furthermore,
I would very much appreciate it in the future if you
would refrain from speaking of me as if I were a beau
ideal. Not only do I find your misguided veneration embarrassing, it makes me question your wits and your ability for sound judgment."

As he'd expected, she looked suitably lowered, crushed
almost, her gay smile fading and her dark eyes growing
liquid with hurt. What he hadn't anticipated, however,
was how terrible he would feel seeing her look so. Truth
be told, had someone else been responsible for that
stricken expression, he'd have been hard pressed not to
throttle him within an inch of his life.

After several tense moments, during which she gazed
at him with wounded eyes and he struggled to refrain
from apologizing, Emily quietly uttered, "I am sorry, Michael. I didn't mean to vex you. I just—just"—she shook
her head, gesturing helplessly—"I just wanted to—"

"I know. I know that you meant well," he gently interjected, unable to remain silent at the sound of the re-
pressed tears choking her voice. "And I am sorry to have
spoken to you so harshly. It is just that I do not wish
you to foster an unrealistic impression of me. To allow
you to do so will only result in pain and disappointment
in the end." Pain for him, disappointment for her. "I am

just a man, Emily, nothing more. One with more than his share of flaws. Please do not make me out to be more."

She returned his gaze solemnly for a moment, visibly searching his eyes, then nodded and looked back down at her kite. Apparently that was to be the end of the matter, for in the next instant she picked up the pencil she'd abandoned when she'd gone to the window, and resumed her work on her sketch. After a minute or two of watching her, sensing that he should say something more, but uncertain what that something should be, Michael, too, recommenced drawing.

They remained like that for a long while, the tranquil coziness of the scene belying the turbulence of the emotions seething just below the surface.

The sewing room, into which Michael had never so much as set a foot until the day before, when Emily had directed him there for their kitemaking venture, was small, with simple but comfortable furnishings and a row of round-headed windows that overlooked the kitchen garden and greenhouses. On the wall perpendicular to the windows, encompassing almost the entire white-stuccoed length, arched an enormous brick fireplace. A fire currently blazed upon the hearth, its dancing flames reflecting off the polished wood floor as it merrily chased away the damp October chill. Though it was only midafternoon, the colza lamps on the walls and table had been lit, and now lifted the cloud-grayed gloom from the room.

As Michael worked, now and again sneaking peeks at Emily to match her features to those of his angel, he couldn't help noticing how tantalizing she looked in the lamplight.

She wore red today, and though the gown was a warm woolen affair with a high neck and prim lace collar, the color did wondrous things for her skin. It made it glow a lustrous ivory, against which the satiny sheen of her cheeks bloomed like rose petals dusted with pearls. Her hair, which she wore in a cascade of curls down her back, shimmered ever-so-slightly with copper fire, imbuing it with a silken warmth that made him ache to touch it and see if it felt as deliciously soft as it looked.

On they worked, the silence of the room broken only by the whispering scratch of their pencils and the crackling of the fire. Now and again the rain splattered violently against the windows, hurled by the driving force of the storm, reminding them of the fury that raged outside.

Michael had just corrected his angel's mouth to his satisfaction and was considering the slant of her eyebrows, when Emily murmured, "Why must you hate yourself so, Michael?"

He glanced up, utterly taken aback. "What?"

She made one final, bold stroke with her pencil, then looked up and solemnly met his gaze. "Why must you hate yourself?" she repeated softly. "It is clear from everything you say and do that you dislike yourself immensely. I do not understand why."

He returned her gaze for several beats, strangely unnerved by her question, then snorted. "I should think it would be obvious."

"But it isn't," she replied, her voice touched with a note of sweet pleading. "I can find no reason whatsoever why you shouldn't feel pride in yourself."

No reason? He stared at her dumbfounded, wondering if she had taken so far a leave of her senses that she couldn't recall all that she had seen and heard during the past month. Determined to remind her, to force her to once and for all desist in her romanticized view of him, he harshly grated out, "Must I keep pointing out that I am an invalid . . . a weak, ineffectual, sorry excuse for a man who must be constantly tended by a nursemaid?" Another snort. "After the way you have coddled me this past month, you, of all people, shouldn't require a reminder of that pathetic fact."

She sniffed. "Stuff and nonsense! I have seen invalids before—real ones—and I can tell you without the slightest reservation that you, Michael Vane, are no invalid. An invalid could not possibly walk out to the moors for a swim, nor would he have your appetite. He most certainly wouldn't have your complexion, which, in case you haven't looked in the mirror of late, has taken on a decidedly healthy glow." She nodded with a resolution that made her curls dance. "You are nowhere near being an invalid."

Another snort from Michael, this one explosive. "Tell that to Eadon and my grandmother. Oh, and while you are at it? Why don't you go before the magistrate and tell him as well? According to the courts of England, I am so invalid that I can be declared incompetent at any time and be stripped of my duchy."

She drew back, her eyebrows drawn together, visibly stunned. "What?"

He nodded curtly. "If you must know, I was divested of my ducal rights and duties during my illness, and have only recently regained them."

"But—why?" She was shaking her head over and over again, as he'd noticed was her habit when she couldn't quite believe what she was hearing. "From what I have seen of a nobleman's duties, you needn't be particularly sound of body to attend them. Indeed, judging from the conversation I heard while in London, most aristocratic business is attended to by solicitors, clerks, estate agents, and any number of other such parties." Her head shaking smoothly transitioned into a nod. "Why, it seems to me that a nobleman's only real duties are to make an occasional decision and sign a few papers, both of which you are, and no doubt have always been, equal to doing."

Michael smiled faintly at her naiveté. "There is a bit more to being a duke than simply signing papers and making decisions, I am afraid, though I must admit that those two acts do figure prominently among my duties."

"Be that as it may, I cannot think that it was necessary for the courts to divest you of your ducal rights, just because you fell ill. Surely your grandmother or some other family member could have attended to matters in your stead until you were well enough to do them for yourself?" She was shaking her head again. "Indeed, I cannot imagine how your grandmother could have allowed the courts to do such a thing. From what I have ascertained from my own grandmother, your grandmother wields a great deal of power in England, both socially and economically. I also hear tell that she has the ears of those high in power. Surely she could have done something to halt the courts' decision?"

"Why would she halt it when it was exactly the decision she sought?" he inquired darkly.

"What!"

"It was she who brought the matter before the courts in the first place, by petitioning to have the duchy turned over to her. Had it not been for her actions, the courts never would have gotten involved."

She was shaking her head so frantically now, that Michael wondered that she didn't make herself dizzy. "Why would she do such a thing? I thought she loved you."

He smiled bitterly. "If you were to ask her, she would most probably tell you that she did it *because* of her love for me. And in her own mind, I do not doubt that she would mean it."

"But you do not believe it?"

"Oh, I do not doubt that she loves me, I never have. However, I also understand how fiercely protective she is of the family titles and know that she would sacrifice anything, even me, to keep them from falling into less than worthy hands."

"Titles?" Her head actually stilled and her frown mutated into an expression of bewilderment. "Is there more than one, then?"

"Three, to be exact," he replied with a nod. "I am the duke of Sherrington, the marquess of Dartnell, and the earl of Grayland."

"Oh." Her frown returned as she considered his revelation. After a moment, her head sprang back into motion, slowly wagging from side to side. "I still do not understand. She didn't have to take the matter before the courts, did she? Surely you weren't so very ill, for so very long?"

He shrugged one shoulder, keeping his voice deliberately cool and his tone clipped as he replied, "If you must know, the infection in my brain was so bad that I wasn't expected to live. The doctors warned that if, by some miracle, I did manage to survive, my mind would be enormously compromised and that I would most likely spend the balance of my days being fed through a pap boat and diapered like a babe."

Again her head was shocked into stillness and her dark eyes grew wide, looking almost liquid, as if they were filled with tears. "Oh, Michael! No! How awful. When I think of you so ill—"

He cut her off with a brusque hand motion. The last thing in the world he wanted to discuss were the details of his illness. The episode with his mistress aside, it was his least favorite topic. "At any rate," he continued, adding an emphasis to the words and a raise of his eyebrows to further dismiss the uncomfortable subject, "my grandmother went to court because she feared that her great-nephew, Owen Pringle, whom she thoroughly abhors and who is, unfortunately, next in line to inherit the titles, would petition for control of the duchy during my illness, thus affording him to begin what she anticipated to be the ruin of the family name and fortune should the worst befall me. Besides, she needed to be able to make decisions on my behalf. When all was said and done, my grandmother ended up with control not only of the duchy, but of my person as well."

Her hands went up to signal a halt. "Your grandmother gained control over both the duchy *and* your person?" When he nodded, she frowned and added, "I have never heard of such a thing as a petition to gain control over a grown man's person."

"Ah, but as I said, the doctors expected my mind to be that of an infant should I, by chance, survive. She sought control over my person so as to ensure that I would receive proper care and not simply be deposited in some squalid asylum, as the Pringles most certainly would have done."

"Then what she claims is true," Emily softly concluded. Her head, which had begun to wag back and forth during his explanation, abruptly shifted into a nod. "She did bring the matter before the courts out of love."

"At first, perhaps. But later"—it was his turn to shake his head—"later, she used her power to control my life."

Her head froze at an inquisitive tilt and her brow creased. "In what way?"

"After it became apparent that I would indeed survive and with my wits intact, she continued running my life. Granted, at first it was because no one knew quite what to make of my seizures and it was feared that they might be the sign of a relapse. But later"—another head shake—"when it was determined that I wasn't going to relapse and that my fits in no way impaired my mind, she used her power first to force me to submit to dozens of supposed cures for my fits, ones, I might add, that make Eadon's look mild in comparison, after which she turned me over to Eadon himself, giving him free rein to treat me as he saw fit. Her last act was to force me to marry you. Of course"—he smiled gently—"I can no longer be angry at her for that. Of everything she has ever done for me, her greatest kindness was giving me you."

She smiled briefly in return, then glanced back down at her drawing. After several moments during which she studied it and made three more bold pencil strokes, she murmured, "Can I ask you something, Michael?"

He let the question float in the air, almost afraid to give his consent for fear of what she might ask. Then he heaved an inward sigh and tautly replied, "If you wish."

"How did your grandmother force you to wed me? I mean"—she looked up, her face troubled and her eyes beseeching—"you hardly strike me as the sort of man to meekly obey such a command. What did she say or do to get you to the altar?"

He returned her gaze for several beats, his mind arrested by her question. Then he glanced back down at his own drawing, making a show of studying it to hide his inner turmoil as he evenly replied, "She threatened to have me committed to Bamforth Hall."

"Bamforth Hall?" she echoed softly in question.

"It's—it's an—asylum—of sorts," he replied, making a silent amendment. The incident with his mistress wasn't his least favorite subject, Bamforth was. Hoping that Emily would be satisfied with his response and leave the subject alone, he picked up his pencil, which he'd laid down during the course of their exchange, and feigned deep concentration as he added a bit more arch to his angel's eyebrows.

But of course she didn't leave it alone. Less than a moment had elapsed before she prodded, "Judging from your bitterness on our wedding day, the place must have a very terrible reputation indeed that you would enter into a match you despised to escape going there."

Though Michael wanted nothing more than to put an end to the disturbing conversation, he knew better than to try. As he was quickly learning, Emily was an exceedingly tenacious chit, especially in matters pertaining to his well-being. Why, if she even suspected how deeply affected he was by the mere mention of Bamforth—

Not wanting to endure the probing that such a suspicion was bound to provoke, well-meaning and gentle though the probing would be, he evenly returned, "On the contrary. The place has the very best of reputations. It is quite genteel as far as asylums go, and takes patients only from the very best families."

"And yet, you fear it so much that you would sacrifice yourself on the altar of marriage rather than go there?"

Michael couldn't help smiling at her melodramatic turn of phrase. "Yes, although 'dread' would be a better word than 'fear' for what I feel toward the place."

"Oh." With that, she fell silent. For a short while thereafter, neither of them spoke as they returned their attention to their kites, each lost in their own thoughts. Michael had just began to relax, certain that the subject of Bamforth had been dropped, when Emily abruptly asked, "What did you hear about it?"

He glanced up slowly, praying that she wasn't asking what he thought she was asking, but dismally certain that she was. "Hear about what?"

She was gazing at him curiously, now and again gnawing on the end of her pencil, which by the looks of it had seen a great deal of such activity. "Bamforth Hall, of course."

Of course. Damnation! Struggling hard to keep his feelings about the place from his voice, he shrugged one shoulder and smoothly replied, "Nothing, really."

"Well then?" she persisted, her gaze latching on to his.

He stared back, trying to think of a response to put her off. After a moment or two during which her gaze never wavered from his and her expressive face took on a look of implacable determination, he gave up. He knew that expression all too well—it was the same one she'd worn the first few times she'd invaded his sickroom. And as he had learned from those exasperating experiences, she would not be put off when she wore that look.

Emitting a noise that perfectly expressed his displeasure at her prying, he abandoned all pretense of nonchalance and bit out, "If you must know, it isn't anything I heard that makes me dread it so, it was my experience there."

"Oh." Another silence. In fact, this one went on so long that Michael again allowed himself to relax, thinking that she was going to let the subject drop at last.

He should have known better. "Would you like to tell me about Bamforth Hall?" she abruptly inquired.

"Good God, no," he ejected, not daring to look up for what she might see in his eyes.

Again silence, then, "It might help, you know."

He glanced up to shoot her what he hoped was a quelling look.

She graced him with a tender smile and a nod. "My father always said that it helps a person to talk about their troubles, that it unburdens their soul. In fact, he made doing so a rule of sorts in our household. We were to talk about anything that plagued us . . . if not to him or each other, then to someone in whom we felt comfortable confiding."

"And it helped?" he softly quizzed, not missing the wistful note that always shaded her words when she spoke of her home and family.

She nodded again. "Yes. Of course, simply talking couldn't always solve our problems or completely heal our hurts, but we all agreed that we felt better for having shared our woes. Have you ever discussed your experience at Bamforth with anyone?"

Michael shook his head. He'd complained about it to

Eadon, his grandmother, and Euphemia, but he'd never actually spoken about the experience itself, not really.

"Then you should," she counseled with yet another nod, this one sage. "I understand that you might not want to discuss it with me . . . after all, there are some things a man isn't comfortable confiding to a woman. However, you should confide in someone. It is apparent that whatever happened to you there is gnawing at your soul. Promise me that you will think about doing so?"

He continued to gaze at her beautiful face a moment longer, now the picture of tenderness, then nodded.

"Good." Smiling in a way that would have prompted him to dub his kite "the angel of compassion" were he to draw her expression, she stretched across the table to give his arm a squeeze. As she did so, she caught sight of his drawing. Standing up for a better view, she exclaimed, "Goodness, Michael. I had no idea that you were such an accomplished artist."

"Only when I am inspired by faultless beauty," he replied sincerely, studying her delicate profile. It was no lie. He had yet to discover an angle from which she didn't look exquisite.

To his pleasure, she blushed at his compliment. "I could say the same for you, you know, that you are flawlessly beautiful, but I fear that doing so would only anger you."

"It isn't that your compliments anger me, Emily. If you must know the truth, they frighten me. I fear that I shall lose you if I allow you to admire me overly much," he admitted, his confession compelled by the intimacy of the moment.

She glanced up quickly, a faint crease marring her ivory brow. "What a queer line of reasoning. Pray do explain what you mean."

"If I allow you to view me in too idealized a light, the shock of seeing my fits might prove too great for you to withstand, and then I will lose you." He went on to elaborate on his theory, during which Emily listened with a thoughtful expression, nodding on occasion, but never once interrupting.

When he had at last finished and had been silent for several moments, she murmured, "May I say something now?"

He nodded. "Please do."

"The light in which I view you is far from idealized, Michael. Indeed, I have seen most of your warts, as my father used to jokingly call our imperfections, so I know how truly human you are. But don't you see?" Her gaze met his again, entreating him to understand and believe in what she said. "That is what I adore most about you. Having seen your flaws makes me feel as if I truly know you, which makes me wonderfully at ease in your company. You have allowed me to be a part of your life, rather than just a spectator, by letting me see you at your best, your worst, and everything in between."

She paused to smile wryly. "Come, come now, Michael. Can you honestly believe that I see you as more than human after all the times I've held your head over the chamberpot in the wake of Mr. Eadon's emetics? If you ask me, I see you in a perfectly clear light, a far truer one than you see yourself."

What she said made sense, he supposed, though holding his head while he vomited was a far cry from what she would see when she finally witnessed one of his fits, which she would eventually do. Nonetheless, as she'd pointed out, she'd seen him if not at his worst, then damn close to it . . . and she still admired him.

That realization fostered his first real spark of hope for their relationship. Thrilled, he smiled and murmured, "Listening to your description of me makes me almost like myself. Too bad I cannot see myself as you do."

She seemed to consider his words for a beat, then nodded. "Perhaps you can." With that, she pushed her sketch across the table. Nodding again, this time to indicate the sketch, she added, "This is far and away better than my first attempt to portray you. At the risk of bragging, I must admit that I captured you rather well."

Loath to tear his gaze from her face, the warmth of which kindled his heart, Michael glanced down at the drawing before him. She was right, she had captured his face perfectly, but the rest of him . . . he frowned. Rather than drawing him clad in the voluminous robe she'd drawn him in on her first kite, his body was gracefully draped in a length of cloth, revealing more than it hid. And what it revealed . . . well, that most certainly wasn't his body. His body no longer looked like that, so strong and well formed.

His frown deepening, he slowly looked back up at her. "I thought you said that you do not idealize me."

"I don't," she replied with a shrug.

"You must to have drawn my head on this body. As I pointed out at the tors, my body is all scraggy and withered, but this—"

"Is an utterly faithful rendering," she interjected firmly. When he opened his mouth to differ, she cut him off with, "Oh, no. Do not even try to argue. This is a perfect example of what I was talking about earlier. You dislike yourself so much that you cannot see yourself as you really are." There went her head again, wagging. "No, Michael. This time you are wrong. You are every bit as handsome as I have drawn you. Indeed, were we to drape you in cloth exactly as I have sketched you and then ask a hundred people to compare you to my picture, I would bet my favorite jade bracelet that their only comment would be that I have failed to do you full justice." The head shake transformed into a nod. "As I told you at the tors, you have a lovely body. Magnificent, I should have said, though I refrained from doing so for fear of making you conceited."

Michael stared at her face in wonder, searching for signs of insincerity, certain that she lied in an attempt to bolster his admittedly sagging confidence. When he saw only truth, guileless and pure, he glanced back at her drawing. Studying it with new interest, he lightly traced the sculpted planes of the angel's chest with his fingertip, marveling, "This is really how you see me, then?"

She expelled an exasperated sigh. "Good heavens, Michael! I am beginning to think that you must be the most slow-witted man in all of England. This isn't how I see you, this is how you look. You are perfectly lovely, and not just on the outside. You are warm, witty, and utterly wonderful on the inside as well. In short, you are a glorious man. How many times must I tell you so before you believe it?"

He critically contemplated the sketch a beat longer, then looked back up, his lips curving into a smile. "If you see me like this, then I suppose that I cannot help but like myself." And suddenly, he did. Oh, he doubted that he was the Greek god she'd depicted him as being, but he also realized that he was no longer the frail, pitifully shrunken shadow of a man he saw every time he looked in the mirror. How could he be when Emily saw him like this? For the first time since his illness, Michael felt a swell of pride in himself. The resulting buoyancy of his spirits was the most exhilarating sensation he'd ever felt, a miracle . . .

As was watching the joy burst into Emily's beautiful eyes. It was like seeing fireworks light up a midnight sky. "Truly?" she inquired breathlessly, her smile matching the radiance of her eyes. "Oh, Michael. I am so glad."

"So am I," he whispered hoarsely, possessed by a strong, impetuous urge to kiss her. So powerful was the impulse that had there not been a table between them, she would have already been in his arms, his needful lips consuming any protest she might raise. The thought of holding her, of caressing her luscious curves and feeling them mold against him as she sighed her sensual pleasure, made his body respond with shattering urgency.

Now struggling to maintain what little was left of his rapidly slipping composure, Michael tore his gaze from Emily's tempting mouth and forced himself to stare back down at her sketch of him. Desperate for something to distract him, anything to get his mind off the erotic vision of Emily with her red lips swollen from his kisses and her bewitching eyes inviting him to steal more, he said the first thing to come to mind. "What other kinds of kites do you make? Surely they are not all shaped like angels?"

"Oh, no. I have experimented with all sorts of shapes—diamonds, rectangles, boxes, circles, even the Chinese lantern—but I always decorate them with angels," she replied, sitting down again.

"Ah. Then you are fond of angels?" Angels? Yes. Perfect. He was hardly in danger of experiencing further arousal while engaged in a theological discussion.

"Of course, isn't everyone?" she retorted. Without waiting for his response, she added, "Besides, what could be a better motif for a kite than an angel? Not only are they beautiful, they can fly higher than anything on earth . . . all the way to heaven." She paused to sigh. When she again spoke, her voice was soft, almost reverent, filled with a wistfulness that made Michael glance back up at her face. "That is my greatest dream you see, to fly. If a person didn't have to die to become an angel, I would be most anxious to join their ranks."

"Then you wish to fly to heaven for a visit?" he gently quizzed, smiling tenderly at her latest bit of whimsy.

She shrugged and nodded in tandem. "Only if I could come back here after my visit. Otherwise," another shrug, this one accompanied by a head shake, "I would be perfectly happy just soaring above the earth and looking down. Can you imagine the sensation of doing so—the thrill, the feeling of absolute freedom? Why, you could see forever and go anywhere."

"Indeed you could," he replied, thinking how radiant she looked in her fanciful enthusiasm. She practically glowed, as if she were lit from within.

Smiling dreamily, she met his gaze, her eyes soft and far away as she pensively murmured, "Have you ever imagined what heaven will look like when you get there?"

He smiled back ruefully. "I used to, when I still believed in such a place."

"What! You don't believe in heaven?" Her raptly introspective expression vanished, and she looked genuinely grieved. "Oh, Michael. No! How very sad. What made you stop believing?"

"Life and the living hell it has become over the past two years, although"—his brittle smile softened into a real one—"I must admit that I am almost inclined to start believing again now that you are here."

"Truly?" At his nod, she nodded back, her voice growing resolute as she countered, "In that instance, I must work harder to help you do so."

"Oh?"

Another nod. "I must strive to create a bit of heaven for you right here on earth. Once you have experienced it here, you cannot help but to believe that there is a place where such joy is possible for all eternity."

"And how do you propose to do such a thing?" he inquired, genuinely intrigued.

"Well, first we must determine what brings you joy . . . something you haven't done in a very long time and wish to do again."

Michael didn't have to think twice to know the answer to that: he wished to make love again. Indeed, he could think of nothing more heavenly than seeing Emily's face transfixed with pleasure and hearing her cry his name in her rapture as he took her. Since that was impossible and since he didn't care to dwell on the vision the thought was provoking, he uttered his second favorite activity, "Riding. I would very much like to ride my stallion, Shurik, again."

"Then you shall," she stoutly declared. "You must."

"Unfortunately, I cannot," he interposed. "It is one of the activities I am no longer permitted to enjoy. Eadon worries that I might take a tumble and hit my head. According to the general consensus of experts, a blow to the head in my condition, even a slight one, could prove fatal, or at the very least cause a drastic increase in seizures."

She couldn't have looked more crushed.

"But I really do not miss it so very much, not anymore," he lied, smiling in a way that he hoped would make her smile back.

She did, halfheartedly. "Still, there must be something I can do. Perhaps—"

"You do more than enough already," he interjected gently, reaching across the table to take her hands in his. "Simply seeing your smile and hearing your voice give me far more pleasure than I could ever express. You, my darling wife, are my angel, and anywhere you are is heaven on earth to me." And it was true. Hmmm. It seemed that he believed in heaven after all.

Chapter 14

As often happens on the moors of Dartmoor in autumn, the rains set in and continued without cease for the next two weeks, keeping Michael and Emily confined to the abbey.

Michael, who had experienced the seemingly interminable storms before and had grown to dread the excruciating boredom and gloom he always suffered in their wake, found himself actually enjoying his captivity. How could he not with Emily by his side? She brightened his days with her luminous smile, her vibrant pleasure in life coloring each gray hour, all of which flew swiftly by on wings of quiet contentment.

Emily, too, savored their time together, especially the evenings they spent in the cozy winter saloon, sprawled on the plush Oriental carpet before the toasty fire. As they lounged against the pile of velvet and silk cushions they had pilfered from the chairs, Michael with a mug of hot milk and she a cup of chocolate, they whispered of their dreams and shared their most treasured memories, spinning a web of intimacy from which neither wished ever to escape.

True, when viewed as a whole, their rainy day routine would no doubt have appeared mundane to those unaware of the special bond between the powerful young duke and his beautiful duchess, tedious even. But to those who knew them best, the servants, who had seen their beloved master's torment and the healing power of Emily's joy, to them those days were a miracle. They understood the significance of the seemingly ordinary schedule of everyday events, and they rejoiced. For after two long, grim years, Michael Vane, duke of Sherrington, was again lord of the manor.

As for Emily and Michael, they arose each morning charged with a heady thrill of anticipation, looking forward to the delightful discoveries they never failed to make about themselves and each other whenever they were together. Thus they endeavored to spend as much time as possible together, a quest that began each morning when they met for breakfast, a relaxed, leisurely meal during which they nourished their bodies with Cook's delicious victuals and their souls with each other's company. After breakfast they would reluctantly part for several hours to attend to their individual duties.

Emily, who with Michael's guidance had gradually adopted the role of lady of the manor, tended to household matters, after which she secretly worked on a surprise she was making for Michael, one which she hoped would enable him to ride again. Michael's time was spent on ducal business or submitting to Eadon's treatments, which he now tolerated with only minor detriment. They would then meet again promptly at three for their daily walk. Because they were unable to venture outside, they took their exercise in the house.

During the first week they strolled through the long picture galleries with Michael acting as a guide, pointing out portraits of his ancestors and other such luminaries, and relating stories of their exploits. When they came to a portrait he was unable to identify, they would make up a fanciful name and history for the person, their hilarity escalating into absurdity as each tried to outdo the other with the preposterousness of their fictitious character's escapades.

Emily loved those moments best, seeing Michael's jewel-like eyes sparkle in his mischievous glee and hearing the unbridled joy of his rich, easy laughter. He delighted in his newfound sense of whimsy and she thrilled to his pleasure. So much so that by the end of their second week of confinement they had thoroughly examined every painting and named every portrait they could find. Loath to see their fun end, Michael had contrived a new diversion, which he introduced that very afternoon.

Thus when Emily met him at their usual rendezvous place by the gargoyles, one of the beasts which now wore a feather-and-ribbon-trimmed cocked hat and the other a fussy leghorn her grandmother had forgotten to pack, she found Michael clad in a dark blue greatcoat, with a lantern in one hand and her red woollen cloak draped over his other arm. Though Emily was warmly dressed, the drafty halls and galleries being chilly on such days, Michael insisted that she don the heavy wrap, saying that he thought she might enjoy exploring the closed wings and deserted upper floors of the abbey, all of which were bound to be cold.

Always game for adventure, Emily obediently allowed him to slip the cloak over her shoulders, busying herself with fastening the front hook-and-eye closures while he turned his attention to lighting the lantern. That done, they were off. At Michael's suggestion they started at the addition off the northeast wing, one he referred to as the old banqueting house.

Built during the reign of Elizabeth, the banqueting house, which had originally stood apart from the abbey but had been joined by an enclosed promenade a century later, turned out to be more of a lodge than a mere pavilion for feasting. Standing three stories tall with each floor housing several rooms full of quaint, antiquated furnishings and once fashionable gewgaws, it proved to be the perfect place to while away a rainy afternoon.

Laughing and chatting as they went, they roamed from room to room, studying the still bright murals and well-preserved tapestries, peeking beneath the covers that shrouded the dated furnishings, and testing the abandoned instruments in the tiny music room, all the while imagining the lives of the people who had once loved and laughed there. Of all the rooms they toured, however, fascinating though they were, none caught Emily's interest more than the ones on the third floor. For at some time in the abbey's long history, early during the past century Michael informed her, they had been used to house the Vane children.

Now standing in the main nursery, the one in which Michael's ancestors had spent their earliest days, Emily was struck by the austerity of her surroundings. With its stark whitewashed walls and hard wood-planked floor, the room was nothing short of dreary—a far cry from the sort of pampered luxury in which she'd have expected the children of one of England's mightiest families to be kept. Indeed, aside from a scattering of sensible furniture, among which were several small cots, a rather lovely swinging cradle, and a trundle bed, no doubt meant for the nurse, the room contained few amenities, none of which suggested comfort or cheer.

As Michael opened the heavy drapes to allow more light for her inspection, Emily stooped down to examine a hexagonal-shaped baby walker, which had once been a bright cherry red, judging from the chips of remaining paint, then rose to study a nearby pair of turned ash high chairs. Both chairs were very elegant, but had no doubt been hideously uncomfortable for their young occupants given the knobbiness of their lathe work backs.

She had just moved to the low oak table with its six child-size fiddle-back chairs and had kneeled before it to contemplate the meager display of playthings arranged upon it, when Michael came to stand beside her. Setting the lantern on the table to further illuminate the toys, he disclosed, "This was my great-grandfather, Edmund Vane's, nursery. I showed you his portrait, remember?"

Indeed she did. How could she forget Edmund Vane when it was from him whom Michael had inherited the handsome cleft in his chin? Idly picking up and examining a piece of the dissected wooden puzzle scattered before her, she replied, "Of course I remember him." A head. The puzzle piece depicted a man's head with curly black hair and a short beard. Curious about the picture to which the head belonged, she set it back down and began shifting through the other pieces, looking for ones that might fit as she added, "As I recall, he was a handsome but exceedingly dour-looking man. And now I know why he possessed such a gloomy disposition. Judging from the bleakness of this nursery, he was given little to be cheerful about in his youth."

"Ah, but you misjudge him. By all accounts he was a most cheerful man . . . one of the great wits of his time," Michael countered, sinking to his knees beside her. Picking up a beautifully carved wooden horse on a wheeled platform, which he proceeded to admire from all angles, he explained, "As I have pointed out on several occasions, you can never trust a formal portrait to be a true depiction of its study. I do not know about America, but here in England it has always been the practice for artists to paint their subjects in the fashion of the day. During my great-grandfather's time it was modish for a man, especially a nobleman, to look like a strong, valiant leader. That being the case, it would never have done to paint him with the smile I am told he wore on most occasions."

"Still, I cannot imagine that his childhood could have been very gay, not confined to a dreary place like this," she retorted, fitting a body in a multicolored coat to the head before her.

He shrugged and set the horse back on the table, giving it a push that sent it charging to the center. "I doubt if it was much worse than anyone else's childhood of the time." At her sniff of disbelief, he gently reproved, "You must understand the views of the day in order to appreciate the truth of what I say."

"Oh?" she challenged, glancing up to shoot him an incredulous look.

He nodded and picked up a puzzle piece near her elbow, carefully examining it as he explained, "From what I have ascertained from reading accounts of the time, childhood was viewed as a necessary evil to be gotten over as quickly as possible. Hence, little concession was made to it."

"But that is dreadful!" she ejected, genuinely shocked. "Childhood isn't something to be rushed and dismissed. It is a wonderful, magical time to be cherished by parent and child alike. Furthermore, it takes years of love and nurturing, and at least a thousand concessions, before a child is ready to move beyond it."

He latched the piece he held, a pair of sandal-shod feet with the name "Joseph" inscribed beneath them, to her colorfully clad man. "That is a lovely thought, Emily, but unfortunately, not one commonly shared by the aristocracy of the last century. Most lordlings of the time were required to be gentlemen by the age of five. Not only were they dressed like their elders, they were expected to parrot their ways and converse in an adult manner. Some could do so in several languages."

"What!"

He nodded. "It wasn't at all uncommon for a five-year-old to be fluent in Latin and Greek. Many knew French as well and had a rudimentary knowledge of the other scholarly disciplines."

"How very sad," she murmured, her heart aching for the noble children and their tragically premature loss of innocence.

He fit another puzzle head, this one with a white beard, to a body wearing a ragged robe holding two stone tablets in its arms. "It seems sad only if you know anything different," he returned with simple logic. "Since it has always been the tradition of the British aristocracy to mold their peers from the cradle, most noble offspring were never exposed to the more frivolous aspects of childhood and thus never missed them."

"I still think it beyond tragic," she maintained, her tone communicating her scorn for his theory. "Thank goodness you nobles have come to your senses and have ceased your barbaric robbery of your children's childhoods."

He shrugged one shoulder and picked up another puzzle piece. "I never said that it had ceased. There are a number of peers who still adhere to what you term as a 'barbaric robbery of their children's childhoods.' To them it is simply the way things are done. Since they were raised in a like fashion and are pleased with the adults they have become, they see no reason not to perpetuate the tradition."

"But—but—" she sputtered, grappling for the words to express her outrage. She found them in the next instant and was poised to articulate them when a new, undeniably hideous thought struck her. "Oh, Michael! Surely you weren't brought up in such an abominable manner?" she cried, stricken by the very notion.

He shrugged again and pressed the puzzle piece he held, which read "Moses" beneath his tablet-toting man. "Not entirely, though you must bear in mind that I was raised by our grandmothers, both of whom naturally have some rather old-fashioned ideas."

"Exactly how old-fashioned?" she quizzed, her eyes narrowing in her terrible suspicion.

"It was their belief that an heir such as I, who bore three ancient and powerful titles at the age of two, must be an infant prodigy in order to do justice to his position in society. Thus, I could read and write by the time I was three, I mastered Latin at four, and had a good grounding in Greek, geography, literature, and algebra by the time I was five."

Emily simply stared at him, too appalled to do more. Then she began shaking her head over and over again. "You poor, poor dear," she murmured, hating the thought of what he must have endured to have had his brain crammed so full of knowledge at such a tender age. "It must have been a grueling ordeal for one so young, learning such difficult lessons. However did you bear it?"

He picked up another puzzle piece, scrutinizing it from several angles as he slowly replied, "I daresay that I had an easier time of it than many boys in my position. At least my tutor never caned me if I was slow to learn, and he very much believed in the benefits of play." He nodded, as if coming to a silent resolution, then concluded, "All in all, my childhood was pleasant enough, though I must admit that I missed not having siblings. At times I got rather lonely for the company of other children."

Emily watched as he tried to fit the puzzle piece to one he'd plucked from the piece pile earlier, imagining a life without the merry company of her beloved broth-

ers. The devastating emptiness she experienced in doing
so made her feel lost and alone and strangely hollow, as
if she'd somehow lost her heart and was helpless to retrieve it. Not knowing quite how to reply in the wake of
the wrenching sensation, she rawly inquired, "Surely you
had friends?"

"Yes, but no close ones my own age." He discarded
the puzzle piece, which had failed to fit. "Perhaps I might
have had better success at friendship had I been allowed
to choose my own company. But of course, that would
never have done. In keeping with her ambition for me,
Grandmother allowed me to associate only with children
from the upper stratum of the peerage. 'Never too early
to begin forging bonds with your peers, my boy' "—he
mimicked the old tyrant's strident tone to perfection—
"she used to whisper as she introduced me to yet another
little lord or lady with whom I had absolutely nothing in
common but our future positions in society." He shook
his head. "Truth be told, my very best friends were the
servants here, though I wasn't allowed to spend nearly
as much time in residence here as I would have liked as
a child."

"From what I have seen and heard here at Windgate,
you are still on friendly terms with your staff," she commented, smiling tenderly at his confession.

"Very friendly, which is the reason I chose Windgate
as my retreat when I retired from society." He pieced
together several more puzzle fragments, revealing a portion of an ark with two lions, a pair of giraffes and an
elephant, then sat back on his heels with a sigh. "Of all
the scores of people who surrounded me when I was a
child, only the servants here ever bothered to notice my
loneliness and take measures to ease it."

"What did they do?" Emily quizzed, wanting, as she
always did, to know everything there was to know about
her magnificent husband.

He smiled faintly and met her gaze, his beautiful jade
eyes soft with nostalgia. "They would steal moments
from their work to play games with me, or tell me stories,
or teach me silly rhymes or gay country songs. Some-

times they just talked to me." His smile broadened, as if in fond remembrance of one of those long-ago exchanges. "You would be surprised at how far a kind word or two will go toward raising a child's spirits."

"No, I would not. I have always thought it extremely important for adults to notice and acknowledge children," she declared, impulsively smoothing a long lock of hair from his forehead, which had tumbled over his brow during their conversation. "It is nice to know that there are people in England who share my belief."

"Just as it is nice to know that you hold them," he countered softly, his eyes glittering from the power of some unfathomable emotion as his gaze locked into hers.

Whatever that nameless emotion was, it touched something deep inside Emily, filling her with a sweet, savage yearning that set her heart fluttering wildly in her breast. Unnerved by her disturbing response, she tore her gaze away, her tongue feeling tied in a thousand knots as she uttered the first thing to come to mind. "Was there—er—anyone among the staff of whom you were particularly fond?"

There was a brief pause, as if he, too, had felt whatever had passed between them and now struggled to regain himself, then he replied, "Phoebe Swann and her sister Agnes were, and still are, special to me."

"I have noticed that they are exceedingly fond of you as well." And it was true. The two women couldn't seem to do enough for him.

He nodded. "I shall never forget how they used to invite me into the kitchen to cut and decorate my own gingerbread men. As I grew older, they let me stoke the oven fire, which was an enormous thrill for a young boy." He paused briefly, straightening back up to resume his study of the puzzle pieces, before adding, "And then there was Isaac Juett, the Windgate carpenter."

"Isaac Juett?" Emily echoed, frowning as she tried to place the man. Though she had been to the carpenter's shop on several kitemaking errands, she couldn't recall meeting anyone by that name.

"Unfortunately, you never had the chance to meet him. To my infinite sorrow, he died several years ago."

"I am sorry," she murmured sincerely. By the tautness of his voice, it was apparent that the man had meant a great deal to him.

He nodded once in acknowledgment to her condolence. "He was much loved here at Windgate and his death was felt keenly by all. I, for one, shall never forget him and his many kindnesses."

"He must have been very wonderful indeed for you to carry such a high opinion of him."

"He was . . . the best of all men, and I shall never hesitate to credit him for being my mentor. It was he who taught me the true virtues of nobility, his counsel I sought when I was troubled or confused, and his words of wisdom that guided me through the difficult transition from boyhood to manhood." His gaze was back on hers, this time glittering with the strength of his conviction. "I can say sincerely and without reservation that I loved him and would have been proud to have been his son, humble though he was in both birth and position."

"It sounds as if he loved you, too," she remarked, her already monumental respect for her husband doubling at the humility and loyalty his confession showed him to possess. "No doubt he would have been an enormous comfort to you during your illness, had he lived."

"No doubt," he agreed with a smile. Tipping his head to one side to view her with the look of admiration she had come to know and cherish, he added in the next breath, "Do you know what I regret most of all about his death?"

She smiled back, shaking her head.

"That he shall never know you. He would have been most pleased to see me wed to you. You are exactly the sort of bride he once counseled me to take."

"Indeed? And what sort of bride is that, pray tell?" she quizzed, feeling herself blush beneath the warmth of his gaze.

"Kind, generous, strong, and spirited . . . with fine hips for bearing children." His lips split into a devastating grin. "You are all of that, my darling Emily, not to mention witty, charming, and a tearing beauty."

"And you are far too kind," she demurred, returning her attention to the puzzle to hide her embarrassment at his effusive praise . . . not that she didn't love hearing him say such wonderful things—she did, far more than was seemly.

"No, my dear, I am simply being honest." The gravity of his voice left little doubt as to his sincerity.

The next few moments passed in silence as Michael and Emily resumed their work on the puzzle, discovering David and Goliath, and King Solomon's feet. As they shifted through the pieces, busily trying, fitting, and discarding the colorful fragments, Emily's mind reeled with questions about Michael.

Sharing his childhood had left her hungry to know more about him . . . greedy, even. Not that her greed was anything new. With every passing day, with every secret they confided and memory they traded, her wish to know everything about him deepened into a keen, wistful yearning.

True, she had learned much about him during the past weeks, but there was even more she didn't know . . . private, personal details into which she hadn't thus far dared to delve for fear that he would become angry and shut her out.

One of those details was his experiences at Bamforth Hall, which she knew haunted and tormented him. The other was his views on children. Though she had promised never to question him on the former, she knew that it was only a matter of time before one of them was forced to broach the topic of the latter. After all, as the duke of Sherrington, it was Michael's obligation to produce an heir. As his duchess, it was her duty to make herself accessible to him and to encourage him to fulfill his responsibility.

Well, at least she thought it was. Having no one to guide her in such matters, she didn't know that for certain, but it seemed to make sense. Of course, before she could encourage him or make her person accessible to him, they would have to discuss the subject. That meant first broaching it.

Stealing a sidelong glance at her husband, Emily wondered if now might not be a suitable moment to do so. After all, they had been talking about children . . . yes, and he was in one of his warm, contemplative moods. Hmmm.

Deciding that the moment was indeed as good as any she was likely to get in the future, Emily fitted the puzzle piece she held, which, appropriately enough, was the infant Jesus in his manger, next to the Joseph that Michael had just assembled, then murmured, "How do you feel about children?"

He shot her a sharp look. "What do you mean?"

She shrugged. "I was just wondering whether or not you like children. Many men dislike them, you know, and wish nothing to do with them."

He seemed to consider her words, his expressive eyes growing oddly shuttered and his handsome face remote, then he looked away again. Making a show of contemplating the puzzle pieces before him, he quietly replied, "I adore them. If I disliked them, I wouldn't be in my current state."

Emily watched as he shuffled around several puzzle pieces, comparing their edges to the one in his hand, wondering what he meant. Unable to make sense of his cryptic response, she admitted, "I am afraid that I do not know what you mean."

"Where do you think I contracted measles?"

"I—I never really gave it any thought," she confessed.

"Neither did I, unfortunately."

Again she was at a loss. "Pardon?"

"Measles. I never gave them or how very contagious they are any thought when I visited Lord Varden's four children in their nursery, all of whom were down with the disease." He paused to pick up one of the puzzle pieces he'd been pushing about, one depicting a pile of straw, and pressed it to the right of the manger. "The children had adopted me as a pet uncle of sorts, you see, and I had brought trinkets to cheer them."

"That was kind of you," she remarked, her heart aching that he should pay such a terrible price for his benevolence.

He passed off her commendation with a shrug. "It gave me pleasure to see them smile. Truth be told, I far preferred their company to that of many of my peers. So much so that I would inevitably end up in the nursery playing with them every time I attended one of the Vardens' dreary social functions." He chuckled and shook his head. "I shall never forget the look of annoyance on Lady Varden's face every time she was forced to trudge up to the nursery to retrieve me. She fancied herself a bit of a matchmaker, I am afraid, and was always trying to shackle me to one of her friends' daughters, despite my protests that I was waiting for her own daughter, Kitty, to grow up so that I could wed her."

"How old was Kitty?" Emily asked, shamed by the stab of jealousy she felt at the affection in Michael's voice as he spoke of the girl.

"Four, and if ever a chit was destined to be a heartbreaker, it is she. I certainly shan't envy Varden when it comes time to bring her out. She will lead him and every bachelor in the *ton* on a merry chase." He laughed softly, shaking his head. "The little minx. I can no doubt thank her for giving me the measles."

Emily smiled faintly, charmed by the animation on his face as he spoke of the child. "How so?"

"Had she not demanded a kiss and insisted on sitting on my lap, I most probably would have escaped the infection." Apparently his fondness for the child outweighed his bitterness over what had befallen him, for his voice remained free of the harshness that usually tainted it when he mentioned his illness.

Thrilled that he had the capacity to care so for a child, she murmured on a sigh, "How very wonderful."

"Which part? Me catching the measles from kissing her, or me catching them from allowing her to sit on my lap?" he inquired wryly, one eyebrow arching in sardonic query.

She waved aside his question with a bubbling laugh.

"Neither. I merely meant that it is wonderful that you have it within your heart to love a child so very much. I always hoped that the father of my children would harbor that very ability."

By his expression, you would have thought that she'd slapped him instead of paid him what she considered to be the highest of compliments. His playful smile faded and the blood drained from his cheeks, leaving his face a ghostly mask of gravity. Alarmed by the hunted, almost wary look that had crept into his eyes, she stammered out, "D-did I say something amiss, Michael?"

He shook his head once, sharply, then closed his eyes and turned his face away, seeming to wage a battle within himself.

She hesitated a beat, watching him with uncertainty, then lightly touched his arm. "Michael?" Her voice had taken on a pleading tone, threaded with a note of tender urgency.

He remained motionless for several more moments, then raggedly whispered, "I am sorry, Emily . . . so very sorry."

"Sorry?" she repeated. She frowned and shook her head, utterly perplexed by his cryptic response. "I do not understand, Michael. What have you to be sorry for?"

"For marrying you."

His reply was like a stab to her heart, slashing it with a viciousness that made it cry out in desolate agony. He regretted marrying her. Feeling as though she would shatter to pieces if she so much as breathed, she stared at him dumbly, her eyes aching and clouded with hurt.

"Oh, I am not sorry to have you for my wife," he added fiercely in the next instant, turning abruptly to face her. "You have been a Godsend to me . . . my saving grace." He shook his head once, his mouth contorting into a grim line. "I am sorry for trapping you into a sham of a marriage. A woman like you should have a real marriage, one with a husband who can love you."

Rather than easing her pain, his explanation made her

feel worse, far, far worse. He didn't love her, and he never could.

Swallowing hard to hold back the sob that had risen from her chest, she desperately clutched at common sense, searching for solace in its clear, cold logic.

She should be glad that he couldn't love her . . . glad, yes . . . relieved, even. After all, it was only right that he didn't love her since she couldn't love him back, what with the curse and all. Of course, Rebecca had said that it might be possible to break the curse, but in order to do so they must love each other with all their hearts and souls. She had also warned that the spell used to banish the curse sometimes failed, which always resulted in dire consequences for the uncursed person, namely Michael. And since Emily was unwilling to do anything that might harm Michael . . .

She gave her head a resolute shake. It was better for the both of them that they remained as they were, simply friends—the best of friends. It was the only way to ensure Michael's safety. Though she still ached inside, Emily managed a faint smile and replied as lightly as she could, "You mustn't feel badly about not loving me, Michael. Truth be told, I am glad you cannot. Since I am unable to love you, what with my curse and all, I would feel ever so dreadful if you loved me and I could never love you back."

"I never said that I do not love you—I do, damn it! I love you with every fiber of my worthless being." He more spat than uttered the words, his voice raw and his eyes glittering with savage emotion. "When I said that I *cannot* love you, I meant love in the physical sense."

Emily's jaw dropped, her mind reeling at his revelation. He loved her . . . her! The knowledge made her giddy with delight. Oh, she knew that she should be distressed, that in accepting his love she risked loving him back and invoking the disaster that always followed in the wake of such an advent, but at the moment she simply couldn't help herself. What woman wouldn't be thrilled to be loved by Michael?

"Damn it, Emily. Did you hear what I said?" he

growled, the anger in his voice piercing her thoughts like a blade.

She frowned, bewildered by his wrath. "Of course I heard you. You said that you love me."

He emitted a frustrated noise. "I also informed you that I am unable to make love to you, which means that I most probably shall never be able to give you the children you so desire."

For several moments she merely stared at him, struck speechless as the meaning of his words began to sink in, then she somehow managed to force out a squeaky, "I see."

"Do you?" he demanded, his face hard and etched with fury.

She nodded vigorously several times, then paused with a sigh and slowly shook her head. "No. I, mean, I am not certain. I—I—" she shook her head twice more, then blurted out, "I do not understand why you are so angry with me. Did I do something to cause your—your problem?"

It was his turn to be struck speechless, his turn to shake his head. "No, oh no! Emily, my love, I am not angry with you," he exclaimed hoarsely, shaking his head yet again. "I am furious with myself because I married you knowing full well that I couldn't make love. Selfish bastard that I am, I never gave a thought to you or how my inability might affect your life. Truth be told, I didn't care. All I cared about was escaping Bamforth." He met her gaze then, his eyes anguished and his voice fraying as he finished, "Had I known how wonderful you are . . . how much I would love you . . . I . . ." His voice gave out then, leaving him shaking his head over and over again, his eyes nakedly begging for the forgiveness his voice hadn't the strength to petition.

Seeing him like that, so humble and vulnerable, his pain radiating from him in palpable waves, made her heart bleed for him. Heedless of everything but her own urgent need to reassure him, she reached over and pulled his tense form into her embrace. Cupping the back of his head in her hand to guide it to her shoulder, she crooned, "There now, Michael. It is all right. Everything will be fine, you shall see." Threading her fingers through his thick, wavy hair, which felt every bit as lovely as it looked, she began gently combing through it in the manner that never failed to calm and soothe her nieces and nephews.

His body remained rigid for several moments, then relaxed by degrees, finally melting against her with a sigh. Emily smiled faintly as he nuzzled his face against the side of her neck, liking the sensation. "I truly am sorry, Emily," he murmured against her neck. "I know how much you desire children. This must be a terrible blow to you."

Truth be told, it was. There was nothing she would have loved more than bearing Michael's children. Indeed, it was her fondest dream, one that reigned even above her desire to fly. That she would never get the chance to carry his babes in her womb, to hold them in her arms, or see Michael's smile when he joined them in their games made her feel achy and hollow inside.

Her throat suddenly dry and fiery from her grief, she huskily replied, "I would be lying if I said that I wasn't disappointed. I want your children, very much. In fact, I want them so badly that I sometimes lie awake at night imagining what they would look like, hoping that they would have your lovely jade eyes and beautiful smile. But"—she emphasized the word—"given the choice between leaving you and having another man's children, or staying with you and remaining childless, I would choose you without hesitation."

He shifted his head to the very edge of her shoulder, tipping it so that he could gaze up into her face. "You would?" he whispered, looking genuinely surprised.

She nodded, smiling tenderly as she smoothed his rumpled hair. "Yes, I would, because you mean more to me than a dozen children by another man."

"Do you really mean it?" he inquired, his brow furrowing as he lifted his head to search her eyes.

She returned his probing gaze steadily, without hesitation, knowing that he would find nothing in her eyes but confirmation of her words. "Yes, Michael. I do."

After a moment or two, his brow cleared and he concluded, "Yes, you do," the warmth of his voice echoed by his sudden, arresting smile. Gazing at her as if she were the moon and the stars and every precious thing on earth, he lifted his face until it was only scant inches from hers. Gently cradling her cheek in his palm, his jade eyes smoldering with tenderness and passion, he trapped her gaze with his, fervently declaring, "I love you, Emily. Dear God, how I love you!"

Caught up in the dark spell of his compelling gaze, she whispered back, "I love you too, Michael." The instant she realized what she'd said, she jerked away from him, gasping her horror. The words had sprung from her heart. She truly did love him.

Chapter 15

He would put an end to this bloody nonsense once and for all. Michael stalked down Windgate's gloomy, Gothic-style hallway, muttering darkly to himself. For two insufferably long, frustrating weeks, ever since the rainy day in the old nursery when they had confessed their love for each other, Emily had avoided him like the plague she thought she was, dodging him and leading him on a not-so-merry chase through the vast abbey and its acres of grounds, a chase in which he had yet to so much as glimpse his quarry. Well, enough was enough! He would be damned if he was going to do without her company for another day.

Clenching his jaw so hard that his teeth hurt, he began climbing the grand tracery staircase at the end of the hall, determined to surprise his exasperating wife in her chamber. So what if it was only six in the morning and he would intrude upon her morning toilet? He missed her, damn it. Life without her gay company was wretched, like being shut away in a prison cell devoid of all light, warmth, and sustenance.

Oh, true, to be perfectly fair he couldn't accuse her of abandoning him completely. She had kept Eadon supplied with the calamint decoction she'd insisted he drink every day, and she still planned his menus. The meals from those menus, however, delicious though they were, failed to pique either his appetite or his interest when served without the accompaniment of Emily's lovely smile and merry conversation. Indeed, so poor had his appetite been of late that the Swann sisters had stormed into the dining room the evening before, demanding an explanation as to why their lovingly prepared meals were being sent back to the kitchen virtually untouched.

Michael shook his head as he stepped onto the second-floor landing and started down the long Jacobean hall, shamed by the memory of the scene and the despicable way in which he'd handled it. His lack of appetite aside, Emily's absence had impacted him in a hundred less-than-agreeable ways, the worst effect being on his disposition. To his chagrin, just about everything anyone said or did these days made him erupt into an outburst of fractious annoyance, in spite of his best efforts to remain even-tempered and patient.

Why, he'd practically growled in response to the Swann sisters' well-intentioned interrogation, rudely reminding them of their station and the fact that as servants they had no right whatsoever to question anything he, their master, chose to say or do. Of course, he'd felt dreadful afterward and had gone to the kitchen to humbly beg their pardon. And of course they had granted it, after which they had sat him at the stout kitchen table as they had done when he was a child, petting and clucking over him while they made him his favorite boyhood treat, a cinnamon baked apple. Though he'd found the delicacy anything but appetizing at that moment, he'd obediently eaten every last bite of it in penitence for his bad conduct.

And then there was the way he had treated poor Eadon of late. As if his brief incident with the Swann sisters wasn't disgraceful enough, the way he constantly snapped and growled at Eadon was nothing short of contemptible. Truth be told, it was a wonder that the man hadn't bled him dry or left the abbey in a huff, so foul had Michael's temper been. As for Eadon's treatments, well, they had become almost intolerable. Not only did the cursed things seem to hurt ten times worse than they had before, they felt as if they dragged on for an eternity now that he was no longer able to look forward to a pleasurable afternoon with Emily. And while he was on the subject of his afternoons, he couldn't say enough about the grievous effect Emily's absence had had on them. Like his treatments, they, too, seemed to stretch on forever, now creeping by in loneliness and frustration as he fruitlessly searched the house and grounds for her, determined to talk some sense into her superstition-stuffed head.

For what most certainly was the thousandth time since the incident in the nursery, Michael cursed the immense size of the abbey. The blasted thing had well over a hundred rooms, not to mention its numerous outbuildings and acres of grounds, which made it impossible to find a person if they truly wished to remain hidden. As for the staff helping in his quest to find his elusive wife, well, they were worse than she when it came to superstitious rot. Apparently Emily had told Mercy about the curse, who in turn had carried the tale to the servants' hall, the result of which had been the staff denying knowledge of their mistress's whereabouts whenever he asked them, clearly believing that they were protecting him by keeping him from his wife's potentially harmful presence.

To say that the situation was maddening was putting his feelings about the debacle mildly. Muttering a string of particularly foul curses that expressed them to perfection, Michael turned from the Jacobean hallway down the adjoining baroque corridor with its magnificent arabesque-figured wainscot walls, stopping before the door to Emily's suite of rooms.

Rather than knocking politely, as he had done on the other dozen or so occasions he had come here over the past two weeks, he wrathfully flung open the door with a force that slammed it into the abutting wall. Bellowing Emily's name, he stalked into her pleasant, if rather gaudy blue and gold sitting room, pausing in the center to glare about him.

Though his wife was nowhere in sight, it was apparent that she had been there recently, judging from the remains of her breakfast on the small table near the fireplace. Wanting to know exactly how recently, he strode to the table and laid his hand against the dainty pink and white porcelain teapot, testing it for heat. It was still warm, giving evidence to the fact that she had broken her fast within the past half-hour.

He smiled. If Emily was like every other woman he'd ever known, she breakfasted first, then dawdled over her toilet for an hour or so, which meant that she was most probably in her dressing room primping and powdering now. Feeling victory close at hand, he continued across the room to the door to her bedchamber, which he tossed open without ceremony. As he marched through the room, he noted several more clues that supported his theory.

The fire, which was doing an admirable job of keeping the late October chill at bay, looked freshly kindled, and the bed was still unmade, both signs that Emily had risen only a short while earlier. Then there was the red, white, and green patterned cashmere dressing gown draped over the chair before the hearth. If Mercy Mildon performed her duties anything like Eadon and his former valet conducted theirs, she was warming the garment for when her mistress stepped out of her bath.

Michael smiled again, this time in triumph. If Emily were indeed in her bath, which he strongly suspected she was, then he had her trapped. There was no way she could flee clad only in a wet bathing shift . . . provided that she wore one at all. Some women he knew had given up the modest practice of bathing in a thin linen chemise, deciding the convention to be uncomfortable and inconvenient. Was Emily such a woman?

Despite his attempt to ignore the provocative question, the lush image of Emily gloriously naked, her silken skin flushed from the heat of her bath and her body beaded with perfumed moisture, burst into his mind, making his groin wrench with a force that brought tears to his eyes. The intensity of his response gave him pause in his purpose.

What if he tossed open the dressing room door, which was several feet from where he now stood frozen, and found her exactly as he envisioned her? Considering how long it had been since he'd had any sort of sexual release, his body's response to the sight was bound to be

violent . . . perhaps even disastrous. Indeed, his doctors
in London had warned him that the high level of excitement provoked by a sensual encounter would most probably bring on a fit, which was the last thing in the world
he wanted to happen in front of Emily.

Still, what choice did he have but to risk it? It could be
a very long while before he was presented with another
opportunity to confront her. Besides, knowing his wife
and her irrational fear of the curse, she might just take
it into her head to leave the abbey altogether in a misguided attempt to protect him, and then where would
he be?

He didn't have to think to know the answer to that
question. His life would be worse than it had been before
she'd arrived, far worse. Having experienced the paradise
of Emily's love and the heaven that came from loving her
back made the notion of life without her unbearable . . .
hardly worth living.

It was the terrible, crushing sensation of loss that possessed him in the wake of that awful thought that made
him stride purposefully to the dressing room door, unmindful of everything but his need to keep Emily in his
life. If he suffered a fit from his lust at the sight of her,
then so be it. Better to risk having her turn from him in
repulsion and know that he'd at least tried to keep her,
than to let her go without a fight.

Clenching his teeth in preparation for the consequences of his bold action, Michael flung open the door,
averting his gaze from the interior of the room as he
gritted out, "Damn it, Emily. I will speak to you and I
intend to do so this instant."

"Yer grace!" he heard Mercy squeal, followed by a
sound he easily identified as the whisper of silk. Nothing
else. There was no startled gasp from Emily, no frantic
splash as she sought to hide her nakedness beneath the
bath water. Just silence.

His eyebrows drawing together in his mystification, Michael glanced in the direction from which Mercy's voice
had come. She stood before the cheval mirror with an
extravagantly plumed court headdress perched atop her

frizzy copper hair, her freckled face flushed the color of
a ripe tomato. At her feet, in a frothy heap of pale blue
silk and crystal-embellished tulle, lay an exquisite ball
gown, leaving little doubt as to the sort of activity in
which she'd been engaged.

Not that Michael cared. Ignoring the servant's transgression, he glanced quickly around the room, his brief
surge of triumph transmuting into frustrated rage as he
realized that he'd again been outmaneuvered by his wife.
She was gone, damn it, though as in the sitting room and
bedchamber, there was ample evidence of her recent
departure.

After several tension-charged moments, during which
he frowned at the floral-painted wooden bathtub, which
still contained water that smelled strongly of French vio-
lets, he looked back at Mercy. She returned his gaze
sheepishly, clearly expecting a dressing-down for pranc-
ing about in her mistress's finery. Her expression of guilt-
stricken misery served only to further annoy him, making
his voice uncharacteristically harsh as he demanded,
"Where the devil is she?"

"W-who, yer g-grace?" the maid stammered, nervously
plucking the headdress from her head.

"You know perfectly well who I mean, damn it," he
shot back, gracing her with a scowl meant to intimidate.

She visibly quelled beneath his rare show of ire.
"B-but yer grace. I—"

"My wife, Mercy. Where the hell is my wife?"

"Out—Out, yer grace. She's out," she muttered, scoop-
ing up the gown she'd dropped in her startlement.

"Out where?" As she opened her mouth to respond,
he irritably warned, "And do not bother trying to tell
me that you don't know where she has gone. From what
I hear, you know everything about everyone from here
to Princetown."

Mercy shook her head, clutching the gown before her
as if it were a shield to protect her from his wrath. "Beggin' yer pardon, yer grace, but I canna tell ye. Not with
the curse. It's fer yer own good."

He advanced a step toward her, fixing her with the icy

glare that had never failed to daunt on the few occasions he'd been forced to employ it. "You are my wife's maid, not my keeper," he informed her in a cold, clipped voice. "As such, it is none of your affair what I do, when, and with whom I choose to do it. It most certainly isn't your place to decide what is best for me."

He paused a deliberate beat, letting the tension mount before curtly adding, "Since you have obviously forgotten your place, Miss Mildon, let me remind you that I am the lord of Windgate Abbey and that you are in my employ. As your master, I demand utter loyalty from you, which means that I expect you to have faith in my judgment in all matters and to abide by my decisions . . . even those with which you disagree. And my decision in this matter is to say to hell with the curse." He took another step forward. "Now where is my wife?"

She mulishly shook her head again. "I'm sorry, yer grace, but I canna tell you. I'd never be able to fergive myself if I told ye and somethin' untoward happened to ye."

Michael had to admire her dedication to him, though at the moment he wished that she was a bit more alarmed by his anger and a little less concerned about his welfare. He heaved an inward sigh. Ah well. Given the choice, he supposed that he would rather be cherished by his staff and suffer the overprotectiveness their affection fostered, than have them hop to his every command and secretly despise him.

After staring at the insubordinate servant for several more moments, wondering what to do next, he decided that a change of tactics was in order. Quickly formulating a plan, he nodded and countered in a reasonable voice, "Very well then, Mercy. If you will not tell me, then I see no choice but to stay here and await her return. Since I cannot risk you warning her of my trap, you must remain with me."

"But yer grace, she'll probably be gone all day," the maid objected, looking none too thrilled with the notion of having him underfoot. "Ye canna really mean to waste yer entire day sittin' around here?"

"My day shan't be wasted in the least, I assure you,"
Michael replied pleasantly. "Neither shall yours, for I
intend to use the time observing you at your duties and
evaluating your performance. I shall, naturally, correct
you as I see fit. My first correction is to insist that you
cease in mooning over my wife's frippery and do something about the state of this room. It is a disgrace." It
was a lie, of course. Everything was in as admirable an
order as one could expect at that hour of the morning.

Nodding to underscore his critique, he marched to the
satinwood tallboy against the opposing wall. After nig-
gling over the organization of the garments in all six
scrupulously tidy drawers and demanding an improvement, he moved to the dressing table where he pointed
out a single ebony hair in Emily's ivory brush. Lecturing
the maid at length on the importance of cleanness and
order, he went on to impugn the placement of the neatly
grouped bottles, jars, and boxes on the table, assuming
the air of a drill master as he tendered precise instructions for their rearrangement. From there he migrated
to the armoire, criticizing everything from the positioning
of the hat and band boxes, to the way the gowns were
categorized and hung.

When he had thoroughly inspected the room and pretended to find fault with everything he saw, he plopped
down on the small needlework-upholstered settee near
the bathtub, making a show of lounging on it by propping
his head up on one arm and draping his long legs over
the other. With a lordly wave of his hand, he commanded, "Well, do proceed. As I have pointed out, you
have a great deal of work to do in order to meet with my
exacting standards. When you have completed everything
here to my satisfaction, we will examine the bedchamber.
From what I have seen of it, it is in as dire need of
attention as this room. From there we will move to the
sitting room."

"Then ye really mean to stay here all day?" As he'd
hoped, Mercy looked far more alarmed by that prospect
than she had by his display of wrath.

Taking pains to hide his satisfaction, he languidly

shrugged one shoulder. "Since I do not have my wife's company to keep me occupied and I have nothing else to do today, yes. I might as well put my time to good use by making certain that you are serving her grace in an acceptable manner."

To Mercy's credit, she managed to withstand his pecking for close to an hour before finally crumbling. Having refolded Emily's chemises a half-dozen times, with Michael finding fault each time and instructing her to redo them, she abruptly blurted out, "The stables, yer grace. Her grace went to the stables."

"The . . . stables?" he echoed, frowning. As far as he knew, Emily never rode unless she was absolutely required to do so. Indeed, by her own admission she was a less than accomplished horsewoman. Eyeing the maid suspiciously, he shifted from his lounging position into a sitting one, quizzing, "What the devil is she doing in the stables? She has never visited them before."

Mercy nervously twisted the chemise she held, shaking her head. "I don't know, yer grace, I swear I don't. I just overheard her tellin' Mr. Grimshaw that she was goin' to the stables and to have Mr. Eadon meet her there."

"Indeed?"

Though the utterance was addressed more to himself than to Mercy, the maid gestured helplessly in response. " 'Tis all I know. I swear," she exclaimed earnestly, shaking her head so hard that a wiry coil of hair sprang from the neat knot at her neck and tendriled down her back.

Michael nodded once. "I believe you, Mercy."

"Then ye'll be goin', yer grace?" She couldn't have looked more hopeful.

He nodded again and rose to his feet. "I believe I shall, yes. And thank you, Mercy."

She seemed to sag with relief. "Yer welcome, yer grace, though I doubt ye'll be thankin' me if the curse is as wicked as her grace claims. Ye will be careful, won't ye?" This last was tinged with a note of anxiety.

Michael smiled faintly and nodded again, then strolled

to the door. He waited until he stood on the threshold before saying, "About the rooms, Mercy?"

"Yer grace?" she tensely responded, clearly expecting more criticism.

"Now that I really look at them, it seems that I was wrong in my initial evaluation. They appear in excellent order. That being the case, you have my permission to take the rest of the morning off." With that, he was on his way to the stables.

Or so he thought. He had hastened downstairs and had just paused before the front door to button his woolen greatcoat, which he'd had the presence of mind to have a footman fetch for him, when Grimshaw came rushing into the entry hall in a visibly flustered state. When the majordomo saw him standing there, a look of profound relief swept across his face. "Your grace, thank goodness," he exclaimed urgently. "I have been looking everywhere for you."

Michael shot him an irritated look, certain that he was about to be detained. "What is it, Grimshaw?" he inquired, not even bothering to try to mask his impatience.

The majordomo bowed. "A visitor, your grace."

"A what?" He more roared than uttered the words in his surprise.

"A visitor," Grimshaw repeated with a faint smile. "Coming up the drive as we speak, I might add."

Michael's brows drew together in displeasure at the news. "Who the hell would be visiting me, especially at this ungodly hour? Everyone knows that I do not receive visitors."

"Be that as it may, your grace, I believe that this is one visitor you will wish to welcome," the servant cryptically replied.

"I doubt it," he muttered beneath his breath. Repenting his irascibility in the next instant, he heaved a long-suffering sigh and added, "Well, out with it then, Grimshaw. Who is it?"

"A surprise, your grace."

A surprise? Oh, bloody hell! He was close, so very, very close to finally catching Emily, and now this.

Though he was sorely tempted to escape through the kitchen door, to avoid being further delayed in his quest, his lifelong commitment to courtesy arrested him from doing so. Seeing no choice but to play the gracious host, Michael nodded and said in a resigned voice, "Fine. I shall go outside now and greet my surprise mystery guest."

"Very good, your grace," Grimshaw intoned, advancing forward to open the door.

As the majordomo did his duty, Michael finished buttoning his coat and drew on his gloves. Pasting a stiff smile on his lips, he stepped outside. The sight of his visitor froze him in his tracks.

There on the drive at the foot of the front steps was the magnificent chestnut Akhal Teké stallion he had purchased from a Russian duke four years earlier . . . Shurik, his favorite horse . . . the one he had been too pained to look at in the aftermath of his illness, realizing that he would most probably never be able to ride it again . . . the very animal he'd banished to his breeding stable at his estate in Shropshire, a vast, luxurious building set far enough from the main house that it would be impossible for him to accidentally see the beast and suffer the anguish the mere sight of it caused him.

It was the exact same anguish he suffered now as he stood staring at the steed with bittersweet longing, yearning to feel its power beneath him, his soul crying out for the exhilarating thrill of freedom he'd never failed to experience as he'd raced about the English countryside on its mighty back.

Hating the sensation and infuriated that he should be forced to feel it, Michael gritted his teeth, glaring first at Howard, his master of the horse at Shropshire, who had clearly brought the animal to Dartmoor and now held its bridle, then at Eadon, who stood beside him with his hands behind his back, grinning like a lunatic. Wishing that he could thrash them both within an inch of their lives for being party to such a cruel joke, he marched down the stairs, growling, "What the hell is that animal doing here? I gave no orders for it to be brought here."

Howard, a short, husky man whose sun-seamed face made him appear much older than his forty years, sketched a brief bow and courteously replied, "Your wife requested it brought, your grace."

"My . . . wife?" Michael repeated in astonishment, wondering what could have possessed Emily to do such a thing.

As if reading his mind, Eadon chimed in, "I believe she is under the impression that you wish to ride it again, your grace."

"Rubbish!" He more snorted than uttered the word in his incredulity. "Her grace is perfectly aware of the fact that I am no longer able to ride, as are you, Eadon." He paused to shoot the man a resentful look. "She must have sent for the beast with some other purpose in mind."

"No, I can assure you that she had it brought for you," Eadon countered with a nod. "Of course, sending for the horse is only half of her surprise. This is the other half." He brought his hand from behind his back with a flourish, brandishing what appeared to be one of the old parade helmets from the armory, which had been stripped of its decoration and painted black.

Michael stared first at Eadon, then at the helmet, not quite certain what to make of either. Finally he shook his head. "I do not understand any of this."

"If you will look closely at the helmet, you will see that it is padded inside," Eadon replied, handing him the article in question for his inspection. "Her grace did the work herself. As you can see, she did a splendid job of it."

Michael took the helmet, turning it over to examine its lining. It was made of supple black leather, beneath which was sewn some sort of thick padding. Looking up again, this time with a frown, he quizzed, "So?"

"So, it will protect your head should you take a spill from your horse," Eadon replied, resuming his earlier grin. "It was her grace's idea, and a very fine one indeed. I wonder that we didn't think of it ourselves."

For several moments Michael simply gaped at the

other man, certain that he'd misread the meaning of his words. Almost afraid to ask, unwilling to crush the hope bubbling in his chest, he finally forced himself to utter, "Are you saying that it is safe for me to ride if I wear this?" He indicated the helmet.

Eadon nodded. "Provided that you do so at a sedate pace and refrain from jumping fences, yes."

Again Michael was reduced to staring, unable to respond for the fierceness of his joy. After a beat or two, during which his lips slowly split into an ecstatic grin, he threw back his head and shouted his happiness. He could—and he would!—ride again. Emily had made it possible. His darling, wonderful Emily. In her love for him she had found a way to give him the bit of heaven on earth she'd promised him. More anxious than ever to find her, wanting to sweep her into his arms and hold her tight as he fervently thanked her for her miraculous gift and declared his love, he urgently inquired, "Where is my wife now?"

Eadon, who shared Michael's opinion of the curse, promptly replied, "Her grace and Isaac set out on the moor a short while ago. She mentioned something about someone named Rebecca and an appointment to collect nettle."

"Did she indeed?" Michael murmured, trying on his gift. It was a bit heavy, but not uncomfortably so.

"Yes, your grace. Should you, by chance, wish to follow her, I believe that Bennie, the coachman's son, has accompanied her and Isaac to this Rebecca person's cottage on several occasions. No doubt he shall be able to guide you."

"In that instance, please ask Bennie to saddle his pony. My first ride shall be to Rebecca's cottage. It is high time I made the woman's acquaintance."

Chapter 16

Bliss, it was pure bliss to ride again. For what had to be the ten-thousandth time in the past half-hour, Michael grinned his pleasure. Indeed, he'd smiled so much that the muscles in his cheeks had begun to ache from overuse . . . not that that was going to stop him from continuing to smile. It was a good sort of ache, as was the one in his thighs and backside, the flesh of which had become tender after his lengthy absence from the saddle.

Not caring that his hindquarters would most probably hurt like the devil come evening, Michael glanced about him with a profound sense of contentment, euphorically drinking in the splendid sights and fresh, earthy smells of Dartmoor in autumn. He hadn't ventured this far out here since he was a boy, and he had forgotten how glorious the moors were at this time of year.

Like all of England in October, the moors were marked by the advancing age of the year. Its herbage and turf, so verdant during their infancy in the spring, were now streaked with hoary fingers of amber and bronze, touched here and there with a stubbornly youthful splash of bright pink campion, purple woundwort, white shepherd's purse, and the inevitable swirls of yellow gorse. Even the moss clinging to the ancient stones had begun to mature with the season, fading from a soft, downy green to a velvety, muted gray. In the distance, bleeding through the haze of the lingering morning mist, were the blurry outlines of several copses of trees, their autumn-dyed hues appearing washed together behind the swirling vapors, like a watercolor landscape left out in the rain.

The grandeur of the sight filled Michael with the intoxicating thrill of simply being alive, spawning a sense of well-being that he hadn't experienced in a very long while. He was happy, genuinely happy. And why shouldn't he be? Not only was his body sounder than it had been in over two years, his spirits were soaring and his life now had meaning. Best of all, he was in love with Emily.

As always happened of late when he thought of his beautiful wife, Michael was consumed by a fierce, almost desperate urge to take her in his arms and tell her how much he adored her. Plagued by the impulse now, he looked over to Bennie, who rode beside him on a sturdy black Dartmoor pony, and asked, "How much further to the cottage?"

"Just o'er that knoll, yer grace." The boy pointed a finger encased in a red knitted mitten at the tawny hill in the near distance. "The cottage is in the dale below it."

Eadon, who rode on Michael's other side, having insisted on coming along to make certain that his patient didn't overexert himself, anxiously inquired for the tenth time since they had begun their pilgrimage, "Are you feeling quite all right, your grace?"

"Never better. I am just eager to see my wife," he replied, feeling an uncharacteristic surge of fondness for the man. In all fairness, the fellow really was rather agreeable when he wasn't inflicting his nasty treatments on him.

"I like her grace," Bennie shyly volunteered, the wind-whipped ruddiness of his round cheeks darkening a shade as he uttered the words. Up until now the boy had spoken only when spoken to, clearly awed at being in the company of the powerful duke of Sherrington. Now gazing at Michael with serious blue eyes, he added, "She's pretty and she knows how to do just 'bout everything. I'm glad ye married her, yer grace. Everyone at Windgate is."

"Not nearly as glad as I am, Bennie," Michael returned with a chuckle. "And I must admit that I rather like her too."

"As do I," Eadon surprised him by contributing. "Her grace is exactly what you have needed all along. Indeed, you are doing so splendidly under her care that I shan't be at all surprised if you cease to require my services someday soon."

"Well, I wouldn't be looking for a new position quite yet if I were you," Michael cautioned him grimly. "Unless we can settle this blasted curse nonsense once and for all, I shan't be the recipient of any more of her coddling. But then, I need not tell you that." He shook his head with an exasperated sigh. "You know how she's been behaving these past two weeks."

Eadon nodded. "I do, and I must say that I am surprised. Her grace has always struck me as a woman of rare good sense. Who would have guessed that she is inclined toward superstition?"

"You do not know the half of it," Michael muttered, sighing again.

"Well, I believe in the curse. If her grace says there's a curse, then there must be a curse," Bennie piped in, loyally defending his adored mistress. "A fine lady like her grace wouldn't make up something like that. Everyone at the abbey says so."

Michael was perfectly aware of the boy's views, having wasted close to a half-hour unsuccessfully trying to coax him into guiding him to the cottage. It was only after Eadon had used the boy's own faith in Rebecca Dare's magical powers to convince him that the woman would keep Michael safe while in her presence that Bennie had finally relented. Reminded now of the boy's belief in mumbo-jumbo and deciding it high time that someone talked some sense into him, Michael opened his mouth to gently argue against the probability of the curse being real. Before he could utter the words, however, Bennie pointed again and exclaimed, "There 'tis, Miss Dare's cottage."

One glance down in the valley below them and Michael forgot all about his lecture. The cottage was enchanting, exactly as Emily had described it. Indeed, so fanciful did it appear with its fairy story facade and unseasonably bright garden, that he was almost inclined to believe that the place was truly magic. Why, just look at the way—

Neigh! Whinny! Michael's horse abruptly reared, almost unseating its rider, shying as a plump brown hare streaked by.

"Careful there, your grace," Eadon shouted, struggling to subdue his own startled mount.

With a mastery born from years of experience, Michael deftly calmed his agitated steed, alternately speaking to it and making soothing noises as he firmly but gently manipulated the reins. When the beast stood perfectly subdued, he took one more lingering look at the breathtaking panorama below, then nodded to Bennie to lead the way down the steep incline into the valley. As he skillfully guided his horse, keeping a sharp eye out for the hare, which had dashed in this direction, he couldn't help noticing that, like Rebecca's garden, the showy display of flora vegetating the slope, too, seemed curiously out of season.

Why, if he wasn't mistaken that was a clump of Lent lilies, or daffodils, as some called them, which everyone knew bloomed in March or April. And weren't those primroses, those pink flowers with five dainty petals? They were. Michael frowned his consternation. How very queer. He couldn't recall ever seeing primroses past May and most certainly not on the moors. And then there were those flowers over there . . . good heavens! Were those bluebells? In late October?

Michael's mind was furiously trying to rationalize what he was seeing and he had just decided that the fantastical plant phenomenon was most probably due to the positioning of the hills and the protection they afforded the valley, when he reached the brook that wound lazily past the front of the cottage. Bennie, whose surefooted native pony had practically flown down the hill, had already dismounted and now stood beside the animal, which placidly grazed on a tall patch of grass.

Smiling in a way that revealed the nubbin of a newly forming front tooth, Bennie informed him, "Ye'll need to leave yer horse here, yer grace. Magellan doesn't like horses."

"Magellan, the goat?" Michael quizzed, swinging from his saddle.

"Oh, he only looks like a goat. He's really a Spanish prince."

Michael shot the boy a sharp glance. "A what?" he ejected. Surely Bennie hadn't really said that the goat was a *prince*?

"A Spanish prince," the boy confirmed, solemnly nodding his flaxen head. "Everyone knows 'tis so, just as they know that fairies dona like it when mortal men trifle with their maidens. Too bad Prince Magellan didn't know it before he seduced six o' their princesses."

Michael drew back slightly, frowning his incredulity. "Six *fairy* princesses, you say?" The goat had quite a reputation, it seemed . . . one that grew more ludicrous with every passing day.

"That's right. Six." Bennie shrugged, clearly unperturbed by Michael's skeptical tone. "Guess he had a way with the ladies."

So innocent and filled with the simple but precious logic of youth was the response, that Michael bit back his cynical retort, suddenly loath to shatter the boy's blissful belief in enchantment. As Emily had said, childhood was a wonderful, magical time to be cherished by child and adult alike. Remembering the fire in her eyes and the way her silken cheeks had flamed in her indignation as she'd uttered the words, he smiled gently and agreed, "Quite a way, it would seem."

"Your grace! Is something amiss?" called Eadon, who had descended the ·hill at a more cautious pace than his companions.

Michael glanced up as the man reined his gelding to a stop next to Bennie's pony, his face marked by worry. "No, no, Eadon. Everything is fine. I stopped because Bennie has informed me that we must leave our mounts here. It seems that Miss Dare's—er—goat"—he shot a droll look at Bennie, who giggled—"takes exception to horses."

Always the model of propriety, Eadon accepted the queer decree without question. "Very good, your grace. In that instance, Bennie and I shall tend to the animals while you speak with your lady."

Nodding his thanks, Michael resumed his trek to the cottage. When he hesitated on the bank of the placid brook, eyeing the slippery-looking moss-slimed stepping stones with misgiving, Bennie came to his side, saying, "We all hop across on the stones, even Magellan. It's easier 'n it looks."

"Magellan?" Eadon inquired politely as he joined them.

Michael and Bennie exchanged a mischievous glance, then grinned at him in unison. "I believe that Bennie is better equipped to explain about Magellan," Michael replied, winking at the boy. With that, he gritted his teeth and leapt to the first stone. If the goat could cross without incident, by St. George, so could he. And he did. It took him only a moment to cross the stream and make his way up to the flower-framed stoop of the cottage. He had just raised his hand to knock on the bright red door when—

"*A-a-a!*" There was a belligerent-sounding bleat from behind him. Certain that he was about to make the acquaintance of the infamous Magellan, Michael slowly turned. It was indeed a goat, an enormous gray one, and it was currently positioned directly at his back, eyeing him with evil intent.

"Magellan?" he ventured, narrowing his eyes in a rush of wariness.

"*A-a-a-a! A-a-a!*" the animal responded, lowering its curly-horned head in a way that could only bode ill.

From behind him Michael heard the door open. In the next instant an exquisitely modulated female voice scolded, "Really, Magellan! Wherever are your manners? That is hardly an appropriate way to greet a guest."

Unwilling to turn his back on the goat, who in his opinion was either demented or possessed by a diabolical being, Michael glanced over his shoulder to put a face with the voice.

The face he saw perfectly matched the voice. The woman was beautiful—not as lovely as Emily, of course, since even the angels in heaven would suffer in comparison to Emily in his eyes—still, this young woman would most certainly cause a stir were she to make an appearance in the *ton*. "Ethereal" was the word that sprang to mind as he looked at her, the ideal inhabitant for this fairy story cottage that sat in this seemingly enchanted valley.

Darting his gaze back to the goat, who had again bleated and now seemed poised to butt him, he murmured, "Miss Dare, I presume?"

"Indeed I am, your grace. Welcome to Greenwicket cottage."

He glanced back at her in time to see her drop into a regal court curtsy. That action, paired with her refined looks and decidedly cultured voice, made him wonder at her origins. So much so, that had he dared to move, he would have bowed in response to her stately curtsy, sensing that it would be fitting to do so. Since, however, he feared that any action would further provoke the goat, he simply nodded and replied, "At your service, madam."

Smiling in a way that left little doubt as to his being truly welcome, she stepped aside and motioned for him to enter the cottage. "Please do come in, your grace. No doubt you are weary from your journey and could use some refreshment."

The goat let out a loud snort at her invitation, again commanding Michael's notice. At his glance the beast jerked its head, as if threatening to jab him in the backside with its wicked-looking horns. Certain that the vile creature would make good on its threat if he so much as twitched in the woman's direction, he remarked, "Er—I do not think that Magellan approves of me."

"Bah! Ignore him. He's just jealous," Rebecca scoffed, shooting the goat a pointed look of disapproval. "He likes being the only man about the place and feels threatened by your presence." Addressing the goat now, she added, "As for you, Magellan, you can stay outside and contemplate the wickedness of your ways."

"*A-a-a! A-a!*"

She frowned and shook her head. "Oh, no. We shall have none of that. Now off with you. I noticed some dandelions growing in with my orpine. Please do tend to the matter." As the goat trotted off, seemingly to do her bidding, making noises that sounded suspiciously like muttering as it went, Rebecca shifted her attention back to Michael. "Now please, do come in, your grace. It is hardly proper for a man of your stature to remain on the stoop."

Though Michael was sorely tempted to quiz her about the goat, confounded by the pair's queer interaction, he resisted doing so, embarrassed by his own absurd inclination to believe that the woman and the beast actually understood each other. Forcing himself to act casual, as if witnessing such oddness were an everyday event, Michael removed his helmet, which he still wore, and stepped over the threshold.

Like Rebecca herself, the interior of the cottage showed unmistakable evidence of gentility. Though the hallway into which he stepped was simple enough with its plain whitewashed walls and smooth stone-flagged floor, the richly carved settle that sat against the wall to his right was grand enough to grace a castle, as was the Oriental rug beneath his feet. And then there was the stunning ebony and brass—or was that gold leaf?—longcase clock regally positioned at the far end of the hall. It was the sort of luxury one usually saw only in the homes of the very wealthy.

After relieving him of his coat and the helmet, his hostess led the way down the hallway, from which he glimpsed a well-appointed parlor through an open doorway. Tossing him an apologetic look as she passed it, she said, "I do hope that you shan't be offended if I ask you to sit in the kitchen. I have bread in the oven which I do not wish to burn. With your permission, I will serve you refreshment in there."

"The kitchen is fine, though you needn't trouble your-

self with refreshment," he replied. "I came only to speak
with my wife. She is here, I was told?"

"She was here," Rebecca corrected. When he opened
his mouth to ask where she had gone, she quickly interjected, "But she will return shortly. She and Isaac are
out gathering nettle for the amulet she wishes to make.
The magical properties of nettle are most potent when
it is still sprinkled with the morning dew."

Magical nettle? Amulet? It was all Michael could do
to curb his impulse to groan aloud at the mention of yet
more superstitious twaddle. Fighting hard to keep his
exasperation from both his face and his voice, and reminding himself that the more he knew about Emily and
her beliefs, the better prepared he would be to reason
with her, he forced himself to ask, "What sort of an
amulet?"

"One to protect you from the curse, of course." She
stepped through the doorway to her right, leading him
into a sunny, spacious kitchen that smelled delightfully
of baking bread.

While Rebecca continued on across the room, Michael
stopped before the kitchen dresser, curiously examining
the wealth displayed upon its shelves. There were several
exquisitely wrought silver goblets and platters, all
stamped in gold with a family crest he vaguely recalled
seeing before; a pair of heavy silver candlesticks; a gilt
salt cellar adorned with what looked to be real rubies;
and a tea service that was delicately painted with scenes
of the Orient and had clearly been imported from China.
Struck anew by the casual display of prosperity in the
humble dwelling, he glanced up and resumed their conversation where it had left off. "Then Emily told you
about the curse?"

Rebecca, who stood peering into the brick bake oven
that was built into the wall beside the fireplace, nodded.
"Oh, yes. We have discussed it at length on numerous
occasions. I am surprised that she hasn't told you."

"You must understand, Miss Dare—"

"Rebecca, please," she quickly interjected, turning
from the oven with a smile.

Dare, of course, he thought, his memory jolted at having again uttered the name. He glanced back at the silver plates. Now he remembered where he had seen that crest. It was emblazoned on the side of Wreford's elegant town coach ... old Laurence Dare, the duke of Wreford. Turning from the dresser, he archly inquired, "I believe that I would not be amiss in addressing you as Lady Rebecca?" He indicated the plates.

She looked momentarily nonplussed, then laughed, a light, silvery sound, and moved to the fireplace, which was charmingly tiled with blue and white Delftware. Checking the contents of the kettle hanging over the low fire, she replied, "Only if we were in a ballroom, your grace. Here, I am just Rebecca. As you can see, I enjoy rusticating, and I find my title rather too grand for the simplicity of the life I have chosen to live."

Michael smiled. "I, too, prefer the country these days, which makes us kindred spirits, so please call me Michael." He could see why Emily was so fond of the woman. She was utterly without artiface, which made her quite comfortable to be around.

"Michael it is, then," she agreed, smiling back. "Now please do sit at the table and rest a bit, while I brew us a pot of tea. Emily will never forgive me if I do not take proper care of you in her absence. She loves you very much, you know."

"Yes, I do know," he acknowledged, sitting in one of the four Windsor chairs at the round oak table. "And I love her, too ... more than anything on this earth, which is why I asked if she had confided her concerns about the curse to you. Not that I, personally, believe in curses, mind you," he felt obligated to toss in. "However, since my wife does believe in them and is highly distressed over what she imagines to be her cursed state, I must naturally do everything in my power to ease her anxiety. You said something about a protective amulet?"

Rebecca, who had retrieved the Oriental teapot from the dresser and had carried it over to the massive corner cupboard near the door, nodded. "There is an amulet that can protect you from the curse, yes. Unfortunately, the protection is short-lived, usually no longer than a week. In this instance it will only last for five days, until midnight on Samhaine, or All Hallows' Eve, as many prefer to call it. At that time the curse must either be broken or you must part company forever."

Michael watched as Rebecca opened the cupboard and retrieved an elegant mahogany tea chest, his eyes narrowing as he digested the tidbit of information. "Then the curse can be lifted?"

"I believe so."

"And Emily is aware of the fact?"

"Of course." Tea chest and pot now in hand, she moved to a small worktable that stood near the fireplace. Setting her burden upon it, she added, "We have discussed the counterspell in great detail. She knows what must be done and—"

"Oh, Michael? No!" interjected Emily's wail from behind him. "What are you doing here?"

Michael jumped up at the sound of her voice, hungry for the sight of her. The vision he beheld left him breathless. She looked beautiful, so very beautiful standing in the doorway in her favorite crimson cloak. Her hair, which was loose, as he preferred it, cascaded from beneath her ruffled hood, tumbling over one shoulder in a riotous, windblown tangle of gypsy wild curls. The autumn chill had kissed her cheeks, flushing them a rich, silken scarlet; her dark eyes glowed with life and vigor, like black diamonds warmed by candlelight.

Willing himself to breathe in his stunned admiration, he huskily replied, "I came to see you, my love. I have missed you terribly."

She shrank back a fraction, shaking her head. "You shouldn't have come. I needn't tell you why."

"The curse?" He shrugged. "Even if it is real, which I sincerely doubt, it hardly seems worth worrying about, what with the counterspell and all."

"You know about the counterspell?" she gasped, visibly dismayed by the news.

His eyes narrowed at her response. "Well, yes. Rebecca was just telling me about it. She said—"

"Oh, Rebecca! How could you!" she cried, eyeing her friend with wounded reproach. "You know that I have absolutely no intention of trying to lift the curse."

It was Michael's turn to be dismayed. "What?"

She glanced back at him, shaking her head. "No, Michael. I shan't be attempting the counterspell. After thoroughly considering the matter, I have decided that it will be best for us both if I simply return to America." Looking away again, as if she could no longer bear the sight of him, she added in a tight voice, "If you must know, I came here today to have Rebecca help me make an amulet to protect you so that I could bid you a proper farewell."

Michael gaped at her, too devastated by her announcement to do more. She was leaving him. And not because of the curse. By her own admission, it could be lifted. She was leaving because she had finally come to her senses and had decided that she did not wish to spend her life tied to an invalid husband. What other explanation could there be?

None, he admitted to himself, afraid to breathe for fear that the sob he felt rising from his chest would escape. And while he was being so brutally honest with himself, he must also concede that he didn't blame her a whit for feeling as she did. How could he? She was so beautiful and vital. She deserved a husband who could love her the way she should be loved—one who could show her the raptures of the marriage bed and give her the children she so desperately desired.

Bitter that he could never be such a husband and hating the unknown man who would someday enjoy the pleasures he was unable to take, Michael suddenly wondered if it was his confession about his inability to make love, rather than his invalid state, that had prompted her decision to leave him.

The more he thought about it, the more likely it seemed. Though Emily had sounded genuine enough when she'd declared her love for him, he now suspected that the words had been false, that she had uttered them in order to use the curse as an excuse to escape him . . .

a theory that made perfect sense when one considered that her declaration had come on the heels of his damning confession. The notion that she, the woman who meant the world to him, had most probably never loved him was nothing short of devastating.

Wanting to scream his pain at her betrayal of his heart, to somehow hurt her as badly as she had just hurt him, yet suddenly too drained to do either, Michael wearily replied, "I see. You do not love me." The words came out in a harsh whisper, breaking in the rawness of his grief.

"No! Oh no, Michael. How ever can you think such a thing?" she exclaimed, her voice rising with each impassioned word. "Of course I love you. I never realized that it was possible to love a man as much as I love you."

"Then why? If you truly love me, why do you not wish to break the curse?" he hoarsely demanded, taking a step toward her.

She put out her hand, as if to halt his advance, shaking her head over and over again. "I do wish to break it . . . oh, Michael, my dearest love! I wish to break it more than anything in the world. And I would most certainly try to do so if it weren't so very dangerous. But if we were to attempt the counterspell and it failed—you—I—" She broke off with another series of head shakes, her eyes growing bright with unshed tears.

"What, Emily? What would happen if it failed that would be so dreadful?" he softly grilled.

"Y-you would be struck down, maybe even killed." There went her head again, frantically shaking. "Oh, Michael. I cannot—I will not!—risk you being harmed. I love you too much to imperil you in such a manner."

"And I love you enough to chance anything, even death, which is why I say damn the consequences," he retorted, his heartache easing at her declaration. What a fool he was! How could he have ever doubted her love? He should have guessed that she only sought to protect him.

"But—"

"No, Emily," he interjected firmly. "Since I am the

one at risk, the decision is mine to make. And I say that we will try the counterspell."

"B-but you do not understand." She shook her head several more times, her anguished gaze meeting his, desperately imploring.

He returned her gaze for a moment, then relented with a heavy sigh. How could he deny her anything when she looked at him with those bewitching brown eyes? "All right, then. Explain to me what I do not understand."

Emily continued to stare at him mutely for several more beats, now and again shaking her head, then she glanced over at Rebecca, clearly seeking her help. "Perhaps Rebecca should explain matters. She is far more knowledgeable about these things than I."

"Fine. Just as long as someone tells me what is going on," he retorted, nodding to Rebecca, who now stood before the oven, removing two golden brown loaves of bread with a wide, shovellike baker's peel.

"I shall be glad to explain as best I can," Rebecca replied, carefully transferring the bread to the worktable to cool. After pausing to rehang the wooden peel on its hook next to the oven, she added, "Since the explanation is bound to be a lengthy one, what with the questions I suspect you will wish to ask, I suggest that we sit and have a cup of tea. I set a pot of my special blend to steep during your exchange. It should be about ready to serve." Without awaiting their response, she carried the Oriental teapot to the round table, followed by three of the matching cups and saucers.

When she had added the finishing touches to her tea service—silver spoons, crisp linen napkins, a plate of walnut cake, the requisite sugar bowl, and a pitcher of fresh milk—Michael, always the gentleman, moved from where he stood in silent communication with Emily, to seat her. That done, he pulled out the chair beside her, glancing expectantly at Emily, who still hovered uncertainly in the doorway.

When she hesitated in joining them, Rebecca said, "This valley is enchanted, remember? It will protect your husband from the curse while he is here. So please, do sit, dear.''

To Michael's relief, Emily accepted her friend's word without question and did as requested, pausing only to hang her cloak on a hook near the door. With the women now properly settled, he claimed the chair to Emily's left, moving it near enough to hers to loop a possessive arm around her shoulders. Smiling in a way that he hoped would coax her to smile back, he gazed tenderly into his wife's troubled face, murmuring, "If you please, Rebecca?"

"As you wish," Rebecca returned, her words accompanied by the homely clatter of china and the faint splash of pouring tea. "I shall preface my explanation by saying that the spell itself is simple, though it does require some rather extensive preparation." There was a soft scrape of porcelain against wood as she set the pot down, then, "Would you care for milk or sugar in your tea, Michael?"

"Neither, thank you. Just tell me what needs to be done," he responded, his gaze never wavering from Emily's face. Though he had managed to make her smile, albeit faintly, her eyes remained shadowed by worry.

"As I said before, the spell must be worked on Samhaine night. So you must travel to Merrivale on Samhaine, to the circle of nine standing stones in the shape of giant maidens," Rebecca replied, her words underlined by the soft clank of silver against china as she stirred something into her own tea. "Within the circle lies a kistvaen upon which is inscribed mystical markings. You must use that as your altar. You will need—"

"What exactly is a kistvaen?" Michael interrupted, wanting to understand every detail, for Emily's sake.

"It is an ancient tomb. The one I am speaking of is the burial place of Deira, a powerful priestess who walked the earth well over a thousand years ago. Her spirit is said to have the power to break any curse, so it is to her that you must appeal."

"And how do we go about appealing to her?" Michael inquired, smiling his reassurance to Emily.

The color drained from her face. "Michael, no. Please, it is too dangerous."

"It will be fine, love. I promise," he pledged, nodding at Rebecca to indicate that she was to continue.

Rebecca remained silent for a beat, glancing from him to Emily and back again, then said, "It might be best if I tell of the consequences first. If you still wish to know the spell afterward, I shall be obligated to tell you." She transferred her gaze to Emily, her expression regretful. "I am sorry, Emily, truly I am, but I have no choice in the matter. As go-between, it is my sacred duty to help mortals right the wrong done to them by magic."

"Sounds fair enough to me," Michael agreed with another nod. "Please do proceed."

Rebecca nodded back. "Deira will accept your appeal only if your love for each other is true. When she looks deep inside of you both, which I promise you she will do, she must find nothing wanting in its nature. That means that your love must be utterly pure and untainted by the slightest hint of uncertainty, selfishness, mistrust, or duplicity. It must be the sort of love that encompasses not just your hearts, but your souls and every fiber of your beings. If she discovers anything at all that she deems unworthy, she will invoke the full wrath of the curse, and you, Michael, shall most probably be destroyed. If she judges your love true, she will banish the curse and you will be free to live and love in peace."

Michael took several moments to digest Rebecca's warning, his eyes slowly narrowing as he looked back at Emily. Viewing her with a slight frown, he quizzed, "Do you fear the counterspell because you doubt my love, or your own?"

There went her head again, shaking. "I love you, Michael. I have no doubt about that. Indeed, if it were I who risked being destroyed, I would gladly stand before Deira and beg for her judgment."

His frown deepened at her response. "Ah, I see. Then you doubt my love for you."

"No! Oh no, Michael, never!" She shook her head so violently that her curls danced. "I have never felt so loved as I do when I am with you. You make me feel safe and warm and cherished. It is just the notion that—

that—" A ragged sob escaped her. "Oh, Michael. I simply could not live for the pain if something were to happen to you."

"And I could not live without you in my life," he countered, taking both her hands in his and pressing them to his heart. "I would not wish to do so."

"Yet you must unless you break the curse on Samhaine . . . this coming Samhaine to be exact, and no other, or all shall be lost forever," Rebecca gravely advised him.

"What is so special about this particular Samhaine?" Michael queried, tenderly brushing away a tear that had escaped down Emily's cheek.

"It is special in that you fell in love this year." At Michael's frown of incomprehension, she explained, "Samhaine marks the end of the witches' year. According to the rules of magic, a couple plagued by the sort of curse you find yourselves under must break it on the Samhaine of the year they fall in love. If they fail to do so, then all is lost and there is no chance for them to ever be together. Thus, they must part company forever, or suffer the wrath of the curse. That fact aside, Samhaine is when the veil between the otherworlds and our world is thinnest, so you shall have the best chance of summoning Deira then."

"Is that all then?" Michael asked, smiling tenderly at Emily, who looked on the verge of shattering.

"Well, there is the preparation of the oils, candles, and such. And you must learn the summoning incantation. But yes"—a nod—"that is all. As I said, it is a simple spell. The question now is: Are you willing to risk the consequences should you fail?"

Michael didn't have to think twice before replying. "I understand and am fully prepared to face whatever consequences come from enacting the counterspell."

"No, Michael. Please . . ." Emily brokenly whispered. "You mustn't risk your life for me. I am not worth it." Her face was the color of ashes now, streaked with tears.

Michael returned her anguished gaze for several beats, searching for the words to ease her fear. When he was unable to find them, he grunted his frustration and hauled her into his lap. Crushing her against him, determined never to let her go, he growled, "To hell with Deira, and to hell with me if my love for you isn't pure enough to pass her scrutiny. I would rather stand before a thousand ghostly priestesses and be killed a thousand times over than lose you." And it was true. Though he didn't believe in the curse now any more than he had before, he would gladly face any peril to keep Emily by his side.

"But, Michael—"

"No, love." He captured her tearful gaze with his steady one, compelling her to see the strength of his purpose. "I have made up my mind. I shall go before Deira, with or without you."

"If you go alone, you shall most certainly perish," Rebecca soberly informed him.

"Then so be it. I would rather be dead than live without the love I have found with my darling Emily. Now do your duty as go-between and tell me how to lift the curse."

The next hour passed with Rebecca explaining the counterspell, during which Michael, who refused to allow Emily to leave his lap, asked detailed questions, making certain that he, and more importantly, Emily, understood what was to be done and why. That task completed, he waited while the women made the protective amulet, unwilling to let his wife out of his sight.

When the amulet was finished, something that turned out to be a small, spicy-smelling linen bag upon which had been drawn several queer symbols, and Emily had hung it around his neck, it was time for them to take their leave. It was then, when Rebecca retrieved Michael's outdoor garments, that Emily saw the helmet.

Her cheeks infusing with soft color, she watched as he placed it on his head, shamefacedly confessing, "I am so sorry, Michael. I forgot all about the surprise in my distress over the curse. Do you like it?"

"Like it? I love it!" he fiercely declared, impulsively

sweeping her into his arms to hug her close. "It is the best gift anyone has ever given me."

She tipped back her head to gaze up at him, her eyes lit with love and her face flushed with pleasure. "Really and truly?"

"Really and truly," he murmured, unable to resist pressing a kiss to her enticing lips. They felt and tasted every bit as luscious as they looked. Left hungry for more, tempted almost beyond salvation to crush her against him and thoroughly ravish her seductive mouth with his, he forced himself to pull away, huskily whispering, "Thank you for the wonderful gift, my love. I shall treasure it always."

Grinning, she rose up onto her tiptoes and kissed him again. "You are welcome, darling."

As Michael stood recovering from the pleasurable shock of their second kiss, he heard Rebecca laugh. "It is apparent that neither of you has anything to fear from Deira," she remarked. "I cannot recall the last time I saw two people so in love."

Pleased by the look of relief that swept over Emily's face at her comment, Michael turned to Rebecca and took her hand in his, wishing to thank her. The instant he did so, he felt an intense tingling that shot up his arm and radiated through his body, vibrating like a hum in his blood.

Power. It was the sensation of pure, raw power, the source of which he could only imagine. Startled and not just a little shaken by the experience, he abruptly dropped her hand and backed away, gazing at her with a new sense of awe.

Could it be that Rebecca Dare indeed possessed magic?

Chapter 17

It was the darkest night that Emily could ever remember seeing, dense and black, as if someone had tarred the sky, obscuring all the stars and most of the moon, leaving only a feeble sliver of light to mark this Samhaine night. All around her the mist seethed thin and pale, rising from the ground like spirits from unhallowed graves, shrouding the Merrivale landscape in a filmy pall of ashen white.

Emily shivered and snuggled deeper into the folds of her heavy woolen cloak, wondering if she would ever be warm again. Not only was she chilled to the bone from the frigid dampness of the mist, her heart was clutched by icy dread and her blood ran cold with fear. For tonight at midnight, a scant half hour from now, she and Michael would stand before Deira and put their love on trial.

Would Deira find their love worthy? Would she judge it pure enough, true enough, that she would banish the curse and allow them to love each other in peace? Or would she rule them as undeserving and—and—

No! Emily's mind screamed, her eyes welling up with tears at the monstrous thought of what would happen if their love was found wanting. Deira would find their love worthy . . . she had to . . . how could she not? She, Emily, loved Michael Vane, the duke of Sherrington, above all else, even her own life, and he loved her in equal measure. She was sure he did. Hadn't he proved it time and again in countless ways, his every word, his every glance and action eloquently expressing the tenderness in his heart? Why, she doubted if there was a woman alive

who felt more cherished than she did with Michael. And
yet . . . yet . . .

Despite everything, despite their undeniable attraction
to each other, despite their steadfast devotion and the
immeasurable strength of their affection . . . what if there
was something deep inside of one or both of them, something which they, themselves, were unaware of, that
somehow tainted their love in Deira's eyes? Or—or—
what if Deira's definition of love differed from theirs?

The sick, gnawing sensation that had plagued Emily
since Michael had announced his intent to attempt the
counterspell intensified at that new and infinitely unnerving thought. There were, after all, millions of different
ways to love, as many ways as there were people on
earth, which meant that one person's perfect mode of
loving might be completely wrong for another. That
being the case, who was to say that one couple's love
was less worthy than another's if all parties involved were
happy and fulfilled in their lives together? As for Michael
and herself, well, who could possibly judge their love as
untrue or impure when they cared so very much for each
other and were willing to sacrifice anything for the sake
of that love?

Oh, true. There were those who would fail to see Michael's sacrifice in what they did tonight. After all, he
did not believe in the curse and thus saw no real danger
in invoking the counterspell. But those people would be
wrong, blind. He was making a sacrifice, an enormous
one. By accepting her belief in the curse and willingly
adopting it to partake in a ceremony that he hoped
would lay her fears to rest, Michael, a man of strong
convictions, was surrendering his tenets of reason and
logic, principles that were as much a part of his being as
his flesh and soul. If such an action did not constitute a
sacrifice for love, then what, pray tell, did? Besides
that—

"I see 'em just ahead, yer grace," Isaac announced,
shattering her reflections and the somber silence that surrounded them.

Since the canon of the counterspell dictated that Mi-

chael and Emily remain apart from the dawn of Samhaine day until half past eleven on Samhaine night, when
they were to meet and commence with the spell, Isaac
and two of the Windgate footmen had been charged with
the duty of escorting her to the stone circle. The circle
lay but a short distance from the quaint inn where they
had all spent the previous night, and where Michael and
Emily had each passed the day alone performing rituals
to prepare their bodies and minds for the coming ceremony. Because the spell also forbade her and Michael
to address anyone but Deira after nightfall on Samhaine,
Emily simply nodded in response to Isaac's announcement and looked in the direction in which he pointed.

There in the distance, radiating through the gathering
fog like a spectral glow, was the eerily diffused blur of
torchlight. The sight sent her heart plunging to the pit
of her stomach. She was almost there. The moment she
had been dreading for the past five days was upon her.

Praying with every fiber of her being, imploring God
and whoever else might be receptive to her pleas tonight
to keep and protect her beloved Michael from harm,
Emily forced her suddenly leaden feet to continue advancing forward. From beneath her boots came the soft
crackling of dry twigs and moldering leaves, fallen from
the skeletal trees surrounding them, their noise like dying
rasps against the whispered warning of the desiccated
grass over which they passed. All too soon she reached
where Michael and Mr. Eadon awaited her outside the
circle of towering stones.

Though Michael, Mr. Eadon, and the footmen had
come to the circle the day before to locate it and to
attend to its preparation, this was Emily's first glimpse
of it. Seeing it now, set against a shadowy, torchlit back-
drop of swirling mist and twisted, barren trees, sent a
frisson of ice slithering down her spine. Rebecca had said
that the stones were shaped like maidens, and they
were . . . nine ancient Amazons standing silent vigil over
Deira's lonely resting place. If Deira was to be their
judge, then these formidable stone giantesses were most
certainly their jury.

Stricken by the sight with a dark sense of foreboding, Emily quickly looked away, her vision blurring with tears as her gaze fell upon Michael. Seeing him standing in the flickering light of the torch he held, his expression tender and his smile reassuring, merely deepened her feeling of doom, fueling her with a powerful urge to throw her arms around him and beg him to abandon his perilous quest.

But of course she didn't give in to her impulse. She didn't dare. To speak out of turn would go against the dictates of the counterspell, thus reducing the likelihood of its success. And since Michael was determined to cast it, regardless of what anyone said or did, she must do everything in her power to afford him his best chance of surviving the experience. And so she simply returned his gaze, mutely begging him to forsake the hazards of magic and preserve himself.

He shook his head once in response to her silent plea, then shot a meaningful glance at the solemn-faced footmen accompanying her. Both servants promptly stepped forward and presented her with the objects they carried. Francis, who flashed her an encouraging smile, bore the leather satchel of sacred artifacts that she and Rebecca had prepared for the spell. The appreciably tense Ralph carried the crude pine branch broom she'd made two days earlier.

When she had relieved the men of their burdens and Michael had taken his own bag of conjuring tools from Eadon, Michael nodded to indicate that the servants were to leave them. He waited until they had melted into the mist before offering her his black-gloved hand, indicating his desire to lead her into the circle. After several heartbeats, during which she frantically grappled for a way to turn him from his purpose and dismally failed to find one, Emily reluctantly did as he bid, her dread doubling with every step she took.

Like herself, Michael was dressed all in black, his somber suit of clothing covered by an ankle-length greatcoat with two wide shoulder capes that flapped in the sodden air as he marched toward his destiny. Rebecca had advised them to don their plainest black garments, saying that Deira would view the act as a symbol of their humility, which would encourage her to look upon them with favor. As Emily followed Michael through the narrow, inky fissure that served as the entrance into the ring of stones, she prayed that her friend was right.

Once in the circle Michael went directly to the kistvaen, a rough, crumbling stone coffin, before which he kneeled in a show of respect. When she, too, had paid homage to Deira, he moored his torch in a nearby pile of stones, which, judging from the jutting remains of charred branches and staffs, had been used as a holder many times before. That done, he busied himself with removing the articles from his bag.

There were four white candles, each incised with a symbol that Rebecca had said represented Deira; a small brass brazier; a pouch that she knew contained a special blend of incense; and two tapers, all items that he set on the tomb, which would serve as their altar. When he had arranged the brazier in the center with the candles forming a semicircle around it, he nodded to her, indicating that she was to empty her satchel.

Gravely nodding back, Emily withdrew four black candles, also incised with Deira's symbol, which she used to complete the circle around the brazier; a vial of consecration oil that Rebecca had helped her prepare; and a muslin bag of dried flowers and herbs. After glancing at Michael, who smiled in a way that made her long to weep from the tenderness it roused within her, Emily picked up the pine branch broom and carried it to the edge of the circle.

Sweeping the gorse-flecked ground with long, fluid motions, she chanted, "I purify the land and make it pleasant for you, Deira, so that you may call upon us and judge our love." Repeating the motion and the chant over and over again, she spiraled counterclockwise around the circle until she had swept her way back to the tomb.

Sweeping with pine branches, Rebecca had explained, purified and sanctified the land for the spirit's visit. The next step was to light a circle of fire around the cleansed area, an act that would seal in the purity and mark the ground as hallowed.

Taking the broom from her now, Michael held it to the torch, setting it on fire. Carrying it aloft, like a beacon of his purpose, he strode to the edge of the circle to light the ring of fagots he and the servants had fashioned the day before. If they had followed Rebecca's instructions, and Emily had no doubt that they had, there were cedar branches to cleanse the air, birch to ward off evil, and rowan to summon Deira from the spirit world, all kindled with dried oak leaves.

Starting at the north edge of the circle, Michael lit the kindling, intoning, "I purify the air and make it pleasant for you, Deira, so that you may call upon us and judge our love." He repeated the action at the east border, followed by the south and west. When they stood within a blazing ring of fire, he turned back to Emily.

At his signal, she picked up her bag of flowers and herbs—rosemary to consecrate the circle, wormwood for evocation, mallow to exorcise black magic, and belladonna to make their souls receptive to Deira's spirit—and walked around the fire, tossing the contents upon the pyre as she recited, "I purify the atmosphere and make it pleasant for you, Deira, so that you may call upon us and judge our love." With each handful she tossed, the flames leapt higher and higher, dancing and writhing as they slowly took on a queer, bluish cast.

Blue, the color of truth, ancient wisdom, and spirit communication. Had Deira arrived then?

Unnerved by the notion, Emily warily backed away from the flames, her wide-eyed gaze never leaving them as she slowly inched backward, watching as they steadily rose against the blackness of the maiden stones, fusing and flickering into what to her mesmerized gaze appeared to be a human form.

Human. Yes. The shape was distinctly human . . . and female. She had just decided that she could see the hourglass curve of a woman's body with a head of shooting sparks for hair, when she felt a hand upon her shoulder.

Too startled to scream, certain that the spirit had somehow escaped its fiery shell and now stood behind her,
she spun around in panic. For several beats she stared
unseeing, blinded by her terror. Then her vision cleared
and she saw that it was Michael, her darling Michael,
who looked back, worry written on every plane of his
handsome face.

Meeting her gaze in silent query, he gently cupped her
cheek in his palm, mutely begging for reassurance that
all was well. She smiled and nodded, readily giving him
what he sought. How could all not be well when he
looked at her like that, so tender and full of love? He
continued searching her eyes a moment longer, as if deciding for himself, then nodded back and released her.
Glancing away now, he pulled his watch from his over-
coat pocket, squinting to see the dial as he angled it into
the light. When he saw the time, he frowned and tipped
it toward her so that she, too, could read the hour. It
was late. Eleven forty-seven. They must hasten to finish
the evocation spell if they were to appeal to Deira at
midnight.

Tucking his watch back into his pocket, Michael
moved to the opposite side of the tomb, where he
kneeled before the white candles. Emily sank to her
knees before the black ones, shivering as the damp chill
from the ground cut through her heavy skirts. After both
had bowed their heads to pay deference to Deira, Michael uncorked the vial of oil.

Made from the essences of fennel, tansy, rue, wormwood, yarrow, fir, and sandalwood, the maceration was
held sacred for its ability to consecrate. Picking up one
of the white candles, white signifying the purity of their
hearts and the sincerity of their love, he anointed the
symbol incised into the wax, saying, "I consecrate thee
in the name of Deira, the wise and the just."

When he had set it back into place, Emily, being the
cursed party, picked up one of the black candles, which
Rebecca had said were used to remove hexes and banish
spiritual discord, and mirrored his actions. Alternating
white and black, they consecrated all eight candles, after

which Michael rose and lit the two tapers from the ring of fire, which continued to burn steadily around them.

Handing one of the tapers to Emily, they switched sides, with Michael lighting the black candles and Emily lighting the white ones, chanting in unison, "With these candles and by their light I welcome thee, Deira, this Samhaine night." When a second, smaller ring of fire burned upon their makeshift altar, Michael moved to kneel next to Emily. It was now time to present their offerings.

Emily's was a fragrant bouquet of purple heather, lavender, mint, and Solomon's seal—the heather to invite the spirit, the lavender to symbolize love and peace, mint for protection against evil, and Solomon's seal to appeal for spiritual aid—which she laid next to the candles, entreating, "Accept my offering and hear my plea for mercy, O Deira, the wise and the just."

Michael's offering was the incense made from sandalwood, anise, and acacia, all of which enticed spirits, with a dash of frankincense to petition the spirit's blessing. Pouring the aromatic powder into the brazier, he lit it with his taper, uttering, "With this offering I appeal to you, O Deira, the wise and just. See our love and lift our curse, grant us the blessing of peace."

They then joined hands and bowed their heads, waiting for a sign that Deira had accepted their offerings and was ready to judge their love. They waited . . .

And waited . . .

And waited . . .

Emily was just beginning to think that they had failed in their quest when she heard what sounded like a roaring sigh issue from the tomb before her, followed by a blast of arctic cold that seemed to cut through her flesh and pierce her soul. Apparently Michael, too, had felt and heard the spirit, for he gasped aloud. Gripped by shuddering dread, terrified of what the being would do next, Emily glanced at Michael in panic.

He stared straight ahead, as if in a trance, his eyes wide and his face frozen in an expression of incredulous awe. Petrified of what she might see, but compelled by

Michael's expression to look, she followed his gaze, feeling her own face mirror his at what she saw.

A shimmering blue vapor had risen from the tomb, swirling and undulating into what looked to be the silhouette of a woman. As Emily gaped, too paralyzed by fear to do more, there was a blinding flash. When her vision cleared a moment later, she saw that the figure had became lit from within, now sparking and flashing like bottled lightning. Floating silently over the tomb, it appeared to be waiting . . . or was it judging? Emily struggled through the sludge of her fright, trying to recall Rebecca's words, to remember what they were to do next.

They must . . . they must . . . yes! It was time for them to prove their love. They must open their hearts and show Deira what was in them. As she glanced back at Michael, poised to plead her case, he abruptly broke from his trance. Rather than look amazed or intimidated by the apparition, he appeared angered by it, a low, feral growl issuing from his throat as he rose to his feet.

His teeth bared and his narrowed eyes staring steadily at the spectral haze, he reached up and savagely ripped the protective amulet from around his neck. Tossing it into the brazier, where it caught fire from the incense and burst into a ball of shooting embers, he snarled, "I stand before you, Deira, with only my love to protect me. So hear me . . . judge me. Look deeply inside me and see the truth of what I say. I love this woman, more than life itself, and there is nothing I would not sacrifice for her. She is everything to me—everything, damn it!— my heart, my soul, my joy, and my passion. She is my very salvation, and I need her as surely as I need the air I breathe, as surely as my heart must beat and my blood must course through my veins."

His fist was raised now, shaking, and he was practically screaming the words. "Judge me, Deira! Judge me now! I gladly risk my life for the chance to remain with this woman, for I would rather die than live without her."

The instant the words left his mouth there was a boom that made the earth quiver violently beneath them, as if it were being torn asunder. A second later a bolt of blue lightning streaked out from the mist, striking Michael's chest with a crash that resonated like thunder. Mindless of everything but her fear for Michael, Emily threw herself against him, collapsing with him to break his fall as he slowly crumpled to the ground.

Crying his name over and over again, she clutched at his still form in panic, her frightened gaze urgently searching his face as she willed him to speak. His eyes were open and staring fixedly ahead, his pupils so dilated that his jade irises appeared swallowed up in blackness. His smooth skin, which had been warm and flushed with health only moments earlier, was cold and strangely waxen, his handsome features frozen into a contorted mask of stunned surprise.

"Michael, love, speak to me. Please speak to me," she begged, this time kissing his pale lips. She didn't detect so much as a whisper of breath. Afraid, more afraid than she'd ever been in her life, she pressed her trembling fingers to his throat, desperately searching for a pulse. Nothing. She moved her hand slightly to the left, still nothing, then to the right, again nothing, frantically groping for something, anything to indicate that he lived. When it was apparent that she would find no sign there, she lifted his limp arm. Weeping now, praying to detect even the slightest palpitation to give her hope, she felt his wrist. There was an utter absence of life.

Her body now wracked with sobs and her soul keening its grief, she violently ripped open his coat and pressed her ear to his chest. It was completely still, utter silence.

"No—no!" she wailed, her voice rising with her sorrow. "No, damn it! I shan't lose you, Michael. I cannot! I love you . . . I need you." Gathering him in her arms, she cradled his head against her breast, dropping kisses on his cold lips as she brokenly pleaded, "Do not leave me, my love. Please come back. Please," again and again. When he remained lifeless in her arms, she raised her tear-ravaged face to Deira, who floated serenely before her, gripped by savage rage at what the being had done.

Her voice low and impassioned, she glared at the spirit,

hissing, "Damn you, Deira. Damn you to hell. He's mine, do you hear me? Mine! And you shan't take him. If I must fight you to keep him, then so be it. I welcome the battle." She was so inflamed now that she shook with the fierceness of her fury.

Laying Michael's inert form upon the damp ground, taking care to rest his head on his flaring coat capes, she staggered to her feet, her fists clenching at her sides and her breath coming out in harsh rasps as she screamed, "I challenge you, Deira! I challenge your powers with the strength of my love for the life of this man!" With that she flung out her arms to invite the wrath of the spirit, heedless of everything but her love for Michael and her desperation to keep him by her side. "Do it, Deira! I dare you!"

"E-Emily?" called a hoarse voice.

Emily glanced down quickly to see Michael struggling to sit up. He looked slightly stunned, but none the worse for his terrifying experience.

"Michael . . . love? Is it truly you?" she exclaimed, her heart filled with a rejoicing such as she had never before felt. Why, she could almost hear it sing, a sound like angels on the wind.

He frowned and shook his head, as if to clear it. "What a queer question. Of course it is me. Who else would it be?" By now he had stumbled unsteadily to his feet.

Her tears flowing freely in her relief, Emily let out a cry of gladness and threw herself into his arms, wanting to hold him close, determined never to again let him go. She had almost reached them when there was an explosive flash of blue and another crash of thunder. Then everything went black.

"Emily, love. Speak to me. Please speak to me!" The voice was frayed and hoarse, raggedly pleading.

Michael. It was Michael's voice . . . coming out of the darkness. Emily groped in the smothering blackness that engulfed her, blindly fighting to find him in the impenetrable shadows. Nothing. She couldn't find him. She tried to call his name, to alert him of her presence, but no sound came out. Again she tried and again she failed.

"I love you, Emily. Dear God, how I love you!" he fiercely declared. Then something fell upon her cheeks, something wet, like droplets from a gentle rain.

"He truly does loves you, as you do him." The words floated through the shadows, as delicate and ethereal as a dream. In the next instant there was a dazzling flash of blue light, one that exploded and flared in the darkness, then a woman materialized in its glowing midst, the most beautiful woman she'd ever seen.

Deira. It had to be Deira. Though she couldn't tell the color of the spirit's eyes, or the texture of her hair, or even the shape of her features for the blinding luminescence surrounding her, Emily saw her with her heart and soul, and they proclaimed her beautiful.

For several moments the spirit simply floated there, radiating power and something else . . . something gentle and serene, almost soothing . . . then she slowly raised one flaming arm, extending it to Emily. "I have judged you and found your love worthy. Go forth and live in peace." With that verdict, she vanished, as did the darkness, and Emily found herself gazing up at Michael.

His beloved face was pale and streaked with tears; his eyes were red, the thick fringe of his lashes spiked with moisture. He was weeping. "Michael?" she murmured, frowning at his tears.

"Emily?" His voice was splintered, breaking with emotion. "Oh, Emily, my dearest love!" he exclaimed, hugging her protectively to his chest. "I thought I had lost you."

All that had happened came flooding back at his words, and she suddenly remembered the sight of him lying lifeless in her arms. Unnerved by the memory, she pulled his face close to hers, wanting to feel his breath, to reassure herself that he was indeed all right. When it fanned across her cheeks, so warm and fresh and comforting, she smiled and fervently whispered, "I love you, Michael. How I love you," then pressed her lips to his, passionately demonstrating the truth of her words.

Michael moaned and eagerly returned her kiss, his mouth moving hungrily over hers, matching her brush for famished brush, nip for greedy nip, lick for ravenous lick, practically devouring her lips in his urgency to savor every luscious inch of them.

It was like a dream, kissing her . . . it had to be a dream. Surely no woman's lips could be so very sweet, so very supple and responsive? And the way she moved against him, sinuously molding and undulating all that voluptuous softness against his love-starved body . . . he moaned again in lustful torment and pulled her more firmly into his lap, fire jolting through his loins as her rounded backside pressed temptingly against his quickening arousal.

Dear God, how he wanted her . . . here and now! He was consumed by an overwhelming need to ease her back and take her upon the grass within this flaming circle of stones. Maddened by his shattering urgency, he shoved his hands beneath her cloak and convulsively clasped her full breasts, the fire in his loins burning hotter when he felt her nipples jutting hard and swollen against her woollen bodice.

"Michael, oh, Michael," she moaned, crushing her breasts against his palms, amorously urging him on.

With a groan he obliged her, his hands moving to the back of her gown where his trembling fingers found and clumsily unclasped the top five hooks. The modest neckline of her bodice now loose and sagging around her shoulders, he slipped his hand beneath the fabric, exploring the layers of flannel undergarments until he at last found her bare nipple. Clutched in the fevered grip of desire, he teased and coaxed it, his lust overtaking his reason as he deepened their kiss, his needful sex thrusting hard against her backside as his tongue masterfully ravished her mouth.

Emily sighed and melted against him, surrendering herself to the riot of pleasurable sensation. His mouth—mmm—how she loved his mouth. The taste was as heady as chocolate, the feel as intoxicating as wine. And the way he smelled . . . ahhh . . . like fresh shaving soap mingled with the spice of the incense . . . and something else . . . something primitive and earthy that stirred and titillated her senses. Then there was the thrilling feel of his arms and how his lithe body cradled hers, wrapping her in his strength and warmth. As for the electrifying way in which he touched her breasts . . . she sighed again, arching her back in voluptuous delight.

Oh! Such pleasure! She felt wonderfully hot and tingly all over, especially in the secret place between her legs, which seemed to melt and pulse with every erotic kiss and caress. Brazenly wondering how it would feel to be touched down there, imagining the rapture of his fingers exploring and stroking her, she wantonly spread her legs and pressed downward, forcefully shoving her now aching flesh against his thrusting hardness. The friction of his arousal rubbing against her served only to intensify the throbbing.

Overcome by desire now, she grasped his left hand, which clutched at her waist while his right one fondled her breast, and shamelessly guided it beneath her rucked-up skirts. Moaning into his mouth, which still hungrily devoured hers, she shoved his fingers against the thin fabric enveloping the now wet recesses of her femininity

He froze for a beat, then emitted a low, guttural growl and cupped her in his palm. She parted her thighs yet wider and squirmed impatiently against it. Pulling her mouth from his to gaze beseechingly into his passion-drugged eyes, she breathlessly implored, "Please, Michael," wiggling against his palm as her own hand slipped downward to stroke the hardness in his trousers.

A look of profound shock came over his face and again he froze, harsh, rasping breaths ripping from his chest as he stared at her. In the next instant he averted his gaze, but not before she saw the crushing ache in his eyes. "I am sorry, Emily. I cannot," he whispered. His voice was fractured and raw, excruciatingly so, as if the utterance had been torn from his soul.

The steamy spell of seduction vanished at his words. Bewildered and more than a little disappointed that their intimacy should come to such an abrupt end, Emily frowned and murmured, "Cannot what? Why? I do not understand."

He squeezed his eyes shut and shook his head once, his mouth drawing into a taut, pain-filled line. "I cannot make love to you. You know that. I explained about my inability to do so."

His inability? Her frown deepened as she became suddenly aware of where her hand rested and the violence of his arousal beneath it. Though she knew little about the actual act of making love, she understood enough from what Judith had told her and the snatches of bawdy conversation she'd eavesdropped from her brothers to comprehend what was involved. And judging from that comprehension, he seemed able enough to her to do the deed . . . more than able, if the size and heat of him were any indication.

Beyond perplexed now, she slowly said, "While I admit that I have limited knowledge about the marriage bed, I do have several married friends who have confided in me, so I am not completely ignorant about what is required from a man to make love to a woman. And unless I have been led completely astray on the subject, it seems to me that you are more than equal to the task." She gave his hardness a pat to illustrate her point.

He emitted a strangled moan and snatched her hand away. Trapping it firmly in his, as if he feared that it might stray down there again, he tersely replied, "You are correct in saying that part of me is equal to the task. Hell, I can barely look at you without getting an erection. You, my dear, are the most desirable woman in the world and there is nothing I want more than to make love to you."

"Well then, if your—you know"—she nodded to his lap—"can get—you know"—another nod—"and you wish to love me, then why can you not do so?"

He smiled faintly, though he looked far from happy. "My—you know—is called a penis and the state it is currently in is called an erection," he informed her, "and you are correct in that an erection and desire are all that are usually required to enable a man to make love.

Unfortunately, my condition is such that the stimulation and excitement from sexual activity can and will trigger a spell, which is why I must refrain from engaging in it."

"Are you certain?" Emily gently pressed, wanting nothing more than to erase the bleakness that had sprung into his eyes. "Your doctors have told you all sorts of things that have proved to be false. Are you so certain that the danger in making love isn't just more of their empty speculation?"

"Damn certain," he ground out furiously from between his teeth.

She recoiled slightly, caught off guard by the virulence of his response. Though she knew she shouldn't ask, sensing that he would resent her prying, she couldn't help quizzing, "How, Michael? How can you be so sure?"

He returned her gaze for several beats, his full lips twisting and his expression hardening. Then he savagely spat, "Because it happened, damn it! I tried to make love and had the most violent fit I have ever had."

"Oh, Michael! I am sorry," she exclaimed, instantly regretting asking for the pain his reply had obviously caused him.

He shook his head, rejecting her apology. Visibly trembling with the power of his emotion, he growled, "Since you are so very curious, you might as well know all the sordid details."

"Michael—" she began, helplessly trying to soothe him.

He cut her off. "It happened with my mistress, Violetta, about a month after my illness."

"Michael, please—" she tried again.

Again he ignored her. "Violetta and I had been together for close to two years when I fell ill. Dear, sweet Violetta." A sardonic smile contorted his lips. "She claimed to love me. Of course, that was before I became what I am now." He paused, seeming to consider something, then sighed and shook his head. "Ah, well. To her credit she did manage to hide the disgust she no doubt felt when I showed up on her doorstep on our last afternoon together, all pale and thin with my head shaved and my scalp splotched with scabs from the doctors' endless leeching and cupping. Then again, I kept her in an exceedingly grand fashion, so it was her duty to be accommodating."

Again he paused, this time to chuckle, a dark, humorless sound. "I must say that she was particularly accommodating that day, using her considerable talents to stimulate and arouse me. I had just entered her and was on the verge of climax when it happened."

"You had a spell?"

He nodded. "A terrible one. Violetta couldn't have been more horrified and disgusted, nor I more humiliated."

"Surely she understood?" Emily inquired, her heart aching at the self-loathing in his voice.

"Oh, she understood well enough," he shot back caustically. "She sent me a note the very next day breaking company with me. Though the note was courteous enough, kind even, she lost no time in circulating the tale of my shame around London, saying that she would rather die than suffer my touch again."

"What a horrible, wicked thing to do!" Emily cried, wishing that the hateful woman were there so she could snatch her bald.

"It was all quite mortifying to be sure, hearing the whispers and seeing the smirks, knowing that everyone in the *ton* was privy to my disgrace. But like all gossip, it soon lost its luster and was cast aside in favor of a newer and juicier scandal." He shrugged one shoulder. "No doubt I would have eventually regained my standing in the *ton* had I not had a fit at Lady Kilvington's picnic a month later. After that, well"—another shrug—"I might as well have had the plague for the way I was shunned."

"You were shunned?" she ejected, genuinely shocked.

He shrugged again, though the gesture was far from nonchalant for the tension in his body. "Oh, I had a few friends who remained loyal, though it has been a long while since I have seen or heard from them. That, of course, is my fault. In my shame, I chose to sever all ties with society. But to answer your question, yes, I was shunned by the majority of the *ton*."

"But—but—that is disgraceful!" she sputtered, outraged that anyone could be so cruel. "How dare those people shun you for something you cannot help."

"They dare because they can," he returned in a reasonable voice. "It is the way of the world, I am afraid, to reject those who do not live up to the standards set forth by society."

"Well, it is not the way of my world," she stoutly declared. "I would never reject you, or anyone else, for simply being ill."

There was a pause, during which he searched her face, then he sighed, a weary, dispirited sound. "I can only pray that you will continue to feel that way when you finally witness one of my fits. Of all the people in the world, you are the one it would wound me most to lose. I truly meant it when I said that I would rather die than live without you."

"You shan't ever be without me. Not for as long as I live, I promise," she vowed, pressing a kiss to his lips to seal her pledge. "I love you, Michael, and nothing will ever change that."

He sighed again, this time as if the weight of the entire world rested upon his shoulders. "I know that you love me, Emily, but I sometimes fear that the love I can give you in return might not be enough. I live in dread that you may someday decide that you want a real husband, one who can give you children and the pleasures of the marriage bed, and that you will leave me."

"Leave you? Oh, never!" she vehemently declared, throwing her arms around him to hug him close. "I promised to stay with you, and I never break my promises."

He hugged her back. "Never?"

"Never," she confirmed, snuggling more firmly into his embrace. "I make it my policy never to tender a promise unless I am absolutely certain that I can keep it. And I have never been more certain of anything in my life as I am of my love for you."

For a long moment thereafter they remained like that, simply holding each other, savoring the feel of each other in their arms. It was Emily who finally broke their silence. "Michael?"

"Hmmm?"

"You believe in magic now, do you not?"

He chuckled and dropped a kiss to the top of her head. "How can I not after all that has happened this night?"

"Rebecca calls autumn the season of enchantment. She says that it is a time when anything is possible." Emily shot him a shy look. "Perhaps—I mean—if you wish—we might—"

"Perhaps," he interjected softly in reply.

Neither needed to ask what the other meant. In their love, they knew and they hoped.

Chapter 18

It was an unusually mild November—everyone said so. The days were cool but sunny, abruptly chilling at twilight when the frost-dusted mist rose from the earth to greet the falling night.

By now the trees had shed their glorious October leaves, casting them to the ground where they lay forgotten and neglected, rotting beneath the gaunt shadows of the barren gray branches that had once nurtured and embraced them. Only the alders and the ivy burgeoned with life, the ivy which flaunted pale green berries and the alders with their purple catkins that dangled like satin tassels from their scraggly, leafless twigs. Even the air smelled different now than it had a scant month earlier, older and brisker, spiced with the dark redolence of earthy decay.

It was the air that Michael now savored as he paused beneath a naked oak tree, smiling as Emily delighted in the soaring grace of a slate blue and buff merlin, or lady's hawk, as she romantically preferred to call the small falcons, one of a pair that had recently adopted the Windgate park as their hunting ground. As he watched Emily's face, as captivated by its enraptured radiance as she was by the majesty of the bird's aeronautics, he marveled over the miracle that was his life.

He loved Emily, the kindest, gentlest, most generous woman in the entire world, and she loved him back, a marvel that was in itself nothing short of wondrous. And not a day had elapsed in the past ten days, since that extraordinary night at the stone circle, that they hadn't freely demonstrated their feelings for each other.

Not as freely as he would have liked, of course. Though Eadon had discreetly mentioned that Michael appeared fit enough to engage in marital relations, Michael, craven coward that he was, had yet to find the courage to attempt the act. And not because he still doubted the strength of Emily's love.

Since that night at the stones, when he had confessed his shame and she had accepted it with unflinching grace, he had begun to genuinely believe that her love was strong enough to withstand the sight of his spells. No, his cowardice did not stem from skepticism of Emily's love. It arose from his fear for Emily herself, from his reluctance to place her in the position to suffer the same sort of horror Violetta had suffered in his arms. The thought of having a fit while loving Emily, of having what should be the most glorious experience of her life turned into an abomination, well, the very notion was loathsome, unthinkable.

As for Emily—a rueful smile touched his lips at the thought of her sweet patience—she seemed to understand his reluctance and had been thoughtfully cautious of his feelings. Not once since the night at the circle had she mentioned the subject of lovemaking, nor had she done or said anything to indicate disappointment in their lack of physical intimacy, though he knew that she was ripe for the pleasures of the marriage bed and eager to bear the fruit of their passion. As always, she was the soul of consideration, demonstrating her affection with a chasteness that was clearly meant to put him at ease. This, however, didn't mean that she avoided all physical contact with him, nor he with her.

Since declaring their love and breaking the curse, their relationship had in some ways become easier, more spontaneous, and they now felt free to touch each other, something they did with unfettered frequency and which he enjoyed immensely. The way Emily hugged and kissed him when she met him at breakfast every morning, her manner casual yet tender, as if greeting him so were the most natural thing in the world—ah, bliss, it was sheer bliss. Then there was the way she slipped her hand into his when they walked together, so warm and trusting, and how she nuzzled her head against his shoulder as they lay before the fire at night, secure in each other's arms and safe in the knowledge of their love. Such moments were pure heaven.

Heaven? Michael chuckled softly. Oh, yes. He believed in heaven now. He had discovered it right here on earth, in the refuge he'd found in Emily's love.

"Oh, Michael! Have you ever seen anything so lovely?" Emily cried, her awed voice intruding upon his spiritual reflections.

Smiling, Michael glanced back over to where she stood, her eyes bright and her face pink with pleasure as she watched the bird glide effortlessly skyward. "Actually, I have. Lovelier, in fact," he sincerely replied, admiring the picture she made this fine autumn morn.

She wore a soft pink cashmere pelisse today, trimmed with wide black velvet ribbon that zigzagged down the front and circled the flaring hem, a motif that was echoed around the gauntlet cuffs and the wide pelerine collar, from beneath which peeked a white lace ruff. Unlike most days, when she went about with her head uncovered and her hair flying in the wind, she wore a hat today in deference to Rebecca and Magellan's visit, whom they now walked out to meet at the edge of the moor.

Michael couldn't help grinning at the sight of her modish headgear. It was an enormous black velvet cottage bonnet, lined in pink silk and extravagantly festooned with puffy loops of pink and white satin ribbon. She hadn't needed to tell him that it had been selected by her grandmother; it was hardly the sort of thing she would have chosen for herself. Indeed, the only reason she wore it now was because Mercy had laid it out and Emily, being so tender-hearted, hadn't wished to hurt the servant's feelings by rejecting her choice.

Seeing him smiling at her now, Emily smiled back, her sparkling gaze locking with his as she returned to his side. Standing on her tiptoes to press a quick kiss to his lips, she lightly scolded, "You, dear husband, are a shameless flirt."

"Only with you, my darling wife, for you are the most magnificent woman in the world," he replied, kissing her back.

She remained on her tiptoes for several more moments, her dark eyes thoughtful and searching as she studied his face. Apparently she was none too pleased by what she saw, for in the next instant she frowned. "Are you quite certain that you feel all right? You look rather pale," she murmured, touching his cheek, as if checking him for fever.

"I am fine . . . more than fine. I feel positively grand," he lavishly assured her, smiling again in a way that he hoped would mask the fact that he lied.

Truth be told, he did feel rather off this morning . . . not ill precisely, but not particularly well either. He'd been plagued by a tired, headachy sort of feeling ever since he'd risen, and there was a queer, metallic taste in his mouth that he couldn't seem to rid himself of, no matter what he ate or drank. Certain that the symptoms were due to his restless lack of sleep the night before and thus seeing no reason to alarm Emily by confessing them, he nodded to reinforce the lie. As protective as she was of him, she would no doubt insist that he take to his bed if she even suspected that he felt as he did, besides which she would spend her entire day worrying and fussing over him.

Not that he found the prospect of her pampering unappealing. To be perfectly honest, there was nothing he enjoyed more than being coddled by his darling Emily. It was just that Rebecca and Magellan were coming to Windgate for their long overdue first visit, and he didn't wish to spoil Emily's pleasure in welcoming them to her home. Besides that, he was looking forward to seeing Rebecca again, hoping that the lavish luncheon he, Emily, and the Swann sisters had planned would in some small measure repay her for all that she had done for them.

Despite Michael's attempt to ease her mind, Emily continued to frown at him, clearly unconvinced of his soundness. When he again reassured her, this time hugging her to demonstrate his strength, she reluctantly nodded. "All right, then. But you must promise to tell me if you start to feel even the least bit tired or unwell. You could be sickening with the ague that has plagued the servants for the past week or so, you know."

He nodded back. "Agreed." Dropping one last kiss onto her delectable lips, this one lingering, he huskily advised, "Now, unless we wish Rebecca to think us rude to the extreme, we must be on our way to meet her."

"Yes, of course. But Michael?" She smiled sweetly, her eyes soft and full of love as she twined her arms around his neck, pulling his face back to hers.

"Hmmm?" he murmured, forgetting all about his duties as host in the seductive tenderness of the moment.

"I was just thinking that—"

Whatever she said next was lost to Michael as his world abruptly turned black.

Sore. He was so very sore . . . and stiff. Every muscle in his body was strained and pulled, his flesh felt bruised, and his bones ached, as if someone had spent the past week mercilessly torturing him on a rack.

Moaning his discomfort, Michael fitfully shifted his throbbing body, a whimper escaping his lips as a stabbing pain knifed through his left hip. In the next instant he felt strong hands upon him, gently easing him over onto his right side. "There now, careful of your hip. You bruised it rather badly when you fell," a deep, familiar voice soothed.

Fell? Michael frowned as he fought through the dusky veils of his unconsciousness, struggling to regain his wits, driven by a sickening sense of dread, as if something were terribly, terribly wrong, something that he should remember but could not. Fell? Hmmm. Had he been injured in some sort of an accident then?

Utterly disorientated, he tried to open his eyes, but his lids refused to lift. They felt heavy, impossibly so, as if someone had placed coins over them, like the villagers often did to their dead. As he tried again, almost desperate now as his inexplicable dread deepened and swelled to the edge of panic, the hands returned, this time smoothing back his hair to place something upon his brow . . . something cold and wet.

He promptly surrendered his struggle to lift his lids, his sluggish brain distracted from its purpose as it grappled to process the new, but infinitely familiar sensation. He knew that sensation, he knew what that something on his brow was. It was—it was—yes, of course. A cloth. Someone had placed a cold, wet cloth on his forehead. In the next instant the hands moved to his tense shoulders, where they began lightly massaging his sore muscles.

Good. It felt good . . . so good that Michael's mind gradually resigned all thought, lulled into an uneasy emptiness by the tranquilizing effect of the rhythmic kneading. Within moments, his rigid body went limp.

"That's it. Relax. Lie still and rest. Everything is fine now," the voice murmured. "Sleep, your grace, sleep."

Your grace? Several layers of his disorientation abruptly lifted as the title seeped into his sopited brain. Ah, yes. Now he remembered. He was Michael Vane, duke of Sherrington. And the voice must be . . . who?

Again Michael tried to open his eyes, wanting to put a face to the voice. He knew that voice, almost as well as he knew his own. If he could just see the man's face . . .

This time he managed to crack his eyes a slit and peer dazedly about him. He was in a bed . . . his bed? Mmmm. His. He recognized the blue and gold tentlike draping above his head. Yes. He was in his domed tester bed, the same one he always slept in when he was at . . . at . . . Windgate Abbey? Yes. He was at Windgate Abbey, lying in the bed that he'd claimed as his own when he was a child. If his memory served him correct, he'd chosen the bed because the draping had looked like something out of *The Arabian Nights,* at least to his young eyes, a book he'd been reading at the time and which had caught his imagination.

Imagination? His mind paused, oddly arrested by the word. There was something about it, something it seemed that he should remember—

"Your grace?" A broad, blunt-featured face with intel-

ligent hazel eyes and a kind smile suddenly dipped into
sight. "Ah, so you are awake."

Michael frowned, his thoughts making a sharp shift as
his mind labored to identify the face. It was, it was . . .
"Eadon?" He more croaked than uttered the word for
the dryness of his throat.

The man nodded. "At your service, your grace. How
do you feel?"

"Like hell," he rasped, weakly struggling to sit up.
Exactly why he wished to sit up, he didn't know. It just
seemed to be something he should do.

"I cannot say that I am at all surprised. You had a
particularly bad spell this time," Eadon replied, bracing
his brawny arm behind Michael's neck and back to lift
his head and shoulders, which he efficiently propped up
on a pile of pillows.

Spell? Michael frowned again, recollection lurking at
the edge of his mind as he watched the servant pick up
a small brown bottle and pour several drops of greenish
liquid into a glass of water. *What did Eadon mean by
a spell?*

As Eadon held the glass to Michael's lips, urging him
to drink, his mind abruptly grasped the evasive memory
and all that had happened came flooding back. The instant he remembered, he pulled his mouth from the rim
of the glass, gasping his alarm. Dear God! He'd had a
spell, and Emily had been in his arms when it had
happened.

More heartsick and frightened than he'd ever been in
his life, Michael darted a glance at the comfortable arm-
chair beside his bed, which had been placed there for
the specific purpose of accommodating Emily when she
visited his sickbed. Ever since she'd come into his life,
he could always count on finding her there whenever
he was unwell, reading or doing needlework, or simply
watching over him while he slept, patiently awaiting him
to wake so that she could coax him into drinking one of
her fortifying caudles.

His soul seemed to shrivel within him at the sight of
that chair, all too aware of the meaning of its vacancy.

Her love for him hadn't been strong enough after all. She had been disgusted by the sight of his seizure, and she could no longer bear to be near him. It was the only explanation for why she wasn't there, and he knew her far too well to try to delude himself into thinking otherwise. If Emily still loved him, nothing on heaven or earth would keep her from his side when he was ill.

"Your grace?" The cool, smooth rim of the glass was back at his lips again.

Michael ignored it. For several agonized moments he continued to stare at the chair, his heart shattering in his chest and his world slowly crumbling around him. Then he ripped his gaze away, suddenly unable to bear the sight of it. He would have the damn thing burned. Hell, he would burn everything that reminded him of Emily— the furnishings in the breakfast room, the cushions they lounged upon in front the fire every evening—the whole bloody house, if necessary. Destroying all traces of her and their love was the only chance he had of surviving the crushing pain of losing her.

Though he didn't particularly wish to hear confirmation of his fears, Michael knew that he would eventually have to ask after Emily and face the devastating news of her desertion. Better to do it now, while the pain was new and raw, for it would only hurt worse later, after the wound had had time to fester and deepen.

After several anguished beats, during which he fought back the stinging tears that now hazed his eyes, Michael forced himself to look at Eadon and query, "My wife?" His voice sounded flat, toneless, dead.

An odd look passed over the other man's face. Regret? Pity? He couldn't be certain. It vanished almost as quickly as it had appeared, replaced by a bland smile. "Out, your grace. Now drink. This will help you rest." Again the glass rim nudged his lips.

Again Michael ignored it. "Out where?" he demanded, determined to hear the searing truth.

"I am sorry, your grace. She did not say and it is not my place to ask," Eadon replied, his voice ringing with a note of finality. "Now drink. You need your rest. Her grace will no doubt be back by the time you awake."

Liar! Michael wanted to scream, bleakly returning the other man's gaze. It was a bloody lie, and they both knew it. Emily would not be back in a few hours' time; she might never come back.

"Your grace, please," Eadon murmured, again urging him to drink. "You will feel ever so much better after you have slept."

Michael shot him a withering look. It would take a hell of a lot more than sleep to make him feel better. Still—

Wanting the world to go away, taking with it the pain and sorrow that it constantly laid at his door, Michael did as he was directed, obediently swallowing every last drop of what he knew to be a powerful sleeping draught. Better to be unconscious than awake and tormented by the knowledge that the woman he loved had left him, probably forever.

It was past nightfall when Michael again awoke. Though he had slept long and hard, his slumber had been troubled, haunted by dreams he could not remember, but which had left him weary and restless and profoundly disturbed. Lying curled up on his right side now, his body comfortably torpid beneath his bedcovers and his mind numb from the narcotic effects of the sleeping draught he vaguely recalled drinking, Michael glanced groggily around him, trying to fix the time and place.

The place was a large but cozy bedchamber decorated in rich, regal shades of blue, gold, and wine. The old-fashioned domed tester bed in which he lay was spacious and soft, luxuriously appointed with mounds of puffy pillows and layers of thick comforters, the latter of which were topped by a silken blue velvet coverlet. Across the room from the foot of the bed, occupying a full third of the gold, marble-painted plaster wall, was a splendid fireplace, its black granite face framed by elegantly gilt double pilasters and crowned by an imposing mirror-inlaid chimney piece. A low fire burned upon the gleaming brass grate within, reflecting off the highly polished andirons to cast halos of soft yellow light upon the sumptuous Savonnerie carpet that spanned a sizable expanse of the marquetry floor.

The place was his bedchamber, of course, and the time was . . . he drowsily transferred his gaze to the row of arched windows with their graceful trefoiled heads, yawning as he squinted through the diamond-shaped panes to see into the night beyond. The fog had completely risen and now clung to the outside of the glass, smudging the moon and stars into indistinct blurs of rippling silver.

He yawned again. Hmmm. Judging from the depth of the darkness, it was well past twilight . . . somewhere around nine o'clock, his sluggish brain guessed, though it could be much later. He often slept straight through the evening and into the wee hours of the morning after undergoing Eadon's more grueling treatments, which he assumed he had suffered that day. What other explanation was there for the way he felt?

Though Michael's mind was still far too muddled to grasp the events of the day, he had experienced the soporific effects of Eadon's sleeping draughts often enough to recognize them now. And since Eadon administered his draughts only on those occasions when Michael was particularly ill or suffering extreme discomfort from his treatments, well, that neatly explained everything. Everything except for—he glanced quickly at the chair beside the bed, frowning when he found it unoccupied—except for where Emily was.

No sooner had the thought entered his head than the cataclysmic events of the day came crashing through the daze of his draught-dulled mind, instantly dissolving the comfortable brain-numbing effects of the drug. He wasn't in bed because of Eadon's treatments; he was there because he'd had a fit. A bad one. In front of Emily . . . and her feelings for him hadn't been strong enough to survive the revolting sight. Emily wasn't by his side because she could no longer stomach being near him.

Desolation ripped through his heart as he forced himself to shoulder the devastating burden of that truth.

Emily, his love and his life, was gone. She'd left him. Never again would he see her radiant smile. Never again would he hear the lilting music of her laughter or be enlivened by her spirited conversation. He would never smell her scent again, so fresh and innocently provocative, nor would he feel the comforting warmth of her body as she melted into his embrace.

Michael closed his eyes, drowning in grief as a powerful wave of sorrow washed over him. As much as he would miss all of those splendid, miraculous things, what he would miss most was the simple joy of looking up and seeing Emily by his side, of knowing that she was there and that she cared about him.

He lay like that for several long moments, engulfed in wrenching misery. Then he slowly opened his eyes and gazed at the chair, which had become the symbol of his loss. He was alone again, unwanted, abandoned, and despised.

Despair sucked him in as he thought of the coming days, which now seemed to stretch before him like an endless chasm of loneliness and pain. Dear God! How was he to bear it? How could he possibly go on living without Emily when she had become his whole reason for being? As long as he'd had her in his life, there had been hope for the future. Truth be told, he'd begun to look forward to the future and had even begun to believe that they might someday have a normal life together, one that included him making her his wife in more than just name. With Emily by his side, anything was possible. He could do anything, be anything for her. But now—now—

He tore his tear-blurred gaze from the chair, unable to bear the sight of it and all it represented a moment longer. Emily was gone, taking with her the light, warmth, hope, and joy that had so briefly made his life worth living.

Wild with grief now and desperate to escape the bittersweet memories that the very sight of the room suddenly evoked within him, Michael emitted a feral growl and ripped back the covers. Ignoring the stabbing pain in his hip and the screaming protest of his aching muscles, he forced himself to stand, not even pausing to gain his equilibrium before he began staggering toward the door.

Shaky and dizzy from the draught, his strength sapped by his fit, he managed only four or five steps before collapsing to the floor. Too weak and wounded to rise again, too defeated to care, he curled into a tight ball where he lay and bitterly wept his devastation.

He hurt . . . dear God! . . . how he hurt. He felt torn and battered inside, as if someone had ripped out his heart and viciously twisted his guts, maiming him beyond salvation. Choking on the violence of his sobs, which tore from his chest with crippling brutality, he huddled yet tighter into himself, rocking in his agony.

This was the position he was in when he heard the door open a short while later. Not bothering to look up, certain that it was Eadon, who would no doubt bleed him within a drop of his life for working himself into such a state, Michael pressed his face yet harder against the tearstained carpet and ignored the presence on the threshold.

"Michael?" There was a soft gasp, then, "Dear heavens, love, whatever have you done to yourself?" followed by the swish of fabric and the sound of light footsteps racing across the room.

Emily? Was that truly Emily's voice he heard? Michael lifted his head to look, his heart seeming to stop in his chest at the sight he beheld. It was his beloved Emily, and she had never looked more beautiful to him than she did at that moment, clad in a plain blue dressing gown with her unbound hair streaming wildly behind her as she practically flew toward him.

His throat too raw from the harshness of his weeping to speak, he mutely stretched out his trembling arms to her, desperate to touch her, to assure himself that she was really there. In the next instant she sank to the floor beside him, making the soothing noises he knew and loved as she gathered him into her arms.

There was no hesitation in her touch, no reluctance in her manner, nor was there the slightest trace of revulsion in her voice as she tenderly comforted and calmed him. There was nothing in her demeanor at all but love and a rather frantic urgency to ease his distress as she clasped his head to her breast, dropping kisses to his hair as she crooned to him softly under her breath.

Swept away by relief, he melted against her, clinging to her as he wept anew, his pain and doubts dissolving beneath his tears of joy. Emily was there and she still cared for him.

"Hush now, love," she crooned, lightly stroking his heaving back. "Shhh. Everything is fine now."

Indeed it was fine, better than fine, in fact, now that he was in his Emily's arms. Determined never to leave them, Michael convulsively wrapped his own arms around her narrow waist, burying his tear-flooded face deeper into the softness of her full breasts.

She tightened her own embrace, snugging him closer. "My poor, poor darling. What has happened to make you take on so? Are you feeling worse?"

He shook his head, his face still nestled against her breasts, the soft cashmere that covered them now damp from his uncontrollable tears.

"Are you hurt then? Did you fall?"

Another head shake, followed by a sniffle.

There was a short pause, during which she smoothed back his hair to kiss his ear, then she murmured, "Perhaps I should get Mr. Eadon. He will know how best to help you."

"No!" Michael raggedly ejected, lifting his head to meet her gaze with pleading eyes. "No, please. Do not leave me. Stay. I am fine now that you are here. I—I just wish to be held."

She smiled gently, her eyes soft with tenderness as she dipped down and dropped a light kiss to his lips. "There is nothing I wish more than to hold you, my love. Indeed, I have ached to do so all day long."

He sniffled again and smiled, pleased by her confession. "You have?"

"Yes, I have." There went her ever-active head, nodding. In the next instant her smile faded and a troubled look settled over her face. "Oh, Michael, I cannot tell you how frightened I was, seeing you like that. I have never felt so helpless or useless in my entire life. I wanted so badly to help you, but I did not know how. It was awful." Her voice seemed to unravel with every word and her eyes grew bright with unshed tears. "If anything were to happen to you. I—I—" She broke off, shaking her head, her expression nothing short of tragic.

It was his turn to comfort her. Smiling with all the affection he felt for her at that moment, he gently reassured her, "Nothing is going to happen to me, my sweet. It was a seizure, just a harmless seizure, and I am no worse for the wear for having had it."

She eyed his dubiously. "Perhaps. It's just that I hadn't expected your spells to look so—so—" Her head sprang back into action, supplementing her failing words with emphatic shaking.

"So what?" he tautly prompted, bracing himself for what he fully expected to be a kindly phrased, yet still unintentionally hurtful expression of repugnance.

"So—so—" Two more head shakes, then she more choked out than uttered, "Painful. Oh, Michael! You looked as if you were in the most dreadful pain. It broke my heart that there was nothing I could do to help you."

Of all the answers she might have uttered, none could have surprised him more. Though he'd heard the sight of his fits described a dozen different ways, usually in cruel and mortifying terms, no one before had ever bothered to care if they were painful. That Emily did, that she was able to look past what most certainly must have been a shocking sight to worry about what he felt, made Michael love her all the more.

Marveling anew that he had been blessed with the love of such an extraordinary woman, Michael smiled faintly and replied, "I can honestly say that I feel nothing when I have my spells. I am completely senseless during them, and usually for a goodly while afterwards. And except for the sting of my embarrassment, the only real pain I experience as a result of them is from the bumps and bruises I inevitably suffer when I fall." He shrugged one shoulder. "Oh, and my muscles sometimes ache for a day or two afterwards. Eadon says that it is from the strain of their rigidity during my fit, but the discomfort is no worse than if I had spent the day engaged in a particularly rigorous sport."

She seemed to consider his words, her gaze anxiously searching his face as if she suspected that he might be lying to spare her heart. When he smiled and nodded, giving further truth to his claim, she sighed, visibly relieved. "I cannot tell you how glad I am to hear that your spells are painless, though I must admit to being concerned about the damage you did to your hip. It was forming the most dreadful-looking knot when I examined it. You also appeared to be getting a rather nasty bruise on your thigh and one on your elbow as well."

"You examined my hip?" He drew back a fraction, caught off guard by her words.

She looked away, blushing. "When I bathed you, yes."

"I see," he murmured, not certain whether to be embarrassed or pleased by the fact that she had attended him in such an intimate fashion.

Her cheeks were now his favorite shade of red, the one he had secretly christened "Emily scarlet," for the fact that the delightful hue was unique to her blush. "I—I hope you do not mind me doing so. Eadon said that it would be quite proper for me to bathe you, me being your wife and all. And I must admit to wanting to examine you myself to make sure that you were truly unharmed."

Pleased. Michael decided that he was pleased at having been tended by her. How could he be embarrassed when it was apparent that she had been neither disgusted nor appalled by anything she had seen or had had to cleanse from his flesh? Adoring her more than he'd ever have believed possible, Michael pulled Emily's prettily flushed face to his, kissing her as he declared, "Not only do I not mind you bathing me, I am pleased that you care enough to wish to do it for me."

"There is nothing I would not do for you. Surely you know that by now?" she countered, kissing him back.

"Yes, I do know." It was true, he did know, with all his heart. He had been a fool to have doubted her love. At that moment, as he gazed into her eyes, so warm and full of devotion, he vowed that he would die before he would ever again be such a fool.

For long while thereafter they simply held each other, secure in their love and wrapped in the quiet contentment of the moment.

It was Emily who finally disturbed their blissful reverie. "Michael?"

"Hmmm?"

"I—I just want you to know that you can always trust me . . . with anything."

He frowned at her odd statement, wondering what had prompted her to introduce the subject of trust. Hoping that she hadn't somehow divined the reason behind his tears, he cautiously replied, "I know that, Emily, and I do trust you. Is there a particular reason for you reminding me of the fact now?"

"It's just that—well—it was just something Mr. Eadon said while I was bathing you."

"Which was?"

She hesitated a beat, as if measuring her response, then haltingly replied, "He commented upon how at ease you seemed beneath my touch. He said that you usually become agitated when he tends to you after one of your spells, because—" He could see the motion in her throat as she swallowed hard before finishing, "Because of Bamforth Hall."

"Ah. I see," he murmured, surprised when he did not feel the usual dread he experienced at the mere mention of the asylum.

She nodded gravely. "He also said that he does not know why you react so, since you have never confided your experiences there to him." She paused, as if deciding whether to proceed, then timidly added, "I know that I promised not to pry into the matter and I do not mean to do so now, but I want you to know that I am here and willing to listen should you ever wish to talk about it."

Michael smiled and nodded, touched by her compassionate little speech. It was odd, but lying here in her arms like this, cradled in her tenderness and the intimacy of her love, he could almost view his misery at Bamforth as a blessing. After all, had he not feared returning to the asylum as much as he did, he would never have consented to wed Emily. And if he hadn't wed her—well, such an existence was simply too dismal to contemplate.

Suddenly wanting very much to tell her about the asylum, to let her know the wretchedness from which she had delivered him by marrying him, he murmured, "I would like to tell you about it now, if you are in the mood to listen."

"Are you certain that you are up to doing so? You have been through so much today," she replied, anxiously searching his face.

"Very certain. It will be a relief to tell you."

"Then I will be glad to listen. Before I do so, however, we must get you off this cold floor. It wouldn't do at all for you to catch a chill on top of everything else. Can you walk, or should I fetch Eadon to help you?"

"I am fine now. I am always fine when I am with you," he replied, the honesty in his voice reflecting the trust in his heart.

"And I intend to see that you are always so," she countered with equal sincerity. "Now let me help you back into bed. It is where you belong, you know."

When Emily had escorted him the short distance to the bed and had tucked him snugly beneath the blankets, she lay down upon the coverlet next to him with her head beside his on his pillow. Her lovely face the picture of tenderness, she murmured, "You may tell me about Bamforth Hall now, if you still wish to do so."

He smiled and moved his head nearer to hers, enjoying the intimacy of having her share his bed. "I do. I just do not know how to begin."

She thought for a moment, then suggested, "Why don't you tell me how long you were there?"

"Six months, though every moment seemed like an eternity."

She nodded at his response, then waited for him to

continue. When he had difficulty doing so, she aided him by saying, "I must admit to being puzzled by your dread of the place. You said that Bamforth is very genteel and respectable."

"It is. And I suppose that it might not have been so very bad were I insane, like most of the other patients."

"What?" She couldn't have looked more flabbergasted.

He nodded. "Bamforth Hall's main function is to provide civilized care for mad members of the aristocracy, though they do boast of superior treatment for peers with seizure ailments as well. According to their doctors' claims, they have had much success in curing them, which is what prompted my grandmother to send me there." He shrugged. "As you can tell from my performance today, they had little success in curing me, though I can assure you that it wasn't for a lack of trying. Indeed, Eadon's treatments are gentle compared to what I was subjected to there."

"Oh, Michael, no!" she cried, visibly stricken.

Michael closed his eyes and nodded again. "Do you know how many different places a person can be bled?" Without pausing to await her reply, he quietly answered, "Twenty-two. And I was bled from them all, regularly. Indeed, not a day went by that I wasn't bled from two or more places. Add the endless leeching, blistering, electrical treatments, clysters, purging, and the thrice daily draughts of saline and opium, and it is no wonder that I couldn't stir from my bed for weeks on end."

He opened his eyes then to see her staring at him, anguish for what he had suffered written on every line of her beautiful face. "My poor, poor love. No wonder you were so terrified to go back there. It is a miracle that you survived six months of such torment," she whispered, her voice raw with sympathy.

"Perhaps, though, it isn't just the treatments, awful though they were, that make me dread the place so."

"I cannot imagine anything worse than daily bleedings," she interjected with a shudder.

His lips twisted into a brittle smile. "The loneliness

and the lack of humanity I suffered were much worse. Oh, I am not saying that anyone deliberately abused me," he quickly clarified. "To be fair, most of the attendants were kind enough. It is just that they were used to treating the insane and handled me in much the same manner. Thus, no one ever thought to talk or listen to me, and I was allowed absolutely no privacy for fear that I might in some way harm myself. I was constantly watched and shadowed during the day, and tied to my bed at night, forced to lie in my own foulness on those occasions when I could not wait for morning to use the privy. As if such treatment wasn't quite humiliating enough, all of my needs, no matter how personal, were tended to by someone else."

"Which is why you cannot bear to be tended in such a manner now," she commented softly.

"Yes. Unless, of course, it is you doing the tending."

Emily's head was shaking now and she looked on the verge of tears. "Your grandmother must be the cruelest woman in the world to have allowed you to suffer so. Surely she saw your misery during her visits?"

"She didn't visit me. Visitors are thought to be overly stimulating by the doctors at Bamforth, so patients are not allowed contact with anyone outside of the asylum until after they have been there for six months. At that point they are considered well enough on the way to being cured to withstand the excitement. When my grandmother saw my terrible condition on her first visit, she ordered me promptly carried to her coach and took me home. She hired Eadon shortly thereafter."

Emily remained silent for several moments, as if considering all that he had told her. Then she propped her head up on her hand, a frown worrying her brow as she reflectively inquired, "Do you really think that she would have forced you to go back there had you refused to marry me?"

"I do not know. Though"—he paused to wince at the pain in his hip as he shifted his body to face her—"I must say that I am glad that she made the threat. Had she not, I never would have wed you and my life would have been much the poorer for never having known you. I really must remember to thank her the next time I see her."

Emily met his gaze, smiling rather shyly. "Truth be told, I am grateful to her myself. I simply cannot imagine my life without you to love. I told Rebecca that very thing today."

Rebecca—he had forgotten all about her visit. Pulling his hand from beneath the covers to brush an errant tendril of hair from Emily's cheek, he ruefully murmured, "I am sorry about ruining Rebecca and Magellan's visit. I do hope they understood."

"Of course they did. In fact, when Rebecca heard what had happened, she told me about a remedy that she thinks might help you. We spent the entire afternoon at her cottage gathering and preparing the required ingredients. Even Magellan helped by going out on the moor and gathering several plants that Rebecca doesn't grow in her garden."

Ah. So that was where she had been when Eadon had said that she had gone out. Touched that she would go to such an effort on his behalf and genuinely intrigued by the notion of a magical cure, he inquired, "Then Rebecca has the power to heal as well as to break curses?" After his experience at the stone circle, he was far less skeptical about mumbo-jumbo than he'd once been.

"In a sense, yes. As with the curse, she has the power to divine what is amiss with a person and then advise him how to remedy it. When she touched you that day at the cottage, she discovered what ails you."

"And she honestly thinks that her remedy will cure it?"

"It might, if you believe that it will. Much of the power of magic comes from simply believing. The rest comes from here." She lightly touched the place just over his heart. "Rebecca can only show each person how to unlock the magic that is inside of them."

Michael considered the theory for a moment, then nodded, deciding that it made sense. Well, at least as much sense as anything else he'd experienced that had

had to do with Rebecca Dare. Eyeing his wife, who seemed to be studying him rather intently from beneath her long lashes, he inquired, "What is involved in the cure? No stone circles and phantom priestesses, I hope?"

"Oh, no. We can do it right here. Though I am not allowed to tell you exactly what is involved, I can promise you that you will find the whole process pleasant to the extreme."

"Indeed?" he countered, becoming instantly suspicious. "And if this spell is so very pleasant, then why, pray tell, are you not allowed to divulge what is involved in working it? In my experience, the worst treatments are the ones that doctors refuse to detail, usually because they are hideous and no one would submit to them if they knew what was involved."

"Ah, but we are discussing magic, not medicine," she reminded him. "Besides, you said that you trust me. If you truly trust me, you will take my word on the matter and allow me to try the remedy on you. If you feel well enough, I would like to do so tonight, since the preparations are the most powerful when they are fresh."

She was gazing at him so earnestly, with such sweet expectation, what could he say but, "All right, then. I put myself in your hands." He only hoped that he wouldn't regret doing so.

Chapter 19

"You want me to do what?" Michael, who lounged in bed sipping the honey-sweetened herbal decoction Emily had bid him to drink in preparation for the spell, stared at his wife aghast, praying that he had misheard her instructions.

"Remove your nightshirt," she repeated, looking up from the circle of candles she had arranged and now lit around the bed. There were gold, green, and orange ones to promote healing and to restore his strength, with several red ones tossed in to increase his vigor. Nodding, she added, "You need to be naked so that I can rub the magical oil Rebecca and I prepared all over your body."

"Everywhere?" He more choked than uttered the words in his dismay. Good God. He shuddered to think of how his love-starved body would react to being rubbed with oil by a temptress like Emily . . . especially if she rubbed a certain place that was quickening even now at the mere prospect of being touched.

She smiled indulgently, as if he had just asked the silliest question in the world. "Of course not everywhere. I am only required to apply the oil from your neck down, though I will initiate the spell by anointing your forehead." Her response was casual, almost breezy, as if what she proposed doing was just another service to be rendered in her quest to heal him.

Then again, to her, perhaps it was, Michael conceded, watching as Emily touched the flame of the taper she held to the wick of one of the green candles. In her innocence she probably didn't realize how hungrily his body would respond to the kind of sensual benevolence she proposed,

nor could she possibly understand the agony he would suffer in the wake of his violent arousal. It would be sweet
agony, true, the sort of erotic martyrdom that most men
would give anything to endure and that they would seductively turn to their own carnal advantage.

Unfortunately he wasn't like other men, who could
enjoy the lustful adventure. He was Michael Vane, the
man who had fallen into a foaming, thrashing fit the last
time he'd been coaxed into a sexual frenzy—the same
man who might possibly experience an equally atrocious
response beneath Emily's unwittingly seductive ministrations, perhaps with identical results.

No, not identical, he corrected himself, his meditative
gaze still on Emily, who frowned as she tweaked the
wick of a red candle, which refused to light. Unlike Violetta, who had cruelly spurned him in the aftermath of
his fit, Emily had weathered the sight of his most recent
seizure without suffering any apparent revulsion or loss
of affection for him. Indeed, if anything, seeing his suffering seemed only to have drawn her closer to him. Though
he found that fact reassuring to the extreme, he was
nonetheless reluctant to tempt a repeat of his morning's
performance, which was exactly what he would be doing
if he allowed himself the measure of arousal the applica-
tion of the magical oil was certain to excite.

On the other hand, it had been a very long while since
he'd had two fits in the same day, not since the earliest
weeks of his illness, which was proof in itself that his condition had improved. Then again, he'd never deliberately provoked a fit on the heels of another. He'd most certainly
never attempted a sexual encounter on the same day he'd
suffered one. So who knew what would happen?

"Michael?"

Michael, who had been staring at the scene before him
without really seeing it, refocused his attention on Emily.
She stood just inside the circle of candles, all of which
were now lit, gazing expectantly at him. She couldn't
have looked more beautiful or tempting.

Her hair, which was always glorious and alluring, tumbled over her shoulders in a lustrous tangle of curls, cap-

turing the fire of the candlelight in a way that made it seem to shimmer from within, as if each midnight strand hid a core of molten bronze that seized and reflected the flames. Her cheeks were flushed a soft, silken crimson, rouged, no doubt by the heat of the room, which she had elevated almost to the point of sweltering with her overzealous stoking of the fire, determined, as always, to ensure that he didn't take a chill.

And then there were her lips, those ripe, luscious lips which currently formed the sweetest of frowns. They were the lips of a temptress set in the face of an angel. As for her eyes, well, what could he say? He could gaze into their brown velvet softness forever and never grow tired of what he saw in their depths. Add her delectable figure to the artless sensuality of her every move, and it was all he could do not to moan aloud in his desire.

He wanted her—dear God, how he wanted her!— worse than he'd ever wanted any woman before. If only he could take her. If only he had the courage to try.

As Michael sat there, watching the vision who embodied his every heated dream of a beautiful woman slowly approach him, he berated himself for not daring to brave that which he knew she wanted as badly as he did. Of course, unlike his own reasons for wishing to consummate their union, which at the moment involved relieving what was quickly becoming his excruciating sexual urgency, the soul of Emily's desire was pure, noble. She yearned to bear his babes, to propagate the Vane family line, and to gift him with the children she knew that he would love as much as she. And though she had tactfully refrained from broaching the subject of children in the wake of his painful confession in the nursery, he knew that she still hungered for them, perhaps even more now that they had declared their love for each other.

Desperately wishing that he had the courage to truly love her, that he was brave enough to at least try to gift her with her heart's desire, Michael looked away from Emily as she sat on the bed beside him, sickened by his own cowardice.

After a beat, during which he stared bleakly into his

cup, she smoothed his tousled hair from his cheek and brow, murmuring, "If you don't feel up to trying the spell tonight, we can do it another time. I shall understand."

Yes, she would understand. Sweet, patient Emily always understood, sometimes all too well, which he suspected might be the case now. If he were indeed correct and Emily sensed his inner turmoil, she was offering him the chance to bow out of the spell without any loss of dignity on his part. He had only to say that he was unwell, and that would be that. She would tuck him snugly beneath the bedcovers, after which she would sit by his side, crooning and stroking his hair until he slept. Then she would leave him alone.

Alone . . . to dream about her and his longing to love her. Alone with his regret and the pain that came with it. Alone, all alone, with the shame of his cowardice.

Though Michael tried hard to master his degrading fear, arguing with it and berating himself for his poltroonery, in the end he failed, crumbling beneath his contemptible cowardice. Now loathing himself more than he'd ever loathed himself before, fervently wishing that things could be different, he opened his mouth to plead illness. As he commanded himself to meet Emily's gaze, determined to at least be man enough to look at her as he uttered the craven lie, he saw the boundless tenderness gleaming in her eyes. She loved him so very much, steadily and unconditionally, far more than he deserved to be loved.

Staring deeply into her unshuttered eyes, seeing her heart reflected in their adoring depths, he felt a sudden, savage longing to be worthy of her unstinting devotion. Damn it, he would be worthy of it! He would be the husband she wished and the man he longed to be. Bolstered by his fierce determination, Michael forced himself to smile and reply, "I feel fine, love. I was just finishing your decoction. You said that I must drink every drop, remember?"

Smiling back, she peered down into the cup. "It looks to me as if you have followed my orders splendidly."

"I am, as always, your servant, madam," he tossed back with an ease he was nowhere near feeling.

"Well, then?" She reached over to take the empty cup from him.

His hand tightened convulsively on the handle. As long as he held on to it, he had an excuse not to move on to the next step of the spell. When she glanced up again, shooting him a querying look, he forced himself to nod and reluctantly eased his grip.

It took her only a second to deposit the cup on the table beside the bed. That done, she again glanced at him, this time expectantly. When he merely stared back, frozen by renewed apprehension, she smiled gently and reminded him, "There is really no need for modesty, Michael. As I mentioned earlier, I saw your body this morning, all of it, and I can assure you that you have nothing whatsoever to be ashamed of. Of course, if you would rather I leave while you disrobe, I—"

"No," he interjected, mentally reconfirming his resolution. "Stay. Please. As you also pointed out, you are my wife, which makes it quite proper for you to see me naked. Besides, it hardly serves me to be modest now when you will shortly be rubbing my body with your magic oil." Praying that his fingers wouldn't be clumsy in his tension, he reached up and systematically unbuttoned his nightshirt. He had just finished and had grasped the hem to lift it over his head when Emily abruptly turned away and began fumbling with the amber bottle of magical oil.

Michael paused to watch her, his eyes narrowing as he noted the hectic, almost feverish flush of her cheeks and the visible trembling of her hands as she lifted the bottle to pour the contents, a viscous green liquid, into a small bowl marked with mysterious symbols. Why, for all her show of serene self-possession, she was just as flustered as he by what they were about to do. More so, judging from her rapidly darkening cheeks.

The sudden surge of tenderness he felt at seeing her so did much to assuage his own anxiety. Easily setting aside his disquiet in his desire to soothe hers, yet sensing that she would be crushed should he mention observing it, given her brave facade, he hastily tossed off his night-

shirt and lay down on his belly, wanting to spare her the
sight of the more unsettling aspects of his nudity. Thus
when Emily finally mustered the pluck to glance back at
Michael, she saw nothing more scandalous than his bare
buttocks. They were nice buttocks, true, taut and muscular, curving into impossibly long, powerful legs, but the
sight was hardly enough to raise a blush, not after a
lifetime spent surrounded by brothers.

Had Michael's face not been turned toward her, Emily
would have sighed her relief. She was rapidly discovering
that seeing Michael naked when he was awake was a far
different matter from doing so when he was unconscious.
When he had lain before her that morning, inanimate
and unaware, she had felt perfectly at ease feasting her
gaze upon his glorious body. Indeed, though it shamed
her now to admit it, she had enjoyed looking at him, her
curiosity overriding her sense of propriety as she had
eagerly surveyed those parts of him that were normally
hidden by his trousers. But now, well, now she wasn't
quite certain where to look or how to act for fear that
he might think her brazen.

Oh dear! Whatever had she been thinking to imagine
that she could work this spell without dying of embarrassment?

The instant the question formed in her mind, she knew
the answer: She had been thinking of Michael, of all he
had suffered coupled with her own desperate desire to
help him. And if this spell was anywhere near as effective
as the one to banish her curse, it would not only help
him, it might very well cure him.

Ordering herself to focus on the virtue of her purpose
and to ignore the ripple of excitement she felt at the
sight of his lovely backside, Emily somehow managed to
inquire, "Are you ready, love?" amazing herself with the
strength of her voice.

He smiled faintly and nodded.

"All right, then. First I must—um—anoint your forehead." Fighting hard to keep her hands steady, she
dipped her fingers into the bowl of oil, using it to sketch
the healing symbol Rebecca had taught her upon Mi-

chael's forehead as she chanted, "With the protective power of sandalwood and mint; with the purifying strength of elder; with the healing might of carnation and the gift of health from rosemary, I command this spell to work my will upon your heart, soul, and flesh."

"Is there anything I need to say or do?" he murmured when she fell silent, gazing up at her with solemn jade eyes.

"Yes. You must close your eyes and concentrate on the motion of my hands—imagine them drawing the illness from your body."

He nodded once, then buried his face into his pillow, waiting for her to continue. A moment later, she did.

After smoothing aside his long hair to expose his strong neck and shoulders, Emily again dipped her hands into the oil, this time allowing their heat to warm it before touching his flesh. Starting at the nape of his neck, she began massaging in the slow, deep, circular motion Rebecca had shown her, repeating the incantation she had uttered while anointing Michael's forehead as she worked.

Taking care to oil every satiny inch of his skin, she stroked down the strong column of his neck to span the impressive breadth of his shoulders, then descended the hard granite of his arms, marveling anew at their sinewy strength. Pausing at his hands to lavish attention on each of his elegant fingers, she smoothed her way back up to his shoulders again, then traveled the muscular length of his back.

As Emily worked, now and again dipping her hands into the bowl, the heady scent of the oil mingled with the natural musk of Michael's flesh, making her all the more aware of the blatant masculinity of the man stretched out before her. Feeling strangely tingly and effervescent all over, she allowed her gaze to wander hungrily over every sculpted inch of his magnificent physique, a delightful shiver of wanting running through her at the sight of him.

Oh, but he was beautiful, so very beautiful with his skin sheened with oil. His body gleamed sleekly in the candlelight, each powerful muscle in his back and arms defined and rippling to perfection. As for his backside—

Her pulse skittered alarmingly and a delicious shudder heated her belly as her hands slithered slickly down the hollow of his lower back to trace the lean line of his hips. Keeping her touch light and her movements rhythmic, she slowly circled up over the firm, rounded curve of his buttocks, savoring the silken sensation of his smooth flesh as she steadily moved inward. Then she dipped between them. He gasped and flinched from her touch, his muscles flexed and his buttocks clenching.

Wondering if she had unwittingly touched a bruise that she had missed during her examination that morning, one that she was now unable to see for the shadows, Emily frowned and murmured, "I'm sorry if I hurt you, Michael. Are you all right?"

Michael jerked his head once to the affirmative. Of course he had lied; he was far from all right. The fire in his loins, which had been sparked when Emily had informed him of her plans to massage him with oil, was now burning high and growing hotter with each passing moment. Gritting his teeth to steel himself against the raging inferno of his arousal, he buried his face yet deeper into the pillow, his body tensing as she resumed her unwittingly titillating ministrations.

Dear God! He didn't know how much more of this exquisite torment he could endure. The feel of her hands moving over his body, so seductive in their gentleness and stimulating in their thoroughness, gripped at his groin with a savagery that made him long to howl with need.

As he lay there stifling his moans, her fingers again slipped between his buttocks. The raw eroticism of the resulting sensation shocked him into breathlessness. Before he could muster so much as a gasp of inflamed protest, her hands slid downward, dropping between his thighs where they lightly grazed the underside of his masculine sac. His whole body jerked in electrified response, his thighs protectively clamping together to prevent her from touching him there again.

"Michael, darling. You really must relax if the spell is to be effective," she softly chided, slipping her fingers between his thighs again, trying to coax them apart.

He shot her a disgruntled look, wondering just how relaxed she would be if it were she lying there naked while he teased her nether regions. The picture that that particular thought invoked merely increased his lustful torment. Now mired in the molten agony of his need, Michael again pressed his face against his pillow, desperately trying to ignore the fact that Emily had somehow managed to part his legs and now caressed the sensitive inner curves of his thighs.

To his eternal gratitude she lingered there only the briefest of moments, skating over the back of his knees and massaging the ache from his seizure-strained calf muscles. By the time she reached his feet, which she manipulated in a way that he found exceedingly relaxing, he had almost mastered his lust.

"There," she murmured with finality, giving the arch of his right foot one last stroke. "You may turn over now."

Turn over? Michael felt his heart drop to the pit of his stomach at the mere thought. Not only did he not wish to frighten Emily with the sight of his erection, which it would most assuredly do, given her inexperience, he was alarmed by the excessive degree of his arousal. Were she to touch his sex, even inadvertently, he would most certainly spill his seed. His fear of another fit now eclipsed by the mortifying prospect of losing control, Michael remained on his belly, pretending that he hadn't heard her request.

"Michael, you really must turn over if we are to complete the spell," she insisted, giving him a pat. When he again failed to respond, she gently inquired, "Is this really so very difficult for you, love?"

After a beat, he reluctantly nodded.

She sighed. "Then we must stop. The last thing in the world I would ever wish to do is cause you discomfort." Another sigh, this one sounding as if it were being ripped from the bottom of her soul. "It truly is a shame, though. The spell is said to be quite effective, and I had so hoped to help you. But if the process is too—"

"I am fine. It isn't all that bad," he gruffly interjected, his resolution renewed by the disappointment in her voice.

After all the trouble she had gone to to prepare the spell, the least he could do was allow her to finish it. If the unthinkable happened, well, then so be it. It would be far easier to live with the embarrassment of losing control than with the knowledge that he had disappointed Emily. Thus determined, he flipped over, not missing the way her eyes widened when she saw his arousal. Glancing down at himself, he had to admit that it did look rather fierce, straining aggressively against his belly.

Looking away again, resolved to ignore it, he nodded to Emily, his voice taut as he bid, "Please proceed."

After a moment of hesitation, Emily did as he directed.

Heavens! she thought, stealing another glance at his manhood from beneath her lowered lashes. He hadn't looked anywhere near as intimidating down there this morning as he did now. True, he had unconsciously hardened when she'd washed him there, but his erection had looked nothing like this one. It most certainly hadn't jutted like that, nor had it been so very enormous. Hmmm. Was this the sort of transformation that Judith had been referring to when she had described the changes in a man's male parts in the marriage bed as startling?

Forcing herself to look away, despite her fascination, she began lightly stroking the healing oil over Michael's throat, working it into his flesh in the prescribed circular motion. Like his back side, the front of him was a miracle of satiny skin and tightly woven muscle, tragically marred here and there by the scars of the brutal treatments he had endured over the years. By the number of them she had noted thus far, it was apparent that he hadn't lied when he'd claimed to have been bled from twenty-two places.

Now gazing at a particularly wicked-looking series of jaggedly healed wounds at either side of his neck, it was all she could do to resist kissing them in the tenderness of her sorrow at what he had suffered. Stoically ignoring the urge and all the others she felt as her fingers passed over scar after heartbreaking scar, Emily worked her way over his chiseled chest and down the tight grid of his belly.

Michael tensed, his body growing rigid as Emily's

hands inched nearer and nearer to his arousal. Bloody hell! It was too much, he couldn't take much more. If she so much as brushed against him now, he would— Michael sucked in a hissing breath as she grazed the dark curls on his groin, his fingers digging hard into the mattress beneath him as he braced himself for the raw shock of her touch.

She was almost to his hardness when she abruptly skirted around it, skimming gently over his hips, her touch growing feather-light as she passed over the tender bruise on his left hip. From there she continued down his legs, not so much as nudging his masculine sac as she again caressed the inner contours of his thighs. When she advanced lower, completely bypassing his male parts, his tension began to recede. So much so, that he had actually begun to relax by the time she reached the tips of his toes.

"There now," she murmured, drawing her hands away at last. After pausing a moment, during which she dipped them into the bowl again, she added, "I have only to rub oil on—uh—you know, and then we shall be done."

Before Michael could open his mouth to protest, her warm, slippery hands were between his legs, gently cupping and oiling his manly sac. The feel of her fingers caressing the sensitive flesh was . . . incredible. So incredible that he was helpless to resist the resulting sensations. His fear of erotic stimulation now forgotten, he moaned his pleasure and spread his legs yet wider, instinctively coaxing her to continue.

To his carnal bliss she complied, intensifying his urgency until he was oblivious to everything but the exquisite sensations radiating from between his legs. So transfixed by his pleasure was he that he hadn't the presence of mind to do more than sob his desperate need when she reached up and grasped his engorged sex.

Shocked by the thrill of her touch, he lay in stunned stillness while she anointed his shaft, his already fevered excitement mounting into a frenzy as she rubbed up his entire length and then down again, repeating the provocative motion over and over again. Gradually his hips caught the rhythm of her hand, moving by their own volition, each intensely stimulating thrust propelling him nearer and nearer to his release. In the next instance she slicked back his sheath and he lost himself.

Hoarsely screaming his rapture, he violently arched his back, tears of pleasure streaming down his cheeks as he experienced the most potent climax of his life. Held in the thrall of his release, he shuddered and thrashed for several long, delirious moments, then fell limp, utterly drained.

"Michael, oh, Michael, my poor darling! I am sorry . . . so very sorry!" he heard Emily cry through the haze of his passion-drugged mind.

It took several beats for his sluggish brain to note her distress and several more for it to grasp why she would sound so. When he finally did, he smiled gently and reassured her, "It is all right, love. I am fine." And he was. Strangely enough, he wasn't the least bit embarrassed by his loss of control. How could he be when he felt so very splendid?

"What?" She stared at him as if she couldn't believe what she was hearing.

He nodded, his smile broadening.

Shaking her head over and over again, she choked out, "I thought—that—that—"

"That I was having another seizure?" he ventured.

The head shake turned into a nod. "The way you were thrashing and—and—this"—she held out her hands, which were sticky with his seed—"I saw this on you down there"—she indicated his equally sticky sex—"when I bathed you this morning. I just assumed—"

"I know what you thought, and I am sorry that I frightened you. As for what you washed from me this morning, well"—he shrugged one shoulder—"it is quite common for men to spill their seed during the sort of fits I suffer."

She glanced back down at her hands, looking all the more bewildered by his response. "If you didn't have a fit, why did you spill it now?"

"What happened to me is called an orgasm, and as with a fit, a man spills his seed while in the grip of one.

Unlike a fit, however, spilling it during an orgasm is an expression of pleasure. Indeed, an orgasm is one of the greatest pleasures of life, one enjoyed by both men and women."

"Oh." Clearly uncertain what to make of his explanation, she reached over to the table next to the bed and picked up one of the linen towels Eadon had left there earlier. Dipping it into the basin of water beside it, also courtesy of Eadon, she wiped the seed from her hands, then gently cleansed him, a process he enjoyed immensely. When she had finished, she sat beside him in silence, eyeing his now flagging sex with a strange expression. When he asked about her thoughts, she sighed and confessed, "I was just wondering how an orgasm feels."

Michael grinned his wicked pleasure at her reply. "Would you care to find out, my love? I would be thrilled to show you." And why shouldn't he show her? It was clear that he was now well enough to do so, though whether his renewed vigor was due to Eadon's treatments or Rebecca's spell, he couldn't say. And it didn't matter. Medicine or magic, he was now able and eager to introduce his darling Emily to the joys of the marriage bed. Who knows? He might even plant the babe she so desperately desired while he was at it.

Emily flushed furiously at his offer. "I—I would like that very much," she replied in a shy whisper. It was the truth—there was nothing she wished more than to be intimate with Michael. Before she quite knew what was happening, he had removed her modest dressing gown and the equally prim night rail beneath it, and was kissing her all over, erasing the last of her maidenly inhibitions as he seductively coaxed her untried senses to life.

Now his lips were on hers, in turn worshiping and ravishing her mouth. Now they were on her breasts, teasing and tweaking her nipples until she thought that she would die from the bliss of it. And now he was between her thighs, kissing and exploring her in a way that made her squirm and moan with pleasure.

She was so sweet, so very sweet in her fervently virginal response, arousing and inflaming Michael all over again. She was also beyond beautiful. Oh, he'd suspected that her body was lovely beneath her clothing; he had just failed to envision its true splendor, perhaps because he never would have believed that any woman could be so very perfect. Her breasts were by far the most magnificent he had ever seen, full and round and soft. Her waist was long and narrow, curving into provocatively feminine hips. Then there was her delectable backside—ahhh! How he loved clasping and kneading it.

When Michael had explored every silken curve and responsive crevice of Emily's body, and had prepared her to receive him, he gathered her into his embrace, holding her close as he slowly entered her. Pausing at every inch to allow her to adjust to his legendary size, he crooned, "Relax, love. Just relax. It will be easier if you relax."

To his surprise she moved impatiently against him, wrapping her legs around him to urge him deeper. "Michael—oh! That feels wonderful," she gasped.

Smiling his delight at her wanton greed, Michael slipped his fingers between her legs and lightly teased the core of her womanly pleasure, hoping to ease her coming pain as he poised himself to respond to her body's brazen demands. When she moaned and strained against him, delirious with need, he thrust deep inside her, rending her virginity in one smooth stroke. Her eyes widened and she cried out, her thighs clamping around him to prevent him from moving within her.

"There, there, love. I know it hurts," he soothed, dipping his head to kiss her. "I shan't move again until you tell me that you are ready."

She gazed into his eyes, her expression dazed and full of wonder, then she glanced down at where they were joined. A faint frown creasing her brow, she whispered, "I never thought that you would fit. You are so large."

He couldn't help chuckling at the amazement in her voice. "Of course I fit. Do not forget that our babes shall spring from that same place, and they are much larger than I shall ever be."

She froze at his words. "Then we are making a baby?"

"I am most certainly doing my best to give you one, though it might take several times of doing this to plant one."

She seemed to consider his words, a slow smile curving her lips as she slanted him a sultry look. "Good. I am finding that I rather like the feel of you inside me. Indeed, it does not hurt so very much now that I am growing accustomed to your size." She relaxed her thighs a fraction to move experimentally against him, then nodded. "Mmmm, yes. In fact, it feels nice."

"I promise that it shall feel much, much nicer—better than nice. I promised you ecstasy, and you shall have it."

"Always a man of your word, eh?" she teased, pressing a kiss to his lips.

"Always," he countered, again parting her thighs to resume stroking her. When he sensed that she was almost to her climax, he clasped her close and thrust yet deeper. She moaned and clung to his neck, her hips rising up to meet him. When it was apparent that she was experiencing nothing but pleasure, he took her the way he had longed to take her from the very first moment he'd seen her, eagerly yet tenderly, plunging again and again until she shuddered and cried her rapture.

The feel of her rippling and contracting in her climax instantly brought forth Michael's release, and together they thrilled to the culmination of their passion.

As they lay warm and drowsy in each other's arms in the aftermath of their ecstasy, Emily breathlessly exclaimed, "Oh, Michael, how can you not believe in heaven when you have experienced this?"

He smiled gently and dropped a kiss to her smiling lips. "Perhaps because I had never experienced it with you. Now that I have, I do believe."

She twined her arms around his neck, amorously kissing him back. "You do?"

He nodded. "Yes. I have discovered it in your arms." With that, he took her again, once more touching heaven.

Chapter 20

"I do believe that he is as pretty as Michael was at his age," Adeline proudly declared, nodding down at her six-month-old great-grandson, Andrew Michael Merriman Vane, the fifth marquess of Dartnell, who sat on her lap single-mindedly masticating the coral teething stick that hung suspended around his neck by a gold chain.

The boy paused mid-chew at the sound of her voice, his jade eyes wide and his expression comically surprised as he stared up at her, looking astonished to see her there.

Euphemia, who sat beside her friend doting over Andrew's twin sister, Lady Aurora Vane, glanced at their mutual great-grandson with a beaming smile. "Indeed he is. He is quite the handsomest boy in England, just as our Aurora"—she shifted her adoring gaze back to where their great-granddaughter lay in her own arms surveying the crowd around them—"is the most beautiful girl child ever born into the *ton*."

"Beautiful," Adeline agreed, lightly touching one of the soft sable curls that peeked out from beneath Aurora's bonnet, "just like her great-grandmother Effie."

"And clever, too, like her great-grandmama Addy. Remember how she said my name this morning? Gre-gran-Eff, she said." Effie nodded. "She said it just like that, clear as you please."

Had Aurora been anyone else's great-grandchild, Adeline would have skeptically pointed out the fact that she

had been fed shortly before she'd emitted the utterance
and that it was most probably the product of gas. Since,
however, the child in question was of her flesh and blood,
she was more than willing to believe Effie's questionable
claim. How could she not when Andrew had said gre-
gran-Ad, which in her mind translated to great-grandmama Addy, just last night?

Thus satisfied that their great-grandchildren were indeed extraordinary in every way, she snorted and tossed
back, "Of course she is clever, and charming, and everything else that makes for a remarkable child, as is Andy.
They are of our blood, after all, and no child with both
Vane and Merriman blood flowing in their veins could
ever be anything less than perfect."

"Mmmm, yes. They are perfect, are they not?" Euphemia marveled, glancing from one dark-haired, jade-eyed
babe to the other, both of whom were dressed in white
muslin gowns with blue satin sashes and elaborate, lace-
trimmed caps. The only concession made to their dif-
fering sexes was the placement of the blue rosettes
adorning their caps. Aurora's was in the center front,
proclaiming her a girl, while Andrew's graced the left
side of his face, as was proper for a boy.

"They are perfect babes born of perfect love," Adeline
pronounced with a nod. The instant the words escaped
her, she smiled wryly. Perfect love? Such sentimental
blathering made her sound like one of those mawkish old
gooses that she and Effie had vowed never to become.
Nonetheless, it was the truth, and she always prided herself on speaking with veracity. Emily and Michael had
indeed found perfect love, the rare, miraculous kind that
charmed everyone who saw them together and prompted
them to remark upon the uncommon depth of the couple's affection for each other.

Thinking of Michael now, she glanced across the sun-
dappled Windgate park to where he stood before a long,
feast-laden buffet table, which had been set beneath the
bud-starred branches of the leafing oaks, laughing as he
shared in some sort of joke with Lords Gilcrest and Kev-

ill. Her smile grew tender, her heart rejoicing at the sight of his merriment.

As she had hoped, Emily had been his salvation. Her strong, stubborn spirit had reached through the midnight of his misery and pulled him from the brink of despair, luring him back into the light of life where she had healed him with her love. And it seemed that he was truly healed. Not only had he been free of spells for over a year now, he was strong and healthy and happy, like the Michael before his illness, only better.

As if reading her thoughts, Euphemia softly remarked, "Our Michael looks well, does he not?"

"Well? Bah!" Adeline snorted, her gaze never wavering from her beloved grandson. "He looks better than well. He looks bloody splendid."

Euphemia sniffed her disapproval of her use of the word "bloody." "You really must strive to guard your tongue when you are around the babes, Addy. As you know, children learn from the example set by their elders, and it would never do for Andy and Aurora to lay hold of inelegant language."

Adeline shrugged, unperturbed by her friend's lecture. As always, she had only spoken the truth. Michael did look bloody splendid, the word "bloody" being instrumental in conveying the satisfying magnitude of his improvement. Indeed, not only had he regained most of his lost flesh, his eyes sparkled, his skin glowed, and he smiled with a spontaneity that bespoke a soul-deep contentment. Most wonderful of all, he had recaptured the easy, genial confidence for which he'd once been so admired, something that she had begun to fear he had lost forever. As Adeline watched, he said something that made the other men laugh, displaying the wit and charm that had made him such a favorite with the *ton*.

Smiling at his obvious enjoyment of his companions, she slanted a glance at a nearby cluster of gossiping noblewomen, all of whom ranked among the finest London hostesses. Judging from the fawning glances they now darted in Michael's direction coupled with the snatches of flattering conversation she'd overheard earlier, it seemed that he was well on his way to regaining his throne as society's darling. That is, if Emily didn't beat him to it.

She shifted her fond gaze to where Emily stood surrounded by an assembly of *ton* leaders, who laughed and clapped with abandoned delight as the extraordinarily lovely, but decidedly eccentric, Lady Rebecca Dare played a helter-skelter game of Graces with her pet goat, Magellan. Adeline had to admit that their performance was diverting, especially the way the beast danced around on its hind legs as it scrambled to catch the hoop that they tossed between them with sticks.

She had just become engrossed in the spectacle herself, a chuckle escaping her as the goat reared up and jerked its head, launching the hoop from the stick it held in its mouth, when Euphemia whispered in a scandalized tone, "Have you noticed the way Lords Bedell, Uppington, and Edmundson are ogling that Dare chit?"

Adeline glanced at the gentlemen in question, snorting when she noted their gawking fascination with the girl. "Egads. One would think that they had never seen a woman before."

Euphemia sniffed. "Well, they have never seen that particular woman before, and you know how men are when they catch the scent of fresh prey."

"Mmmm, yes. Indeed I do. And I suppose it is only natural that prey like Lady Rebecca should excite such interest. Between her fetching looks and her father's plump pockets, I daresay that she will create quite a stir when she finally makes her bow to society."

Another sniff from Euphemia. "Well, she'd best do it soon if she wishes to make a decent match. She isn't exactly in the first blush of her youth, you know."

Adeline smiled down at Andrew, who had begun to make soft cooing sounds, his head drooping drowsily in the warm, late-afternoon sun. "I would hardly call twenty-five past one's prime, though I must confess to being at sea as to why she hasn't had a Season yet. Her father is the duke of Wreford, after all, one of London's most prominent citizens, so it isn't as if she lacks the

funds or the connections to enter the *ton*." She paused
a beat to ponder the puzzle, then theorized, "You don't
suppose that Wreford forgot to bring her out in his grief
over his wife's death, do you? I seem to recall that she
died eight or nine years ago, which was about the time
the gel should have come out."

There was a short silence, as if her friend contemplated
her hypothesis, then she replied, "Perhaps. However, I
tend to believe that if such were indeed the case, the
oversight would have been rectified years ago." A nod.
"If you ask me, I think that Wreford decided the chit to
be far too eccentric to be offered at the marriage market,
what with her fondness for goats and other such
queerness, and decided it best to simply give in to her
desire to rusticate here in Dartmoor. After all, he does
have his younger daughter to consider. Perhaps he didn't
wish to risk her chances for an advantageous marriage
by allowing the older one to taint the family name with
her oddness."

"Hmmm, yes," Adeline mused, seeing merit in her
friend's reasoning. "Now that you mention it, I did hear
something about plans for the younger chit's coming
out."

"Indeed?"

Adeline nodded. "Lady Calthrope was complaining
just last week that her dressmaker, Madame Minott, had
turned away her request for a new ball gown, saying that
she was too busy preparing a wardrobe for the duke of
Wreford's daughter's coming out. I daresay that it is his
younger daughter her ladyship was referring to, because
she confided that the poor gel is going to need all the
help she can get in compensating for her freckled nose
and unfortunate red hair. I hear tell—"

"Poor chit," interjected Michael's voice, his tone laced
with wry amusement. "And whose reputation are you
wicked old dragons ruining today?"

The two women looked up with a start, both having
been too engrossed in their speculation over the duke of
Wreford and his daughters to note his approach. Quickly
recovering herself, Adeline tartly retorted, "I daresay

that you would be able to guess had you and Emily come to London for the Little Season, as Effie and I begged you to do."

Michael shrugged and reached for his daughter, who chortled and eagerly stretched out her chubby arms to him. Handling the babe with practiced ease, he swung her high into the air, making her shriek with delight as he replied, "In case you have forgotten, Emily gave birth to your grandchildren in early September. She was hardly in any condition to go gadding off to London so soon after lying-in."

Adeline emitted a derisive snort. "Stuff and nonsense! I have never seen a woman have an easier time of it than Emily did. She was more than fit by the beginning of the Little Season."

"And eager to go to London, I might add," Euphemia corroborated with an affirmative nod. "Indeed, I seem to recall her begging you to go." A head shake accompanied by a clucking noise. "The poor dear! I can only imagine how hungry she gets for company, living in this godforsaken place."

Michael dipped his head to kiss Aurora, who giggled and clung to his neck. It was true that Emily had begged him to go to London, but not because of any eagerness on her part for the society of the *ton*. No. She had wished him to go for his own sake, knowing, as they both did, that he would never be completely healed until he faced and conquered the last of his crippling fears. That fear was, of course, returning to town and reentering the *ton*, though he no longer dreaded doing so for the same reason he had before meeting Emily.

Where he had once been frightened for his own pride, shrinking with shame at the remembrance of the humiliation he'd suffered in London, loving Emily had prompted him to put aside his worry for himself and to fear for her instead. She loved him so much, fiercely and with such staunch loyalty, that she couldn't help but be hurt by the mocking smirks and stinging cuts that he knew would greet him were he to try to regain his standing in the *ton*.

When he had confessed his fears to Emily, she had hastened to reassure him, holding him close as she gently coaxed and reasoned with him. But her tender urging had been to no avail. He'd held firm to his resolution. And so they had remained in Dartmoor, passing first the fall and then the winter in the quiet bliss he had come to cherish.

Truth be told, he had thought the whole matter of London and the *ton* to be settled until he had stepped outside with Emily earlier that afternoon to greet their arriving grandmothers. Today was his thirtieth birthday, and like the twenty-seven preceding it, his grandmother and Euphemia were to be present to help him celebrate it. What he had found awaiting him was not only his expected guests, but an assembly of London's finest society with the makings of a lavish gala set up in the Windgate park.

Though he had wanted nothing more than to flee, uncertain what to do, or say, or what to expect from the silent, watchful crowd, he had allowed Emily to lead him down the front steps to where their grandmothers sat enthroned on a pair of gilt-wood armchairs, both visibly pleased with their day's work. What followed was still a bit of a blur in his stunned mind, though he did seem to recall that it was his boyhood chum, Viscount Langcliffe, one of his few friends who had remained loyal after his fit at Lady Kilvington's picnic, who had come forward first.

Warmly clapping Michael on the back, he had grinned and murmured, "Missed you terribly, Sherrington. London is a dreadful yawner without you. Do remind me to take you to task later for refusing to receive me when I tried to call."

After that he had been besieged by *ton* members. Some had greeted him with ease, chattering and laughing as if they had seen him just the day before, seemingly having forgotten his disgrace. Others had approached him with caution, their smiles taut and their manner tentative, as if they were as uncertain of him as he was of them. Still others had gazed at him with shamed apology, their eyes mutely begging his forgiveness as they humbly congratulated him on his beautiful wife and babes, and tendered wishes for many happy returns on his birthday.

His forgiveness he gave freely, gladly. How could he not? Had these people not driven him from the *ton*, he most probably would never have wed Emily and his life would have been so much the poorer for it.

As always happened when Michael thought of Emily, he smiled, his gaze hungrily seeking her in the aristocratic mob. Though she had remained by his side while he had greeted their guests, every inch a duchess in both beauty and poise as she had graciously acknowledged his introductions to his elegant acquaintances, they had been separated shortly thereafter. Since then they had been unable to steal more than a moment or two together, so in demand were they by their guests.

Hoping to steal another moment now, he continued to comb the crowd, his smile broadening when he at last found her at one of the buffet tables, directing the footmen as they replenished the feast. His pulse racing and his gaze adoring, he savored the picture she made, reverently admiring everything from the flattering fit of her lilac and green diamond patterned gown to the way her modish cottage bonnet with its green gauze puffs and silk lilacs framed her prettily flushed face. He was about to go to her, determined to spirit her off and kiss her breathless, when she looked up and caught him smiling at her.

Smiling back, she said something to Henry, the fifth footman, who nodded, then she started toward him.

Michael watched her approach, his heart swelling with pride. He must have done something very good indeed at some time in his life to have been blessed with such a glorious wife. With Aurora now tucked firmly in his right arm, he held out his left one to receive Emily, wrapping it around her shoulders to draw her near when she walked into it. Hugging her close, he pressed a kiss to her smiling lips, murmuring, "Thank you for the wonderful surprise, love. I could not have asked for a better birthday."

"Much of the credit belongs to our grandmothers," she replied, kissing him back. "It was they who lured the *ton* here. I merely planned the feast."

"Ah, but it is you who gave me the strength to face the *ton*. Without your love, I could never have—"

"Well, well, Emily, my gel. It seems that you have taken the *ton* quite by storm," interrupted Adeline's voice.

Michael and Emily reluctantly tore their gazes from each other to look at her.

She nodded and added, "Ladys Buxton and Hawkshaw, whom I might add are two of London's most discriminating hostesses, have both promised to hold soirees in your honor once the Season is in swing."

"Yes, and Lady Kilvington has invited you both to her picnic next month," chimed in Euphemia, "though I am certain that everyone will understand if Michael would prefer to decline that particular invitation."

Michael shrugged, pleased to find himself unperturbed by the prospect of visiting the site of his final disgrace. A year ago the very notion of doing so would have been unthinkable. Well aware of why he now felt as he did, he smiled tenderly down at Emily, replying, "I shall leave that decision up to my wife, just as it is for her to decide whether or not we will attend the Season this year."

"Pish! Of course you will attend," his grandmother retorted. "After the pains Effie and I took to ensure your welcome back into the *ton,* it would be exceedingly rude, not to mention ungrateful, of you to stay away."

"Ah, yes. My welcome. I have been meaning to ask how you managed the Herculean feat of securing it," he countered, arching one eyebrow in sardonic query.

The women exchanged a rather guilty look. After several beats, during which they remained in silent communication, Euphemia sighed and explained, "It was quite simple, really. We merely put it about that you had married and that your wife had restored you to health. When the *ton* heard of your improvement, they were more than eager to welcome you back into the fold. As so many people here today have remarked, your charm and wit have been sorely missed."

"Just like that, eh? Easy as crossing the road?" he quizzed, wondering if they truly thought him so very gullible.

Apparently they did, because they bobbed their heads in unison.

He snorted. "I think not. I know the *ton* far too well to believe that the matter was so easily settled. Do try again."

"Well, the babes did have something to do with the *ton*'s decision," Euphemia slowly conceded, trading another glance with Adeline.

Adeline nodded and confirmed, "Yes. After that business with—a-hem!—well, you know"—she shot Emily an apologetic look—"the news that you had fathered twins did much to give validity to our claims of your improvement."

"Indeed?" he drawled.

Another nod from his grandmother. "Yes."

"And?" he prodded, certain that there was more to the tale. There had to be.

"And what, dear?" Euphemia inquired, her face the picture of perplexed innocence.

Michael made a derisive noise. "Come, come. Surely you do not think me so very obtuse?"

Euphemia sniffed. "I cannot even begin to imagine what you mean by that remark."

"You know exactly what I mean, and do not imagine that you can convince me otherwise. Now please do me the favor of crediting me with some wits and tell me how you accomplished all of this." He gestured to the crowd around him.

Another look passed between Euphemia and Adeline, this one lingering. At length, Adeline shrugged and shifted her gaze back to Michael. Picking up the gauntlet he had tossed with his words, she replied, "While it is true that most of the *ton* was willing to take you back on the strength of our report, we will admit that there were a few members who required a bit of—er—persuasion."

His eyes narrowed with suspicion. "What sort of persuasion?"

"The sort that comes from the advantage of being in the *ton* for close to seventy years." This was from Euphemia. "After such a lengthy time, one cannot help but to collect a few—ummm—choice bits about London's finest families."

Michael's eyes were little more than slits now in his distaste for what he was hearing. "Are you saying that you blackmailed the *ton* into taking me back?" he ground out.

"Of course not," his grandmother snapped, looking indignant at the mere suggestion that she would be privy to such underhanded methods. "What we did was remind the less forgiving *ton* members of their own transgressions, after which we pointed out how they had been pardoned and suggested that they show you the same charity." A shrug. "When we then reminded them that your fits had come about through no fault of your own, thus illustrating the inequity of your expulsion from society, they all came around smartly enough. Most went on to express delight in welcoming you back, saying that they have sorely missed your presence. Indeed, by the time we left London the town was abuzz with excitement over the prospect of your return."

Michael simply stared at her, rendered speechless by her words. That she and Euphemia would risk their own lofty positions in society to ensure that he was not only accepted, but eagerly welcomed back, into the *ton* spoke volumes about the depth of their love for him—not that he had ever doubted that they loved him. He hadn't, not once. It was just that he had never before realized what a treasure their love was, at first taking it for granted, and then dismissing it in his selfish bitterness over his misfortune.

Now understanding the richness of their gift, yet another legacy of loving Emily, Michael slowly smiled and said, "Have I ever told you sly old dragons just how much I adore you?"

To his amusement they flushed like a pair of schoolgirls being flattered by their very first beaus. Looking suspiciously misty-eyed, his grandmother snorted and tartly returned, "If you care for us so very much, you will come to London so that all of our hard work shan't be in vain."

"As I said, I shall leave the decision to Emily." He transferred his gaze to his beautiful wife, who smiled at the byplay between him and their grandmothers. "If she wishes to attend the Season, then I shall be glad to escort her."

At that moment Aurora kicked and let out a screech, a precursor of louder squalls to come. Nodding to the twin's nurses, who stood a watchful but discreet distance from their charges, indicating that they were to take the tired babes back to their nursery, Emily replied, "I think that we should go. Not only would the society do you good, I should like to see Mr. Eadon again and tour his new hospital."

Eadon, who had left Windgate shortly after the birth of the twins, having deemed Michael cured, had just opened a small hospital in London, the purpose of which was to treat and study the sort of seizures that had once plagued Michael. According to the letters they had received from him since, the enterprise was thriving, thanks to recommendations from the venerable dowager duchess of Sherrington and her bosom-bow, the dowager viscountess Bunbury. He was also happily courting a young widow, whose daughter he was treating, and whom he hoped would accept his proposal when he tendered it in the summer. Being fond of Eadon, Emily secretly planned to do everything in her power to promote the match, wanting him to find the same sort of happiness she had found with Michael.

Slanting a flirtatious look at the man who had made all of her dreams of love and family come true, she sighed and added, "That is, if I can find time for such a visit. I daresay that I shall be kept beyond busy fighting off all of the women who will wish to steal you from me once they see how handsome you look."

Michael kissed first Andrew and then Aurora, who

were being claimed by their nurses, grinning as he bantered back, "I can assure you that I shall be far too busy fending off the hordes of men who will be trying to steal you from me to notice any other woman."

"My word! Will you look at that?" Euphemia abruptly ejected, pointing to the sky in the distance. "What in the world is that doing here, do you suppose?"

Emily glanced in the direction her grandmother pointed, her eyes widening as she caught sight of a pale blue balloon with a passenger basket shaped like a Venetian gondola floating over the trees at the edge of the park. As it drifted nearer, she saw that the balloon was emblazoned with an angel. "Oh, Michael! Have you ever seen anything so very wonderful?" she exclaimed, filled with longing at the thought of soaring so high above the earth.

Michael chuckled. "After being married to me for almost two years, you should know the answer to that question: you, my dear, are more wonderful than anything else in creation. However, I must say that I am glad that you like the balloon, because it is my birthday gift to you. Your dream to fly is about to come true."

"What?" She tore her gaze from the balloon to gaze at him in confusion. "But it is your birthday, so it is you who should be receiving the gifts."

"I am receiving one, the one I desire most in the world."

She shook her head in bewilderment. "I am afraid that I do not understand."

"Having you by my side, knowing that you are mine and that you love me, is the greatest gift I can imagine."

"Indeed?" she purred, twining her arms around his neck to draw his face to hers.

He nodded.

She sighed. "Then I suppose that I must resign myself to having an exceedingly spoiled husband, for it is a gift that I intend to give you every day for the rest of your life." With that she kissed him, demonstrating the sweetness of her promise.